"LET ME MAKE LOVE TO YOU, RAINE...."

"Not here, Bran—not now," she whispered back, her words as gently caressing as the lips that parted to nuzzle his chest hair.

"No one will know," he countered, impatient.

"I'll know."

"You're damned right you'll know," he growled with an urgency that ignited her own smoldering passion.

"Bran, please! What I meant," she went on more softly, "is that if we do this now, I'll never know if you put me onstage because I was a good dancer—or a good lover."

"And once you're a success, then what?" he demanded.

"I can't answer that." Raine drew away from his hungry embrace, even as she ached inside from wanting him....

Casey Douglas

DANCE-AWAY LOVER

A SUPERROMANCE FROM
WORLDWIDE

TORONTO · NEW YORK · LONDON

Published August 1983

First printing June 1983

ISBN 0-373-70075-X

Printed in Canada

CHAPTER ONE

RAINE CAMERON'S HAND rested lightly on the barre as she bent her knees, muscles automatically tightening to form the *demi-plié* of classical ballet. The pain was there, too, running up from the long bone of her left leg to the flexed knee. But she was used to that. It had been her constant companion since the accident, though mercifully its severity had begun to diminish in the long months of recuperation.

She forced herself to ignore the sharp jabs of sensation as she went through her brisk series of exercises at the long wooden barre. From time to time she would bend down to massage the aching muscles. Beneath the bulky woolen leg warmer, her leg was as slender and shapely as it had ever been. There were no outward signs of injury. There was nothing but the damned unsteadiness of her limbs, as much psychological as physical, that made her afraid to dance full out. The fear and the pain were somehow tied in her mind, but again she disciplined herself to ignore them.

Sometime later, as she paused to wipe her perspiring face with a towel, Raine became aware of the morning sun pouring in through the long eighteenth-century window of the studio. In her intense concentration she'd almost forgotten where she was, until the sunlight, picking up the gilded molding of the high ceiling, reminded her that this was Paris—three thousand miles from New York and a year distant from the Kingsley Ballet and the horrible fall that had threatened to prematurely end her dancing career.

Though she shut her eyes tightly against it, the ugly memory invaded her thoughts as if on cue. She envisioned the tricky balance in the duet that John Kingsley had choreographed for his short ballet, *Winter Morn*, and the subsequent lift when her partner had swung her high overhead. The movement had been designed to suggest endless flight, but something had gone disastrously wrong. Raine's forehead grew clammy as she relived the fall...the shattering impact of her knee with the stage, the lower leg twisting unnaturally beneath her before she blacked out....

The cheerfully plunked keys of a piano in another studio down the hall recalled her to the present, and Raine went on with her exercises even more briskly than before. But the specter she'd lived with for so long continued to haunt her.

Winter Morn had been created specifically for Riva, but when a much longer and more flamboyant ballet had been included in the same program, she had demanded the larger role instead. Kingsley, Riva's lover at the time, had reluctantly acquiesced and given the shorter solo to her sister.

Raine, of course, had jumped at the opportunity. She'd always danced in the shadow of Riva's technical brilliance and longed to prove herself in a small showpiece number. Unfortunately no one could have foreseen the tragic outcome of that decision.

Riva had left the Kingsley company while Raine was still in the hospital. Her unexpected resignation had been given not, as the press averred, because of what had happened to her twin, but for more personal reasons.

Along with the bouquets of flowers and baskets of fruit, Raine's friends in the corps de ballet brought her the up-to-date company gossip. They told her that John had broken off with Riva and refused to create any more dances for her. There had been a typical, hair-flying scene before the aspiring prima ballerina had stomped out of his office.

Riva made no mention of all this in her visits to the hospital, and in fact the two women had surprisingly little to say to one another. Riva brought an enormous and outrageously expensive bowl of orchids to the room the first day Raine was allowed visitors, but her eyes slid away—refusing to meet Raine's—even as she bent down to brush her lips against the injured dancer's cheek.

John Kingsley's own visit later was painfully similar. He insisted on mumbling a long and embarrassing apology even after Raine told him that she blamed no one for the accident. She'd known the risks when she'd agreed to the role, but he refused to accept the fact that she bore no grudges. He himself was feeling guilty at the thought that he'd allowed his personal involvement with Riva to affect his artistic judgment. He'd pushed Raine into the role too quickly. In the end Raine couldn't bear the pity in his eyes, and she asked him curtly to leave.

As her days in the NYU Medical Center stretched into weeks, and it became general knowledge that the orthopedic surgeons who'd operated on her leg were questioning whether she would ever dance again, the pity and the sympathy began to be reflected in the eyes of her other visitors. Raine came to dread their visits and their well-meant condolences, secretly vowing to prove them all wrong. That inner promise had given her the courage to undergo the long months of slow and painful physiotherapy.

Even in those first weeks of Raine's hospitalization, Riva's visits grew less and less frequent. Finally, after one long absence, she called Raine and breathlessly informed her that she was at the airport awaiting an overseas flight. The undercurrent of excitement in her voice was unmistakable as she told her sister that she had accepted a job with the Paris-based Ballet du Monde.

Thereafter, while Raine took her first faltering steps as if she were a toddler, gradually reeducating her limb in the most basic movements of flexion and extension, she marked her snaillike progress by the monthly cards she received from Riva—postmarked Vienna, Amsterdam, Copenhagen and Athens. But though the glamorous locales had changed with monotonous regularity, the message was inevitably the same: "I, I, I...."

After the last of Raine's unemployment checks and workers' compensation had been spent on hospital charges and extra therapy sessions, she had been forced to give up her Greenwich Village apartment and accept the kindly hospitality of her Aunt Helen in western Pennsylvania.

Helen Dexter had never got over the shock of her younger sister's leaving her hometown at eighteen to make a name for herself as a costume designer in New York. The shock and dismay had only intensified when the lovely impetuous Jenny had married Andrew Cameron, a handsome but penniless actor, and within the year had borne a set of twin girls. When Andrew was killed in a car accident a few years later and Jenny was forced to perfect her costuming skills in order to provide a living for her growing daughters, Helen had regarded the matter as an act of God.

But to Raine and Riva, their childhood was anything but a retribution. They loved to traipse along behind Jenny as she fulfilled one design contract after another for off-Broadway productions, operas and of course ballets. There had even been a one-year stint in Paris that still loomed magically in Raine's mind, and no doubt, in Riva's, too. The girls had grown up with a love for the theater, and their mother had encouraged them in their dancing. It had been the ultimate joy of Jenny Cameron's life to see her nineteen-year-old daughters embark on promising careers with the Kingsley Ballet Company. She'd died not long afterward, and the ever watchful Helen had regarded that, too, as an act of God.

Five years later she had welcomed her injured niece with open arms, and over the months she was always ready with a shoulder to lean on and a ceaseless flow of gentle encouragement. When Raine finally lost the last traces of a limp, her first task was to walk into the small dance school in downtown Clairton and sign up for private lessons. Under Angela Ricetti's expert tutelage she slowly began to recover the old skills. Even as Angela marveled at her progress, however, Raine kept a bitter secret within. While she did fine at the barre, Raine discovered that she was terrified to leave its support for adagios and other floor exercises in the middle of the room. Somehow the mere thought of it always conjured up the vision of center stage and the dreadful accident. Despite these secret fears, she continued to regain the strength and grace of her limbs.

It was the ever patient Aunt Helen who finally broached the subject of Raine's recovery. The two women were seated on the front porch, sipping iced tea as the humid afternoon drifted toward evening. Helen looked up from the piece of embroidery in her hand to regard her niece thoughtfully. "Don't you think it's time, dear, that you found a job?" she ventured. "It'd be good for you—help you forget things."

Raine glanced up swiftly at that. "But what could I do?"

The older woman dropped her sewing in her lap, ready for just that question. "Well, I've been talking to George Kaufmann. He's an old family friend who runs the big hardware store down on Route 51 and he's offered to take you on and teach you secretarial skills. It would be real practical training."

Touched by the woman's concern, Raine got up and kissed her dry cheek. "Thanks for thinking of me, Aunt Helen, but I'm. . .I'm not sure yet what I want to do."

A few minutes later Raine descended the porch steps, strolling along the hilltop that overlooked the steel mills and coke works. The red glow from the furnaces mingled with the last dying rays of the sun to bathe the sky and the lazily flowing Monongahela River in a vivid coppery light.

Even as she walked, Raine knew she had to leave the little town that had been her refuge for the past eight months. Already she could anticipate her aunt's objections. "But Raine, dear, you aren't the same person Riva is," Helen would say, disapproval evident in her soft voice. "You can't think the ballet world is still yours—not after what's happened."

"Maybe that's precisely why I have to leave," Raine murmured to herself. "I have to prove what *I'm* capable of." Once again she was reminded of the covert pity in so many eyes, and her resolve hardened.

Later that evening in her own room, she dug out the postcard she'd received from Riva just the day before. The newsy message embellished the dancer's favorite theme of her meteoric rise to principal soloist in the small but elite company. But the card also mentioned that the Ballet du Monde was back in Paris for the summer break before fall touring, and that the company's director, Madame Nina Tarsamova, was seeking an assistant artistic director. Without further hesitation, Raine took out stationery and pen from the desk drawer and wrote a carefully worded letter to the Russian ballet mistress.

That had been two months ago. Summer was nearly over now, and Raine had made her way to Paris at the woman's invitation.

Again Raine's nostalgic thoughts were interrupted by the enthusiastic plunking of keys on a distant piano, reminding her that the day was about to begin at the French dance company. She had just arrived in the city the night before, and this was her first morning at the studio.

Raine had come early so that she could be assured of a long workout at the barre without anyone seeing her. The warm-up might help dispel her nervousness, too. Madame Tarsamova's letters had been filled with penetrating questions. Finally the woman had invited Raine to Paris to size her up in person, promising that the post of assistant artistic director would be hers only if her work proved satisfactory during their mutually agreed upon trial period.

Raine hadn't mentioned her aspiration to dance again, since she herself wasn't certain what she was capable of. The strength was there, but she didn't know if she possessed the courage and drive that were also required. Until that time she would work alone. She had finally managed to conquer the numbing terror that overcame her every time she moved toward the center of the room, the metaphorical "center stage," the thought of which still caused nervous spasms in her stomach. But simple slow movements away from the barre were a far cry from exquisite variations in a demanding pas de deux.

As she stood there, willing herself to be calm, the notes trailed off in a rippling harmony of chords, and she wondered if the beginners' class was already over.

Then, through the long windows that opened onto a private courtyard, came a music far different from the energetic but amateurish piano rhythms. Someone in the adjoining studio must have put on a record, because a moment later a full orchestra sounded a passionate theme, dominated by a strident high trumpet followed by shreds of wind-instrument melody.

Raine stood as if transfixed in the center of the studio, caught in a beam of warm sunlight. There was a fine sheen of perspiration on her delicate features, and she had long since discarded the bulky leg coverings needed for warm-up, so that her graceful length of limb was revealed in pink tights and satin toe shoes. She wore a simple black leotard with a pink ribbon around her small waist, and her hair was pulled back severely from an oval face as beautifully faceted as a gem.

The pain and fear were momentarily forgotten as the music washed over her; the easy breathing of the melody seemed to call her. She hadn't listened to a single phrase of classical music since the accident. Purposely she'd cut herself off from it, grateful for the buffer of the small, blue-collar mill town that had offered few reminders of her other life.

Now, without warning, she felt her body and emotions responding to Falla's music. She'd recognized the vivid Gypsy ballet from the very first strains, because for one night she had actually danced the lead in *El Amor Brujo*, the understudy pulled from the chorus to perform after the company's ballerina had sprained an ankle. Raine had only been twenty-two at the time—still too young to bring any emotional depth to the role—yet the critics had praised the ethereal delicacy of her form. She could remember most of the steps, and now in the empty studio she felt the music swirling around her with irresistible force.

As tentatively as a piece of thistledown blown on the wind, Raine rose on pointe. As if listening itself to the music, her body moved, and she became completely a part of the music. Quick little leaps and slow turns in the "Dance of Terror" gave way to a muted, almost Oriental spell. If her pirouettes were a bit shaky and the little cutting steps of the *coupés* were less than sharp, Raine's arms bespoke a graceful lyricism of their own. They told the story of a young girl haunted by the ghost of her dead Gypsy lover, who refused to let another man take his place, and of her efforts to break the spell.

Then a solo cello announced a beautiful slow melody, evocative of a southern Spanish tango, and Raine half closed her eyes as she swayed in the imaginary arms of the Gypsy girl's new lover, Carmelo, the one destined to free her from the old specter.

Raine's eyes flew open with a sense of shock a moment later as she felt a pair of hands encircling her waist from behind, propelling her across the floor from shadow to sunlight and back again. Behind her own slender figure in the mirror, she caught the reflection of the unknown partner at her back. A shock of tousled black hair fell across his forehead as he looked up, and for an instant her luminous dark gold gaze met his penetrating blue stare.

She stumbled and hesitated, but the pressure of his hands and the brush of his muscular thigh against her hip impelled her to continue in the dance. In fact, she suddenly felt that she had no choice but to move along with this dynamic presence at her back.

Curious now, she kept darting sharp little glances over first one shoulder and then the other, trying to get a better glimpse of him. But he was too quick for her and brought his head across to the opposite shoulder, never missing a beat in the swaying seven-eight time of the Cadiz tango.

Finally the music slid into the slower tempo of the song of love and destiny, and her partner took one hand from her waist while the other remained in place, as if in tacit recognition that she might need that subtle support in her single-toe balance. She stepped down into a *demi-plié* then, wincing almost imperceptibly from the resultant sharper pain, and continued the dance, now face to face with her mysterious partner. As her feet and limbs executed the well-remembered steps, Raine studied him.

He was lithe and lean in his gray sweat shirt and black tights that molded his rugged musculature, and she sensed at once a sharp intensity and passion about him as he danced. She was fascinated by his quicksilver shifts in movement, the toughness of a boxer that gave way to pantherine twists. Beneath the animallike quality, she sensed, too, a certain moodiness and a smoldering sensuality that didn't quite break through to the surface.

So caught up was she in studying the man and the way he moved that Raine nearly forgot the climax of the old ballet, in which the Gypsy girl and her lover exchange the one perfect kiss that will break the sorcerer's spell. As the music evocative of Gypsy camps in the dark Andalusian mountains continued to swirl around them, Raine glided with practiced ease into the danseur's arms. She remembered now the embrace in dramatic pantomime that preluded the bell-chiming finale of the ballet and waited with breathless anticipation for his response.

She was startled a second later when her partner broke the rhythmic impulsion of their dance, his hands dropping to caress her arms with familiar intimacy. He whispered to her in French over the low keening sweetness of the music, "I've never seen you dance with such feeling, Riva."

Her troubled and confused gaze met his as she opened her mouth to protest. "But—"

There was no time to phrase her denial, however, because his mouth swooped down to cover her parted lips. The kiss was hungry, explorative, as if he were discovering new depths in a woman he thought he knew so well—and liked what he was discovering.

Raine found herself momentarily giving way to the passion of this stranger's embrace. She swayed against him and savored the brush of her small uplifted breasts against the steel-banded muscles of his chest. The moment was electric, as if the stylized choreography of the dance had spilled over into hot consuming emotion that was all too real.

But it lasted only an instant. Raine struggled to pull away, the unexpected and engulfing bliss of the moment giving way to chagrin and humiliation when she recalled the circumstances of the kiss. He had called her Riva, had thought the woman in his arms was her twin.

Finally she managed to twist her lips away, their rose-petal softness a vivid contrast to the hard topaz sheen of her eyes. He returned her stare, the smoldering emotion in the midnight depths of his own giving way to reckless challenge.

"I'm...I'm afraid you're mistaken," Raine informed him icily in her schoolbook-perfect French before reverting to English. "I am *not* Riva. I'm Raine Cameron."

His brow dipped in an angry question toward the narrow bridge of his nose, but when he replied it was in cool American slang that gave only a hint of a French accent. "What the devil do you mean?"

That took her by surprise, but she regained her composure at once. Giving him a cool wry look, she replied without missing a beat, "We were pretty much interchangeable as kids and we had a lot of fun tricking our friends. But that was the past." She broke off then to move toward the barre, where she'd draped her small hand towel earlier. Lifting it to her face, she pressed it against her forehead, flushed cheeks and finally her lips in an unconscious attempt to wipe away the last vestiges of that all-too-intimate and consuming kiss.

That done, she came toward him with fluid grace and regarded him for a long moment with her clear golden gaze. After a while she went on, "Riva and I have grown to be two very different people and about as interchangeable as, well, chalk and cheese. I hope you'll remember that, Monsieur...?" Her manner still frosty and bristling with hauteur, she extended her small hand to him.

"Du Rivage," he muttered in return as their fingers touched. "Brandon du Rivage." He spoke his name in a tone that mixed anger and pride.

She felt a fleeting pang of disappointment at that tone, as if it erased once and for all the restrained sensuality and underlying sweetness of their impromptu duet. But she steeled herself to ignore such a regret. After all, he was probably another in Riva's long glittering string of lovers. Raine forced herself to ask distantly, "You're the principal danseur of the company, Monsieur du Rivage?"

"No," he responded with equal coolness. "I'm the choreographer."

Her eyes flashed. She knew she'd been right in assuming he was another of Riva's conquests, another male whom she'd charmed into helping catapult her more quickly to the top. "I see," was the only reply she made at last.

Meanwhile he continued to observe her, his perplexity giving way to curiosity. "Riva never mentioned she had a sister who was a dancer."

A dry smile briefly touched her pretty lips. "No, she wouldn't."

"In fact," he went on, "the only dancer I've heard her even mention from her New York company was someone who'd had an accident and would never dance again. But you...she never mentioned once. Which company have you performed with since Riva's been in Paris?"

A bitter anger darkened Raine's eyes for a moment at her sister's blithe assumption that she would never dance again—at Riva's pretending that she no longer existed! But with a struggle she quelled it; there was no point in airing dirty family linen.

She remembered the choreographer's question then. "I haven't been with any company. I...I've been out of commission this past year," she informed him after a moment's hesitation, some imp of perversity keeping her from telling the simple truth—that she was the one who had been hurt and whose career had been threatened. Raine wanted no more pity.

In response to her vague reply, Brandon automatically glanced down toward her ring finger and made a quick assumption of his own. He'd seen the same situation so many times before: the dancer either bored or fed up with her slow progress in the ranks and deciding suddenly that she was in love and would retire from the ballet in order to marry and raise a family. A year or two later she'd be back, divorced usually, demanding her old position in the corps as if she'd never gone.

"So," he observed at last, a cool taunting edge to his pleasantly low baritone, "you intend to pick up where you left off? Hoping that no one'll notice the shaky pirouettes, the less-than-dazzling leaps?" There was no mistaking the sarcasm in his tone.

Once again the warm flush of anger crept into her cheeks, lending unwonted brilliance to her pale complexion, so that she seemed even more fragile next to the cool and proud du Rivage. But the fragility was only an illusion—it was actually supported by discipline and by muscles that had been forced through pain to recover their steely strength.

Raine longed to lash out at him for his cheap accusation. Yet she found his biting cruelty much more preferable to any kindness born of pity. She swallowed the sharp retort that had risen to her lips and replied instead, "No, Monsieur du Rivage. I don't intend precisely to 'pick up where I left off.'" The soft-spoken words were gently mocking. "Madame Tarsamova has hired me as assistant art director to the company." The brilliant sapphire of his eyes

darkened in surprise, and he had no reply whatso-
ever.

Falla's rich orchestral suite had long since died
away in a clash of drums and cymbals, so that they
faced each other in deepening silence. Then, as if in
comic relief, the slightly out-of-tune strains of the old
piano filled the air once again. Raine caught the
briefest glimmer of a smile in Brandon's eyes as the
piano chords mingled with the impatient bleep of a
Citroën horn in the boulevard outside the studio.

She might have smiled, too, except that the comically imperfect piano playing that followed the
melodic sweep of the Gypsy ballet reminded her all
too forcefully of the imperfections in herself, the
feared loss of her own lyrical grace. She managed to
hide the old fears behind a mask of cold determination, so that looking at her, Brandon saw nothing but
the reflection of her sister's ruthless ambition.
Without warning the warmth fled from his eyes, and
it was Raine's turn to regard him with a faintly perplexed air.

Next door someone had switched on the stereo
again, so that the vibrant music swelled into the
studio. Brandon reached for her, a gleam of mischief
in his eyes as his large hand caught her waist. "Shall
we see exactly how you dance, *mademoiselle*?" he
teased, the hint of challenge reawakened in his tone.

Despite the subtle shift in his attitude, Raine
longed to go through the steps with him as they had
earlier. In the sheltering support of his arms she had
managed to forget for a while all the pain and uncertainty. She had sensed as well an intuitive rapport
and sensitivity between them that had gone far

beyond mere motor timing. She'd never sensed that with any other danseur before—nor with any man, in fact.

Still she wrenched free from his touch. She wanted nothing from one of Riva's lovers. The two sisters had always competed on a professional level, with Riva invariably coming out the winner through her technical bravura. But Raine had neither the desire nor the will to compete with him for the attentions of a man. She wanted to prove one thing only to Riva—that she still had a place in the dance world.

Brandon seemed to have guessed her thoughts. "Are you afraid, Cameron?" he whispered as she turned her back to him. The words were like an insolent whip lashing at her neck. "Are you afraid of being compared to your sister?"

She whirled around again at that, eyes ablaze like molten gold. "I'm not afraid of anything," she flung back at him, furious that he'd seen through her carefully constructed defenses.

Her body reflected a tense delicacy as she ran back toward the barre to retrieve her things and get away from her tormentor as swiftly as possible. Yet even in her anger Raine projected the natural grace of a woman born to move poetically, an image that wasn't lost on Brandon's experienced eye.

They both looked up then as the double doors to the studio opened and an elderly woman entered to stand silently observing them both. Despite her age, she still dressed with élan. Beneath her calf-length black ballet skirt were pink leotards and tights, while her severe gray bun was caught back with a length of wispy chiffon in a complementary shade of rose.

Watching her glide into the room with a step that had lost none of its aristocratic elegance in half a century, Raine knew without being told that she was about to meet her new employer.

As Raine moved away from the barre, the graceful ballerina addressed her in clipped austere French. "I'm delighted to see that you have arrived early for a change, Riva."

Raine hurried forward, resigning herself to the inevitable confusion in people's minds. She inclined her head and knee in an impromptu half curtsy before the woman, sensing that nothing less than the formality of a balletic reverence would do for this lovely dowager of the art.

"I'm afraid you're mistaken, Madame Tarsamova," Raine replied, her softly accented French respectful but firm. She straightened and lifted her wide pansy-gold eyes to meet the woman's gaze. "I'm Raine Cameron, not Riva. I flew into Paris last night."

Madame Tarsamova's expression sharpened in surprise, but all she said was, "Come along with me to my office, then, Mademoiselle Cameron, and we'll have a little chat."

As the woman turned abruptly on her heel and left the studio, Raine grabbed her tote bag and black wraparound skirt from the chair where she'd hung them. Nodding curtly to Brandon, she followed her employer.

He stared after her thoughtfully. As sunlight continued to fill the studio with its bright warmth, his attention was drawn to the place where Raine had stood to do her morning workout. The short length of barre was still damp from the sweat of her palm, and he wondered how long she'd been at work before he'd arrived.

Raine adjusted the tie of her swingy skirt as she ran lightly to catch up with the company director. She'd had no time to change out of her pointe shoes, but there was no help for that now. It was already apparent to her that *madame* was not a woman who liked to be kept waiting.

While she walked with the director to her office at the end of the long hall, members of the corps raced by one another en route to the first class of the day. Their cheery cries of *"Bonjour, madame"* and "Good morning, Madame T" rang out along the corridor. Raine herself was greeted with sullen closed looks and an occasional "Hi, Riva" from a hopeful male dancer. None of the women spoke to her.

For the first time she wondered if she hadn't made a mistake in coming to a company where Riva's coldly ambitious reputation had preceded her. Could she ever be judged apart, on her own merit? *Never mind,* she chided herself briskly. *You didn't come here to dance but to assist Madame Tarsamova.*

The director's cluttered office was cool and quiet. The walls were covered with photographs of famous dancers of the past, while beyond the open window a deep ledge housed overflowing pots of carnations. They provided a spicy accent to the jasmine-scented breeze wafting into the room from the small courtyard below.

Raine glanced around her with appreciation as Madame Tarsamova gestured airily for her to take a seat on the floral-printed chaise adjacent to the desk.

A moment later she was handed a small glass of tea set in a filigree holder, which the Russian woman had filled from the brass samovar next to the window.

Sitting down then herself, she retrieved a beaten-silver flask from one of the capacious desk drawers and poured a drop of what appeared to be vodka into her glass of tea. She caught Raine's interested glance, and the merest hint of a smile touched her thin disciplined mouth. "Age brings with it certain privileges," she observed with a blend of arrogance and humor.

They sipped their tea then for a while, neither speaking until *madame* finally fixed her new employee with an eagle eye and murmured half to herself, "The likeness is astonishing. I find it fascinating that neither of you thought it of enough consequence to mention that you were identical twins."

Raine shrugged her shoulders lightly. "I saw no need, and I suppose Riva felt the same. We're two quite different women."

"That remains to be seen," the ballet mistress rejoined at once. "Riva can be difficult, but she pushes herself hard. I like that. Can I expect the same of you?"

Raine wasn't daunted by this peppery cross-examination. "I'm not accustomed to flying three thousand miles on a lark, *madame*."

"And I'm not accustomed to hiring employees sight unseen. I suppose I must chalk it up to an old woman's weakness—curiosity." There was a short silence. "Why did you come?" she asked then, apparently impatient with the subtleties of conversation.

Raine was momentarily taken aback by the bold
question but decided that it demanded an equally
direct reply. "I was hungry," she told the director
with a self-deprecatory little laugh. "I needed a job,
and secretarial work didn't appeal to me."

Madame Tarsamova seemed to approve of her
forthrightness. After a moment she picked up a gold
pen from her desk blotter and toyed with it thoughtfully. "Riva told me that you would never dance
again, and you yourself in your letter informed me
that you no longer dance. Yet you were in the studio
just now with Brandon." She looked up from the
desktop and shot a sharp inquisitive look at the
younger woman.

Raine flushed. "Maybe I should have said that I
can no longer dance the way I want to. If I can't have
perfection, I don't want anything at all." Her chin
lifted proudly.

"Shades of Riva?" *madame* inquired.

"The quest for ambition and the quest for perfection are not at all the same thing, *madame*," Raine
countered at once. Although her tone was still
deferential, her eyes flashed the uncompromising
message that she wouldn't tolerate people's assump-
tions about her based on their experiences with Riva.

Madame Tarsamova lifted the glass of tea to her
lips and sipped delicately, so that Raine wondered if
the strange little interview was over. But the keen-
eyed ballet mistress wasn't done with her yet. "You
must tell me, *mademoiselle*," she began at last,
"what precisely did happen to you. In your letters
you mentioned only an accident."

Raine let out a long sigh and began to talk softly.

Soon she found herself pouring out the whole story and as she continued, she began to sense a growing sympathy beneath the Russian woman's imperious facade. Though Raine hadn't mentioned the terrors and insecurities that had dogged her in that nightmarish year, and still haunted her, *madame* must have felt their powerful undercurrent tugging at the young ballerina.

When the whole story had finally been told, Madame Tarsamova lifted her still graceful hand and idly fingered the oval, brushed-gold watch pinned to her bosom. Raine was charmed by the gesture, which gave the woman the air of a turn-of-the-century schoolmistress. Again she waited for the old ballerina to speak.

Madame Tarsamova sighed almost imperceptibly, and once more her tone suggested she'd forgotten there was another person in the room. "A broken spirit can be infinitely more difficult to heal than a broken bone," she murmured before shaking her head and glancing down with crisp efficiency at the hands of the little watch. "That should do for now, Mademoiselle Cameron. Report to this office tomorrow morning at eight-thirty sharp. Now," she added, as she stood up from the neatly organized desk, "I have a class."

Raine rose at once and regarded the woman in astonishment. "You still teach, *madame*?"

A ghost of a smile touched Madame Tarsamova's patrician features. "The Ballet du Monde is a small struggling company, my dear. More often than not our expenses are greater than our income. Pointe shoes alone cost us five thousand francs a year," she informed Raine, shaking her head like a weary bureaucrat. "As a result, we all have double roles. Besides, I consider it my solemn duty to carry on the old Russian traditions of ballet in the West—and to maintain standards. Heavens, but you should see those long-legged ten-year-olds sinking down into their *grands pliés* and waiting—like worn-out old ladies on a park bench!"

Raine laughed in delight at that vivid bit of imagery and was pleased to find an answering wintry sparkle in the old woman's piercing black eyes.

Madame went on more seriously. "Yes, I tell them, 'Don't sit on your heels, children!' I repeat it over and over again, just as it was drummed into this thick head when I was a little sprite in the Kirov school." Her gaze seemed to turn inward then, as if she were flipping through the pages of the past to her long-ago education in St. Petersburg. With a will, she recalled herself to the present. "But to answer your question, *mademoiselle*, I most definitely teach—as does Brandon, even though he has a busy schedule as choreographer staging old productions and designing new pieces of his own. We strive for the eclectic approach in our little company, because we, too, are ambitious and strive for perfection." Her black eyes sharpened a little, not missing the flash of mingled pride and irony in the young dancer's luminescent gold eyes.

Raine lowered her gaze then as she briefly inclined her head and murmured a gracious thanks to the company director for her time. She turned and crossed to the door in two long graceful strides.

Hurrying along the polished corridor, Raine felt the little prickles of anger rising along her neck as she thought over *madame*'s parting words: "We, too, are ambitious and strive for perfection." Had the woman been mocking her, she wondered. *No,* she answered herself in almost the same breath as she relaxed a little. *Testing my mettle is more like it.*

At the end of the hall, she found that the double doors to the studio where she'd been exercising earlier that morning stood ajar. Unable to contain her curiosity, she pushed them open a little farther and stepped over the threshold. From the small record player in the corner blared the wild and diabolical music of Mussorgsky's *A Night on Bald Mountain*. Her eyes were drawn at once to Riva practicing *fouettés*, the lightning whipping turns that are a hallmark of a ballerina's brilliance.

One of the male dancers at the barre happened to glance toward the doorway then and did a swift double take, his confused gaze darting from Raine to Riva and back again. He nudged the person next to him, and soon the entire row of dancers was abuzz with curiosity and whispered speculation.

But Raine didn't notice them, because her gaze had settled on Brandon du Rivage as he called Riva to the front of the studio, and they began to demonstrate a particularly tricky choreographed movement before the long mirrored wall. Even in class Riva went through her paces with an unbridled fiery exhibitionism, as if demanding that her fellow corps members be an adoring audience as well.

The ballerina moved like a precision instrument, but it was her partner who held Raine's attention. Once again she felt herself drawn irresistibly by Brandon's sinuous quality, his emotion-charged energy.

At the same time there was a brashness about him, a bold charm and sexual magnetism that seemed to radiate from his rugged body without his even being conscious of it.

Against her will she found herself imagining Riva and Brandon in bed together, their sleek and sensuous give and take on the dance floor extended to a far more intimate realm, and Raine was rocked by the jealous anger she felt. She was surprised, too. Never before had she felt anything but indifference toward her sister's wild escapades both in bed and out, but somehow this wasn't the same. Without pausing to analyze her confused and angry feelings, Raine turned on her heel and fled the studio.

The struggling but critically acclaimed little ballet troupe was housed in the Richelieu Theater, a former cabaret on the boulevard de Clichy. Raine was familiar with the area, because it was here that her family had lived twelve years earlier while her mother fulfilled her design contracts at the well-known Lido and Moulin Rouge nightclubs. An adult herself now, Raine could appreciate the irony of the ballet company's locale as she strolled down the street past the seedy hotels and striptease joints that were typical of the legendary Place Pigalle. By day the area had the feeling of a shabby amusement park. Nevertheless, Raine was charmed to find herself again in the neighborhood of the famous Moulin Rouge, whose gaudy revues and operettas were so vividly captured in Toulouse-Lautrec's turn-of-the-century paintings. A few minutes later she passed the home of Edgar Degas, another nineteenth-century artist, whose depictions of ballet dancers she adored.

Raine's steps brought her at last to a small winding lane that led upward to the picturesque quarter of Montmartre, where the bistros and art studios tumbled down in quaint profusion from the white sanctity of Sacré-Coeur church like a host of fallen angels. She turned into a quiet little square ringed by gray buildings with copper mansard roofs that were stained a dull mottled green from centuries of exposure to the weather. Raine gazed up in delight at the long shuttered windows that opened onto wrought-iron balconies. *At least I have to admit that Riva has exquisite taste in living quarters,* she conceded to herself with a laugh.

Not yet ready to make the long climb up to the third-story flat, she slipped into one of the chairs in the square's open-air café and ordered a Campari and soda. Automatically she reached down to massage the supple ridge of muscle along the aching long bone of her left leg. She had forced herself to walk the mile and a half uphill from the studio because she was still intent on building strength in her weaker leg, not to mention the fact that the cost of taxis in this lively city was prohibitive, a little luxury she could ill afford.

As she leaned back to sip the bittersweet aperitif, Raine caught the rustle of chestnut leaves overhead. The air itself was alive with the scents of fresh bread and new wine, and for the moment at least she felt happy to be in the charming French capital. Paris, the city of light... and of lovers, she reflected ruefully, trying hard not to remember the image of Riva in Brandon du Rivage's arms on the dance floor.

Somehow Raine had never managed to make any

emotional commitments in the long years that she'd been a dancer. There had never been time, and she was not one to give herself lightly to any man. Now, of course, she had to devote herself wholeheartedly to her work. One entire year had been lost and could never be recovered. Love was something that for now could have no part in her life.

Leave the sultry affaires de coeur and hot lovers' quarrels to Riva and her stable of admirers. *To hell with her and Brandon,* Raine thought with unexpected ferocity. She would do what she had to do without leaning on anyone for support.

Yet a strange undercurrent of sadness rippled through her prideful anger. She knew, of course, that life was never as simple as that. . . .

CHAPTER TWO

A CLOUD OF STEAMY MIST, fragrant with violets and musk, followed Raine out of the tiny bathroom as she towel-dried her hair and padded barefoot into the living room. She'd wrapped a white terry bathrobe around her slim figure.

What Riva's third-story walk-up lacked in modern conveniences, it more than made up for in quaintness. Filmy lace curtains, much mended over the years, billowed at the window, and the room boasted a lovely rococo fireplace. But it probably hadn't worked in fifty years; instead, an efficient electric heater had been tucked inside the hearth.

From the square below came the raucous shouts and laughter of kids at play. Raine stood before the open window a moment, breathing in the delicious scent of croissants and éclairs that wafted upward from a bakery around the corner. In early September, Paris was still hot. The previous evening when she'd flown into Orly Airport the night sky had been ablaze with heat lightning, rippling sheets of incandescence more dramatic than any stage revue. Still she detected a subtle presage of autumn on the wind, and she shivered a little.

Sitting down on the dainty sofa with its faded tapestry-print covering, Raine pushed aside the folds of her robe. Then she opened the jar of medicinal balm that she'd carried from the bathroom and began to massage her leg with therapeutic thoroughness. As she rubbed she was aware of the muscle, bone and sinew that had been knitted into a finely sculpted line, as beautiful and responsive as a costly musical instrument. A dancer's leg.

She sighed as she worked, and once more her thoughts turned to the approaching winter. Its inevitable dampness and cold would play havoc with the limb. Ruefully she wondered if she'd be like the old farmer with arthritis, his creaking joints a faithful harbinger of snow and rain.

When she'd finished, Raine laid her head back against the sofa and let her gaze move idly around the silent room. For all its quaintness, the space seemed impersonal to her. Riva had invested no part of herself in the apartment, which seemed somehow out of keeping with a woman whose sense of style was otherwise so flamboyant. Then Raine realized that her sister conserved all of that—color, drama, emotion—as raw material for dance.

Raine wondered how long the two of them could live together under one roof. At first when Riva had somewhat condescendingly insisted that her twin room with her, Raine had balked at the idea. Then pride had given way to practical necessity; she knew she had no choice. She had only a small nest egg tucked away for emergencies, and the salary she'd be getting from the company would be a pittance.

Her "room" was no more than a curtained alcove with a narrow iron bedstead, but it did possess a half-moon window through which she could just glimpse the jumbled Parisian rooftops. It was enough.

Snapping out of her reverie, she sat up and began to flex her leg. The heat-generating balm had done its work, and the pain had subsided to a faint throb. Months ago the doctor had given her a prescription, but she'd never bothered to have it filled. She used the pain as a gauge to determine how long and how hard she could work out without causing further injury to herself.

She'd just lowered the leg again when the front door flew open and Riva breezed in. Over her sleeveless black leotard she wore tight jeans and high-heeled sandals, and she carried a straw shopping basket in one hand.

"You found your way up, I see." Coming over to the sofa, she leaned down to brush her cheek against her sister's.

Raine smiled ironically to herself at this less-than-effusive welcome, considering how long it had been since they'd last seen each other. "Thanks for having me" was all she murmured in reply. "It's good to be here."

Riva made no answer to that. Instead her nose crinkled in disgust as she demanded, "What are you using on your leg? That stuff reeks!"

Raine ignored the remark as she stood up and followed her sister to the kitchen. She leaned against the doorway of the dark narrow cubicle with its World War Two-vintage appliances. "I saw you in class today," Raine said. "You looked ravishing, as always."

Riva looked up swiftly, observing with deceptive

lightness, "I see you didn't waste any time today getting around. Bran was asking a million questions about you."

Raine's color deepened at that, and she was glad that Riva was too preoccupied putting groceries away to notice. She watched as the milk and yogurt, protein powder and raisins were stashed away, along with a piece of sticky honeycomb in a jar—more raw material to feed a dancer's energy.

"I'm sure he's intrigued," Raine replied at last in as cool a tone as she could muster. "It's just like having another you around." Reaching over, she picked up the blue enamel kettle from the stove top where it had been simmering.

Riva regarded her sharply. "What's eating you?"

"Nothing." Raine flung back with equal tartness as she prepared two cups of strong black tea and stirred in overflowing spoonfuls of honey. Picking up her mug, she went to curl up in the overstuffed velvet chair that looked like a refugee from an Art Deco movie theater. "Nothing at all," she went on as Riva followed her into the room with her own cup and stretched out on the sofa. "I guess I'm simply getting tired of stumbling over your lovers—you leave them strewn around like broken toy soldiers."

Riva leaned over to retrieve a cigarette from the brass box on the coffee table. She never inhaled, Raine knew—she was far too mindful of her vital lung capacity needed for breathtaking leaps and *soubresauts*—but the action kept her nervous hands busy.

Raine observed her as she lighted the cigarette, and her eyes gleamed with humor. Here they hadn't seen each other in at least a year, and they were both wearing exactly the same shade of rose-colored polish on their fingernails. And Raine had known without asking how much honey to put in her sister's tea, had known she would prefer lemon to milk. Their biological clocks were identical as well, both were night owls who loved nothing more than to sleep late in the morning. But beyond those gut-level similarities they had hardly anything in common.

Riva had been watching her, too. "Did Bran tell you that—that we're lovers?"

"No, but he didn't have to." Raine's eyes darkened to amber glints as the memory of the sweetly invasive passion of his kiss rose unbidden in her mind. But she forced herself to forget it.

Riva stood up in agitation and went over to the long window overlooking the square. The afternoon sunlight caught the fine planes of her face; she was like a piece of living sculpture. But though Raine's eyes followed her, she really didn't see her sister. It was too much like looking in a mirror, she thought, so that she was unaware of the effect of her own delicate oval face framed with long chestnut hair, the short straight nose above the generous upper lip that combined to create a subtle air of sensuality, in contrast to the petite grace of her body.

"Bran and I have to be discreet, you know," Riva said at last in a soft feline purr. "Otherwise the rest of the dancers might get jealous."

Her sister's rippling contralto laughter sounded at her back. "Since when has that been your credo?" Raine couldn't resist needling her.

To her surprise Riva whipped around, her lovely

features marred by anger. "Why did you come to Paris anyway—just to hassle me, *chère soeur*?" The words "dear sister" spilled from her lips with biting irony.

Shaken by this unexpected attack, Raine set her mug down carefully and looked up at her sister with large eyes grown somber in their intensity. "I don't know exactly why I came, Riva, but I'm here now. And I do intend to stay." She hesitated, then, as if debating whether to go on, finally deciding that they might as well clear the air right now. "There's one other thing I must know," she demanded quietly. "Why have you been telling people that I'll never dance again?"

"Because it's the truth!" Riva spat out, her eyes still flashing with anger and other emotions.

Raine sensed it then, the unspoken animosity fueling their argument. Riva couldn't stand the idea of having to face her sister once more in the competitive milieu of dance. Somehow that realization served to give Raine strength. In the past she'd thought she was the only one to feel the competitive sting that made her ache to possess her sister's technical virtuosity. But what did she possess that Riva might envy? She couldn't resist asking herself that, though no answer came to mind.

Raine addressed her sister quietly. "I've been doing barre work again, Riva, and a bit of adagio, too. I'm not quite washed up yet."

Riva's gaze slid away as if she was unwilling to accept her sister's words. She puffed nervously at the cigarette in her hand before observing, "You're crazy if you think you can steal dance time away from your work with Madame T. The old lady can be a real harridan.'' Stubbing out her cigarette, she gulped down the rest of her tea. ''Look, I've got to run. I have an appointment with a podiatrist to have the kinks massaged out of my feet. By the way, Bran is having an informal little get-together tonight at his place, and a lot of the corps will be there.... He said it would be all right if you came along,'' she added with a touch of reluctance.

Raine couldn't tell from the way Riva had phrased the words whether Brandon had extended the invitation or whether Riva had mentioned the idea to him first. Somehow it was very important for Raine to know; still, she wouldn't ask directly. The last thing in the world she wanted was for her sharp-eyed sister to sense that she had even the faintest interest in Brandon.

Raine's lips curved upward in a wry smile. ''I suppose the question now is whether it's okay with you if I come to the party.''

Riva read the affected deference, the touch of challenge in the clear golden depths of her sister's eyes, and she swore in exasperation. ''I don't give a damn what you do! Just remember one thing, Raine—you're no longer hibernating in some backwater coal burg. So I'd advise you to borrow something suitable to wear out of my closet.''

With that cool pronouncement Riva left the apartment, slamming the door so hard behind her that the door frame shook. Gradually the clatter of her high-heeled sandals on the narrow wooden staircase faded away.

Raine seethed quietly. ''Damn her!'' she swore at

last, still smarting from Riva's insinuation that she was less sophisticated and less chic: an innocent country girl come to town.

This latest little contretemps between the two sisters caused Raine to completely revise her plans for the rest of the afternoon. She had intended to visit the Tuileries gardens and the Louvre, and to prowl through the museum shop in search of a few inexpensive Degas prints. But that could wait. For now, a little more serious shopping was in order.

Street map and transport guide in hand, she caught the *métro* in the rue des Abbesses and rode the modern, bullet-quick underground into the heart of the city. From the Place Vendôme with its gracious seventeenth-century buildings and distinctive Napoleonic column, Raine caught a bus that traveled a route past the elegant couturier houses on the rue du Faubourg St-Honoré and on to the rue de Rivoli with its bright arcades.

At the Pont Neuf she disembarked, deciding to cross Paris's oldest bridge on foot. The meandering Seine sparkled brightly in the sun as she made her way to the Left Bank, where the Sorbonne and a dozen other academies rose in stately juxtaposition to the nearby rows of jazzy boutiques Raine had read about.

She lingered awhile among the little booksellers' stalls that lined the quay above the river, enjoying the art show of old prints and new postcards dangling on clothespins from the sides of the carts. Then, after having an ice cream cone from a corner vendor, she made her way at a leisurely pace to the rue de Sèvres.

Later, Raine tried not to think of the mortal blow

she'd dealt to her savings account after an afternoon of poking around in the dazzling boutique racks that carried everything from avant garde metallic shirts to bright folkloric prints. But as she'd shopped she'd been forced to admit to herself that Riva's point, for all its condescension, had been well taken.

She'd been so intent during the past year on the inner woman and her vicissitudes that she'd nearly forgotten the externals. For a change, she let go and pampered herself, and as she boarded a crosstown bus with her armload of packages, she reflected that for the first time in a long time she'd begun to feel good about being Raine Cameron.

As the churches and weatherworn monuments of old Paris merged in an imposing streak of gray and ocher beyond the bus window, Raine thought ahead to the coming evening. She hated to admit to herself how much she was looking forward to seeing Brandon again, even though that anticipation was dimmed by her knowledge of his relationship with Riva. His touch had struck a responsive chord deep within her, and she knew that it would take all the acting skill she possessed to pretend she didn't care.

The afternoon had nearly gone by the time the laboring bus climbed the hills of Montmartre, past the neon-lighted bars of Pigalle, their tawdriness a sharp contrast to the lovely small streets on the Left Bank. Raine's cheerful mood stayed with her as she climbed down from the bus and made her way back to the apartment. She'd walked much too far. If only she could forget the throb of pain in her leg and the network of tortured memories tied to it in her mind. . . .

THE EVENING SKY was a black silken banner as Raine crossed the wide stone bridge linking the two islands that were situated in the middle of the Seine. To her back was the cathedral of Notre-Dame, its spot-lighted buttresses like rows of massive arms bent under the weight of history. Ahead of her, protected by a double frontier of trees and water, lay the tiny Ile St-Louis with its silent quays and seventeenth-century gray stone facades, unchanged in three centuries.

As she walked along the deserted cobblestone side-walks, Raine idly wondered how Brandon could afford a home on the prestigious island. From what she'd heard, its real estate prices were the most astronomical in the city, and she knew from her own experience that ballet companies couldn't afford to pay their members generous salaries. Telling herself firmly that it was none of her business, Raine hurried along toward the address on the Quai de Bourbon that Riva had written down for her.

A few moments later she stopped in the light of an old-fashioned street lamp to tighten the strap of one sandal, readjust her cotton challis shawl over one arm and brush back the soft curling tumble of chest-nut hair that glinted with russet and gold highlights. Beneath her shawl was a full-sleeved peasant blouse in a soft rose that contrasted beautifully with the creamy expanse of her bare shoulders. Gathered around her waist was a rose and fuchsia skirt shot through with gold threads.

Five minutes later she stepped into the elegantly carved entryway at number 15 and climbed the stairs to the second story. Evidently these enormous mansions from another era had been subdivided into modern condominiums. Raine knocked loudly, hoping to be heard over the wave of melodic jazz that penetrated even the massive oak barrier of the front door.

It was opened at last, and she was whisked inside by several smiling guests, none of whom she recognized. Her shawl and bag were spirited away, and a glass of wine was thrust into her empty hands. Left alone then, she was able to catch her breath and glance around the apartment with curious eyes. Neither Brandon nor Riva was in sight.

His quarters had a lean Spartan air about them, like an unfinished abstract painting. The windows were curtainless, the floors were without rugs and a plain gray leather sofa faced the marble fireplace. One wall was taken up by an elaborate stereo, scores of albums and several piled boxes that looked as though they were waiting to be unpacked. Filled bookshelves lined another wall. She caught sight of a row of gleaming trophies on the top shelf, and once again she found herself speculating curiously on Brandon's background.

At that moment Riva came into the room from the kitchen, and the two women spied each other at the same time. Riva's eyes narrowed as she took in her sister's softly feminine attire, which hadn't come from *her* closet. Raine sighed, realizing she should never presume to involve herself in a game of one-upmanship with Riva where drama was concerned.

The ballerina wore a black skirt with a provocative slit halfway up the front of it and a tight-fitting red-and-white-striped jersey. Her hair framed her face in a series of dizzying little waves that had been set in place with a crimping iron. This was Riva's witty salute to the famed French women of the night, a look of unadulterated sexiness designed to show off her exquisite dancer's body to maximum advantage. There was nothing subtle about her.

Riva inclined her head in her sister's direction, a set smile on her lips. The message in her eyes was unmistakable, however: come in if you like, but don't expect me to smooth the way.

"Hellion!" Raine swore under her breath. But as she turned her back on her sister, a self-mocking little laugh escaped her lips, because she knew that she herself could be just as arrogantly stubborn when she chose.

As she turned, Raine's eye was caught by the large oil canvas on the wall adjacent to the foyer. Her eyes drank in the original artwork with its muted colors and bold sweep of expressive line. The dynamic painting affected her in the same way that she'd hoped her dancing might touch a member of the audience; it was full of emotional depth, yet sparkling with life. She definitely approved of Brandon's taste in art.

Her thoughts were cut short when the front door swung open, and she found herself standing face to face with a robust-looking man, his ruddy cheeks agleam like Normandy apples above his short beard. His brown eyes went liquid at the sight of her, and in that moment he seemed to pale a little.

"Riva, how gorgeous you look tonight!" he exclaimed thickly. "God, you don't know what torture it is for me—"

"Hello," Raine interrupted him coolly. Her pretty brows had arched subtly in a here-we-go-again expression as the anguished French syllables washed over her. She'd spoken as quickly as possible to stem the flow before any embarrassing revelations were made, but the moment was still quite awkward. How many more of Riva's lovers, current and past, would she have to stumble over before the night was through! "I'm Raine Cameron, Riva's sister," she introduced herself, feeling like a scratched record that repeats one phrase endlessly.

He looked stricken. "*Ah, pardon, mademoiselle.* She never mentioned a sister. I—forgive me."

"Never mind." Raine smiled at him, her eyes full of teasing warmth. She felt sorry for the man, yet instinctively she found herself liking him as well. "It's been that kind of day," she added in mock exasperation.

"Ah, I can well imagine." He smiled a little in return, although it was apparent that he hadn't quite recovered from his embarrassing but highly understandable faux pas. "So," he began again after an awkward pause, "how do you like the painting that you seemed to be studying so carefully when I came in?"

"I like it very much," she answered at once. "Usually I'm not a big fan of abstract art, but this is terrific. It's so alive."

A boyish grin transfigured his features then. "Thank you, *mademoiselle*. You see, I'm the artist," he explained with a laughingly executed little bow. "Pierre Junot at your service."

His good humor was infectious, and Raine found

herself laughing, too. "I'm glad I gave it a good review," she teased before adding more seriously, "Do you show at local galleries?"

The animation in his warm brown eyes dimmed a little. "When I can. Unfortunately, my output isn't that great. I have to work to support myself by means other than my canvases. As a matter of fact, I'm the set designer for the Ballet du Monde."

"If your sets are anything like this, they must be superb," Raine told him with genuine enthusiasm. "I'll look forward to seeing them."

"Thank you. I only wish Riva shared your enthusiasm for my art." The man's smile was crooked. "But it seems that the people I care for most are the ones who care the least about my work."

"Riva's quite an art fan," Raine protested, not knowing quite what else to say.

"She's also a fan of all the finer things in life that only money can buy."

She bit her lip at that wry observation, knowing full well Riva's penchant in that direction. But why on earth had she strung Pierre along in the first place if she knew he had neither connections nor money?

Their conversation was interrupted as a brown hand clapped down on Pierre's shoulder, and they both looked up, startled, into Brandon's face. His glance ricocheted between them, only to return more slowly to Raine and rove with interest over a wave of soft shiny hair to the velvety expanse of her bare shoulder. His eyes, with their compelling electric-blue intensity, continued to flick downward, lingering on her rounded curve of breast, the subtle swell of her hip and shapely calf.

Bran's slow arrogant appraisal made her feel like a prize Thoroughbred filly on the auction block, but she also realized that through his eyes she was made more deliciously aware of her own femininity. It was a heady feeling, yet a potentially dangerous one. She reminded herself that she wanted no part of this man, even as her heart began to beat a little more quickly in her breast and a warm flush of anticipation stained her cheeks.

"What is this, Junot?" Brandon demanded of his friend with exaggerated severity. "Are you trying to corner the market on the Cameron sisters?"

The two men laughed, although Raine sensed the subtlest hint of tension beneath Brandon's easy geniality. She understood at once, imagining the two must have been rivals for her sister. He'd tried not to show it, but the dark smolder in Brandon's eyes indicated his jealousy. Seeing that look, Raine felt a highly uncharacteristic pang of dismay.

Chiding herself for being such a fool, Raine began to edge away from the two men, hoping to lose herself in the anonymous laughing crowd gathered around the fireplace. But someone had come up to Pierre and engaged him in an animated conversation, so that she found herself standing alone with her host. The dark look had vanished from Brandon's eyes, to be replaced with an objective teasing glint as he cocked his head and inspected her with the same slow measuring look that had discomfited her a moment earlier.

"You'd better come with me," he murmured at last, his low laughter softening the words somewhat. "I hate the sight of a hungry dancer. Lovely little starvelings tend to arouse my . . . concern."

Raine's eyes flashed warningly. "You're a real philanthropist, is that it?" she replied with a touch of irony. "Offering your board and—"

"Bed?" Brandon concluded for her with a wicked grin, enjoying the golden flicker of anger in her eyes. "But you're not quite right about that, Raine Cameron. Usually it's the woman who offers first."

Her cheeks flamed with indignation. "I hate to destroy your egotistical illusions," Raine retorted more hotly, "but I don't use satin sheets as stepping stones in my career."

She made a move to turn away, but his hand had shot out more quickly to imprison her arm, and Raine was being propelled through the crowded living room to the candle-lighted dining area, Brandon's deep baritone chuckle goading her as they moved across the floor.

Raine momentarily forgot her anger as her gaze took in the dining table with its tempting array of food, and she was forced to admit to herself that Brandon had been right on the mark with his teasing observations about a hungry dancer. She was in fact starved, having eaten nothing all day but the ice cream cone she'd bought from the vendor on the quay above the Seine.

There were elegant molds of Strasbourg goose-liver pâté, a selection of ripe cheeses from Brie to Pont l'Evêque, long crusty loaves and a bounteous assortment of *crudités*, along with a casual arrangement of orchard-fresh peaches in a long wooden bowl. After Raine had filled her plate to overflowing, she felt Brandon's proprietary arm once more on her elbow as he urged her along, this time through the narrow door that led into the kitchen. With one hand he pulled out a leather-backed bar stool and gestured for her to sit down.

He seemed to forget her then as he busied himself, retrieving bottles of beer from the refrigerator and arranging them in ice-filled copper tubs. Raine watched him in silence, her edginess abating a little as she ate several morsels of cheese and bit into the pâté with its delicious hint of apple brandy.

As she observed him, Raine reflected that Brandon du Rivage hardly fitted the image of a dancer. His features, the slightly crooked nose and wide cleft jaw, seemed hewn out of granite, and he radiated an almost pugnacious vitality that was all male. She realized that he mustn't have been exaggerating a bit when he'd told her with a grin that it was usually the woman who did the pursuing.

Unexpected she smiled, thinking how wrong he'd be to expect the same of her. And she waited. Her gaze grew curious as she saw him pull a vintage bottle of Moët & Chandon champagne from the lower shelf of the refrigerator. After deftly uncorking the bottle, he filled two slender glasses and handed one to Raine. Then he reached out with his glass and clinked it lightly against hers.

Not trusting herself yet to raise her eyes to his, Raine focused on the pale gold of the wine, shot through with a thousand crystal bubbles. "What's the occasion, Monsieur du Rivage?" she demanded finally, willing her expressive eyes to reveal nothing more than an amused watchfulness.

"To your arrival in Paris, *mademoiselle*," he answered at once. For all their teasing banter, his words held the light warmth of a caress. Brandon's eyes sought hers, and their gazes collided like a storm-tossed sloop against a rocky shore.

Perturbed by the effect of those glinting ultramarine depths, Raine glanced hastily away. She was determined to get their interchange back to safe neutral ground. "How did you come to dance, Brandon?" she asked him at last. "I noticed the line of trophies on your bookshelf, and I know for a fact that there aren't any Oscars or Emmies for dance. What precisely did you excel in?" Playfulness and unabashed curiosity mingled in her tone.

Grinning at her inquisitiveness, Bran dragged another bar stool out and sat down facing her, straddling the stool so that his arms rested on the leather back and his knees nearly touched hers. "I played professional soccer for six years, and four of those six I made the national team," he explained matter-of-factly.

"You must have been good," Raine observed as she sipped at the exceedingly fine dry champagne.

Brandon shrugged. "I'd built up the speed, endurance and agility from dance. I studied ballet from the time I was eight to the time I was eighteen, when I became a professional athlete."

"Why did you give it up?" she asked softly, her playfulness giving way to intense interest.

"Why did I give up ballet, or why did I give up soccer?" he countered.

"Both."

The choreographer, too, seemed to have forgotten their badinage of a moment earlier. His eyes grew thoughtful, and Raine noticed the way his fingers moved restlessly around the rim of his wineglass. "I was a pragmatic man," he observed finally. "I made good money in soccer, invested it well and decided to retire and devote my time again to ballet."

"Why did you choose ballet in the first place?"

The muscle along his jawline tensed for an instant before he replied in a brusque tone, "My mother was a dancer. She came to Europe from New York and studied with Nina Tarsamova. Ballet was something out of my childhood that I could never quite get out of my blood." His curtness left as much unsaid as his words revealed.

Raine's gaze traveled once more over his angular and somewhat battered features that seemed to meld humility with a commanding arrogance. "You're actually American, then?"

"Not quite. My father was born in Paris." He grinned suddenly. "It makes for an interesting amalgam. I suppose I get my practicality from my French blood."

"And from the American half?" Raine couldn't resist asking.

He shrugged. "Not much, I suppose, except for my great liking for other Americans." Brandon caught her chin then and lifted it, so that she had no choice but to meet his blue gaze and read the sparkle of mischief that gleamed there.

After a moment he got up restlessly from the stool and went to stand before the small bare window that looked out onto the medieval towers and gargoyles of Notre Dame.

Raine followed him with her eyes. "And you still dance?" she persisted softly.

When he turned back slowly to look at her, she saw that the laughter had fled from his eyes. "No," he answered at last, the word an explosive sigh. "At first I believed that those six years I'd given up to professional sports wouldn't matter. But I was wrong, of course, and I soon found that my body was always giving less than my imagination could create. I knew I could never be a great dancer, so...I began to create steps and movements for other dancers who could attain the perfection I knew I'd never be able to reach. Can you understand that?" Brandon demanded almost angrily, his brows dipping in a brooding furrow above his eyes, as if he were already regretting having spoken so frankly.

He turned away then, but Raine's clear gold gaze continued to bore into his darkly sculpted profile. "Yes, I do understand," she murmured as she stood up. "I've been fighting similar demons of my own this past year, Brandon."

His head swiveled to assess her sharply, eyes aglitter with unspoken questions. Raine never would have confessed even that much if he hadn't opened up to her first. Madame Tarsamova was the only person in whom she'd confided, the only one who had guessed the extent of the emotional scars she still bore. Raine was nervously debating how much more she should say to Brandon, how much more she should trust him, when their brief moment of shared understanding was broken as Riva breezed into the kitchen.

"Ah, getting acquainted with my sister, Bran, darling?" Riva inquired archly as she came up and slipped her arm possessively through his. "Lovely, isn't she?'' she went on teasingly, eyes brimming with coy mischief.

"Yes. Yes, she is," Brandon reverted to English, his low voice once more cool and controlled.

There was a long moment of awkward silence, until Raine sensed that the two lovers were waiting for her to leave so they could be alone. The realization cut her deeply, and she found herself almost hating them both in that instant. Nevertheless, she managed to say in a light tone, "You'll both have to excuse me. I think I should mingle with the other corps members, or they'll start to think I'm a snob."

As Raine turned to leave the kitchen, Riva's equally offhand voice sounded at her back. "Yes, you *do* have that reputation, sister, dear."

She went rigid at that softly flung taunt but didn't bother to turn around again to confront Riva. Raine had no intention of exchanging barbed words and accusations with her sister as Brandon looked on in amusement. She had too much self-respect for that sort of cheap display. Instead she pushed open the swinging door and went on through the dining area, wondering with an angry little sigh what cleverly distorted stories had begun to circulate in the company about her.

And indeed, while the other dancers in the living room didn't go so far as to pointedly exclude Raine from their conversation, neither did they invite her into their midst. Again she found herself gravitating toward the friendly bearded artist.

"Ah, did du Rivage let you go at last, the *salaud*?" Pierre inquired amiably as she came up to him. "When my friend decides he wants something he goes after it, and there's no stopping him. That's what made him such a hotshot scorer on the soccer field.''

Raine couldn't help but be intrigued by Pierre's observations about Brandon. "Really? And he never felt his masculinity was threatened by dropping out in mid-career and turning to dance, as so many men would have?'' she asked.

"He was teased by his compatriots at first, until they found out that their women were still chasing after du Rivage. Believe me, his friends have a healthy respect for his male attributes.'' Though he said that laughingly, Raine didn't miss the bitter little sigh that escaped his lips.

She looked at him for a long moment, her eyes warmly sympathetic. "Are you still in love with Riva, then, Pierre?''

He shrugged, his shoulders lifting in a typical Gallic gesture that could say so much, or so little. "I hope that you and I can be friends at least, Raine,'' he said, charmingly evading her question.

Their conversation was interrupted then as the upbeat jazz on the stereo was replaced by the passionately strummed chords of a Spanish flamenco, and a moment later a gaminlike woman with short blond hair jumped up onto Brandon's low coffee table and began dancing to boisterous cries of "*Olé*, Tracey!'' From the battered condition of the sturdy tabletop, Raine guessed that such impromptu party performances were not a rare event, and she was soon laughing in delight at the dancer's irrepressible antics.

The woman wore snug black jeans, a matching

short toreador jacket and a white ruffled blouse that really made her look like a fearsomely proud Spanish flamenco dancer. Her performance enhanced the image as her heels struck the wood with machine-gun rapidity, and she spun with taut grace, sharply clapping her hands in faultless imitation of castanets. As the music dissolved in a Latin fury of strummed notes, Tracey bowed low. But when she rose again, her face had lost its forbidding lines, replaced by a wide pixieish grin, full of energy and life.

Raine found herself laughing and applauding as exuberantly as everyone else in the audience. A few minutes later, after the tumult had died down, Pierre commented to Raine, "It's a good thing your sister was preoccupied in the kitchen. Otherwise, we'd have had a real dance battle on our hands."

Raine grew thoughtful. "Is Riva jealous of this Tracey?"

Pierre smiled a touch grimly. "Not of Tracey per se, but of anyone who might threaten to upstage her in any way. Riva is the undisputed queen, and she won't let anybody forget it. And you must admit she's right. No one can touch her as far as sheer talent is concerned."

Raine's chin lifted at that. "Is that supposed to be a friendly warning to me, Pierre, not to throw myself in Riva's path?" she demanded in a tone that was only half teasing, though her eyes glinted now with wry humor.

"You know your own sister, Raine. I didn't. I had to learn the hard way about her."

Raine's heart went out to him. "She must have

known from the start what you were, didn't she, Pierre?"

He brushed his long sensitive fingers down his beard. "She knew I was an artist from a wealthy family."

"I...I see."

Pierre laughed. "You don't see at all, I can tell. Your sister must not confide in you. But never mind. I refuse to bore you with the details of my life." His eyes narrowed then as Riva came over to join them.

"So you two have met," she said with a mischievous smile, raising her hands to her slender but well-delineated hips in the sexy black skirt. "Do you like what you see?"

Though Riva's teasing eyes had slid to her twin's features, Pierre's gaze was still riveted on Riva. "Appearances can be deceiving." She laughed archly before drifting off to join the crowd in front of the fireplace, leaving Pierre to stare after her broodingly.

"She's a selfish woman," he whispered bitterly, half to himself.

"Single-minded might be a better word, or ambitious," Raine surprised herself by protesting.

Pierre shook his head. "You defend her because she's your sister, but I get the feeling you're not like her underneath."

"Are you saying that you think she'll always get the better of me?" Raine demanded quietly.

"All I'm saying is that she'll get what she wants."

"Which is?"

The look Pierre shot her was angry, resigned. "To have du Rivage in the palm of her hand."

"I thought she already had him there," Raine

eplied a little too sharply. But Pierre refused to answer that, perhaps because he didn't want to know himself. After a while she ventured, "Have you known Brandon a long time?"

"Yes. He was ahead of me in school, so I always looked up to him and relied on him for advice. But for all that, I don't know him well. He's a hard man to get close to."

Raine looked at the artist with new interest. "Why?"

Tugging meditatively at his beard, Pierre considered that. "Who can say, really? He is a man who is always at war with himself. He and I share that much at least." The brooding look returned to his eyes. "That binds us despite everything else. But for him the problem is that his destiny is tied too closely to that of his family, while for me it is not tied closely enough."

Raine's gaze darkened questioningly. "I don't understand."

"Nor do I sometimes, I'm afraid." His gaze shifted to Brandon and Riva, where they stood deep in conversation by the window. "Now if you will pardon me, I must leave."

After he'd gone, Raine wandered over to the bookshelves to take a closer look at the gleaming trophies that seemed to guard the room with an air of benevolent assurance. Just as she stepped behind the immense Kentia palm, whose large pottery base and lush foliage nearly filled the corner adjacent to the shelves, a couple of people strolled past and paused there a moment.

Though they spoke in quiet tones, their conversation drifted back unmistakably to where Raine stood alone in her partially hidden position.

"All we needed was another little American bitch to try and take over everything for herself."

"Like two peas in a pod."

"*Oui*—both rotten."

Raine clenched her fists at her sides in silent dismay. Speculation must have run rampant in the company after Raine's unexpected arrival. Perhaps they were justified in assuming the worst about her; still, it angered and hurt her to be judged so viciously by strangers.

Deciding that she'd had enough, too, Raine began to move toward the front door, until she realized that she wouldn't get too far without her shawl and bag. Turning, she made her way down the long deserted hallway. She had seen her things disappear in this direction earlier in the evening.

At the end of the corridor a door stood ajar, and soft light emanating from a bedside lamp seemed to beckon her inside. Raine glanced around the spacious master suite with interest, her eyes taking in the masculine relaxing color scheme of gray and hunter green. The room had a very different air from the unfinished quality of the rest of the apartment.

Set on the dark gray carpeted platform that dominated the center of the room was a low bed, its rich designer comforter tucked in with precision. Directly behind it, a pair of French doors opened onto a balcony. Through the open doors came the distant sound of Parisian traffic, its screech and roar muted to a low pleasant hum, buffered by the river and the rustling chestnut trees along the quays.

After Raine had found her things among the heap on the bed, she stepped up onto the platform and moved toward the empty balcony. From where she

stood, the view of Sainte-Chapelle, its miraculously
slender spire seeming to float above the dark silhouette of the Conciergerie, was more enchanting
than anything she could have imagined. She found
herself reluctant to leave. Far below her, the river
gleamed like old silver as it flowed languorously
around the island. Raine followed the silent currents
with her eyes, letting the beauty and tranquillity of the
scene invade her senses until she began to relax at last.

Her quiet mood was shattered, however, as a low
urgent voice rang out from the doorway. "I was
wondering where the devil you'd disappeared to."

As startled as if she'd been caught trespassing in a
very private domain, Raine whirled in confusion to
face Brandon. "I...I was just leaving," she murmured even as he crossed the room toward her in
three loping strides.

A moment later he was beside her on the balcony,
and his hands reached out to grip her arms. "Why is
that?" he demanded. His eyes deepened to indigo in
the moonlight as they bore intently into hers.

Raine glanced away, once more seeking the delicate
tracery of the Gothic chapel before her own eyes could
reveal how his very presence disturbed her, how his
touch infused her with warmth and an inexpressible
need. At last she turned to face him and drew a shaky
breath. "I guess I'm not quite used to French hospitality," she replied. Though her lips curved upward in
a half smile, her eyes glistened like hot spilled brandy.

"What happened?" Brandon asked more quietly.

"Nothing much," she laughed, then just as quickly bit her lip to keep from crying. "But I suppose it's
never pleasant to find yourself so cruelly prejudged."

He relaxed his iron grip on her arms and shook her lightly. "Is that all?" he countered, his low voice edged now with irritation. "Aren't you woman enough, Raine, professional enough to know that backbiting and vicious gossip are as much a part of ballet as the harmony and grace displayed on stage to the world? If you want to hear stories about jealousy and feuding, about ground glass poured into the toe of a slipper and shoes stolen before a performance, talk to Nina."

Raine stiffened at his lack of sympathy. "Just because it happens doesn't mean I have to like it!" she retorted.

"No. But I think there's an American saying." Brandon paused and shot her a mocking grin. "'If you can't stand the heat, get out of the kitchen.'"

Raine's bruised feelings were eclipsed by anger, and her eyes reflected the hard polished sheen of topaz. "How dare you lecture me as if I were a child," she replied as she lifted her chin to a defiant angle.

"Why not?" he countered. "You're behaving like one."

Her cheeks flamed with indignation. "I am not one of your corps de ballet, to be ordered around like a puppet." She bit off each word in turn and flung it at him.

"No, not yet, *mademoiselle*, not yet...but you will be." Although he spoke with aggravating assurance, his blue eyes gleamed like the hot core of a flickering flame.

Infuriated by his calm presumptions and air of superiority, Raine made a move to step around him and leave the apartment. But once again he was far too swift for her, moving with lithe pantherish grace to block her path.

An ill-controlled blend of fury and excitement blazed in her eyes. "Is this a new dance you're choreographing, Brandon?" she taunted. "You can call it *Cheap Seduction*. It should be a new twist for a man who boasts of always having to run from pursuing women."

The harsh laughter in his eyes spilled downward to slash his lips in a crooked line. "You're full of surprises, Raine," he rejoined, an unexpected intensity simmering beneath his raillery. "If you'd channel those hot emotional depths to the stage, you could be another Pavlova."

She regarded him in stony disbelief. No one had ever before compared her to the legendary Russian ballerina.

Brandon laughed more easily now. "Don't you trust me?" he demanded, the intimacy of his tone washing over her like the heady aroma of aged cognac.

"No," she whispered, even as his dark hands came up to frame her face and draw her mouth slowly to his.

Their lips met as softly as two leaves that brush and chafe against one another in a shadowed secluded bower, only to cling more urgently as if a sudden wind had whipped them into an ungovernable frenzy.

"No!" she whispered again as she shook her head. But the murmured syllable had quite the opposite effect, only serving to open a sweet pathway into the moist dark harbor sought by his ravishing tongue.

Stunned by the invasive power of a kiss that went

far beyond the almost playful intimacy of their studio encounter, Raine lifted her arms to push him away. In response Brandon's hands dropped to hers and encircled them, forcing them down to her sides, so that the tiny hairs on his fingers grazed her breasts through the thin cotton of her blouse. Raine felt the traitorous response of her body as he pinioned her hands to either side of her on the iron balcony rail.

The burning pressure of his mouth on hers eased then as he allowed his mobile lips to slide down across her chin to the velvet contours of her pale throat. His mouth explored wantonly, here pausing to flick a sensitive hollow with the tip of his tongue, there biting gently into the bare gleaming ridge of her collarbone.

He released her arms, and his hands were now free to slide upward past the indentation of her waist. Raine drew in her breath sharply as his fingers skimmed the ruffled neckline of her peasant blouse. Once more he lowered his head, and his mouth followed the teasing tracery of his fingers.

Her breasts grew warm and flushed. His lips sought their shadowed valley with an intensity that was at once teasing and hungry. Questing mouth and hands joined in an irresistible duet as Bran gently pushed her blouse farther down her arms until the thin fabric only precariously covered her.

Frightened by the intensity of feeling that threatened to overwhelm her precious self-control, Raine at last managed to twist away from his slow sensual onslaught.

"No, Brandon!" she rasped as she turned her back on him.

"Why not?" His voice was hoarse as he reached for her again.

"Don't touch me." Despite the ice in her tone, Raine's shoulders shook a little with the aftermath of emotion. Each word was an effort. "I'm sure you've practiced that same duet countless times with Riva. You don't need me to perfect it."

"Damn it, listen to me," he swore angrily.

But before he could say anything more, Riva's light inquisitive voice floated up toward them from the bedroom doorway. "Bran, darling?"

With a quick intake of breath, Raine regained control of herself and stepped back into the room. "I was just leaving, Riva. I came in to get my bag, and Brandon was kind enough to point out some of the sights from his balcony," she went on in an even measured tone. "He's been a thoughtful host," she added with the merest trace of irony.

"Yes, hasn't he?" Riva answered, her eyes narrowing to gold slits as she observed Brandon and Raine together.

Not wanting to prolong the conversation, Raine moved down the platform steps with lissome grace and paused only as she reached the doorway. She turned back, her delicate silhouette softly edged by the low lamplight. "Good night," she murmured. "And thanks very much for your hospitality, Brandon." Again her light voice echoed with gentle irony.

"Raine!" Bran's low voice, deepened by angry impatience, rang past her down the long hall, but she didn't stop.

She'd let herself out the front door and was halfway down the stairs to the second-story landing, when another voice, feminine and unfamiliar, called out her name. Whirling swiftly, she found herself staring up into the features of the blond gamine who'd danced the tabletop flamenco.

Raine relaxed and smiled a little as the dancer went on in an engaging but somewhat unusual accent. "I thought I'd introduce myself before you took off in such a tearing hurry. I'm Tracey Markham."

"I very much enjoyed your performance," Raine responded laughingly.

"Thanks." Tracey grinned in return.

"Are you English?"

"Lord, no!" Tracey replied, crinkling her eyes in amusement. "I'm Australian, from Melbourne."

"You're a long way from home," Raine observed, warming to the other woman's uncomplicated friendliness.

"So are you. It should be fascinating to have identical twins in the same ballet company. This new season could be exciting."

"Then you're one of the few to register any enthusiasm for the idea," Raine put in dryly.

"You know, everyone really thinks Riva is the bee's knees, even if she can be a royal pain in the neck."

Raine laughed, her expression curious. "The bee's knees?"

"Yes, you know—terrific, hotshot. But everyone's jealous that an American has begun to dominate a European company," Tracey elaborated.

"What about you? You're as exotic as any American," Raine said with a smile.

The woman shook her head. "I do love to dance,

but everyone knows I have no burning ambitions—
except to travel round the world. That's how I pay
my way. I've danced in Malaysia, Japan—you name
it. But in the end it's back to Australia for me, to
marry my one true love." Once more she smiled with
exuberant self-assurance.

Raine had grown thoughtful. "And now the other
company members are wondering how this new Cameron will turn out—if she'll be a carbon copy of her
sister."

Tracey cocked her head, regarding Raine with new
intentness. "There's a rumor that you don't even
dance."

"I did...once."

"Do you think you'll try for a comeback?"

Raine sighed, her shoulders lifting uncertainly. "I
honestly don't know. I'm not even sure I can."

Tracey grinned. "Brandon is always looking for
new blood. He may be a regular bastard sometimes
but he's a terrific teacher."

Raine flushed, remembering the way he'd kissed
her. "Yes, I'm sure he is," she said hastily. "Well,
I'd better be going."

"Okay. I won't hold you any longer," Tracey replied, her eyes still bright. "I just came out to say
hello and welcome you to Paris."

"Thanks," Raine replied, touched by Tracey's
cordiality.

After she'd dashed back inside to the party, Raine
slowly descended the stairs to the street and walked
toward one of the bridges that led from the island,
her footsteps beating out a lonely echo on the rough
cobbles.

A few minutes later she heard the throb of a car engine beside her and looked up to find a battered taxi drawing to a halt beside her. "A cab, *chérie*?" the driver inquired as he leaned his head out the window of the Deux Chevaux, a common French economy car.

Raine was tempted to climb in and fall back wearily against the seat. But remembering the depleted state of her pocketbook, she shook her head ruefully. "Thanks, but I guess I'll walk."

To her surprise, the cabby didn't screech off in search of another fare. Instead he spoke again in his clipped staccato Parisian accent. "Listen, *mademoiselle*, the gentleman back at number 15 called up and ordered this cab for you. The trip's already been paid to Montmartre, so you might as well get in."

She turned around, startled, and glanced back along the deserted cobbled street in the direction of the last mansion on the Quai de Bourbon. Without further protest, she got in and relaxed against the worn leather of the back seat.

The cab rumbled across the old stone bridge toward the Right Bank and sped off silently in the direction of the Place de la Concorde. Raine leaned forward to glimpse the towering obelisk that graced the center of the square.

"A beautiful sight, *non*?" the cabby interjected. "More civilized, perhaps, than the guillotine that stood there before it. That's where Louis XVI lost his head."

A moment later the obelisk was behind them and they were swept up in the river of light that coursed along the elegant Champs-Elysées with its fragrant gardens, crowded cafés and brightly lighted store windows. Far ahead Raine glimpsed the imposing silhouette of the Arc de Triomphe that Napoleon had built as a monument to his victories. A short while later the cab was circling the vast square from which twelve avenues radiated like the points of a star. Turning into the busy avenue de Wagram, the driver continued to speed northward, and Raine asked curiously, "Is this the quickest route to Montmartre?"

He shrugged without turning around. "All I know, *mademoiselle*, is that the *monsieur* paid handsomely for you to be driven home—by the most scenic route possible. You're not appreciating the beauty of Paris by night?" he demanded incredulously.

She sat back with a perplexed air, not bothering to answer his question. What was she to make of Brandon du Rivage—a man who was arrogant, strong-willed and demanding, a man whom friend and colleague alike referred to with amiable respect as a "bastard." Yet he'd seen fit to order a taxi for her and provide a lovely surprise tour of the city.

Raine thought back to something the artist, Pierre, had said in passing. "When my friend decides he wants something he goes after it, and there's no stopping him."

What was it he wanted of her, Raine asked herself as the taxi at last drew to a halt in the quiet, nineteenth-century square that for now, at least, was her home.

CHAPTER THREE

RAINE'S FIRST WEEK at the studio passed in a never-ending flurry of activity, and in that short span of time Madame Tarsamova had grown to depend on her young assistant, who willingly took on any assignment. Raine had done everything from substitute teaching for Madame T's class of giggly ten-year-olds to balancing the little company's monthly accounts. A touching warmth was blossoming between the old woman whose stage life had long since ended and the young dancer whose career had never quite begun.

She had wanted to go back to the light-filled studio to watch Brandon work with the corps, but something had held her back. Raine tried to convince herself she was satisfied to have just a peripheral role in the ballet world, but deep down she knew it wasn't true. She wanted desperately to dance again, and fleetingly she wondered if Madame Tarsamova had sensed her discontent.

The ballet mistress had gone out to lunch that day, leaving her assistant in charge. Raine had taken care of the dozen chores and minor problems that had cropped up, posting rehearsal schedules and tracking down an electrician to look over a short circuit in the stage lighting downstairs. As she poured a kettle of tepid water over Madame T's windowsill carnations, Raine told herself with wry amusement that her new job was about as artistic as the secretarial position her Aunt Helen had wanted her to take.

Swallowing her bitterness, Raine sat down in the desk chair and swiveled to look at the photographs arranged on the wall. She wondered if Riva would ever be among the handful of greats in *madame*'s collection. Her twin certainly had the technical virtuosity to make it, something that Raine—accident or not—would never have achieved. Still she knew that greatness required far more than technical skill.

Long before the week had passed, the staff and other dancers had come to distinguish between the sisters, realizing that they were identical only in outward characteristics. Even the least observant person would have found it difficult to mistake Riva's flamboyance for her sister's quiet delicacy. Raine was greeted by name in the halls now with rather more curiosity and less hostility than when she'd first arrived.

A FEW AFTERNOONS LATER, she was alone in the small studio adjacent to Madame T's office. The class she'd subbed in was over, and the little girls in their pink leotards had disappeared in a clatter of shouts and laughter down the corridor. Going to the small record player in the corner, Raine put an album on the turntable.

It had been cloudy all day, and now a dull silvered light poured through the long window, leaving most of the room in shadow. Not thinking of anything in particular, she gazed down into the courtyard, watching as the last of the attractive Parisian matrons collected their children, and a stray tabby cat prowled on the cobblestones. Prokofiev's haunting violin melody with its sadness and longing filled the space around her.

In the shadowy protection of the studio, she began to move across the floor, tentative yet graceful, as the music washed through her veins. Raine could no more have stood still than she could have willed herself to stop breathing. The steps flowed in succession until, rising on pointe, she dipped in a graceful arabesque. For that instant the dancer was a sculpture in space, the purity of her line giving the impression of utter aloneness.

Then the moment was over, the music ended, and Raine stepped down onto her heel like an angel who'd given up flight. She had begun to walk toward the record player when a shadowy movement in the doorway caught her eye, and she glanced up with a startled intake of breath. A small elegant figure in black was framed there.

"*Madame*, I didn't see you," Raine murmured in a rush of French. "How... how long were you standing there?"

"Long enough," the woman replied with a touch of asperity.

Silence fell between them, broken only by the monotonous whir of the record on its turntable. Raine hurried to switch it off, her thoughts guilty, confused. "I'm sorry, *madame*," she began quietly. "I know I should have been—"

"Sorry for what?" the woman countered, her Russian-accented French making the words sound heavy and stilted. "Why apologize, Raine—because you've a body gifted for movement, a finely tuned instrument longing for expression?" Raine stared at her, taken aback. Madame T went on in the same acerbic tone. "If you apologize for anything, it should be for not trying, for giving up what you were born to do."

Raine's eyes flashed at that. "That's much easier for you to say than for me to believe. I know what my body was once capable of, and I refuse to be a ghost chasing after myself."

The woman's lips curved slightly upward in a smile. "You have a poetic bent, Raine. That's one of the things I like about you; it's the spark of a great dancer. You know, of course, that ballet is art, illusion. You start with the dream, the expression and gesture." She paused, her sharp black eyes boring into the younger woman's. "The strength will come later of its own, bit by bit."

Raine positively sparkled now, her excitement undercut by wariness and disbelief. "What are you trying to say, Madame T?" she demanded softly.

"You must dance again, Raine, if for no one else other than yourself," the woman replied, crossing to the window with her long graceful stride, staring out into the gathering dusk. "I've watched you this past week, the way you are drawn to music. For you not to dance is for a painter to have lost his sight." Madame T's head swiveled sharply, her intense gaze sweeping down her young assistant.

Raine's heart leaped at the words. She knew they were true, yet she knew desire wasn't enough. "You may be right," she replied carefully. "Still, I'm a practical-minded woman. I came to Paris to work, not to dance. I don't think I'm strong enough yet to do both.''

Madame T's high-flown Russian romanticism gave way to Gallic practicality. ''Let me worry about that.'' The woman's reply was crisp, abrupt, but she softened it with a smile. ''There are just two requirements: you have to work full-time as a dancer, and to do that you must find a patron.''

''A patron?'' Raine laughed as she repeated the word that seemed to belong to another century. ''Where on earth—''

''That you leave up to me, too,'' Madame T interrupted. ''Tomorrow I want to see you in class with the rest of the corps, bright and early. *Tu comprends?*''

Although her smile was tremulous, Raine's eyes danced fire. *''Oui, madame.''*

RAINE SLIPPED UNOBTRUSIVELY INTO POSITION at the end of the barre, aware of the low murmurs that rippled away from her like waves from a pebble thrown into a still pond. Word traveled fast in the tightly knit company; they knew Raine had joined the troupe now as a dancer.

Ignoring the whispers, Raine went through a quick stretching routine. The injured calf felt limber and almost hot after the vigorous massage she'd subjected it to that morning, but Raine was taking no chances. She wanted desperately to prove she was strong enough to handle the rigors of a professional class again.

One of the double doors that opened onto the hall

swung wide, and Bran came into the studio, his rest-less eyes sweeping down the row of waiting dancers. He wore a cutoff sweat shirt over his gray unitard, the thin stretch fabric emphasizing the rugged lean-ness of his musculature. His long powerful thighs and taut haunches exuded the lithe sensuality of an animal in its prime.

Raine willed herself to control the flutter of ner-vousness in her stomach as his eyes flicked down her—once. Had Bran's cool gaze been assessing, challenging? She wasn't quite certain. They hadn't spoken since the night of his party except for quick hellos when they'd passed in the studio corridors. Of all the company, he was the only one who hadn't seemed to make a distinction between the two sisters, and Raine couldn't help wondering if he'd already forgotten that moment of still intimacy on his apart-ment balcony, when he'd taken her in his arms. Per-haps that was his democratic approach to all the new women in the company. With a little smile, Raine chided herself for even thinking that a spark of some-thing deep and real might have flown between them. Such romantic fancies were totally unlike her.

Her thoughts were interrupted as Bran's deep authoritative voice rang out, and there was no mis-taking he meant business. "Let's get going. We've got a lot to go through this morning."

As he turned to the waiting pianist in the corner, the studio door slowly creaked open, and a blond head peeped around the edge. Raine recognized at once the gamin features of Tracey Markham.

The tiny dancer raced over to the barre, grinning at Raine as she took up the last position. "Welcome aboard," Tracey whispered warmly. "I'd heard Madame T put you in the company."

Raine nodded, though any reply was frozen as Bran's voice grated between them. "You're late again, Tracey. If it happens once more, I'll throw you out on your ear."

"Sorry, sir," she replied contritely. But when he'd turned away, Tracey shot Raine a wicked twinkling look from beneath her lashes that seemed to say, "See, what did I tell you—a regular bastard!"

Tracey's mischievousness somehow gave Raine heart, and she couldn't resist grinning in return.

The pianist struck a sonorous chord, and the workout began. One step followed another in military precision, the dancers' erect backs in contrast to the suppleness of arms and legs that lifted and extended with feline grace. Bran called out the combinations in a brisk monotone, the simple deep stretches of the *grands pliés* giving way to more intricate combinations that demanded every ounce of Raine's concentration.

As she raised on pointe, her left foot beating swiftly against her right ankle in a series of feathery light *petits battements*, anyone might have been convinced of the ease of her movements. That was the art, the illusion that Madame T had spoken of. The reality was the perspiration that started on her temples and coursed down to her chin; the inevitable pain that began as a throb in her lower leg and radiated upward. But Raine steeled herself to ignore it. She knew her own limits, and she hadn't yet begun to reach them.

Bran walked up and down the length of the barre,

pausing here to correct a dancer's posture, there to adjust the turn-out of a hip. His voice rang out at her back, though he never addressed her directly, never touched her. Sensing his watchful eyes on her from time to time, she redoubled her efforts.

Even through her haze of concentration and exhaustion, it was inevitable that Raine would remember the first time she'd been in this studio. Her mind lingered an instant on the fleeting joy of his partnering and the delicious warmth of his unexpected kiss. But inevitably, too, she remembered the cold criticism that had followed. Raine had been too proud to tell him the real reason she hadn't danced in more than a year. She had feared his pity.

Now perhaps he needn't ever find out. She wanted no special consideration. She wanted only to dance, to regain the lost ground that would make her a strong member of the corps. Raine had no illusions about being a star. That she would leave to Riva.

She felt relief and not a little satisfaction at the way she'd kept up at the barre. Still the old tremor of anxiety began to nag at her as Bran called his dancers into the center of the room. She managed a quick smile at the danseur assigned to partner her. All dark eyes and shy smile, the boy couldn't have been more than nineteen. Paul was his name. He had the slender build and tensile musculature of a racehorse.

Her eyes slid over him, automatically measuring his strength. Raine prayed that the new dance Bran was working on would call for no difficult lifts, would give her no access to those sudden flights of panic that had haunted her dreams for a year.

The routine began slowly with supported pir-

ouettes and *penchés*. Inexorably, however, the tempo
and the challenge increased. Unable to quell her un-
reasonable fear, Raine tensed as Paul began to lift
her above his head. Her timing was off and her body
went rigid, causing the whole sequence to look awkward.

"Sorry, Paul," she murmured as he set her down
again.

Gallantly he attempted to assume the blame, but
Bran's cutting voice overrode their exchange. "What
the hell do you think you're doing, Raine—trying to
break Paul's back? I was watching you—you didn't
spring off, you didn't even try to give him an assist in
the lift." His tone was grating, angry. "I won't put
up with dancers who strain their partners just so they
can make the lift seem effortless. Do you understand
me?"

The studio went deadly quiet, all eyes turned to
Raine.

"I was not purposely making myself deadweight,"
she argued coolly, although her face was pink from
his stinging rebuke.

"The hell you weren't," Bran swore in return.
"Give Paul a hand for pity's sake and stop worrying
about yourself."

Her humiliation was complete, but she swallowed
back any further retort. Raine feared he might probe
her fears, and she didn't want that. "I'm sorry," she
said finally between clenched teeth.

The last half of the class was a nightmare for her.
Despite Bran's lashing command, Raine couldn't
forget herself or her fears. Each time Paul swung her
up and over his head, she envisioned a ghostly dancer

sprawled on the floor far below, like a broken doll.

Again and again she tried but she either pushed off too hard or not hard enough. The whole routine was stiff, her own attempts woefully amateurish. Bran didn't say anything more. Still she felt his eyes raking her the whole time, sensed his growing anger and frustration.

It was finally over, and the last chord had barely died away when she grabbed her towel and skirt, ready to bolt for the door. But Bran's curt voice held her back, her name a sharply clipped syllable on his lips. She stood rigidly at the barre as the other dancers streamed past into the corridor, her eyes fixed on the white wall.

Though he stood right behind her now, his voice still seemed distant. "What was wrong with you today?" he demanded. Gone was the fluid French he'd used in class. He spoke to her in curt, impatient English. "Nina told me you were a professional."

Her head shot around at that, eyes flashing with hauteur. "I *am* a professional."

"Then what was going on? You were acting like a scared kid."

Her lashes dipped protectively to brush against her flushed cheeks. "I don't want to talk about it."

When he didn't reply, Raine made a move to brush past him to freedom. His arm shot out to imprison her. "Don't walk out on me." Although his voice was quiet, the warning in it was clear. "If you don't want to discuss what's bothering you, that's your affair. But your performance in class *is* my business. If you refuse to talk it out, then we'll work it out—now."

Her eyes swooped up, their golden depths filled with a reckless light. She was still smarting from the humiliation he'd administered before the others. "And if I refuse?"

"How badly do you want to dance, Raine?" he shot back.

Her chin lifted. Although she said nothing aloud, her glance spoke the truth with compelling simplicity. In her eyes Bran read her passion for the art, her vital need to dance, and he was a little shaken by their depth of expression.

"Okay," he said roughly. "Let's start, then."

Bran filed away the Paganini violin concerto with its implicit demand for virtuosity and selected a softer sonata.

Raine had moved back to the center of the studio and stood with head down, the foot of her weaker leg cocked slightly in a relaxed pose as if she were a proud Thoroughbred in a lonely pasture. The impressionistic landscape of the music swept over her, and she'd almost begun to relax when Bran's hands, suddenly holding her waist from behind, caused her to stiffen again.

"You *are* frightened of something, aren't you?" he said, his voice questioning and intense against the easy swell of the music.

Gone was the rough impatience that had driven her in class. All that Raine sensed now was the warmth and power imbuing him, the dark undercurrent of sensuality she found at once exciting and magnetic. Again he spoke over the rich melody, his voice a note that she found could touch her as deeply as any music. He was talking her through the lift as if she'd never done one before. "Bend your knee slightly so you'll spring off from the ball of the foot. Lift the rib cage...that's right. Now draw in your breath...."

And it was done. There was only a little stiffness this time as she was swung effortlessly above her partner's head, but in a little while even that had disappeared. It was as if the languorous rhythm of the music and his touch had lulled her senses. She could imagine sweet wine flowing through her veins, infusing her limbs with magic.

She felt the spark of rightness in their shared movements. There was no hesitation; their minds seemed to leap at the same instant toward identical points. She felt the old fear surge and then gradually recede as Bran's grasp repeatedly propelled her upward. For an instant she would float in a void, her back arched and supple below the gilt ceiling.

And always there were his hands, a touchspring of strength, guiding and somehow protecting. Banished now was the fear of falling. There was nothing but the exultant joy of imagined flight. Bran sensed her letting go and responded with increasingly daring lifts. His fingers were warm against her thigh, the palm of his hand sure and strong when it cupped the small of her back.

Yet beneath her exuberance as a ballerina being partnered by the ideal danseur, she was a woman aware of Bran as a man—acutely aware of his touch, which for all its impersonality spun a web of pleasurable warmth around her limbs. In class an hour earlier, the lesson had dragged on interminably, an exercise in frustration and fear. Now she wished their intimate pas de deux would never end.

But inevitably it was over. She was brought back down to earth as the muted call of French horns gave way to voices in the hall, young and high-pitched. An instant later a dozen girls, gangly as colts and abrim with nervous energy, trooped in, awkward ducklings who would emerge in a few years as lovely swans.

Raine crossed the room to retrieve her hand towel from the barre, then turned back to Bran with a quick smile. "Thanks for your time and help," she told him as she caught her breath and pressed the cool terry to her throat. "Sorry I was such a disaster in class."

His eyes flickered over her in that objective, assessing way that was becoming so familiar to her. "Why didn't you just admit you were afraid...of whatever?"

"In front of the whole world?" she flung back, her laughter tinkling and sweet. "When I can't even admit it to myself most of the time?" she added in a rush, surprised by her own frankness. Somehow the noise and bustle encouraged confidences, as if any ill-advised revelation would be safely hidden in the innocence surrounding them.

"Where are you headed now?" he asked casually.

Raine hesitated, her dark gold eyes shimmering at the unexpected question. "Home, I guess, to soak these tired old legs." Another tentative smile hovered at the corners of her lips.

He surprised her again with a quick grin. "How about a walk in the Bois instead?"

Her brows lifted in subtle inquiry. "Don't you have a practice session with Riva?" she couldn't resist asking.

His mouth hardening into a thin line, Bran replied, "Your sister has a penchant for standing me up. It'd do her good to get a taste of her own medicine."

Raine had the distinctly unpleasant suspicion that she was being used to make Riva jealous, and the warmth that had so animated her eyes a moment earlier was hidden now by a hard protective sheen. "Sorry, Brandon," she told him curtly, "but I've got to run."

"I'll drop you off where you're going." He followed her out into the hall.

"That won't be necessary."

"Won't it?" He mocked her new coldness, even as his hand slipped easily under her elbow. He didn't relinquish his hold until they stood outside the changing rooms. "Meet you back out here in ten minutes," he said, and strode quickly away.

Raine threw her toe shoes into a locker and grabbed a brush. As she uncoiled her tightly pinned hair and shook it free, she caught a glimpse of her expression in the mirror. It reflected an anger and hurt that were not just the result of injured pride; that look couldn't be denied.

Impatiently she pulled the brush through her gleaming chestnut waves. In the past she'd been indifferent to Riva's entanglements with men. Why should this particular affair and this particular man affect her so differently? Raine's eyes stared back at her, luminous and huge against the pale contours of her cheeks. Though she might try to fool herself, those eyes didn't lie. In some indefinable way she needed him. She realized instinctively that he'd sparked that need in her, a need that went far beyond the give-and-take of dance. But she'd be damned if she'd let him know or give Riva the chance to guess. She'd had enough hurt; she couldn't handle any more.

Quickly she pulled off her leotard and tights, savoring the coolness of her lavender-and-gray print skirt against her bare legs. After tucking a gauzy lavender shirt into the waistband, Raine picked up her oversize straw bag and hurried outside.

She was still blinking in confusion against the bright afternoon sunlight when a silvery Fiat Spider roared to life beneath the covered portico. Bran backed it out into the courtyard and drew to a stop beside her. "Get in!" he called.

To her ears it sounded perilously close to a command, but she was too tired to argue. At least she'd be spared the mile and a half climb to her apartment. Raine slid into the bucket seat beside him and leaned back against the headrest as the little car merged into the endless surge of traffic on the boulevard de Clichy.

She glanced up a minute later when they stopped at a traffic signal. "You're headed the wrong way, Brandon. I live in Montmartre," she informed him, half-tempted to add that he was probably all too familiar with the path that led to Riva's door.

Oblivious to her simmering annoyance, he glanced at her with another of his rare, charmingly crooked grins. "You looked hungry to me, so I thought we'd have lunch first. I like my dancers lithe and leggy, but you're carrying that a little to extremes. Besides," he added, teasing still, "I've noticed the little worry lines around your eyes. It's a challenge to me to try to get rid of them."

Against her will she found herself responding to his teasing warmth and smiled in return, a smile that deepened the amber glints in her eyes but didn't quite banish the subtle lines that his observant glance had picked up. Raine was tired and realized she was not yet fully recovered from the old accident. But there were only two antidotes for that—time and hard work on the dance floor. Even as she told herself firmly that she needed nothing else, the memory of the strength and animal vitality that she'd felt in Bran's arms washed over her. With an effort she quelled the thought.

Leaning back again, she closed her eyes, savoring the warmth of the late-summer sun and the cool wind rushing toward her while Paris slid by in a kaleidoscopic blur of chic cafés, corner markets and stately residences. The little sports car slowed down as it turned onto a stone bridge crossing the Seine, and Raine opened her eyes. Directly ahead of them lay a towering iron structure, its profile quixotically old-fashioned against the sleek urban skyline of twentieth-century Paris.

Again she found herself smiling. "The Eiffel Tower!" she exclaimed with a laugh. "How did you guess I hadn't been here yet?"

Bran shrugged. "It wasn't too hard, since you seem to have been spending every waking moment at the studio this week. Time out, Pavlova!"

They skirted the long park with its grassy meadows and rode in a creaking elevator to the tower's highest observation deck. Far below, the city seemed to slumber in a bluish haze. From this height even the river seemed little more than a sluggish green serpent, its back scored at regular intervals by narrow gray bands.

The summer crush of tourists had long since gone, so they found themselves practically alone. With the wind whipping through her hair and all of Paris at her feet, Raine felt curiously alive and free. Leaning one elbow on the rail, she turned to Bran. "Tell me, do you play hooky from the studio like this very often?"

Bran answered with a grin. "Even dedicated artists need an occasional break. Besides, I get a lot of inspiration from Parisians. Have you noticed the way they talk so animatedly? I try to echo some of that in the dances I create."

"I'll look forward to seeing them performed."

"That doesn't sound to me like a dancer talking," Bran shot back, his eyes taking on that curiously penetrating expression that could so unnerve her. "Maybe I'll choreograph a dance sometime especially for you."

Raine laughed at the idle suggestion, though the sound was rather hollow in her own ears. "There's not room enough for two stars in a small company, Brandon, and you know it."

"You're assuming a lot, aren't you, Raine?" he replied casually. "I didn't say I'd make you a star."

She tossed her hair back over her shoulder with a proud gesture. "Good, because I wouldn't want the role anyway. I've seen what it does."

Her bravado didn't fool him a bit, and Raine felt his insistent eyes on her until she was compelled to meet his gaze. Bran startled her then by saying, "You envy your sister, don't you? You say you don't want to compete for roles, but you do, Raine."

"That's a lie," she retorted calmly.

"Then why did you come to Paris?"

But she refused to answer, leaving the rail and moving toward the elevator, pressing the button impatiently. She breathed a sigh of relief when another couple strolled up beside them, forestalling any more of Bran's relentless probing.

The elevator deposited them at ground level again, and they walked back through the park, she wrapped in her own thoughts while Bran idly whistled a musical score to himself. The silence between them was broken unexpectedly as a black-and-white soccer ball bounced down in front of them, followed by a tow-headed boy running breathlessly after it.

Bran, his hands still in the pockets of his white, loose-fitting trousers, intercepted the wayward ball and began to kick it effortlessly along the ground toward the boy, using the side of his foot. The rest of the pint-size team ran up and let out a gleeful little cheer as Bran joined in their game for a minute.

Strolling across the grass, Raine observed the action with a little smile. She admired the lightning play of his feet, the lithe movements of his body that indicated his incredible balance and quick reflexes. They were the skills of a successful soccer star but, Raine reflected, they were quite close to the precision and speed demanded of a good danseur.

Eyes brimming with amusement, Bran rejoined her and they stopped shortly afterward at a food stand, coming away with two bottles of sparkling cider, thinly sliced ham and cheese tucked into crusty baguettes and a pair of shiny red apples. They carried their picnic feast to a wooded area in the shadow of the tower and sat down in the grass.

While she hungrily devoured her sandwich, Raine gazed across the river to the lawns sloping upward to a great curving building on a plaza that sparkled with splashing fountains. Bran shot her an amused look as she tossed the few remaining crumbs to the gathering cluster of pigeons. "It's nice to see a woman enjoying her meal for a change," he observed lazily. "Most dancers eat like birds."

"I *was* starved," Raine conceded. She leaned back against the tree trunk, legs outstretched and crossed at the ankles. The pain she'd experienced that morning in class was only a faint throb now, and Raine was grateful for that. After a while she reached out to idly pluck a blade of grass. Twirling it in her fingers, she looked over at Bran, her eyes faintly questioning. "Who's your principal male soloist?" she asked, studiously casual.

His brow dipped in a slight frown. "We don't have one really. It's simpler just to rotate the roles."

Raine glanced up through the gently stirring leaves that cast a flickering web of light and shadow over the ground. "I watched you on the soccer field earlier," she began softly, "and I felt the strength in your arms when...when you lifted me in class. You're better than any of your young danseurs."

He swallowed a long draft of cider, and for a moment Raine thought he was going to ignore her. Then his disconcertingly intense blue gaze came to focus on hers. "That's a pretty sweeping statement for someone who's been with the company only a few weeks, and as a dancer for less than a day."

"I'm not blind. Anyone could see that in five minutes." She bridled at his implication that she was hardly a judge of such matters, and anger made her bold. "Why don't you dance, Brandon?"

His eyes flashed now with mingled defiance and humor. "Are you always so direct?"

"Does it bother you?" she countered at once, telling herself that she was only paying him back in his own coin.

"Only because I don't have a pat answer to give you." His gaze flickered impatiently away from her, then back again. "Performing is an all-out thing. It consumes you until there's no time for anything or anyone else." His voice was tight, as if he were holding back a flood of feeling he didn't care to face. "Believe me, I know. So I prefer to observe from a distance. Life's a series of choices. I've never regretted the ones I've made."

Raine's gaze was thoughtful and faintly questioning still. "Pierre Junot said something about you the other night at your party. He told me your destiny is tied up too much with your family. I didn't really understand what he meant."

Bran frowned. "Pierre speaks too freely."

She shot him a quick glance. "He told me you're a difficult man to get to know. Now I'm beginning to understand why."

"Pierre can be a fool."

Harshness in his tone put Raine on edge. To her mind the words had the unmistakable ring of some dark emotion. "Why?" she flung back. "Because he might still be in love with Riva?" Only with great effort did she hold back the other jealous retort that hovered on her lips: *because you feel guilty about taking her from him?*

But Bran must have sensed her thoughts from the look in her eyes. To her great surprise, he threw back his head and laughed. "It's hard for me to believe now that I mistook you for her that first morning in the studio," he said, laughing still. "You're not anything at all alike. All your feelings are right there on the surface to read, like a child's—no pretense, no games."

The dark glimmer of laughter shone in his eyes as he leaned toward her and brushed a stray crumb from her lips. His touch, for all its teasing casualness, was electric, and somehow this new lighthearted mood between them angered her. Remembering the tempestuousness of their confrontation on the dance floor and the hungrily demanding sensuality of his mouth moving against hers, Raine found herself hating this easy sense of camaraderie.

He could afford to joke and laugh with her, reserving his passionate air of possession for Riva. She remembered, too, the jealous smolder in his eyes when he'd confronted his rival, Pierre, at the party. She'd read in Bran's expression that Riva was his— and what did that make Raine herself? A plaything, a moment's comic interlude to divert him from the tense sexual battleground of his affair with Riva?

In one swift graceful motion Raine stood up, not looking at Bran. But he had sensed the new undertone of turbulence and rose beside her, his hands lightly on her upper arms as he whirled her to face him. "What is it, Raine? What's the matter?"

She shook off his touch. "Nothing you'd understand."

"Try me." His tone was curiously earnest.

She knew his voice could move and delight her, but she willed herself not to listen. "No, thanks," she retorted.

"Let's go, then," he said abruptly. "I've got to get back to the studio."

"Yes. Riva's waiting," she bit out.

At mid-afternoon the Parisian boulevards were nearly deserted, as if the city had fallen into a state of suspended animation. The whine of the Fiat punctured the silence as they raced along the slumbering treelined streets behind the Ecole Militaire.

Raine was eager now to be away from him. She'd been a fool to let herself be maneuvered into coming along in the first place. To Bran she was nothing more than a machine in need of fine tuning, a new cog to be fitted into his smoothly functioning dance company.

Her bitter musings were confirmed as they climbed into the maze of lanes cobwebbing the picturesque quarter and the car squealed to a halt in the square beneath Riva's apartment building. She stiffened as he leaned over her to snap up the handle and fling the door wide open. "You'd better get to bed early, Raine," he ordered in a cool peremptory tone. "I don't want a repetition of what happened today in class. I don't know what the bloody hell your personal problems are, but I really don't care. Just see that they don't interfere with your performance." Bran's eyes raked over her pitilessly.

Stung to the quick, Raine fought back the tears that burned the back of her throat. With a supreme effort she managed to keep her tone as indifferent as his. "I've told you—I'm a professional, Brandon. Nothing counts but that."

Their hard gazes met and clashed. "We understand each other, then," he muttered as she swung her legs out onto the hot pavement. An instant later the silvery Spider raced away in a mad squeal of tires.

Slowly Raine climbed the narrow stairs to the apartment, exhausted by the emotional and physical rigors of the day. Her lips twisted in a rueful expression, remembering that she'd been afraid to confide in him because she feared his pity. *He doesn't know the meaning of the word,* Raine thought angrily as she paused on the second landing. She was moving now with a barely perceptible limp, brought on by weariness and the trailing edge of pain. But she willed herself to climb the last flight of stairs at a brisker pace, taking strength from Nina Tarsamova's assured counsel: "The strength will come...bit by bit."

Raine fitted her key into the lock, but the door handle turned in her fingers before she'd even twisted the key. Her fear that she'd hurried away that morning without properly locking the front door turned to surprise as she stepped into the living room and found Riva standing before the lace-curtained window overlooking the square.

Riva turned and stared at her sister in silence. Raine closed the door and leaned against it. "Hello," she began evenly. "Somehow I didn't expect you to be home at this hour. Aren't you in the midst of rehearsals for an especially difficult number?"

Riva's voice was an echo of her own. "Yes, I should have been—except that my partner never showed up." The eyes beneath her raised brows glinted with rising anger.

"That was no fault of mine, you know," Raine answered her in a tone of defiance.

"Oh, really?" Riva's disbelieving laughter was sarcastic. She moved away from the window then with a quick controlled movement that revealed her tenseness. Her breasts were boldly delineated beneath the thin white tank top she'd tucked into her close-fitting jeans. Always flaunting what she's got, Raine couldn't help thinking. But her amusement died as Riva's strident voice cut in. "What kind of a fool do you think I am, Raine? I heard Bran's car, and I saw your heads together in a sweet little tête-à-tête."

"Stop it, Riva. You're blowing everything out of proportion."

"Am I?" her twin flung back, regarding her slyly out of the corner of her eye. "I heard about your disaster in class today. And I can guess the rest of the scenario. You had to cry on Bran's shoulder about the tragedy that befell you."

"He doesn't know about the accident. I haven't told him." Wearily Raine kicked off her sandals and dropped her bag and sunglasses on the entry table.

"You know, I'm really sick of your act of noble stoicism," Riva whispered cruelly.

Raine's head whipped around at that, the anger she'd been so determined to control now threatening to explode. Her eyes, glinting beaten gold, bored into Riva's, their gazes colliding like a clash of heavy metals. "Don't mistake your responses for mine. If it had been you instead of me, Riva, you'd have played the role of tragic queen to the hilt. But that's not my style. I don't want to manipulate anyone by playing on his pity. The past is done with.''

"Sure it is,'' Riva taunted. "That's why you had to follow me to Paris—to punish me. Why didn't you go back to the Kingsley Company? They'd have taken you.''

"Out of pity,'' Raine flung back softly. "I want to make it because I'm the best I can possibly be, not because someone feels they owe me.'' A deep current of passion rippled through her words, for an instant transforming her expression to one of beautifully compelling intensity.

"But why here?'' Riva demanded petulantly. "My life was set up—''

"So cozily,'' Raine sardonically finished for her, her mouth lifting in an unwilling smile. "With at least two men wrapped around your fingers, and only God knows how many more.''

Her attention momentarily deflected from the argument, Riva's brow furrowed. "Two?''

"Yes. Have you already forgotten poor Pierre Junot?''

"Oh, him,'' Riva replied in a coldly dismissing voice.

"You're too quick to hurt people,'' Raine chided her.

"Look who's talking!'' she was mocked in return. "Don't you think you hurt me by showing up on Madame T's doorstep?''

Raine regarded her twin in thoughtful silence for a long moment. "You really do see me as a threat, don't you?'' she whispered, half to herself.

"No!" Riva's retort was a bit too sharp. "You're just a thorn in my side, an irritation."

"Naturally," Raine answered dryly. "You're still trying to make me the lesser satellite orbiting around your stardom."

"Quiet little Raine," Riva needled her. "You've never learned to handle being second best, second chosen."

"That's all going to change." Raine's pretty, musical voice was undercut by a subtle note of challenge that surprised them both.

"Keep out of my way, Raine," her sister warned her at last. "I've fought too hard for what I've got."

Exhausted by their pointless quarreling, Raine left Riva standing alone in the middle of the living room and went to draw a bath for herself. She opened the faucets full force and sprinkled a handful of perfumed salts into the claw-footed tub. She slipped out of her clothing with effortless grace. Anyone who knew her well would have recognized that her figure had just now begun to take on its customary rounded contours after months of recuperation, though her face was still a little thin. The sculpted hollows of her cheekbones were a frame for hauntingly expressive amber eyes. Their depths still reflected a hidden pain, but it was offset by an unexpected stubbornness of will and determination.

Raine's vision of herself vanished as the fragrant mist from her bath touched the glass. Turning, she climbed into the tub, breathing a sigh of pure pleasure as she eased down into the steaming water. A minute later she heard the front door slam resoundingly, and she was grateful to be alone at last in the little apartment.

As soon as her finances allowed, she had to find her own place. Otherwise who knew what further mischief the women might cause each other? They were like matching time bombs waiting to explode, Raine thought with a sad shake of her head. Lying back then against the cool curving rim of porcelain, she gave herself up completely to relaxation. Through the high open window above the tub came the scent of late-blooming roses and freshly baked bread.

She was thinking of nothing in particular when the question suddenly hit her again: why *had* she come to Paris? Brandon had asked, and so had Riva.

Raine's thoughts drifted back far into the past. From the moment they'd been born, the twins had been competing—first for their mother's attention, later for teachers' smiles, for toys and friends, a coveted spot in a dance company. And always Riva had managed to come out the winner. Perhaps she'd always won because Raine had never been willing to fight for what she wanted. But the past year had changed things. Now Raine planned to prove, as much to herself as to Riva, that she was ready to compete.

Lifting her leg out of the water in a languorous extension, Raine found herself thinking about Bran. Would he be worth fighting for, she wondered. . . .

CHAPTER FOUR

STREET CLEANERS TRUNDLED their carts along, sweeping up the debris of the night as Raine hurried past them. The early-morning air was cool and clear. There were no crowds to jostle past in the hilly lanes, since the city was barely waking up. Raine had been the only customer in the café where she'd taken her croissant and coffee, eating quickly because she'd overslept a little. In bed that morning, Raine had been only dimly aware of Riva's heels clattering on the stairs, but it was enough to jolt her awake and remind her she would be late for class. There had been no time to baby her leg with slow warm-up stretches and massage, but that couldn't be helped.

Raine crossed the wide deserted boulevard just as a bus drew up at the stop to discharge its passengers, and she ran almost headlong into Tracey Markham as the two women made for the ballet studio's front gate.

"Good morning, Tracey!" Raine greeted her teasingly. "Looks like you took Brandon's threat to heart."

"Haven't I just!"

Although the blond dancer laughed, Raine couldn't help noticing the dark circles beneath her eyes. "You look a little tired," she ventured.

Tracey managed another grin. "Wouldn't you be if you'd been up half the night?"

"Oh, were you sick?" Raine's expressive eyes were sympathetic.

"Hardly that," Tracey retorted with an air of sly mischief. "I'm moonlighting."

Raine's sympathy dissolved in curiosity. "Where?" she asked as they crossed the courtyard and headed for the back stairs.

"The Folies Bergères."

Raine stared in astonishment at this casual pronouncement. "You mean one of those sexy topless revues?"

"Oh, that stuff I leave to the statuesque showgirls, and they're welcome to it," Tracey said airily. "I'm in one of the *entractes*, a spoof on Peter Pan. I'm Tinkerbell. I wear gossamer wings and a jungle-green maillot cut up to here." Tracey flashed a wicked smile as she indicated a point halfway up her hip, and Raine couldn't help but laugh at her irrepressible good spirits.

"Why do you do it?" she asked, laughter still tinging her voice.

"Two reasons," the dancer replied forthrightly. "It's fun, and the money's good. I'm saving up what I call my trousseau fund. But actually I'm not all that interested in clothes. I'm going to buy my Tom a wedding present—a small sailboat."

"He doesn't mind you traipsing around the world?"

Again the irrepressible grin. "We Aussie women are every bit as liberated as you Yanks."

"Bravo!"

Tracey gave a little mock bow. "Thanks. Actually, you see, Tom's a professor of history at Melbourne University. He's the quiet type who doesn't have much use for travel. So he told me to go and sow my wild oats before I settle down to married life," she added with a laugh.

"When are you going home?" Raine asked over her shoulder as they climbed the steps.

"As soon as I've saved enough for Tom's sloop—probably a couple of months."

Raine was about to say something in reply when a sudden spasm in her leg caused her to breathe in sharply. She leaned down to massage her muscles.

Tracey watched her curiously. "Are you okay, Raine?"

She nodded, biting her lip. "It's just a cramp."

Tracey was silent a moment, as if debating with herself. "It might just be psychological," she offered hesitantly. "You're not afraid to go into class after yesterday, are you?"

"No, of course not!" Raine said rather too sharply. She straightened up and flexed her leg, relieved to find that the worst of the cramp had passed. They had hurried up the flight of stairs and were just passing Madame Tarsamova's door, when the old woman stepped out into the hall and gestured for Raine to join her inside.

Sitting at the desk in the small outer office was a young woman from a temporary agency. With her brown hair bobbed at chin length and the oversize glasses perched on the bridge of her nose, she looked like a thoroughly efficient secretary. *At least I'm not missed here,* Raine thought as she smiled down at the woman, who didn't glance up from her work.

Madame Tarsamova closed the door to her private office with a decisive click, giving Raine the uncomfortable fleeting sensation that she was an unruly schoolgirl being brought to task before the principal. She turned to face the older woman, waiting.

"There's not much time to talk. I know class starts in a minute," the ballet mistress began in her husky accented voice, her coal-black eyes on the young dancer with fixed intensity. "So I'll get directly to the point. Rumors have been rife about what happened yesterday when Paul Devore was partnering you. I asked Brandon about it, but he was rather short with me. He said only that you'd frozen, that you were afraid."

"True on both counts," Raine replied without any attempt to defend herself. "Did he say anything more?" Her clear eyes followed the older woman as Madame T crossed the small space to stand directly in front of her.

"No." The woman's eyes were questioning. "That's the reason I called you in." There was an infinitesimal pause before she asked quietly, "Do you want to forgo center-floor exercise for the time being?"

"No, I do not," Raine answered firmly.

"You're certain?"

Raine nodded, willing her thoughts away from the telltale edge of pain that was still there in her leg. "I think someone said once that the first step in overcoming fear is to face it." Her French came effortlessly now, despite the real uncertainties she felt.

"Just see that you don't break your neck in the process," *madame* said dryly, a faint smile deepening the black gleam in her alert eyes.

Not if I had the security of dancing in Bran's arms, Raine thought bemusedly as she left the office and hurried down the long corridor to the studio. *Not that that's likely to happen too often.*

Her stomach contracted with tension as she slipped into class. Bran, his back to her, must have arrived just a moment before she had. Raine was oblivious to the smiles of commiseration, to the eyes that slid away from her in embarrassed remembrance of her debacle in class the previous morning. There was only one pair of eyes in the room that mattered to her, but he didn't even glance in her direction. She raced through her preparatory stretches, finishing as the battered piano sounded in a gliding crescendo of chords and class began.

The barre work went quickly. Bran was in an impatient mood that spilled over into his direction of their brisk floor workout. He was adapting a Bournonville ballet for the company, and the quick animated steps required every ounce of the dancers' concentration. Raine realized gratefully that the sequence didn't call for lifts, though her gratitude was dimmed a little by the sudden suspicion that Bran had planned it that way to spare her further humiliation. But she dismissed the idea as swiftly as it had arisen. He'd made it clear that the company was his life and that he had scant patience for the individual foibles of his dancers. They were there for his benefit, not vice versa.

So Raine danced, oblivious to the perspiration

trickling down her spine as she went through the little twists and hops on pointe that lent such charm to the allegro sequence. The next choreographic phrase called for a *cabriole devant*. The diagonal leap, in which the dancer appears to defy gravity for a breathtakingly long instant as her legs fly out to one side, made severe demands on the body. The art was in making it appear effortless, jubilant. Raine tried to do just that, concentrating on the graceful impulsion of her limbs.

Though the leap was executed perfectly, Raine sensed the problem at once as her left leg bent in *plié* and the compression of her landing reverberated up her calf. The force of it sent another spasm through the muscles. Gamely she attempted to continue, but now each step was an effort.

Though Raine was half hidden behind two rows of dancers, Bran saw what was happening and threaded his way back to her at once, signaling the others to finish the routine. "Did you hurt yourself?" he inquired roughly.

Raine swiftly shook her head. "No, it's just a cramp. I'll be fine."

Not content to take her word, Bran squatted down beside her to have a look at the leg. The music had ended; all eyes were on them. Raine felt the hot flood of color rising from her throat as his hands came up to examine her calf with professional care. Then his sharp blue eyes met hers again. "What the devil did you do—run a marathon last night?" She bridled at the implied criticism in his tone, but before she could reply he was speaking again. "You'd better sit out class before you do any more damage."

Damage to what? To your precious company, she longed to retort. But she bit back the words and went over to the chair in front of the window. Class went on, the wooden floor reverberating each time the danseurs came down from their high leaps. As Raine's eyes returned to Bran, she saw at once that he was holding back. He merely implied the motion with a quick gesture, leaving it to the others to give full balletic impulse.

Raine couldn't help contrasting his attitude to her own. Where she vowed to dance again no matter what, he seemed curiously determined to deny his own abilities. Yet Raine had felt the strength in him, emotional as well as physical. Why did he keep it leashed?

Her musings were interrupted as the studio practice came to an end and everyone dashed for the door, eager for a cold drink or snack before the next work session. Raine stood up, holding on to the back of the chair and gingerly flexing her ankle. Though the calf was no longer cramping, it was still a bit tight.

She glanced at Bran as he sauntered toward her. "How is it?" he demanded, his eyes raking her face for an answer.

"It's fine—really it is," she added protestingly as he disregarded her assurances and leaned down again to look at it, running thumb and forefinger gently up from the ankle to where the taut muscle rounded outward.

His casual touch left a trace of warmth, but the sensation faded as he stood up and addressed her abruptly. "Go home." He must have read the stricken look in her eyes, because he went on in a more softened tone. "Soak for an hour in the tub with the water as hot as you can stand it, then keep the leg elevated for another hour. After that do a series of slow stretches. That should leave plenty of time for you to meet me back here at the studio at noon. And don't walk back to the apartment. Take a taxi."

Embarrassed, she tried to protest. "But—"

He cut her off with a return of his old impatience. "Don't argue with me. If you're going to dance, it's going to be done my way. You've got too many ragged edges for my satisfaction." He turned then and strode away, leaving her alone in the quiet studio.

From working with Madame T and typing up the daily schedules, Raine knew Bran's hours by heart. He was tied up from morning to evening with practice, choreographing sessions, paperwork and discussions with Nina. Only at noon did he have two free hours to himself, and Raine was humiliated that he felt compelled to use them in coaching her.

RAINE SLIPPED INTO THE DESERTED STUDIO just as the bells from a distant church chimed the hour. She'd exchanged her black leotard of the morning for one in a dusty rose color. Shining against her pale tights were her crisscrossed satin shoe ribbons, their newness in contrast to the scuffed toe shoes themselves. She'd reblocked them three times and knocked the wooden pointes against each other until they felt just right. In a way the old shoes were her talisman, her link to the past when she couldn't face looking ahead to an uncertain future. Like her dancing, they, too, had ragged edges.

Ignoring the nervousness in her stomach, Raine went to the window and stared out. After a while she closed it against the heat and noise of the street, savoring the cloistered silence of the studio. Her left leg was cocked in its familiar resting position, even though it felt as limber and strong as the other now. She had followed Bran's instructions meticulously. That morning lesson had been another costly one for her in terms of ego. Never again would she show up for practice without having physically readied herself.

Raine heard the door swing open, and she turned around. She and Bran faced one another across the room in silence for a long moment, each taking the other's measure. The moment was broken as Bran moved toward her with his rhythmic stride. A thin film of perspiration glistened on his neck, and she knew he must be exhausted from his long morning schedule. Again the guilt she'd felt earlier assailed her.

"Why are you doing this for me?" she suddenly asked as he came to stand beside her at the window.

"Because you need it. Because you haven't disciplined yourself in a year, and once you move away from the barre it shows badly." If he was exhausted, there was no sign of it in the cutting coolness of his voice, nor in his eyes.

Raine stiffened at the criticism that he'd made no attempt to soften. "If I'm that awful, maybe I should just leave."

"Go ahead." The bright intensity of his gaze

pinned her. "Taking the easy way out can become a habit."

"Damn you," she enunciated softly, her voice vibrating with the emotion she couldn't quite subdue. "Don't judge me, Brandon, when you don't know what I've been through."

"The only thing I'm interested in judging is your performance, and for the most part that's been second-rate."

Angrily she turned away from him, her quick lithe steps propelling her halfway across the room until common sense stopped her dead in her tracks. He'd only been speaking the truth. Raine turned back again slowly, the unselfconscious movement expressing at once her fragility and her air of injured hauteur. Her pride was still warring with her basic self-honesty.

With narrowed eyes Bran watched this personal battle, sensing it in the electric tension of her arms and the subtle tilt to her head. But he waited, saying nothing.

At last Raine lifted her chin at a stubborn angle. "Why don't you just take me out of company class for a few months, if that's the way you feel?" she suggested, the hurried words betraying her reluctance and her fear that he might actually agree to the suggestion. "I don't want to be the cause of the company's being held back," Raine went on more firmly.

Bran closed the distance between them, his whole demeanor exuding impatient energy. "You've wasted a year as it is, Raine. Time is a luxury you can no longer afford."

She stared up at him, searching his eyes. Their

clear depths were flecked with midnight blue, tempering their intensity. She found neither compassion nor solicitude in his gaze, only devotion to his art. That revelation somehow wounded her to the quick, and Raine glanced down. But after a moment she looked up again, her own expression composed and determined. "I suppose you're right," she conceded reluctantly. "Shall we begin?"

Bran kept her at center stage for almost the entire two hours, his voice at her side, her back, following her across the room as she worked to give her movements a sharper polished edge.

"Do the *échappés* over again, and this time I want them to flash like knives," he exhorted her even before she had time to catch her breath from the previous set.

Raine shot an exasperated look over to where he stood, one foot planted on the wooden chair seat, his elbow resting casually on his thigh. Had she imagined the grin that briefly twisted his lips when he noticed her irritation? She couldn't be certain, because his back was to the window and the afternoon light flooding into the room cast him in shadowy bas-relief. For all her concentration on the dance, the image of his silhouetted form impressed itself on her mind.

When he straightened and crossed his arms over his chest, eyes following her graceful pirouetting form, Raine used him as the focal point to spot each turn. Each time she spun, her head whipped around in swift pursuit, and Raine could for an instant imagine he was a sculpture lifted from an ancient Greek frieze: a male in his prime, proud and sufficient unto himself. As she thought that, a fleeting sensation of loneliness crept up on her.

"They need a hell of a lot of work." Bran's grating tone cut into her thoughts. "You're rusty, but I don't think I have to remind you of that."

The private lesson—private torture might have been more apt—went on as Bran switched her from simple turns to the more demanding leaps and *tours en l'air*.

As the tempo picked up, so it seemed did his anger. "Go beyond yourself—reach—let go!" He shook his head in exasperation at one point and massaged the tight muscles in his neck as Raine paused, fighting to regain her breath. She longed to tell him she'd had enough, but she was far too stubborn for that. She vowed to show him that her feisty determination would make up for any rustiness in her skills. But a moment later she sighed in pretended defeat as his fingers snapped and the punishing pace resumed.

"Can't you liven it up a little?" he demanded. "You've got about as much spirit as the loser in a cat fight."

Raine bristled at the unflattering comparison. "At least I put up a fight," she flung back at him sarcastically, but he ignored her.

They were standing face to face now. Gone was the cool proud demeanor she'd exhibited at the start of their session; after two punishing hours Raine did look a little like a bedraggled kitten. Yet even though she was beaten down by exhaustion, there was an intensity about her that had been lacking before. Her pale cheeks were flooded with healthy color, and the angry eyes she flashed at Bran brimmed over with life.

Bran stared down at her, his gaze absorbing and measuring the subtle transformation. Cocking his head at an inquisitive angle, he demanded quietly, "Do you see what I'm after now, Raine? You have to give more of yourself."

She shot him a glance from beneath her lashes, her amber eyes seeming to catch and hold the shifting sunlight. "Just what is it I'm supposed to be giving?"

"Passion," he answered her almost roughly. "You have to funnel every ounce of it into your performance."

For some reason his offhand reply sparked defiance in Raine. "Oh, yes," she mocked. "God forbid that we should have any feeling left over."

He was angry, but the only sign of it was in the telltale tightening of the muscle in his cheek. "Passion on stage is an illusion." Each word as he spoke it was clipped and emotionless. "It's not meant to draw dancers together. It's only a tool to fuel their art."

"I'll remember that," Raine bit out just as impassively, though her eyes still shimmered their defiance.

IN THE AFTERNOONS that followed Raine tried to accept that philosophy, even though her heart told her it was a lie.

She and Bran had slipped into the routine of a private noon workout, each session as traumatic and draining as the first. His initial quiet demand that she give more of herself became a pounding refrain. He goaded her with subtle psychological pressures that were far worse than his arrogant bullying. Raine wanted to scream at him, to slap him and say she wanted to be left the hell alone. But she did none of those things. She bit her lip and disciplined herself to carry on.

Implicit in Raine's submission to his harsh tutelage was her own unyielding stubbornness. Even when he bullied her, inquiring sarcastically if she couldn't get her left leg higher, Raine didn't give in to the temptation to confide why the leg dragged at times and was a little slower than her right. She had vowed to make Bran respect her on her own terms.

But she didn't say that to him. They, in fact, had remarkably little to say beyond the professional quick commands and questions exchanged in class. Though the private sessions continued, it was as if an invisible wall had been erected between them. They were nothing now but master and pupil. No longer did they share even those fleeting moments of intimacy when the music had ignited a powerful spark between them.

Bran gave that spark no chance to burst and engulf them again. He never touched her, never spoke except in a businesslike voice. Not since that first day when she'd made such a disastrous showing in his class had they danced in each other's arms, their joined rhythm an impulse of sharing and joy. It was that touch she wanted and needed, that connection alone to give deeper meaning to her art. Now the choreography was little more than a series of steps that, with his help, she was honing to technical excellence. Despite all the hours he was devoting to her, she felt almost cheated.

Raine was aware that she was being pushed to her limits as a dancer. And grudgingly, for all her dissatisfaction, she had to admit that she was growing stronger day by day under his relentless direction. She felt the new confidence and certainty in her balance, the exciting momentum of her leaps, the satisfaction of muscle and nerve interacting in split-second harmony.

Still she resented feeling as though she were a machine being built to Bran's exacting requirements. Never satisfied with anything less than her utmost, he pushed her to do increasingly difficult routines.

One day, after her unsuccessful attempt at a difficult combination, Bran ran tense fingers through his hair. "Damn it, Raine," he swore impatiently. "Do I have to drag it out of you?"

Something must have snapped inside her, because without warning she rounded on him with tigerish ferocity. All the anger and the need she'd been suppressing now threatened to overflow. "I'm not a carbon copy of Riva!" she shouted. "I don't pretend to be a finely tuned machine. I'm a woman, Brandon. Dance is meaningless to me unless it expresses emotion, feelings."

He listened unperturbed to her tirade. His legs straddled the wooden chair and his forearms were crossed on its slatted back. When she'd finished, his cool amused stare seemed to ridicule her. "You're a hypocrite," he accused softly. "I haven't seen any sign of the emotions that you claim mean so much to you. In fact, I might as well have been working with a display mannequin."

Raine listened aghast to this totally unexpected

criticism. "I don't dance in a void, Brandon. I mirror what's around me. Didn't you stop to think it might have been your coldness that damped any feeling in me?" she accused in turn, moving angrily toward him. "I don't give a damn if I can never do the world's most breathtaking leaps. Dance to me isn't a Guinness book competition. I don't want to set a record!" She was standing directly before his chair now, her proud gaze boring down into his. "I want to touch and move an audience in far more subtle ways than that."

Bran sprang up from the chair, brow furrowed thoughtfully above the cobalt intensity of his eyes. "Hold on to that inner rage," he ordered. "Put it to use."

Raine was still seething as he went over to slip a tape into the cassette player, and the haunting strains of Prokofiev's *Romeo and Juliet* imbued the room with its sense of tragic foreboding. Almost reluctantly she began to move, as if an invisible hand were pushing her from behind.

She rose on pointe, regretting the slight waver of her ankle as she sought her balance. Then the little false step, the uncertainty were forgotten as the poetry of the score drew her. Gone was the cold machine Raine had felt herself to be in class. The fluidity and lightness of her upper body produced a vision of perfection that her legs and feet strained to match.

Now she *was* Juliet, defiantly risking her family's fury to give herself to her lover. Raine's slightest gesture and movement managed to convey passionate youth, the dreamy grace of a maid on the trembling brink of womanhood.

Bran was behind her now, hands light on her waist as he whispered, "Good. The emotions have unreined a little." Then, amazingly, he was teasing her. "Now you see how far a little anger can go."

Though his touch was barely perceptible, it was enough to lend her strength and confidence in the controlled delicacy of her adagio. Raine moved into a pirouette supported by his arms, elation rising at her perfect execution. It wasn't only the anger, she longed to tell him. It was the magnetism of his touch that freed the nascent poetry of her body.

Bran's forearm slid around to grasp her waist more firmly, and as he lunged forward Raine's back was molded to his chest. His hand held hers by her side, while their heads arched back in a timeless gesture of ecstasy. Again they danced as one. Raine's heart leaped, and her feet dutifully followed.

She spun away, and he drew her back in a rhythmic duo of tension and release that suggested the powerful interplay of emotion. Bran was fire to her ice, his driving male force giving new intensity to her every step and movement.

The low tremolo of the music that spoke of such compelling intimacy faded into a sprightly echo of horns, and Bran and Raine drew apart. While she struggled to quell the tumult of emotion that still engulfed her, Bran had already slipped back into his teaching role. "You're getting there, Raine, but you've got a hell of a long way to go."

Stung by his impersonal reply, Raine spoke in a tone that was brittle and quick. "Am I supposed to say thanks, or should I just rake you with my nails?"

"Usually we compromise and the dancer offers her bed." Bran's eyes glimmered wickedly.

Though she knew he'd said that only to tease her, Raine couldn't resist sniping in return, "You're not worried about making Riva jealous?"

He seemed genuinely puzzled. "Riva?"

"She can make life hell on earth if she thinks a lover has crossed her."

Bran's eyes narrowed at that. "Where the hell did you get the idea that Riva and I were lovers?" Although Raine's gaze didn't waver, a veil of wary watchfulness hid their amber depths. When she didn't reply, Bran guessed the truth at once. "Riva told you herself."

"Not in so many words," she denied stiffly.

Bran's breath escaped in a soft explosion of anger. "It's none of your damn business, but for the record, she's been the pursuer. I won't deny I've been tempted. I'm sure that fiery tempestuousness has driven more than one man over the edge." His eyes hardened, and Raine wondered if he was thinking of the hurt Riva had caused Pierre. Bran went on in a distinctly sarcastic tone. "No, I hate to disappoint you, but your sister is climbing the ranks solely on her own. That's one damn good reason for my staying out of her way. I don't want to hear any cries of favoritism from the others."

"I suppose that's meant as a warning to me," Raine responded softly.

A hard grin touched his lips for an instant. "Take it as you will. I don't give favors and I don't accept them." He paused. "But you might remember something else—the bottom line is that I do what I want.

And if I want something badly enough I generally manage to get it.''

''Are you always so ruthless?''

''I like fighters, Raine; I like them in my company. That's why I admire your twin. She may be arrogant and selfish but she goes after what she wants.''

Raine flashed him a look of defiance. ''And what about you, Brandon? What do you want from me?''

He grinned again. ''I haven't quite decided.'' Realizing he was toying with her, Raine turned away to leave, but his next words drew her back. ''I have to admit you intrigue me, Raine. There's a hidden part to you I haven't quite been able to reach. I've read the edge of pain and sadness in your eyes.... He must have been one hell of a bastard.''

A slow flush stained her cheeks at what he'd so wrongly assumed, but she covered it by replying tartly, ''Funny, but that's the same epithet people apply to you.''

''Including you?'' He surprised her then by asking.

''I haven't quite decided.''

Bran's sharp laughter echoed between them.

He turned and walked out of the studio, leaving Raine alone with her thoughts. Rather nonplussed by the conversation that had just taken place, she sensed that their relationship had switched footing unexpectedly and taken them both by surprise. But she hadn't an inkling where it was leading to.

THE GYMNASIUM SAUNA was deserted, Raine saw with relief as she stepped inside. Wearing a bikini, with a towel wrapped around her middle and another draped over her head, she climbed up onto the second wooden tier and stretched out on her stomach. The gym was only five minutes from the ballet company, which paid a fixed monthly sum so the dancers could take advantage of its facilities.

Raine sighed as the dry heat enveloped and relaxed her. Head turned to the wall, she closed her eyes and almost dozed off. It must have been a few minutes later that she was startled by the opening of the sauna door, because her whole body was wreathed in a healthy flow of perspiration. Although she was awake, Raine didn't stir—not until her mood of drowsy relaxation was shattered as the two newcomers, who settled themselves comfortably on the sauna's lower benches, continued a conversation that must have begun a lot earlier.

"Oh, you can't blame him! He loves *madame* and would do anything for her."

The voice was vaguely familiar to Raine, and she opened one eye. Then the other woman spoke. "But why should Madame T be so concerned about the new *Américaine*? She can't hold a candle to Riva."

Raine stiffened, every nerve in her body seemingly on alert. She recognized both voices now. Violette and Mari were members of the Ballet du Monde corps.

Now Violette replied knowingly to her friend, oblivious or uncaring of the fact that there was another person in the sauna. "*Madame* will have her certain pets, no rhyme or reason to it. So poor Brandon is forced to give up his lunch hours to work with her. It isn't fair!"

"But if *madame* decrees it...!" The dancers

laughed at what must have been an old joke between them.

As their conversation flitted around in dissections of other dancers' performances, Raine lay above them in tense silence. The heat was beginning to suffocate her, but she was determined to outwait the other two dancers. Meanwhile she fretted, her own thoughts scattering in a dozen directions. She couldn't help wondering if what Mari had insinuated was true, that Bran was devoting time to her on Madame T's orders.

After what felt like hours but was probably no more than five minutes, Mari broke in petulantly, "Ooh, it's too hot in here. I have to jump in the shower."

Raine waited a minute more after they'd left, then slid down from the upper bench. Outside she dropped her towels on the poolside deck and dove into the cold water, swimming with long vigorous strokes. Again and again the women's conversation replayed in her mind, and she knew it was true. Bran's sharp comments about favoritism fitted too neatly to be denied. He'd agreed to work with her not because he believed in her potential but because he had no other choice.

"My damned ego!" she swore angrily. She'd mistaken his gallantry for caring, but his devotion was to Madame Tarsamova and to the company; all the rest were chess pieces, expendable pawns he moved around to suit the ballet's needs. "He *is* a cold-hearted bastard," Raine whispered angrily to herself as she swam. Yet she couldn't help remembering the hot sweetness of emotion that had arced between them when they danced.

She had pulled herself up out of the pool and grabbed a towel by the time Violette and Mari appeared around the corner from the shower room. She didn't miss the quick glances they exchanged but pretended not to notice. Tucking the towel into her bikini top, she brushed past them and nodded distantly, not caring what they thought.

CHAPTER FIVE

RAINE SAT PERCHED on the deep windowsill in the
apartment, her legs drawn up under her chin. Beyond
the rusting filigree of the fire escape, the sun shone
brightly in the square below. It was filled with people, men laughing and talking beneath the Campari
umbrellas and women dressed in bright summer
florals, ready to embark on the pleasant ritual of
Saturday shopping. She had the impression that the
city was preparing itself for a last frolic before the
season ended and autumn winds sent brown leaves
tumbling across the cobblestones. With a quick little
sigh that might have been one of contentment or
vague dissatisfaction, Raine leaned her head back
and lifted her mug of coffee to her lips.

Riva had dashed off a half hour earlier with bolts
of tulle and vibrant silk beneath her arms, en route to
a tailor in Montparnasse. She didn't trust the ballet
company's seamstress and was determined to super-
vise her own costumes for the coming season. A
fighter, Bran had called her. Prima donna was more
like it, Raine told herself.

The phone rang, and uncurling gracefully from her
window perch, Raine hurried to answer it. "*Bonjour.
Cameron ici,*" she said softly into the receiver.

"Riva. Good morning." She recognized the low

fluid voice at once, and her vague discontent gave way to a quickening excitement. "This is—"

"Brandon, hello. Sorry to disappoint you, but Riva's already gone out."

His laughter washed over the line to her, and when he spoke her name it was almost a teasing caress on his lips. "Raine. This is the first time I've heard you on the phone. You sound—"

"Yes, I know," she cut him off again. "We sound exactly alike." The irony in her tone was obvious.

There was a long pause. "Don't put words in my mouth." He seemed to make an effort then to swallow his annoyance. "I was about to say that you sounded sleepy and relaxed. Hope I didn't wake you."

"Not at all," she returned with crisp finality. "Shall I take a message for Riva, tell her you called?"

"I wanted you, not her." He spoke with a trace of his old impatience, but Raine was less aware of that than of his choice of words. Had it been subconscious, or had he meant to put it so baldly? She waited for him to go on. "The reason I called is to ask you to go with me this morning to the flea market. Nina's birthday is tomorrow. I wanted you to help me choose something for her."

"I'm sorry, Brandon," she lied. "I've already made other plans."

"Cancel them."

"Why should I?"

"Because I'd like to see you."

Raine bit her lip angrily at that. "You're a very clever actor, Brandon. You should have chosen drama over dance."

He made no attempt now to hide his annoyance. "What the hell are you talking about?"

"You never once let on all week that it was Nina who ordered my private tutoring sessions with you, even when I asked you point-blank." Anger sharpened the contralto of her voice. "Was it she who suggested this little outing?"

Brandon ignored that last little thrust. "Who the devil told you that? Riva again?"

"No, it wasn't Riva," Raine went on in the same injured tone. "But it doesn't really matter who told me."

"Damn it, I thought you might be above all the petty intrigue that goes on in the company—" his voice had hardened "—but I see you're as avid for gossip as the rest of them."

"Only when it concerns me," she replied spiritedly. "I have my pride."

He swore in exasperation. "Will you stop being so bloody insufferable? I just wanted to surprise Nina with something special for her eighty-fourth birthday."

"It really is tomorrow?"

"Yes. You and she have gotten so close, I thought you'd have a few ideas."

"She *is* quite special," Raine said softly.

"Finally we agree on something." She detected an edge of laughter in his voice now. "I'll be at your place in half an hour."

"Brandon—" She hadn't agreed to accompany him anywhere, but he'd hung up before she could protest. With a sigh she replaced the receiver.

Flinging down the French novel she'd promised

herself she would read that weekend, she began to
riffle through her narrow clothes closet, glad to be
getting out of the apartment and into the sunshine.
She told herself firmly that her suddenly buoyant
spirits had nothing at all to do with Bran.

The dress she chose was a summery design with
spaghetti straps, its millefleur print in warm russets
and golds picking up the highlights in her chestnut
hair. She tied a silky shawl Gypsy-fashion at her
waist and slipped into a pair of comfortable
espadrilles.

She had just put a sweep of blush high on her
cheekbones and was slicking amber gloss on her lips
when the door bell rang. Knowing that it was too
early for Bran and that his arrival would be announced by the loud roar of his car in the square
below, she moved with unhurried ease to answer it,
thinking it was probably their neighbor, Yvonne.

But the pretty smile on her lips gave way to surprise, then a little frown of confusion. "You're
early! I didn't hear the Fiat in the square."

He was lounging in the doorway, looking all too
attractive in blue gray trousers and a darker blue shirt
with rolled cuffs. "What I'm used to is, 'Brandon,
how delightful! Won't you come in?'" he teased,
eyes glinting at her mischievously.

"I'm sure you are," Raine said dryly. "But at least
I can offer you some satisfaction—won't you come
in?"

He grinned crookedly. "At least I know where I
stand with you."

Raine ignored that as she stepped aside, and he
brushed past her into the apartment. "Would you

care for a cup of coffee?'' she asked. "Our neighbor,
Yvonne, has taught me to make a wicked espresso.''

"I'd just as soon be on our way." His eyes had
cursorily swept the room before coming back to rest
on her. She felt the color rising slowly in her cheeks
beneath that male gaze. "But I *will* take a rain check
on that offer."

He was altogether too sure of himself. "You just
may not get another," Raine said coolly, her flashing
eyes like newly minted gold.

Brandon laughed. "Then I'll just have to make
coffee for you sometime." Raine didn't know what
she'd expected, but it certainly wasn't that. Against
her will she found herself laughing back at him.

When they came out into the square downstairs,
Raine automatically looked for his car. "Where's the
Spider?"

"In the garage," he replied at once, eyes aglow
with the same mischievous lights. "I thought we'd
just let ourselves be carried along by the madding
crowd."

"Good." She smiled up at him. "Now I'll get to
see how really civilized the French are."

"Believe me, it's only the thinnest of veneers,"
Bran teased as he slipped his hand under her elbow
and let his fingers slide down in casual intimacy to
grasp her arm. His laugh was low, and the look he
shot her set the blood coursing recklessly through her
veins.

Their easy mood had changed infinitesimally, their
light badinage not quite masking the electric current
of sensuality that charged the atmosphere between
them. Their relationship was no longer master and

pupil or employer-employee. He was a man and she was a woman, simple as that, and the whole day stretched before them.

They moved easily together across the square, dodging the elaborate prams being pushed along by proud *mamans* and pausing to smile at an old woman with her bread crumbs, who'd become a Pied Piper to the pigeons flocking around her bench. Down in the rue des Abbesses the sidewalks bustled with the quicker tempo and clamor of foot traffic.

Kids on bicycles, their baskets overflowing with crusty loaves, careened past in high spirits, nearly colliding with a burly-shouldered butcher carrying a slab of beef across his back. Half turning in their direction, the man cursed the boys roundly as he readjusted his heavy load and staggered on. He might have bumped into Raine if Bran hadn't circled her waist with his arm and deftly slipped her out of the butcher's way.

His warm protective touch had that inevitable feeling of rightness she'd recognized before, and it was with a certain reluctance that they drew apart and walked on. Truce there might be between them, but lovers they were not. The unsettled mood created an odd constraint, as if both knew they were poised on the edge of something from which they might not be able to withdraw.

The cool *métro* station was less crowded than the streets above, though there were no seats on the train they boarded. Raine faced Bran across the wide aisle, her arm looped around a supporting pole. As the train picked up speed, she closed her eyes and felt herself propelled along by the swaying motion of the ride. When she opened them again, it was to find Bran watching her, his disconcertingly direct look full of questions he seemed in no hurry to find answers to. Her own eyes slid away in an altogether cowardly fashion, and she cursed the telltale blush that crept into her cheeks.

They reemerged into the sunlight at the Porte de Clignancourt and were swept up in the tide of strollers headed for the shadowy maze of alleys that comprised the old flea market. To Raine's eyes, each stall was an antique trunk that had burst its hinges and scattered contents helter-skelter in every corner. There were porcelain-faced dolls in silk dresses, Tiffany lamps from the States, long-barreled dueling pistols, coins blackened by age.

Raine glanced up at Bran, laughter in her eyes. "Tell me, did you have anything particular in mind?"

"No. That's why I brought you along," Bran replied as he took her arm to guide her around a gilded rocking horse that had been straddled by a toddler. Once past, Bran didn't relinquish his hold, and she was content to let him move her along the colorful passageways.

They came to a row of furniture sellers with the most intriguing collection of goods Raine had ever seen. In one stall was a battered chaise longue whose graceful lines might have supported the reclining figure of Napoleon's empress. In another corner was an ornately carved stool that the proprietor swore had been a camp chair of the Roman emperor, Trajan.

"Think what importance such a piece would add

to an ordinary hall!'' the dealer enthused, eyes sharply twinkling beneath the beret he'd pulled low over his forehead. ''Ah, I can spot young lovers at a glance! You're furnishing an entire apartment, I'll wager.''

Laughing, Raine looked away, but not before Bran caught her eye and winked. He had joined in the game with the amiable hustler. ''I think *madame* wants something more practical.''

When the old dealer saw Raine's glance move toward a musty armoire with a cracked glass, he pounced again with the slyness of a cat. ''Now that, *madame*, I don't know if I can part with. It belonged to my great-grandmother and was saved when Paris was sacked by the Prussians back in 1871.''

Raine grinned at him. ''By all means, you should keep it then, *monsieur*.''

Knowing he was beaten, the dealer chuckled in return. As they started to stroll on, he called after them, ''You're a handsome couple. May you have a house full of beautiful *enfants*!''

''Crazy old guy,'' Bran murmured once they were out of earshot. ''He must assume all the world are lovers.''

''What's the matter with weaving a little web of fantasy if it makes his life more bearable?'' Raine couldn't resist retorting. ''Isn't that what your work and mine is all about?''

Bran stopped to look at her, leaning back against a brick wall that caught a narrow shaft of light between the awnings. He crossed his arms and draped one foot casually over the other as his eyes roamed lazily over her features. ''Somehow I get the feeling I'm far too practical for your tastes, Raine.''

Something about his stance made her feel as if they were back in the studio again. "Practical *and* hard driving," she answered with rather more vehemence than she'd intended. "Your American blood coming through."

"That sounds like a reprimand," he said.

Raine shook her head, unaware of the play of light on her hair that made it gleam like dark damask shot through with cinnabar. "No, let's not reprimand each other today," she replied swiftly, not wanting to breach their tenuous truce. For a long moment they stared at each other. Then the moment passed, and Bran took her arm again as they ducked back into the seemingly endless maze of stalls.

They were now in a row that specialized in items of copper and brass, and Raine's curious eyes skimmed over bed warmers, spittoons, kettles and Chinese woks. But what held her attention was a simple, beaten-copper pot. She imagined it planted with flowers on the apartment windowsill, providing a sheen of warmth and color throughout the winter. But the inner debate as to whether or not to purchase it was brief; she needed no reminder that it was another pretty luxury she would simply have to forgo.

As they walked on, Raine's brow furrowed in thought, and she turned suddenly to Bran. "I just thought of something Nina might love if we could only find it. She seems to remember her childhood days in St. Petersburg fondly. It would be nice to get her something that reminded her of that time in her life."

After an hour of poking around in different cor-

ners of the market, Raine found what she was looking for in a small back-alley shop filled with medals,
keys, ancient engravings and religious ex-votos—all
in need of a vigorous polishing and dusting. Propped
on a shelf in the rear of the shop was a Russian icon.
When she rubbed away a square of dust and grease,
Raine found a rich motif edged around with gilt, the
colors still brilliant. The haloed figure in the center
had an air of still grace, the pose of the hands and the
folds of the gown giving mute testimony to another
world and another life far away.

She turned around and handed it to Bran. He, too,
rubbed a window through the decades of grime and
stared at the richly painted icon for a long while. "I
think you're right," he said finally. "Knowing Nina,
she'll treasure it."

Bran spoke to the shopkeeper, and after haggling
briefly with the woman, he agreed to a price that made
Raine gasp. It was far higher than she would have
dreamed, but Brandon paid for it without a qualm.

"Done." Bran grinned as he joined Raine outside
and dropped the small wrapped package into the
pocket of her capacious straw bag. "Now, is there
any shopping of your own you want to do?"

She laughed and shook her head regretfully. "I'm
afraid I'm more the Sunday stroller than the Saturday buyer type. My eyes are far bigger than my
pocketbook!"

He laughed, too. "That sounds like no woman I've
ever known. How about lunch, then? Are you hungry?"

"Well, actually...." She wavered only an instant.
"I'm starved, as a matter of fact!"

A few minutes later they were facing each other over a small window table that was resplendent with white damask and elegantly scalloped silver flatware. Elevated from the street, the little restaurant looked out on the sophisticated passersby. Over a rich tureen of vichyssoise and a delicately sauced shrimp casserole, they enjoyed the panoply beyond the curtained window, neither one of them speaking much.

The Provençal wine Bran had ordered was wonderfully light. Lifting it to her lips, Raine was reminded somehow of the sun and sea, of distant southern shores. Like the gleaming copper, it was a talisman of warmth to ward off the winter.

She set the glass down and looked over at her companion. "Thanks for today, Bran," she said simply. "I think I've seen more of the real Paris in these past few hours than I've seen in the past two weeks."

But it almost seemed that he hadn't heard her. His gaze was playing over her features with that intensity that could hold her against her will. "Your eyes are sad again, Raine," he murmured, his left brow raised in a manner that was half-teasing, half-questioning.

Her betraying eyes slid away from that penetrating gaze that made her feel curiously naked and vulnerable. "I was just thinking about the approach of winter, that's all." She looked down at the table, where their hands rested close but not touching on the cloth. His were dark and veined, the long tapering fingers toying idly with the base of a water goblet. Restless even in repose, they seemed to generate energy and strength, while her own fingers were pale and still. She and Bran were so incredibly different.

He spoke again, his voice low and insistent, teasing still. "So why should winter make you sad?"

She shrugged with a pretense of offhandedness. "I suppose I'm already missing the scent of flowers. . . ." Her nose crinkled unexpectedly and an infectious grin appeared as she tried to make light of the whole thing. "And the taste of strawberries."

But Bran's persistence was stronger than her stubbornness. "And. . . ?" he prompted.

"Nothing else." But her shrug was evasive.

"You're lying," he accused quietly, waiting.

Raine leaned her elbow on the table and ran nervous fingers across her brow. "Look, Brandon," she began with a quick little sigh, "I haven't been totally honest with you. I know what you assumed about the year I lost. But you were wrong. It was nothing like that—no shattered romance. You see, I. . .I had a bad accident."

"On stage?"

"Yes."

Raine looked up and saw his eyes flicker with sudden understanding. "So you were the 'friend' Riva mentioned, the one she said would never dance again."

She nodded. "My doctors in New York said the same thing."

"Nina knew about this?" he asked suddenly.

"Yes, of course."

"For God's sake, why didn't you or she tell me?" he demanded, his fingers drumming now with suppressed impatience on the tablecloth.

She observed him for a long moment across the table. The new dusting of freckles across her nose lent a heightened air of fragility to her features that was deceiving. Blazing beneath was a strong and stubborn will. Bran sensed that will, too, in her deceptively quiet reply. "I thought it had no bearing."

He shook his head, as if still not quite believing her. "I might have been easier on you," he finally muttered.

"I doubt it!" There was a sparkle of laughter in her golden eyes. "Besides, that's just what I didn't want."

The waiter brought two demitasses then, and over coffee, Raine's story, or rather what she chose to tell of it, came out: her wanting to dance and her fears that the injured limb would hold her back, especially once the weather changed. She didn't dwell on the accident, or on how the twins had drifted even further apart in the aftermath. Such things were far too personal and painful to discuss.

"So you see," Raine concluded with a soft laugh, "there was no bastard screwing up my life. It was just bad luck. Fate."

"Good," Bran laughed in return, the sound like a low purring growl. "Because every time I looked into your eyes I had the urge to beat up the guy."

Although he'd meant to tease her, Raine sensed immediately that there was no lightness in the feelings underlying the words. She'd caught the fierce protective glint in his eye, an air of warmth and caring that lighted a treacherous flame of desire inside her. "You see, all that storm of emotion wasted on nothing," Raine replied in a curiously breathless voice that she hoped sounded amused and light.

But he'd caught her mood, and a slow grin spread over his features. "Not wasted...never that," he retorted softly, his eyes glimmering like hot blue flames.

Raine glanced away in confusion, gratefully fixing her attention on the group of itinerant artists who'd set up their wares on the narrow sidewalk outside. Fortunately the waiter returned at the same time with their check, so that by the time Bran had settled the bill, she'd managed to recover her composure quite well. "Do you mind if I poke around those artists' stalls outside?" she said, standing up from the table. "Maybe I'll find something to brighten up Riva's apartment."

Once outside, Raine took her time, stopping to examine and admire the handmade ceramic vases, handsome watercolors and charming French street scenes painted in miniature. At the last stand a woman artist was draping her hand-dyed challis scarves over a low wire fence.

The brilliant colors caught Raine's eye at once. "Aren't they something?" Raine smiled up at Bran. "She's got a real dramatic flair."

Bran's eyes narrowed critically. "They remind me a lot of Pierre's abstract stuff. Maybe that's why you find them so attractive." He shot her an odd little look, his eyes darkening subtly. And for a second Raine imagined crazily that his jealousy the night of his party had been sparked, not by the artist's devotion to Riva, but by Pierre's interest in Raine.

The thought made her spirits soar unaccountably. "Maybe so," she conceded, eyes alight with mischief as she leaned forward to examine the fabrics.

"Bonjour, monsieur et madame," the artist greeted them in atrociously accented French. "May I help you with something?"

Raine straightened up, taking in the fair complexion, tiptilted nose and heavy red hair. "Hi!" she responded in English. "I'm afraid your accent gave you away. British, aren't you?"

"And you're American." The artist chuckled in return. "No mistaking that accent, either." As she laughed, her long silver earrings danced against her cheeks. "I'm Margrit Blake, by the way."

"Nice to meet you," Raine replied, finding the other woman's laughter contagious. "We were just admiring your scarves. They remind us a lot of a friend's abstract paintings."

There was another burst of delighted laughter. "How flattering! Are you both artists, too?"

"We're with a ballet company here."

"Wonderful! I adore ballet and the theater. In fact I used to do a little work for the Cambridge Playhouse." Her eyes flickered speculatively between them. "Say, you wouldn't by chance have a need for a costume designer, would you?"

Raine looked inquiringly up at Bran, who replied at once in a low easy voice, "The company's always in need of creative talent, but I have to warn you—we pay slave wages." He shot the woman a warm engaging grin as he searched his pockets for one of his business cards.

The card found, Margrit accepted it eagerly. "A choreographer, eh?" she said, her hazel eyes dancing as she tilted her head to one side. "I'm quite impressed. Perhaps I'll ring you in a day or so, before you forget that you offered me a job." She grinned at her own boldness, causing Bran to laugh.

"Believe me, you don't know what you'd be getting into," he said. "It gets so hectic in season, you don't have time to think."

"Think!" Margrit echoed, a chuckle rising again in her throat. "Who wants to do that? My boyfriend pushed off and left me without warning—after five years of being together. So I decided to push off myself," she said frankly. "I wanted to do something romantic and crazy, and Paris was about as far in that direction as my pocketbook would take me. Monsieur du Rivage, I'd be delighted to drop by and talk business."

Raine admired the artist's air of jaunty self-confidence, her breezy manner of dismissing a part of her life that must be hurting her deeply. Margrit wasn't precisely pretty, but with her quick hazel eyes and bright hair, she radiated an earthy animation that was quite appealing.

After addresses and phone numbers had been exchanged, Bran and Raine made their way back to the Clignancourt *métro*. Neither of them spoke, but it was a comfortable silence borne along by the memories of the morning and a sense of shared discovery.

"Are you tired?" Bran asked as they stood side by side on the subway platform.

"Not at all," Raine admitted. "I think Margrit's effervescence spilled over onto me."

Bran's answering grin was quick. "Good, because I've got a bit more of Paris to show you."

Raine's eyes swooped up, startled, to meet his. Somehow she hadn't expected that.

"What's the matter?" he teased. "Don't you want to?"

"It's not that," she demurred. "I suppose I just assumed you had work to do."

"On a sunny Saturday afternoon?" he retorted with incredulity. "Come on, Raine. I'm a man, not a machine."

"Original sentiment," she answered dryly, at once irritated and amused at the clever way he'd managed to throw her own words back at her.

Any answer he might have made was swallowed up as a train roared into the station and they boarded. It whisked them back into the heart of the city, where they disembarked at the Tuileries. The formal gardens, which extend to the Place de la Concorde from between the wings of the Louvre, were developed more than four hundred years ago for the pleasure of the courtiers.

Bran took Raine's arm, and they headed off toward one of the pavilions at the eastern end of the gardens. "The Jeu de Paume," he told her succinctly. "My favorite museum."

And as they stepped inside, Raine understood why. A tribute to the Impressionists who'd blazed a new direction in art a century earlier, the museum was human-scaled, almost intimate. Wandering in delight among the small rooms, she scarcely noticed that the sky beyond the windows had begun to darken. Within the museum's walls, the paintings threw a clear wash of light that needed no assistance from the sun.

When they came out two hours later, Raine glanced up in surprise. A gray cloud veil hovered high above the city, its far edges rent by traces of lightning. Occasionally there was a rumble of thunder, so distant that it sounded no more threatening than a purr.

"Do you think it'll storm?" Raine asked Bran anxiously.

"What are you worried about? Afraid of melting?" he teased.

"I don't have ice in my veins, if that's what you're insinuating," she retorted evenly. Without waiting for his reply, she struck out across the busy rue de Rivoli as soon as the signal changed.

Amused, Bran swiftly fell into step beside her. "Where are you going?"

"We're not far from the Place Vendôme, right? I've got a sudden taste for elegance." Raine shot him a sideways glance from beneath her lashes. "I'll buy you an aperitif in one of the cafés."

"Thanks, but this day's on me."

Raine came to an abrupt stop on the far sidewalk, oblivious to the crowd of pedestrians milling past them. "Stop being so damn macho," she replied irritably.

To her amazement, when she looked up into his face Raine saw that he was laughing, a faintly wicked sound. "That's the first time a woman's ever accused me of being too male."

She ignored the challenge in his tone, trying with less success to ignore the little pinpricks of delight that followed in the wake of his eyes as they touched on her lips and the bare smoothness of her shoulders. "Brandon," she began uncertainly, "you don't owe me anything."

The laughter went out of his eyes, in its place the

raking intensity that seemed to probe and measure. "Don't you get tired of struggling under that great burden of pride?"

Raine tossed her hair back over her shoulder in an angry gesture. "It's all I've got," she told him slowly. "If I can't believe in myself, then how can I expect anyone else to believe in me?"

"Touché," he murmured, his reply at once rueful and self-mocking. "I'm coming to find that your air of fragility is nothing but a clever disguise. Beneath it all you're as ruthless as your sister." He grinned. "And that scares the hell out of me."

Her color deepened at this new insinuation. "Don't worry," she whispered. "There's only one thing I want, and that's to dance my best."

The teasing light that had filled his eyes suddenly faded. "We'll see about that."

The café he took her to was situated across the square from the Ritz hotel, where limousines and taxis discharged their wealthy clientele in a never-ending stream. After the waiter had set down the Pernod and water he'd ordered, Bran looked over at Raine, amused. "Elegant enough for you?"

"It's a world away from Clignancourt." Raine laughed softly as her eyes swept past the limousines and the women in their haute-couture silks to drink in the lovely symmetry of the square itself. Her gaze slid back to Bran. "But you seem to fit equally well in both worlds."

He smiled strangely. "Are you always so perceptive? Though I don't know about fitting in; I feel like I've been walking a tightrope between the haute monde and the demimonde my entire life. My father came from an aristocratic family and built a multinational corporation from the ground up.''

Raine's eyes sparkled with interest. ''Is your mother still alive?''

''She's retired and has a place on the Riviera.'' Bran's words were clipped, and Raine sensed the subtle shift in his mood. Whether he was expressing anger at her for asking or some hidden irony whose meaning she couldn't begin to fathom, Raine wasn't certain. Yet she had to know more.

''So your mother danced here on the continent?''

Bran's affirmative nod was curt. ''That's right. But I only saw her occasionally after she divorced my father.''

''He mustn't have been too happy with your choice of career, then.''

''No, he wasn't,'' Bran admitted dryly.

''Yet you came back to dance.''

''My father died the year I gave up my sports career. I decided my life was my own.''

''And dance was an important part of it. You love it, don't you, Brandon,'' she interposed gently. ''I sense it every time you work with me. Your mother must be proud of you.''

He shrugged. ''She has her own life. Our worlds don't overlap.''

The finality with which he said that made Raine's heart constrict painfully. She wanted to ask more, but she sensed that Bran had begun to retreat into himself. Respecting his tacit wish not to be pushed into further revelations, she turned her attention to the drink in front of her. They were both startled by a loud clap of thunder overhead.

Bran laughed over at her, banishing the constraint in his eyes. "You were right. Looks like the storm was headed in this direction, after all." He stood up and threw several franc notes on the café table, then pulled out Raine's chair. "Come on, we'll go rout out the Spider. For all your denials, I'd still hate to see you get caught in the rain," he teased.

She was laughing, too, as she stood up. "Somehow I get the awful feeling you keep confusing me with the Wicked Witch of the West from *The Wizard of Oz*."

"Sorceress is more like it," he murmured, switching to the more intimate phrasing of French. "Come on, let's go."

Raine thought she would remember that day as much for its particular aromas as anything else: the mustiness of the flea market and the fiery licorice sweetness of their aperitifs. Now the diesel fumes from the buses roaring past on the elegant boulevards had been replaced by the sharp smell of ozone.

An instant later, another deafening clap of thunder reverberated around them. Hurrying along the Quai de Gesvres where the bird sellers were drawing covers over their caged inventory in anticipation of the storm, they ducked into a bakery. Its well-lighted interior was an oasis in the gathering darkness beyond the windows. Here a whole new batch of delicious scents assailed Raine's nostrils as she waited for Bran to complete his purchase.

But it was only a moment's respite, and they were back outside again, rushing hand in hand across the Pont d'Arcole to Notre-Dame, across the pretty square fronting the cathedral, only stopping to catch their breath once they'd reached the tiny Pont St-Louis.

"You're crazy!" Raine exclaimed as Bran delved into the white paper bag and drew out one of the bakery confections.

He grinned. "You won't think so after you've tasted this."

"But I've already gained five pounds today!" Raine protested, laughing still, her protests cut off as he lifted the meringue to her lips, and she bit into the light crust that was filled with a spice-laced crême Chantilly.

Happy though she was at that moment, Raine felt an odd sense of guilt, and she turned to her companion with a faintly troubled expression. "Brandon, I thought you didn't believe in showing favoritism to your dancers. So why are we together like this today?"

"Let me worry about that," Bran answered slowly as his thumb came up to brush away the smudge of cream on her lower lip. Then he lowered his face to hers.

His lips were deliciously warm against her own. The sweetness of his tongue as it tasted the corner of her mouth and tentatively probed its dark recesses evoked in her an almost unbearable wave of pleasure. His hands cupped her face, his thumbs languidly caressing the silken column of her throat. Her hands came up to close on his. Yet for all the need his kiss awakened in her, Raine knew she meant to pull his hands away, to break the spell that held them both. She had no desire for a part-time lover; no desire for a schizophrenic existence in which they were master and pupil throughout the week and man and woman only in stolen weekend moments.

But he mistook the tension of reluctance in her fingertips for growing desire, and his hands slid downward over her warm shoulders. Slowly he pulled her close until her breasts grazed his shirt and passion raced between them, the treacherous languor of her limbs overcoming the proud reservations in her mind. The moment was broken by the intrusion of cold reality—in the form of great splashing raindrops.

Raine drew back with breathless laughter. "Don't you think we should make a run for it? I might be a sorceress, after all!"

His response was low and caressing. "At this point I wouldn't doubt it at all."

The warning spatter gave way within seconds to a gusting deluge of rain and wind. They sprinted across the bridge, agilely dodging puddles and leaping from doorway to doorway once they'd reached the sanctuary of the Ile St-Louis.

Outside Bran's gray-stoned apartment, they were stymied by a wide puddle deeper than the rest. Oblivious to her wet clothes and the goosebumps on her skin, Raine laughed up at him through the raindrops clustered like diamonds on her lashes. "Now if this were a more romantic era, you'd already be tossing off your cape and laying it down for me to walk across."

"No," he countered with a laugh. "I've got a better idea." Without warning he bent down and picked her up, sloshing through the ankle-deep water blocking the entryway. Still holding her, he began to climb the inside stairs.

"You can put me down now," Raine said evenly. When Bran ignored her and continued climbing, she began to prickle with irritation. "You said you would drive me home. Don't tell me the Spider is parked in your living room." He climbed up the last flight as she continued her halfhearted protest. "Put me down, Brandon. I'm no invalid."

The front door loomed at last, and he eased her down beside him, whispering as he did so, "Haven't you figured it out yet, Raine? The more stubborn you are, the more stubborn I become. You can't win."

"Can't I?" she retorted coolly, though her confidence began to ebb as she grew more aware of his hand on her waist, his thumb tracing a leisurely arc from the high point of her hip bone to the sensitive rib beneath her breast. She remembered the sensuous tracing of his mouth over hers a few moments earlier, and she licked her upper lip nervously, knowing her pretense of control was only that. She felt the blood pounding through her veins like the surge of a normally quiescent creek at flood tide, and hot color flooded her cheeks as she saw his eyes hungrily follow the innocent flicker of her tongue over her dry lips.

Reluctantly Bran tore his gaze from hers and reached into his pocket for the apartment keys. A moment later the door swung inward, and the hand at her waist gently nudged her inside. She stopped just past the threshold, her eyes following him as he crossed to the fireplace and busied himself arranging several logs in the grate.

"I think I'd better go," she said in a subdued voice. "It's getting late."

"Don't be a fool," he flung back over his shoulder impatiently. "You're wet and cold, and it's still pouring outside. Besides, you'd better give that leg a rest."

That last was a timely reminder. In the turmoil of other feelings she'd almost forgotten about it. Gently she gave a little practice flex of her calf and knew he was right.

Bran had straightened up and was regarding her. "Why don't you get comfortable? I'll be back in a few minutes."

He left her alone, and Raine found herself drawn to the fire, its cheerful hiss and crackle a pleasing counterpoint to the drumming cadence of rain against the windows. Slowly she untied the wet shawl knotted at her waist and laid it before the grate to dry. Then she eased down onto the floor and began running her fingers through her damp hair with long gliding strokes until it fell in a soft doeskin cloud over one shoulder. Though the warmth invaded every part of her, the muscles of her weak leg still felt tight and cold. She raised the knee slightly until her skirt slid along her thigh, and leaning forward, she began to massage the calf with light quick fingers. Yet she couldn't quite relax.

The sound of a door softly closing at the end of the hall caught Raine's attention and she looked up, waiting. Bran came around the corner of the kitchen, a bottle of brandy and two glasses in hand. He'd exchanged his street attire for a short black cotton robe, and his hair was tousled. His mood of quiet unselfconscious intimacy touched Raine in an indefinable way. The rain, and the fire, the brandy and his dishabille formed a cozy web that surrounded them both, still practically strangers but somehow ready now to trust.

There was a thick white towel draped over his shoulder, which he pulled off and flung onto the leather sofa. ''I thought you might need this, but it looks as though you've done just fine with the fire alone,'' he murmured, never taking his eyes off her as he dropped down beside her and set the bottle on the black slate hearth. The firelight cast a warm sheen over her hair and skin, the soft shadows contouring her beautifully defined legs up to where they disappeared into the bright tumbled linen of her skirt. ''How's your leg?'' he asked finally.

Her lashes dropped protectively against her cheeks as she sought to avoid his questioning gaze. ''Just fine,'' she lied.

''You're a rotten liar, Raine. Your eyes and face are far too expressive.'' He laughed softly as he reached out to run his hand along the silken musculature of her calf. Before she could draw away, his strong fingers had begun to knead and massage the tight knot of muscle and sinew.

His warm touch was utterly delightful, a practiced massage that for all its therapeutic thoroughness sent little rivulets of desire up and down her spine.

''You shouldn't have stayed on it all day,'' Bran said without looking up.

Raine leaned forward, crossing her arms on her upraised knee. ''And just whose fault do you think that was?'' she replied teasingly.

His hand stilled for a moment on her leg as he shot her a swift raking look. Then he grinned and reached for the warming bottle of spirits. "I stand corrected." With one hand he poured brandy into each glass, then lifted his own to touch hers. "Here's to the end of a lovely afternoon."

Raine laughed gently. "I'll drink to that."

She let her head fall back and shook out her hair, enjoying the brandy that warmed her within and the trailing edge of Bran's fingers, his long teasing strokes setting her more recklessly afire. "That feels wonderful."

"I'm glad you approve of my touch," he teased, his eyes glinting like hard sapphires. Bran leaned toward her, his fingers still sliding along her bare leg in a soft glissando. His face hovered an instant above her trembling mouth, reminding them both of another poignant moment in the apartment when they had hesitated on the brink before his hungry mouth had captured hers. But they were alone now, with no threat of intrusion from raucous party guests.

His lips tasted and enveloped hers with unhurried ease. His teeth nipped gently at her upper lip and grazed the full contour of her lower lip in a slow ravishment that ignited flickering sparks along her whole body. Lifting her hand, Raine gently stroked his neck, her fingers trailing downward to slip into the V-neck of his robe. They skimmed his chest, their tips, featherlight, circling his flat nipples and the lush mat of black hair. He groaned beneath the sweet sorcery of her touch, and Raine knew then how much she wanted to give as well as take, to taste his pleasure along with her own.

Bran sensed her feminine exultation, and its sweetly hungering power ignited something deep inside him. Raine's heightened senses responded at once to her unspoken plea, her heart leaping as their tongues touched and mingled in a devastatingly intimate kiss that pushed her beyond the boundaries of mere sensuality.

With a slow shudder of delight, she felt his hands pushing her skirt farther up her thighs, felt the hot tracery of his fingers as they splayed across that smooth shadowed warmth. Gently then, Bran eased her down onto her back and lay beside her, the soft mat of hairs on his bare legs grazing against hers in a way that prickled and teased maddeningly.

Yet for all the slowness of his touch and the tender depth of his kisses, Raine sensed something wild and untamed that he held in check. She longed for him to unleash those feelings as he had for fleeting moments when they'd danced together across the studio floor. But she knew that in tempting him she would be tempting herself. They were no longer on a stage. . . .

Her thoughts blurred again as his mouth reluctantly relinquished hers and slid downward to drop kisses on her shoulders. He tugged the thin straps of her dress over her arms, lips trailing in pursuit. His playful mouth grazed and tickled the hollow where her upper arm pressed against her breast, until she gasped with mingled laughter and desire. Then his hungering tongue was tracing the upper edge of her bodice, which still clung precariously to the rounded swell of her breasts. Her nipples thrust protestingly against the confining fabric, until her muffled gasp gave way to a cry.

She reached forward to loosen the belt of his robe and knead his hard torso, yearning to touch and caress him as much as she wanted to be touched. Now Raine moaned as his mouth sought the tender peaks of her breasts, as his fingertips left a trail of fire over her pliant thighs and gently curving hips.

"I want to undress you, Raine," he murmured huskily. "Your body's perfection. I want to see all of it in the firelight."

As he spoke, Bran pulled her up again into a sitting position, her back half turned to him. She gasped aloud as she felt his hands on her spine, the quick ripple of a zipper in its track. As the bodice fell forward, she caught it instinctively to her breasts.

Suddenly Raine felt as if she were a performer being led through a well-practiced sequence, and the thought brought her back to reason, back from the tempest of emotion that had engulfed her. They *were* no longer on a stage; this was life. Whatever happened now, she, at least, could not walk away once the music had faded into an empty silence. Yet she feared that Bran could all too easily. . . .

Raine felt his lips, intimate against the small of her back, as if they'd lain just this way together for countless afternoons. The thought of such delightful easy communication between two lovers, sure and confident in their shared love, sent a wave of need so deeply through her that it was almost a shock. Bran felt her tremble, but mistaking it for simple passion, he slid his hands around her waist and tried to pull her back down beside him.

She shook her head in a quick gesture of impatience. "It was wrong of me to come here," she whispered, her face still turned to the hot fire in the grate.

"Why?" he murmured distractedly, his lips still caressing her back, so that each word was a softly breathed kiss that sent little waves of pleasure lapping over her bared skin.

"Because I don't quite trust you. You're either hot or cold, Brandon—no in-between," she said in a soft rush, steeling herself against the ever spiraling desire that his mouth and tongue elicited. "You frighten me."

Mistakenly believing it was his sexuality that she feared, Bran took her arms, and with gentle force pulled her around to face him. "There's nothing to be afraid of," he whispered slowly, his eyes feasting on the beautiful flush of warmth and desire that spilled downward from her cheeks onto her naked shoulders.

"Isn't there?" she retorted, her voice defiant now. "How can a woman know where she stands with you? You told me yesterday that you never get personally involved with your dancers, yet today you sought me out. Yesterday in the studio you made me cry and rage inside, and now you want to make love to me." Raine broke off, her sigh at once perplexed and angry. "Brandon, aren't we breaking all the rules?"

"What if we are?" he responded roughly, the caressing sensuality of his voice overridden by impatience. "We've got no one to answer to but ourselves."

"That's just the point, Brandon. I'll have to live with myself tomorrow," she replied. "Besides, I get the feeling you've choreographed this same little scene over and over again."

"You and your damned pride." He laughed shortly. "Though I have to admit that part of you fascin-
ates me, Raine."

She wasn't mollified. "And when the fascination
ends?"

Bran shook his head, his eyes like hard uncut
stones. "I can't answer that."

With as much dignity as she could muster, Raine
zipped her dress with quick trembling fingers and
stood up, pulling her shawl protectively over her
shoulders. "Life's nothing but a stage to you, isn't
it?" she observed quietly, all her anger burned out.
"A series of sets that you can enter and leave at will,
without really giving anything of yourself."

"What the hell do you think I gave you last week
in all those hours we spent alone in the studio?" he
raged, rising to his feet beside her.

The dark gold flash of Raine's eyes in the refined
composition of her face was the only hint of the con-
flicting emotions roiling beneath the surface. "You
gave your expertise," she countered softly. "There's
a difference."

"You've got your nerve," Bran said, incredulous
now. "Raine, you're the one who's leaving, the one
who's so afraid to give."

"You don't know me well enough to say that."

"Don't I? I know your kind too well." There was
a curious bleakness in his gaze that she'd never seen
before. "Your ambition overrides everything else."

She regarded him stonily. "If I were ambitious, I'd
still be lying in your arms." Raine turned to pick up
her bag with shaking fingers, retrieved the wrapped
icon and dropped it onto the sofa. "Goodbye, Bran.

Wish Nina a happy birthday for me and . . . and thank you for today.''

In three quick strides she was at the front door. Afraid that he might call her back, and that she would go to him, Raine flung it open hurriedly and raced down the stairs.

Outside, the initial fury of the storm had spent itself; the rain falling was only a misty silver curtain. Raine turned her face up to it, enjoying the coolness against her burning cheeks.

Gradually her lingering desire gave way to perplexity. Why had he suddenly accused her of being ambitious, as if it were a crime? The words had been a challenge, yet she'd sensed a fleeting trace of vulnerability in his tone that had caught her off guard. Raine wondered how much of him lay hidden beneath that self-possessed facade.

Turning away from the silent mansion, she slowly made her way toward the bus stop on the far side of the gray river.

CHAPTER SIX

RAINE THREADED HER WAY between an elderly woman en route to Mass and a man in his Sunday suit, his ruffled and beribboned daughter on one arm and a package of fresh pastries balanced on the other. Montmartre had come alive beneath a pallid autumn sun that didn't quite warm the brisk air blowing off the hill.

For three hours on that quiet Sunday morning, she had danced full out in the lonely studio, the settling creaks and groans of the old building a mutinous protest to the uncustomary invasion. And as she danced, Bran's accusation had reverberated again and again through her mind—that she put her ambition above all else. Why should he care?

Now as she climbed the stairs to the apartment, Raine was thinking of nothing more than a hot shower and a cold drink. But when she opened the door, what she found on the low coffee table made her forget those things at once. Bewildered, she walked over and lifted up the antique copper pot she'd admired just the day before in the Clignancourt market. It was filled now with masses of blooming lilies. Thoughts still reeling, she set it back down.

Riva sauntered out of the bedroom and leaned back against the doorway. "That's not all," she said, her observant eyes full of curiosity and the merest tinge of envy. "A basket of hothouse strawberries was delivered from Fauchon's. I put them in the fridge. You're a fast worker, Raine. Who's the admirer?"

Raine ignored this needling cross-examination as she leaned down to bury her face in the profusion of exotic blooms, wondering why on earth he'd sent them. With a veiled expression, she looked up at her sister. "Was there a card?"

She hadn't actually expected one, so she was surprised when Riva crossed to the phone desk and retrieved a small white envelope from the message basket. With a flick of the wrist, her sister extended the card between two fingers, eyes still watchful.

Raine opened it and read to herself: "Here's hoping this taste of summer will get you through the winter." For all the anger and tension in their parting the day before, he'd remembered the things she'd confided in him in the Clignancourt restaurant. Though this example of Bran's thoughtfulness touched her deeply, it left her a little unsettled, as well. Again she wondered what lay behind the distant, self-contained demeanor he presented to the world.

Riva interrupted her silent musings. "Are you going to share the good news, Raine, or are we not dropping names now?" There was more than a touch of malice in the question.

Raine shook her head, unaware of the color that had crept into her cheeks and the bright intensity of her gaze. "Sorry," she murmured in a soft distracted voice, "but I don't feel like talking about it."

"Are you in love?" Riva cried in disbelief, watching her twin's eyes darken in response to that entirely unexpected question.

"I did not come to Paris to fall in love," Raine snapped. "I'm not that naive." For all her denials, Raine's hands were gentle, almost caressing as she picked up the copper pot and carried it to the windowsill.

"You're right." Riva spoke thoughtfully at her back. "You're not naive. I might have said differently a few weeks ago, but not now. Somehow you're not quite the same person."

Raine's head spun around at that, her eyes gleaming with curiosity. "In what way?" she demanded.

Riva shrugged. "I don't know—tougher, I guess."

Raine's brow dipped in a subtle frown. Her sister's words should have pleased her, since this was Riva's reluctant admission that she thought of her as a professional again. Yet deep down, the statement worried her.

"Wake up, girl!" Riva chided her out of her meditative mood. "Now, come on...what's the guy's name?"

"Sorry, but I'm not saying," Raine insisted stubbornly.

A pillow came winging through the air, just missing Raine's head. "You sly witch!" Riva exclaimed, but she was laughing a little now. "By the way, are you having lunch with Yvonne and me?"

"Just give me fifteen minutes to soak in the tub."

When Raine emerged from her bath, she found Riva and Yvonne chatting in the kitchen. The Frenchwoman had whipped up a quiche and invited

them to share her Sunday feast. After Riva made a
salad and Raine uncorked a bottle of inexpensive red
wine, the three women trouped out onto the fire
escape for a picnic.

They enjoyed a leisurely meal, laughing and gossip-
ing as they drank the wine from small tumblers. Raine
volunteered to carry the leftovers inside and returned
a few minutes later with the bowl of washed hulled
strawberries and a bit of thick cream for dipping.

Yvonne, her nose crinkling in delight, exclaimed
over the luscious red fruit. "What did you do?" she
teased her American friends. "Rob a bank to buy
these at Fauchon's?"

The glitter of Riva's gold cat's eyes was shuttered by
the flutter of her thick lashes as her gaze swooped in
Raine's direction. "They were a gift, Yvonne. Raine
has an admirer."

Yvonne flung back her short-cropped black hair.
"Mon Dieu! How romantic! Is he a secret admirer?"

"Only to the rest of us," Riva responded. *"She*
knows who he is."

Yvonne winked conspiratorially at Raine. "Let me
guess, *ma chère*. He's the wickedly handsome guy
with angry blue eyes and shoulders like an Adonis's
who called for you yesterday."

Raine blanched, realizing their neighbor must have
been home yesterday and couldn't resist peeking out
her door when Bran had come up the stairs. Feeling
Riva's sharp eyes on her, Raine decided to laugh off
Yvonne's words as an amusing joke. "We should all
be so lucky," she retorted, her lips curling in a deter-
minedly rueful smile. "Are all Frenchwomen such
dreamers?"

Yvonne leaned her head back against the warm brick wall with a sigh. *"Oui*, I suppose so."

Raine relaxed as she saw Riva do so, though she wasn't quite certain if her twin's suspicions had been completely put to rest. Raine knew it was ridiculous to attempt to hide the fact that she'd seen Bran outside the company. Still, her fears of another bout of sisterly competition were strong.

Later that evening, after Riva had gone out, Raine picked up the telephone and slowly dialed Bran's number. He answered at once, his voice mellow and relaxed. She pictured him in his short black robe before the fire, and her pulse quickened.

"Bran, this is Raine," she began, hoping he wouldn't notice the slight tremor in her own voice. "I . . . I wanted to thank you for the gifts you sent."

His laughter was low. "So you approved of my peace offering?"

"Is that what it was?" She laughed in return. "I didn't realize we were at war."

"Isn't that what it always boils down to between a man and a woman?"

But she ignored his cynicism. "Now that you've buttered me up, I suppose you're expecting an apology for the way I walked out of your place yesterday."

"No," he said quietly. "I wasn't expecting that. Just a chance for us to get started off on the right foot again."

"Is that a choreographer's pun?" she couldn't resist teasing.

He chuckled. "You're a real comedienne. At least I know I'll never be bored with you around."

"Nope," she replied mischievously in pure American slang. "I'll keep you on your toes."

He groaned. "Will you spare me the bad jokes if I bribe you?"

"Depends on what it is," she retorted, envisioning his crooked grin.

"How about the theater after rehearsals tomorrow?"

Raine hesitated, wanting to be with him, yet wondering at the propriety of any personal involvement. But her feelings won out. "What are you taking me to see?"

"A surprise," he replied warmly. "Something I know you'll enjoy."

"Good. I like surprises."

"Okay, then," he said more crisply. "See you in the studio tomorrow morning at eight sharp."

"Yes, sir!" she snapped back as he reverted without even a pause to their company roles.

THE DAYS HAD ALREADY BEGUN to shorten with the onset of autumn. Raine noticed the darkening sky beyond the window as she walked down the long studio hall, a towel draped around her neck. Mondays were always like that for dancers—long and tough, she reflected. But the workouts had been good, and her lifts in class, even if they hadn't attained the poetry of flight, were at least decent.

She savored the memory of her private noon session with Bran, too. Though he was still a hard taskmaster, there was a new tentative closeness between them that made those hours together something special. And as she'd relaxed, Raine had felt a resurgence of self-confidence that lent animation to her gestures and smoothed over the occasional shakiness that still clung to her limbs.

Now she had the coming evening to look forward to. She'd grab a light salad and a handful of raisins, so there would be plenty of time to nap before Bran came over. Ceasing her mental note-taking for a second, she popped her head around Madame Tarsamova's office door to say good-night.

The ballet mistress was bent in concentration over the papers on her desk, but she glanced up at once when she heard Raine's cheery voice. "Ah, good," she murmured crisply. "I was hoping to see you. Come in, child. I've something to say." Her black eyes gleamed in the spilled lamplight.

Reflected, too, in the soft light was the old icon, cleaned and burnished now to a rich gloss. *Madame* had set it on the small table amid her silver-framed grouping of family photographs. Raine was touched to find it there, taking a place of honor with all the other things the woman held dear. But it was a poignant reminder, too, that the studio was *madame*'s life, her home, her very heartbeat.

The ballet mistress spoke again, her sharp voice reflecting an unmistakable iron will. "Sit down, please. You must be exhausted after your long day," she observed before launching without preamble into the topic that was uppermost in her mind. "Now, you remember our discussion about finding a patron for you."

Actually Raine had forgotten all about it, perhaps because the idea was a little distasteful to her. "I really don't think it's necessary, Madame T."

"Quite the contrary, dear," the Russian woman corrected with a subtle lift of her thin brows. "You've not got Riva's stamina to do guest spots with other European companies, and somehow I can't see you selling shoes at Printemps." Her sarcasm, sparingly used, was effective.

"I've talked to Tracey about the Folies. She says the money's good," Raine interjected swiftly. "I might apply—"

"Nonsense," *madame* rapped out. "Your style is poetry, not vaudeville." She uttered the last word as if it were poison. "No, you must listen to me. I know the kind of woman you are—living on lettuce leaves and air. You don't have the strong instinct for self-preservation necessary to the prima donna. Such women drive themselves mercilessly, but then they pamper themselves with luxury. So," she concluded with a satisfied air, as if everything had already been decided, "in your case, we'll have someone else do the pampering."

Raine's answer to *madame*'s little speech was a somewhat wary smile. "What do I have to do in return?"

"Nothing, of course, beyond fulfilling simple social obligations. Just be your lovely youthful self. He will take you to all the 'right' places, and you will enjoy his company." *Madame* paused then as if to marshal her thoughts. "I'm sure you must be curious about the man I've chosen. Pierre Santandre's birthright goes back to one of the baronetcies of the Norman conquerors. He is a congenial man and a great supporter of the arts. By assisting you, he assists the ballet."

Raine bit her lip. "It sounds as though I have no choice."

Once again, a sense of unwavering purpose was clear in the elderly woman's husky voice. "I am thinking of you, and I am thinking of my company."

"But, *madame*, what if...." Raine hesitated, not certain how to phrase the awkward question. "What if the man's attracted to me?"

The Russian woman chortled. "*Mon Dieu*, what a mind you have! The man is a gentleman, not a lecher. He is a lover of beauty and gentle wit. He will appreciate you as a person, and you must appreciate him."

Again Raine sensed the subtle but unmistakable emphasis in Madame Tarsamova's tone, the words that were not so much an admonition as a command. "But what if I hate him?" she threw out perversely.

There was impatience in *madame*'s sigh. "He is a patron, not a husband. If there's to be any marriage, it will be between Monsieur Santandre and the Ballet du Monde. We desperately need that kind of support." There it was, out in the open—the bald practicality. "I should also mention that this patron business will go no further than the three of us. I don't want to generate any unnecessary jealousies among the others. The primary reason I am doing this at all is because I believe in you."

"I appreciate your confidence and your concerns, *madame*. Still I think Bran has to be told about—"

But *madame* shook her head with the same air of brittle impatience, cutting her off. "Brandon disapproves of my old-fashioned diplomacy. Nevertheless," she added crisply, "I find it works. He needn't know where I squeeze my pennies from."

"But I'm certain if you explained to him—" Raine went on doggedly.

The old woman's laughter was sharp, unexpected. "No, he mustn't get wind of it. He and I respect each other, but we've had our battle royals in the past. I refuse to battle with him over this."

"That's downright machiavellian!"

"No, just practical," Madame Tarsamova countered as she shot Raine one of her rare smiles, conspiratorial and full of devilry.

Raine understood, then, that this was the way it must have been done in Russia at the turn of the century, when ballerinas didn't simply dance, but became involved in murky intrigues and were affected by the treacherous shifting sands of imperial influence and design. *Madame* thrived in that kind of environment, but Raine had begun to have real misgivings about what she was in for. At heart, though, she had to admit that she agreed with Madame Tarsamova's goals. She wanted to dance, without all the little worries of how to make ends meet pressing in on her—and she wanted the ballet company to thrive.

"Very well, *madame*," Raine said in a firm voice as she stood up. "When do we meet this courtly figure?"

A loud knock sounded on the outer office door. "Is now soon enough?" the Russian woman countered with lifted brow. *"Entrez!"* she called out in a louder voice as she, too, stood up and came around the desk.

The door burst open, and a rotund, genial-looking man burst into the room. He had a white fringe of hair circling his balding head, lively eyes and bright red apple cheeks. Raine nearly laughed aloud at her own misgivings. He looked like a grandfather every child would adore having. The only hint of his seignorial forebears was in the thin stubborn line of his lips, though even that was erased as he smiled at the two women. Raine suddenly realized that there was something vaguely familiar about the man, but that thought was forgotten as he took her hand and pumped it vigorously.

"Mademoiselle Cameron, I am enchanted to make your acquaintance. Madame Tarsamova has told me a little of your history," he said, his eyes warm and sympathetic. "You are a courageous young woman."

But Raine shook her head. "There's nothing courageous about doing what you have to do," she told him simply.

"Well said, well said!" His round dark eyes flashed then, and Raine could almost imagine the swift machinery of his mind. "Mademoiselle Cameron, I know this is short notice, but I've received two tickets to the opening of the Bolshoi Ballet at the Opéra tonight. I would like to bring you as my guest."

Raine was about to shake her head regretfully when she caught Madame T's glance, eloquently expressing both a plea and a command. Knowing she had no choice, Raine sighed and nodded her head. "Thank you, Monsieur Santandre. I'd be honored." Even as she said it, she wondered how on earth she would explain to Bran.

But the ballet mistress and the spry French aristocrat had no such concerns. They were beaming at each other, and at her.

After Pierre Santandre had taken his leave with a promise to call for Raine that evening, Madame T took her aside again. "I knew the man would be enchanted," she said decisively as she moved to a small closet behind the door. "Now, there's just one more thing. You will need an evening dress. I'm well aware of the lamentably casual style American women are so fond of."

Raine stared at the enormous box *madame* held out to her. "Where on earth did you get it?"

"A long story, but a simple one. One of my most beautiful dancers was involved in an affair with a designer, who lavished gifts of his latest creations on her. When she rejected him for another man and ran off to Italy, she bequeathed her collection to the ballet. The wonderful couturier silks didn't make up for the loss of a great dancer, of course; still, I knew they might be useful someday," she explained with an air of satisfaction.

THE RUSTLE OF CLARET-COLORED SILK against her stockinged legs was deliciously unfamiliar. Raine turned this way and that in the hall mirror, taking in the vision of herself in the strapless confection with its gathered bodice and narrow waist. It was far more revealing a gown than Raine would have chosen for herself, though she had to admit it set off her pale shoulders rather nicely. The only jewelry she wore was a tiny diamond pendant on a slender chain that had been her mother's last gift, one each, to her daughters before she died.

Raine had gathered up her hair into a soft knot, leaving her bangs free to sweep low over her forehead in a gleaming mahogany wave. The effect was almost regal in its simplicity, yet Raine was less aware of that than of the deepening furrow of worry between her eyebrows. She reached for the phone and dialed again.

Her concern over how she would explain to Bran had so far turned out to be academic, because she hadn't been able to reach him anywhere. After leaving Madame Tarsamova's office, she'd sought him out. But all the practice rooms had been empty, his own office door locked. Raine had telephoned his apartment first thing when she'd arrived home; all she got was his answering machine. How much could she say in thirty seconds? Raine had informed him tersely that though she very much regretted doing it, she had to cancel their date.

Her worrisome speculations were interrupted by a sharp rap on the front door. Whirling to open it, she came face to face with a chauffeur in full uniform.

"Bonsoir, mademoiselle." The man gave a polite half bow. "Monsieur Santandre awaits you downstairs in the car."

Raine swallowed her astonishment, and muttering a quick "Good grief" under her breath, turned to pick up the beaded evening purse she'd bought in a Greenwich Village thrift shop. She folded her soft daytime shawl over her arm, hoping she wouldn't need it, since it would look out of place against the sumptuous gown.

She felt ridiculously like Cinderella dressed for the ball, although Madame T seemed a rather unlikely fairy godmother. Deciding that she had no choice but to put the best face on the whole affair, she forced her lips into a determined smile and followed her new patron's chauffeur down the stairs.

Outside, her eyes widened as they took in the silver Rolls drawn up in quiet splendor before the building. The door was opened for her, and as she slid inside, her host leaned forward to greet her in courtly, old-fashioned French. "Mademoiselle Cameron, will you forgive an old man for not calling in person? I'm afraid these arthritic old legs couldn't take a three-story climb."

Raine was haunted by the odd sensation of something familiar about him, tugging elusively at her mind.

By the time the car had reached its destination, Raine and Pierre Santandre were chatting like old friends. She'd learned that he was a businessman who owned one of the biggest plastics-manufacturing firms in the country, and she was intrigued by the blend of aristocracy and commerce in his background.

"Oui, mademoiselle," the elderly man was saying in response to her question. "The Santandres, for all our distinguished lineage, have been men of business for the past two hundred years. My great-great-great-grandfather escaped the bloody excesses of the French Revolution because he was at sea with his merchant ships. Yes, commerce and business have literally been our lifeblood, passed down from father to son in unbroken tradition."

For all his pride of ancestry, Monsieur Santandre hadn't mentioned his own family at all. "Your son will carry on the business when you retire?" Raine ventured politely.

"I had no son, only a daughter—and both she and her husband are dead." The words were spoken with a bitterness that shocked Raine.

"There is no one else?"

"No." His acerbic tone was overlaid now with a curious stony stubbornness, and Raine sensed some angry emotion festering below the surface.

But there was no time for speculation, because the car had drawn up into the Place de L'Opéra, and the chauffeur was opening the door for her.

Raine stepped out onto the pavement, waiting to take Monsieur Santandre's arm. They mingled with the other theatergoers beneath the elegantly proportioned porticoés of the opera house as Raine glanced around in delight at the other gowns of silk, taffeta and tulle that flashed like jewels in the brilliantly lighted square. All the color, movement and sense of drama that she loved about dance were mirrored spontaneously on the steps outside the opera. Monsieur Santandre nudged her forward, and they were drawn into the stream of people feeding into the opulent foyer.

A deferential usher led them up a magnificent staircase and saw them installed in their box. Raine leaned forward eagerly, her eyes sweeping the palatial red-and-gold auditorium with its massive stage and Chagall mural on the ceiling. The environment stirred a breathless excitement within her as she imagined being on that stage before a crowd of over two thousand. What a tremendous feeling to have that power of enchantment, however brief, over an audience!

"*Sorceress,*" Bran had called her. Is this what he'd

meant? She smiled to herself in quiet pleasure, until a feeling of deep regret washed over her because she wasn't with him. But the watchful Monsieur Santandre had caught her subtle frown and leaned forward attentively to make certain there was no problem.

Raine smiled over at her host and forced herself to return to the optimistic thread of conversation they'd begun in the car before the talk of family had so disturbed him. "It's a lucky thing that generous benefactors like you exist, Monsieur Santandre. Otherwise many of us would be out in the cold."

"I'm glad you think so, *mademoiselle*," he responded with evident satisfaction. "The Santandres have supported the arts for centuries. It's a fine pastime—so long as it doesn't interfere with the real business of living."

"I love my art, *monsieur*," Raine shot back, piqued by his attitude. "And every artist who devotes himself to his craft is the same. His art is his life. If you take that from him, what does he have left? If that isn't the 'real business of living,' then nothing is."

He had the grace to color then, belatedly realizing that his attitude might be offensive. "I wasn't referring to you, child. I was speaking only for myself."

"Yes, of course."

His brows drew together in a slight frown. "You're a headstrong young woman, aren't you?"

She smiled unexpectedly. "I know what I want."

"You come from a family of dancers?"

Raine shook her head. "My mother was a costume designer on Broadway, and my father was an actor."

Santandre beamed. "There, but you see, the theater is in your blood. You are doing only what you must. You are being true to your own family's tradition."

Her eyes danced impishly at this tiresome emphasis on the past dictating the future. "Would I be less true if I decided my talents lay in being a secretary or a business executive?"

He harrumphed at that, his ruddy cheeks flushing an even deeper carmine. His aggravation was apparent; still, he made no answer.

Now Raine leaned forward in anticipation as the curtain finally rose. The Bolshoi dancers, with their incredible acrobatic leaps, did not disappoint. Their colorful showmanship was rather different from the classical aristocratic style and lightness of movement that Madame Tarsamova had brought to the Ballet du Monde as a legacy from the Kirov school. Appreciating the dramatic flair of this evening's show, Raine was reminded of her sister. It was the type of performance she excelled at. In *madame*'s company, Riva was a vivid red bloom in a field of delicate white roses.

Suddenly Raine laughed at herself. She'd been wrong all these years to aspire to Riva's electric bravura; her own particular gift as a dancer lay elsewhere. She now knew it was the Ballet du Monde that would summon it forth, though she was afraid to speculate at what personal cost to herself.

Would she have to choose between her impulses as a woman and a ballerina? She'd told herself proudly that she wanted no schizophrenic existence, torn between work and feeling. Well, she'd taken a step in a definite direction tonight by accepting Mr. Santandre's invitation over Bran's. It was her career she was putting uppermost. "Ruthless," Bran had also once labeled her, only half teasingly. Despite the warmth of the theater, Raine shivered a little.

As the curtain rose for intermission and the theater lights brightened, Pierre Santandre reached out and lightly touched his guest's arm, concern in his expression. "You're enjoying the performance, child?"

Though her eyes were vaguely troubled, Raine's smile was full of warmth. "Very much so."

"Good. Would you like to stretch your legs for a while? We could go take a glass of champagne at the buffet."

Raine smiled to herself as they threaded their way back through the well-dressed crowds milling in the galleries. It was apparent that the long intermission was designed as much for upper-class Parisian society to see and be seen as it was for the performers to catch their breaths between acts.

At the top of the massive white marble staircase, Raine paused to gather up the rustling weight of her skirts before descending. They were just taking the last step down to the grand foyer, when Raine looked up to see her sister's familiar profile not thirty feet away. With that telepathic perception that sometimes exists between twins, Riva turned at the same time to fix Raine with a surprised look, her eyes sliding from the sumptuous silk of Raine's gown to the portly man at her side.

As Riva turned, so did her escort, and Raine recognized Pierre Junot. To her intense surprise, she saw that the artist's attentive if rather abject expression positively darkened when he, too, saw Raine's escort.

Glancing back at her own companion, Raine saw Pierre's look mirrored less openly in Monsieur Santandre's eyes.

The awkward moment was interrupted when Pierre, seeking relief from the old man's cold hard stare, glanced distractedly toward the foyer doors. A moment later his voice boomed out unexpectedly, "Look who else is here! Come join us!"

Raine's relief at this new development was short-lived when she looked around, and came face to face with Bran du Rivage. Completely ignoring his friend's greeting, Bran flicked his gaze between the two women. His penetrating blue stare took in Riva's clingy gold-sequined sheath and the bared shoulders of Raine's elegant gown. It was apparent that he hadn't yet figured out who was who, though his eyes lingered a bit longer on Raine's burning cheeks. Confused and stunned, she couldn't open her mouth to speak. She guessed at once that this must have been the surprise theater date he had intended for her... if she hadn't stood him up.

Riva's tinkling laughter broke into the awkward silence that seemed to have paralyzed everyone else. "Hello, Bran," she teased. "Are you picking up any ideas tonight?"

"A few," he answered curtly, his eyes still flashing narrowly between the twins before coming to rest with a certain cold finality on Raine's face. "Funny no one mentioned today that they were going to the Bolshoi."

"It was a last-minute thing." Two mouths spoke the words at the same time, though Raine's reply was fainter than her sister's.

Bran laughed abruptly, a harsh sound that held no real mirth. "I'll just bet it was."

"What's the matter, Bran?" Riva inquired archly. "Losing your touch where the *femmes* are concerned? Couldn't you get a date?"

Raine drew in her breath sharply, paling at the vicious thrust. Riva couldn't have twisted the knife with more deadly skill if she'd been planning the line for months. With a control born of desperation, Raine turned to Monsieur Santandre before Bran could reply and said brightly, "I don't think you've met Pierre Junot."

The two men glared at each other, radiating hostility. "We're well acquainted," the old man announced in frigid tones. Pierre lifted his head a little higher, a look of pride and pain in his eyes.

Raine bit her lip in dismay. She felt like an unwilling player in a sharp drawingroom comedy, whose darker undercurrents were tugging at them all. When she looked back at Bran, she saw that his harsh mirthless grin hadn't changed. "Now if you will all excuse me, I'll leave you to return to your pleasures."

Raine felt his sarcasm like a slap in the face, yet she couldn't leave it at that. As he turned away, she impulsively followed. "Bran, you got my message?" she whispered up at him.

"Yes, I got it," he snapped. His eyes gleamed like blue vitriol, hot and caustic, as they raked her slowly. Gone was the rough tenderness and growing respect, the shared laughter of that afternoon. She read nothing in his expression but contempt.

"I'm sorry, Bran, believe me!"

"I'll just bet you are," he ground out with extraordinary bitterness. "You're just like all the rest, Raine—you go after what you want no matter who's hurt along the way."

Her eyes flashed angrily at that. "Brandon, for God's sake. Don't I at least get a chance to explain?"

"Don't bother. I've seen it all quite clearly for myself."

But she persisted. "Monsieur Santandre is a friend to me and to the company—nothing more." Raine felt she could say that much without breaking *madame*'s trust.

His breath escaped in a hiss. "How angelic you can look when you practice your little deceptions."

"Bran, don't." She touched his arm, but he shook it off. Helplessly she watched as he strode away, wanting to follow yet feeling Riva's eyes boring into her back. With great reluctance she turned back to join the others.

As soon as she reached Monsieur Santandre, he took her arm, and with a curt nod to Riva, propelled his guest back in the direction of the marble stairway. To Raine, as she sat and watched the dancers on stage, it seemed as if all the joy and excitement had gone out of the evening. Glancing over at her companion, she sensed that he felt the same way.

"Do you mind if we leave now, *monsieur*? I think I've had enough for one evening."

He nodded wearily. "Perhaps the ballet wasn't such a good idea, after all, this evening." His hand was hard and cold on her arm as he led her from the opera house. Nor did she miss the way his eyes hardened as they swept the foyer entrance, where they'd run into Riva and Pierre earlier in the evening. What bound the two men with such animosity?

"What is Pierre Junot to you?" she bravely asked.

"Now? He is nothing to me."

Yet his denial posed more questions than it answered.

MUCH LATER THAT NIGHT, as she lay in bed tossing and turning, Raine mulled over the disastrous course of the evening. Not only had she risked losing Monsieur Santandre's patronage with her forthrightness, but she had hurt Bran—and the latter result disturbed her far more.

She knew now that she'd had no right to accept an invitation when she'd already agreed to spend the evening with Bran. Madame Tarsamova would have been annoyed, but Raine would far rather have faced that than Bran's unforgiving anger. Though she hated to admit it, he was right; she was putting her career above personal feelings.

Come on, she finally upbraided herself. *You made the decision with your eyes wide open. Now you'll just have to live with it.*

But it would be a difficult and painful task.

CHAPTER SEVEN

RAINE WOULD NEVER AGAIN envy a cat its nine lives. She found that living two simultaneously was quite enough. Contrary to what she had feared, in the following weeks Monsieur Santandre had evolved into a most attentive and thoughtful patron. There came a steady trickle of offerings to the Cameron apartment—cuts of filet mignon, tropical fruits and the best of the country's cheeses.

By night, she toured the Parisian haute monde in his company. They dined at Maxim's and La Tour d'Argent and in exclusive, out-of-the-way restaurants known for their *nouvelle cuisine*. Each time they met they picked up the thread of their old argument, begun in his box at the Opéra, until they made a half-bantering pact, agreeing to disagree.

One evening while they were dining at Castel's, her patron declared he was in no hurry to stir from the comfortable red plush booth. The after-dinner entertainment was over, and he was in a strange mood, confiding, almost sentimental. They were the last couple in the restaurant.

"I admire you, child. You have spirit," he told her with a bemused expression. "You remind me of my wife, Sylvie. Since she died I've been rudderless."

"You have no friends?" Raine asked, feeling gen-

uine sympathy for the hard-nosed old business ty-
coon.

"No. A businessman needs allies, not friends," he
rejoined automatically, as if he'd said the same thing
to his vice-presidents at Plastique, S.A., countless
times, until he had come to believe it himself.

"You're wrong, you know," Raine chided. "I
think we've become friends."

His cynical expression softened a little. "You're
not much like that sister of yours, are you?"

Her eyes widened in surprise. "You know Riva?"

"I know that she and Junot were involved at one
time." His chin quivered slightly at some remembered anger.

"What did Pierre do to you?" she demanded impatiently.

Monsieur Santandre's confiding mood vanished at
once. "You are an impertinent young woman. Don't
ask questions that don't concern you."

They stared at each other for a long moment. Then
with a frustrated sigh, Raine stood up from the table.
"Shall we go, *monsieur*? I've had a lovely evening,
but I've got an early class tomorrow."

BY DAY, Raine worked like a demon in the studio.
Her relationship with Bran had disintegrated to one
of cold formality, although simmering beneath it was
a tension that kept Raine constantly on edge. A good
part of it was sexual. For all their coldness toward
one another, the sparks of awareness were more hot
and potent now than they'd ever been. Although he
may have attempted to deny it to himself, Raine felt
the unconscious intensity of desire each time he

needled her in class. Yet there was anger, as well, fed
by the memory of their accidental meeting at the
Opéra.

Today, he was pacing back and forth along the
row of dancers at the barre. Raine followed him in
the far mirror with her eyes—the pantherine strut of
his long legs and the rhythm of his taut haunches as
he moved. When he turned, Raine felt an answering
warm excitement and perturbation whirling inside
her, waiting for the critical comment he might toss at
her this time.

She felt his eyes burning into the nape of her neck
as she began the series of quick *ronds de jambe en
l'air* that ended in an extension of the leg in an almost
vertical position to the side.

"Can't you lift that leg higher, *mademoiselle*?" his
deep voice taunted.

With eyes fixed straight ahead, she complied.

"Higher still," he commanded softly, and she
flinched as if she'd been touched by a burning match
when she felt the cool pressure of his forefinger
against the ridge of her Achilles tendon, gently
pushing and lifting.

Again she complied, though it was much harder this
time. He was pushing her to her limits, and they both
knew it. Slowly she lifted higher, up and away from
the hot brand of his fingertip, gritting her teeth from
the exertion and from the anger his needling invariably aroused. Though her expression was pleasant
and seemingly indifferent to his presence, Raine knew
he was far too practiced a dancer not to read the tension that clamped her neck muscles. She could have
sworn she heard his soft laughter as he moved on.

Bran stopped several times along the line of dancers, counseling and correcting, but never with the sharpness in his tone that seemed reserved for Raine alone. She noticed, too, with growing aggravation that he never corrected Riva, who stood in the last position at the barre. It was as though he was taunting Raine with her sister's technical perfection.

The twins had been working in rehearsals together, like matching bookends enclosing the rest of the troupe, ever since Madame T had announced a revised schedule for the upcoming season: the company would tour for six weeks on the continent, and only the best of her dancers would go. The excitement of the pending announcement and the tension it generated lent a new animation and tempo to each session.

Raine feared being left behind as much as anyone else, so she worked harder than ever, willing herself to ignore Bran's small daily humiliations in class, his prodding.

Suddenly he was beside her again, squatting as he reached out with his thumb and middle finger to trace the long sinewy contour of her thigh muscles. "Never forget, *mademoiselle*, that a ballerina's power comes from her thighs."

His touch at once tingled and stung like a scorpion's bite. Her face flamed, but she forced herself to stare blankly in front of her, ignoring his raking gaze. Raine's only reply was to increase her turn-out even farther, confident now in her body's responsive flexibility, which had returned far more swiftly than her strength.

Damn him, Raine swore inside, aware that he was still subtly taunting her about Santandre. Her personal life was none of his concern anyway.

A FEW DAYS LATER, she and Bran found themselves alone together quite by accident. Though he no longer worked with her at noon, Raine had fallen into the habit of practicing during those hours by herself.

Now she sat on the floor before the deep-silled window, legs extended far to either side. Bending with catlike suppleness from the lower back, Raine touched her forehead to the cool polished grain of the wood and held the stretch for a long moment. The serenity of her pose was disturbed by the faint creaking of the studio door. With slow grace Raine straightened her back and sat up.

They stared at each other in silence, the crackle of tension charging the wide empty space between them. Believing for an instant that he could no more stand the solitude of those once-shared sunlighted hours than she could, Raine felt her heart begin to beat a little faster. "You wanted something?" she demanded softly.

Raine saw as he approached that his eyes were cold. "Yes. The studio."

"Ah, yes. Of course," she replied, her tone tinged with sarcasm. Walking over to the upright piano, she retrieved the skirt she'd flung over it. Bran ignored her as he arranged the pages of a musical score, and somehow that angered her far more than the barbed remarks he flung at her in rehearsals. Her golden eyes glinted up at him, and then she spoke. "You told me once that we all make our choices in life, remember?''

He lifted his gaze slowly to meet hers, the dark blue velour depths curiously veiled. His voice was subdued, faintly questioning. "I remember."

Raine lifted her chin. "Well, I made mine, too. The only one I could make."

"So you're taking the easy way out, after all," he accused her, his expression stony.

"No, I'm not!" Her reply was fierce, quick. "What you don't realize is that I don't have enough strength yet to channel in more than one direction. I can't work part-time like the others do and still have energy for class. The decision I made has freed me to think of nothing but dance."

Raine's eyes begged that he try to understand, but his gaze had already swept away down her graceful form, touching like a pulse point of fire where it lingered. "Well, it's a mistake. You're a woman first," he murmured, "and a dancer second."

His eyes swooped up again to meet hers. Though his tone was light, the words branded themselves in her mind, their truth reinforced by the rush of warmth through her belly and the hot pulsing throb in her neck.

Feeling naked beneath his unrelenting appraisal, Raine turned away and flung herself down onto the windowsill, where the sunlight collected like warm water in a shallow pool. She drew her knees up in a childlike gesture of self-protection, though there was nothing of the child in the bold womanly look she threw at him. "Life would have been much simpler, Bran," she slowly whispered, "if you hadn't reminded me of that fact."

"So what do you want?"

"You can stop judging me."

Bran sat down beside her and leaned forward, arms resting on his thighs until his face was inches from her own. "That's my job," he replied. "Judging all my dancers honestly so that I'll know which ones are weak and which are strong."

"But you've no right to judge my life outside of dance!" Her warm voice seemed to ripple with vehemence.

"Who said I was?"

Raine sighed in frustration. "You've been furious with me ever since you saw me with Pierre Santandre."

"I think I had a right to be angry," he countered harshly. "Did you play on his sympathy the way you played on mine? I don't trust women who use men."

"Now who's listening to cheap backstage gossip?" she bit out, so intensely aware of his closeness that the rest of the world might have vanished in that instant. "You're so wrong about me, Bran. I never used you; I never asked for anything."

"You don't have to ask in words." A dark fire glimmered in his eyes. "You can be far more subtle than Riva...and far more dangerous."

"Dangerous how?" she retorted softly. "Because I somehow got you to feel, too, when we danced together?" In her intensity Raine leaned forward, aware of the way her breasts nearly grazed his taut biceps.

"So you did!" he shot back with a bitter little laugh, his head cocked slightly so that his caressing eyes could play over the high enticing curve of her breasts and the rose-clad contours of her hip.

Raine's intensity didn't waver. "Don't make fun of me, Bran."

Though his expression was angry and hard, the forefinger he lifted to trace the line of her cheekbone and the sensitive edge of her lower lip was oddly gentle. "You're full of demands, aren't you?"

She nodded, savoring the touch of his fingernail where it rasped teasingly along the indentation of skin. "I suppose so," she murmured, the words like a kiss against his upraised finger.

As if that were a spoken invitation, Bran leaned forward until his chiseled lips hovered above the silken moistness of her mouth. Then the studio door creaked warningly, and they drew back so swiftly that the sensuous web entangling them dissolved as if it had never been.

Standing up, Bran turned back to the piano. Raine slid off the window seat and ran out of the studio, brushing past the three dancers who were just coming in without even seeing them.

WHEN THE DOOR BELL RANG at the apartment that afternoon, Raine swiftly folded the newspaper she'd been reading and got up to answer it. The friendly eyes of a delivery boy peeped over the edge of a box marked with the distinctive lettering of one of the city's most famous couturiers.

After tipping the boy, Raine brought the package inside and propped it against the door while she opened the attached envelope. She'd known at once whom it was from, and the embossed note signed,

"With affection and deep respect. P.S." confirmed it. Pierre Santandre.

Raine shook her head as she eyed the elegant box dubiously. From the very beginning of her friendship with the charming old man, she'd got the impression that Monsieur Santandre was so eager to give her things because he had no one else on whom to shower his gifts. Often enough she had sensed his loneliness, so that his continued generosity saddened her in a way.

Her musings were interrupted when Riva came out of her bedroom, wrapped in Raine's fleecy white robe as she toweled her hair dry. "Who was that?" Riva demanded as she flung back her head and glanced toward the front door, not missing the elegantly wrapped package propped next to it. Her eyes narrowed as they moved from the box to her sister. "Now what's this?"

"I don't know," Raine replied, settling back down into the sofa. "Steaks and Persian melon were one thing, but this looks like a whole different ball game."

Riva crossed over to the door with long impatient strides. "Aren't you going to open it?"

Raine watched her as she stared down at the package, could almost see her mind whirring. From the start Riva had assumed the worst about her sister's friendship with Monsieur Santandre, especially when Raine had begun to appear every night in a different evening gown. Raine's patient explanations that the dresses were on loan from Madame Tarsamova didn't diffuse her twin's jealous anger. In Riva's eyes, she alone was the one who deserved the fine clothes and the wealthy benefactor. After all, she was the company ballerina, while Raine was little more than an upstart.

Raine looked at her sister's tense back, finally answering her in a firm voice, "I don't think I should."

Riva whipped her head around. "Don't be ridiculous!" she cried impatiently. "You have to at least see what it is." Before Raine could object, Riva tore the ribbon off the package, and with reverent fingers lifted a short ermine jacket from its tissued nest. Again without a by-your-leave, Riva slipped her arms inside the wrap and lifted the white fur collar up against her cheeks as she preened before the hall mirror. "This is appalling," Riva murmured at last, even as her fingertips continued to stroke the lustrous fur.

Raine's answering laughter was wry. "You look anything but appalled, Riva!" And she had to admit that Riva looked quite lovely, a woman born for luxury.

Riva's gold eyes swooped angrily back in her direction. "No, that's not what I meant. I mean it was wrong to buy this for you when Pierre is practically starving."

Raine let out her breath in an impatient sigh. "What are you talking about? Pierre Santandre is a rich man."

"I'm not talking about the old man." Riva came around to perch on the arm of the velvet easy chair, still swathed in the priceless wrap. "I'm talking about his grandson—Pierre Junot."

"His grandson?" Raine repeated in disbelief.

"Oh, don't act as though you didn't know."

"I didn't," Raine insisted. But even as she denied it, all the little clues fell neatly into place. Pierre Santandre had made far too many bitter references to family betrayal and destroyed traditions. "Are they really estranged?"

"The old man has disowned him!"

"Because Pierre is frittering his life away as an artist, no doubt," Raine observed ironically.

"The old coot is a jumble of inconsistencies," Riva observed disrespectfully.

"Aren't we all?" Raine shot back. "Santandre may love the arts, but he wants his grandson to follow in his footsteps."

"Pierre's a naive idealist."

"Because he gave up wealth and power to do what he really loves?"

Riva frowned. "Whose side are you on, anyway?"

"Neither. I sympathize with them both."

"Well, I don't," Riva replied impatiently. "Pierre was a fool. If he'd listened to me, he could have had it both ways."

Raine's smile was cool, shrewd. "You little hellion. Pierre's grandfather resents you. How on earth did you get involved?"

Riva shrugged as if she'd grown bored with the discussion. "Oh, I simply encouraged Pierre to sue Santandre, so that granddad would be forced to release the trust money he's holding for his grandson."

"What!" Raine cried, aghast. "That would have made them enemies for life. At least now there's hope for a reconciliation."

"I doubt it."

"Yes. I'm sure if you thought there was still a chance you wouldn't have given up the Santandre fortune so easily."

"I don't intend to be a struggling ballerina my whole life," Riva snapped.

"Always the realist, aren't you?"

"Look who's talking. You're getting exactly what you want." There was a drop of venom in the words.

Raine's eyes flashed. "I'm getting just one thing— the chance to devote myself to my career."

"Oh, God, how well I know that!" Riva retorted in an impassioned voice. "I've seen you in class—and I know why you've suddenly acquired this rich friend, too. You've found out that the quickest way to Madame T's heart is through the company bank account. If *monsieur* will contribute so many thousands of francs, you're hoping to get all my plum roles!"

"I'm not a fool, Riva. I don't want your roles, damn it, because I know I can't match that kind of technical perfection." She waited a second for that to sink in. "But I *do* want my own role," she added, the conviction in her tone no less for all its lilting softness.

"A dance choreographed especially for you?" Riva asked with equally deceptive softness, somewhat mollified by her sister's admission, though her suspicions still lurked beneath the surface.

"Why not?" Raine shrugged with a pretense of offhandedness.

To her surprise, she saw Riva throw back her head

and laugh in rich amusement. "You're far more ambitious than I ever dreamed, sister, dear!"

Annoyed at the way Riva had seen through her facade to the competitive ballerina poised in the wings, Raine responded with a subtle accusation of her own. "I've had a good teacher all these years," she noted, her eyes boring sharply into her sister's.

Riva's amusement had fled. "You know that two can play at this game—"

The rest of the sentence, with its hint of bravado and an implied threat, was swallowed up in the loud quick rap of knuckles on the front door. Their argument was left to simmer on a back burner as they both chorused, "Come in!"

Mari, one of the other company dancers, stood in the doorway. *"Ciao, amies,"* she greeted them in a breezy voice. "I've come to borrow back the costume pattern Madame T said you had," the visitor went on, her gaze sliding between the sisters before coming to rest in wide-eyed wonder on the fur jacket. "Whose new bauble?" she demanded eagerly.

Riva's eyes glinted with sly mischief as she switched to elegant French. "It's Raine's. She's got what we all dream of having, Mari—a rich and doting patron."

Mari's eyes shone with new respect and not a little envy. Then unexpectedly she giggled. "Riva, you're slipping," she teased. "Somehow we always supposed that you'd be the one to pull off a coup like that."

Riva's smile was confident, serene. "It's never too late, is it?"

Abruptly Raine stood up. She knew now that she'd

been inexcusably naive to think her friendship with Monsieur Santandre would go unnoticed. Without a word, she went over to her sister and pulled the expensive fur from her shoulders.

"Ooh, possessive, too." Mari giggled again.

"It's not that, Mari," Raine said at once. "I just don't want it to get dirty, because it's going back to Dior's right now. And you shouldn't take everything Riva says seriously. She has a real gift for colorful exaggeration." Her light words were belied by the sharp look she gave Riva.

But despite her attempt to play down the gift, Raine saw that the damage already had been done. She knew from personal experience the power of Mari's wagging tongue.

HEATED WHISPERS and speculative glances followed Raine around the studio wherever she went. She hadn't underestimated Mari's talent and capacity for gossip; the dancer had done a thorough job.

"But I can't stand it!" Raine exploded behind the closed doors of Madame Tarsamova's office.

The old woman looked up in surprise from the carnations she was tending. "And what do you care?" she retorted with scarcely veiled exasperation. "You look healthy. Our *monsieur* has been seeing to it that you get lovely meals and that you go out and relax in the evening rather than brood. Your dancing has improved. There's a new edge to it."

Raine smiled ruefully to herself, knowing that the edge to her dancing was a reflection of the growing tension between her and Bran. Invariably he was the spark, the catalyst.... She returned to her list of grievances. "*Madame*, you never told me that Monsieur Santandre and Pierre Junot were related and involved in some sort of awful feud. Now everyone is spreading ridiculous rumors, suggesting I've somehow come between them."

"Gossip is an inescapable part of this kind of life," *madame* replied serenely. "Why let it disturb you?"

"I'm disturbed because two people are very unhappy," the dancer came back with unwonted sharpness. Sometimes *madame*'s coldness where anything other than her company was concerned infuriated Raine. "I've come to regard the two of them as my friends. And I know they're both lonely."

The elderly Russian woman crossed her arms and came around the desk to squarely confront her stubborn young dancer. "That is no business of yours; nor is it any of mine. They have to resolve their own quarrels."

"Do they hate each other?" Raine persisted. "If they both love ballet, can't they have other things in their lives to share?"

Madame's lips curved wryly. "They share a love of art, but from irreconcilable perspectives." She shook her regal head impatiently as she sensed another question forming on Raine's lips. "So soon again I must remind you? It's none of your concern. Your only business is to dance and to dance well."

Although she nodded in reluctant agreement, Raine wasn't so certain she shared Madame T's singleminded vision. For seventy-five years the ballet had been Nina's life, lover, husband, child. She had sublimated everything to that. Raine didn't know if she wished to make the same sacrifices in her life, especially not after having known a man like Bran, who could remind her so potently that passion wasn't limited to an artificial world on stage.

All personal discussions shelved for the moment, Nina and her dancer moved side by side down the long hall toward the studio. Raine glanced over at the clipboard the ballet mistress held in front of her. She knew Nina and Bran were in the process of deciding which dancers would tour. "How many will go?" Raine suddenly asked her.

"Just twelve," Nina answered calmly. "Five will be left behind."

"The ultimate decision will be yours...or Brandon's?"

"His, of course. I trust him implicitly."

"And the feeling's reciprocated?" Raine couldn't help needling just a little.

Madame's black-currant eyes sparkled. "Of course not! He realizes I'm much too devious. But that doesn't matter, child. What matters is that we both know we're working toward a common goal."

Their conversation broke off as they entered the studio and Raine went to take her customary position at the barre. She noticed at once that Riva wasn't in attendance. Had she been detained somewhere? Raine released a muffled sigh of aggravation. More likely Riva was simply displaying her particular brand of arrogance. Of all the corps, she was probably the only one who didn't fear being left behind in Paris. And what aggravated Raine most was that her sister's confidence was justified.

Her quick warm-ups were interrupted time and

again as the rest of the dancers trooped in and made a point of greeting Raine by name. The women's smiles were feline, sometimes sharp with envy, while the danseurs treated her with new deference. *All of a sudden I'm a rising star,* Raine reflected ironically, knowing this new treatment had far more to do with her supposed "connections" than with all the work she'd put in these past weeks.

Tracey Markham dashed breathlessly into the studio just then, one step ahead of Bran, and squeezed into position ahead of Raine. "I hear you're a real femme fatale," Tracey whispered teasingly. "The latest rubbish circulating is that you're going to marry Pierre's grandfather and cut the poor boy out of his inheritance."

"Guess I'll just have to weather the gossip storm," Raine replied with a frustrated sigh. "It's bound to blow over eventually, and I can go back to being just another member of the corps."

"Never that, love," Tracey shot back as she gave her friend's arm a reassuring squeeze. "You're far too good."

A Russian folk melody rippled from the piano keys, and the dancers warmed up to the lively strains of Stravinsky. They were rehearsing *Petroushka*, a funny-sad ballet revolving around the antics of a group of puppets at a winter fair.

The rehearsal was going quickly and surprisingly smoothly, perhaps because everyone was making his or her utmost effort before Madame T's sharp eyes. Bran was aware of it, too, and kept his critical remarks to a minimum, not looking in Raine's direction at all. Instead his gaze returned again and again to the studio door as if he were expecting someone. Raine, watching him, felt a little stab of jealousy.

Halfway through rehearsal, Bran lifted an arm and signaled for the pianist to break off for a moment. "Okay, group, things are going well," he told them all. "I want to work this thing through as if it were a full stage rehearsal. The only problem is," he went on, his gaze at once sardonic and angry as it flickered over them, "the Ballerina appears to be missing. So I'll need one of you to fill in."

The Ballerina was the principal female character in *Petroushka*. But everyone knew he was making an oblique reference to the company's own errant ballerina, Riva, who hadn't bothered to show up on time for rehearsal.

So wrapped up was she in her own thoughts that Raine didn't notice the dancers around her drawing back; she suddenly found herself all alone, facing Bran. His expression was teasing as he held out his hand to her. "I guess you win the part by default, Raine."

Her eyes swooped up angrily to meet his, and she took the hand he offered without hesitation. The music resumed in a clash of chords, and Raine leaped into the role of Ballerina to Bran's comically portrayed Moor, as he demonstrated to Paul and the other danseurs just the sense of movement and expression he wanted from them.

Raine found herself laughing inside at his hilarious interpretation of the hedonistic male puppet, and her soaring spirits gave a buoyancy to her own dancing. She was so enjoying the amusing pas de deux that she didn't hear the studio door open.

Seconds later as she stepped out of a cool pirouette, Raine looked over, startled, to see Riva dancing the same steps on Bran's right side. The ballerina gave them an attack and brilliance that were obviously meant to overpower Raine's captivating and far more subtle interpretation.

Raine might have slipped back quietly into the corps if it hadn't been for the cunning look of triumph Riva shot her. An imp of perversity seemed to take control of Raine's limbs then, and she continued dancing, much to the amazement of everyone else in the studio. The rivalry lasted less than a minute as the twins whirled past each other, mirror images in everything but style.

Bran's head whipped around as he turned, revealing a comic confusion that wasn't entirely feigned. Laughter and teasing shouts of "Bravo!" filled the studio as the music trailed off, but neither Raine nor Riva noticed. They were too busy glaring at each other.

As Raine hurried over to the barre to pick up her towel and mop her face, Riva was right beside her. "You little bitch," Riva began threateningly, though anything else she might have added was overridden by Bran's angry voice.

He'd dismissed the other dancers and stood facing the two of them, his eyes playing over Riva's stubbornly set features. "I warned you about playing the prima donna on me. Come in late like that again and you're out."

In a twinkling her expression was contrite. "I'm sorry, Bran," she whispered in a dulcet voice that grated on Raine's nerves. "You've every right to be furious with me."

Raine was about to turn away in aggravation, when Bran's low tones pinned her with scathing sarcasm. "And what about you, Raine?" he demanded. "If Fokine had wanted a pas de trois in that scene, he'd have written it."

Her chin lifted at a pugnacious tilt, and there was no mistaking the angry gold sparks in her eyes. She wasn't about to fawn or apologize to him. "You chose me," she countered proudly. "So I decided you should finish the dance—with me."

Before he could say anything in reply, Raine turned her back on both of them and walked out of the studio with a controlled grace. *Damn them both,* she swore to herself as she made her way through the dancers milling in the hall. Raine did her best to ignore the amused questioning looks that trailed after her, but suddenly she'd had enough. She had to escape, to have a few minutes alone.

Raine found the back stairs that led to the theater and slipped down them. A few stage lights had been left to burn, though they were quickly lost in the murky half light. Down in these shadowy caverns of the ballet company was a make-believe world held together by canvas and ropes, painted backdrops and cardboard props. It had an air of mysterious abandonment that had soothed Raine's jangled nerves on several other occasions.

She wandered past the false-front balconies and illusionary forests that now leaned almost drunkenly after a year's idleness. Even though they were half-hidden by scaffolding and carelessly flung tarpaulins,

Pierre's vibrantly designed sets still beckoned. Raine became so engrossed in looking around that she lost track of where she was going and tripped on a tapestry-covered stage bed left over from an old production of *Romeo and Juliet*.

Sitting down, she swiftly untied her shoe ribbons. Luckily the wooden pointe of her slipper had absorbed most of the shock, but her toe still throbbed. Raine pulled off the shoe and threw it behind her on the bed before reaching down again to gingerly examine her foot for any injury.

A sound from the opposite corner of the stage caused her to look up quickly from her task, but she couldn't see much in the gloom. "Who's there?" she demanded. Her own voice, high and nervous, echoed back to her from the catwalks and ropes that reached toward the blackness arching high above.

Then a familiar voice, seemingly out of nowhere, replied, "Imagining the limelight already?" A moment later Bran stepped out of the shadows and grinned at her.

For all the casual teasing in his question, she felt the sting behind it and looked away, her glance drawn to the slumbering black cavern of the auditorium. "I like the feel of a real theater," she told him coolly. "It's a solace to remember there's a reason behind the daily torture you put me through in rehearsals."

"So you can't wait for the applause?" He stood before her now, looking vital and sleek-muscled as a cat in the dark unitard that molded to him like a second skin. There was a devilish aura about him, as if he were still the Moor he'd danced in rehearsal.

"No, I don't care about that," she retorted. "I dance for myself."

"And for me," he reminded her.

Remembering Riva's honeyed apology after class, Raine shifted her eyes to clash boldly with his. "If you expect me to simper and fawn in order to get what I want, then you'll be disappointed, Bran."

He laughed softly between his teeth as he strolled behind the bed, idly examining the bits of scenery and carpenters' tools ranged around it. "You think a rich lover's going to smooth the way."

"No!" Her head whipped around. "I don't want anything handed to me."

"Not even expensive furs and fine foods? 'Nothing but friends!'" He ridiculed the lame excuse she'd given him about her relationship with Pierre Santandre. "Damn it, I thought you were different, Raine."

She swiveled around farther on the bed, leaning forward on her palm. "You're not listening to me, Bran. I *am* different, damn it. I don't want furs or applause. Besides, you've got your bloody nerve," she exclaimed, her eyes shooting golden flames. "You with your lovely apartment and fine wines, that fast little car. You earned your money kicking a ball around on a field of glory and came home the conquering sports hero. Only then did you give yourself the luxury of choosing whether or not you'd go back to dance. What do you know about struggling for what you want, the pain and fear? How much do you know about giving everything and then being told that it's not quite enough—and having to give more until you don't have an ounce of strength left?"

His eyes glimmered impatiently out of the shadows. "The sermon through?" he demanded roughly. She nodded, spent. "Good," he went on, "because I don't like being preached to."

Her head came up again, but now her eyes held a faintly mischievous gleam. "You can dish it out, but you can't take it, is that it, Bran? You followed me down here just to chastise me. But I'll be damned if I'll listen to your sermon, either!"

"Fair enough." He shrugged with a pretense of indifference, even as he bent down across the bed. Only too late did she realize what he was up to. Before Raine could stop him, Bran had snatched up her toe shoe by its trailing ribbons. Grinning, he tied the ends and hung it over the tall wooden screen beside the bed.

Despite her anger, Raine wanted to laugh then. His unexpected gesture had changed the mood of the moment. The fragile pink shoe lent an unsettling air of intimacy to the deserted cavernous theater. They were no longer professionals battling it out on an empty stage. Suddenly they were alone within the confines of a boudoir, a man and a woman engaged in a very personal battle.

Raine grew acutely aware of him, his eyes teasing her and the dark-veined hand idly caressing the shoe he'd stolen. "Why *did* you follow me down here?" she asked softly, her pulse quickening as she became even more conscious of her womanliness in exquisite opposition to his virility.

"This was my refuge before it was yours, Raine," he retorted in a wistful tone that matched her own. "This is where I come to get away."

"To get away from what?" she demanded curiously.

"You have to ask, after that last little scene in class?" Unable to see the expression on his shadowed features, Raine saw only the glint of his eyes as he went on. "You and Riva are driving me crazy with your competitiveness. The two of you are going to tear this company apart if I don't stop you."

"Why don't you fire one of us, then?" she flung back, jealous that he'd dragged Riva into the conversation.

"Any suggestions as to which of you should go?" he countered dryly, still withdrawn from her, standing in the gloom cast by the wooden screen.

Raine flushed, knowing that if it were to come to that, she'd be the first one out. She had a long way to go yet to prove herself. Though she might almost despise her twin sometimes, in a way the two women needed each other: their warring ambitions spurred them both on.

Bran sensed her inner turmoil. "Are you afraid the company will lose Riva, or is that what you're hoping for?"

Raine stared down at the imprint of her hand on the dusty coverlet. "A little of both, I suppose," she confessed, her vulnerability achingly exposed by his probing. She looked up as a new thought struck her. "Aren't you worried about losing Riva to a bigger company?"

Bran grinned. "No. She won't leave the Ballet du Monde, because she hasn't gotten what she wants yet."

Raine needed only an instant to figure that one out. "You." She breathed the word softly.

His rippling baritone laugh washed between them. "You're very quick, Raine—but then maybe that's because you want the same thing."

The words, for all their teasing, infuriated her. "I've had it with your arrogance," she grated. Light and agile as a kitten, Raine climbed onto the bed to reach for the shoe he'd draped over the tall screen, but his own response was lightning quick. One hand shot out to grip her wrist while his other arm came down to imprison her waist, so that suddenly Raine found herself lifted, her hips and thighs crushed against his torso. His laughing eyes, shot through with midnight, raked upward between the soft valley of her breasts. "Put me down, Bran."

He grinned at the implied threat in her voice. "Or what?" As he spoke, he relaxed his firm grip to let his hands snake around to either side of her waist, his thumbs just grazing the gentle undercurve of her breasts. He lifted her higher, and Raine's hands automatically gripped his wide shoulders for support. For an instant Bran held her poised above the stage floor, until in an exquisitely slow sensuous movement he began to let her slip through his hands. . . inch by inch.

Raine let her head fall back, closing her eyes as she savored the hot enravishing opposition of their bodies sliding past each other. As she slithered through his hands, she felt the pressure of his chest against the soft globes of her breasts. Then his jaw rasped the silken column of her throat, and his mouth caressed it fleetingly in a brushstroke kiss that inflamed and tantalized.

The floor rose to meet the ball of her foot, but that contact with reality dissolved again in a void as Bran's hand swooped downward past the swell of her hips to capture her legs and set her down gently across the tapestried bed. He sank beside her, his knees bending to imprison her thigh as his fingertips made delicious traceries down her side.

He kissed her closed eyelids, the fevered warmth of her cheeks, teasing and tantalizing again as he hovered above the moist beckoning embrasure of her mouth. Sweet expectation and their mutual need escaped in a mutual explosion of sensation as his lips closed over hers, warm and caressing against the gossamer trembling of her own. Raine lifted her arms to encircle his neck and draw him closer.

No longer shy, she hungrily explored his mouth, and as the kiss deepened, it was as if they'd never left the rain-washed intimacy of that afternoon in his apartment. She let her hands slip down to his shoulders, marveling at the sinew and muscle beneath her fingers. She traced the hard ridge of his biceps, his dark forearm that rested across her torso, the sensitive strength of his hand, down to his gently undulating hips.... The tender hungering inquisitiveness of her touch must have ignited his own desire to fever pitch, because he released a muffled groan and reached up with urgent fingers to pull her sleeveless leotard down over her shoulders.

Though the thin nylon she wore outlined her female contours in naked detail, the neck-to-toe cover-up was as confining and chaste as any garb a jealous medieval husband might have invented. When Bran's groan became a sigh of impatience as he struggled with her clothing, Raine couldn't suppress the low delicious giggle that welled up inside her.

He lifted his head, resting his chin lightly on the creamy swell of her breast. "What's so funny?" he growled, although Raine saw that his eyes were dancing, too.

"Nothing. Everything," she chuckled softly in reply. "You."

He lowered his head again, murmuring against her breast, "I like your laughter, Raine. It's like a summer wind."

"Good," she whispered, still laughing. "Then maybe you'll be more interested in making me laugh than suffer."

"Yes, I do know how to make a woman suffer." He laughed softly in return, even as his hand came up to teasingly draw away the edge of her bodice and his tongue dipped inside. With exquisite slowness it circled her breast, until the aureole gleamed moist and dark as sweet wine. Then he caught the engorged peak between his teeth and nibbled it lightly until her laughter trailed off in a low purring moan.

Through the haze of her exploding desire, Raine heard the faint sound of footsteps in the distance. Tangling her fingers in his black hair, she'd meant to gently push him away, but instead found herself holding him to her with fiercely passionate abandonment. Raine felt as though she'd tumbled into a deep well, its cool dark walls imbued with a musky male essence that was Bran himself. She no longer felt the perspiration that slicked their overheated bodies, no longer smelled the dust that rose in lazy whorls from the long-abandoned bed each time they moved.

But the footsteps, less distant now, were accompanied by voices, and Raine tugged at Bran's hair with playfully urgent fingers. "Someone's coming," she whispered.

He drew himself up beside her, trailing kisses across her shoulders and up her throat. "Damn it," he muttered irritably. "I'll throw them out."

Raine pushed him away and sat up, readjusting her leotard. "You always have to be in control, don't you, Bran?" she observed with a half-humorous, frustrated sigh.

He laughed shortly. "That's because I learned the hard way—you can't depend on anyone but yourself. Anything else weakens a man—or a woman." Standing up, he swiftly raked his fingers through his hair, then reached out to grab her shoe and toss it down on the bed beside her.

"That's a lonely way to live," Raine argued, not looking at him as she undid the knot in the satin ribbons and slipped the shoe back on her foot. She stood up, too, wanting to confront him face to face. "Listen, Bran, I want to set the record straight. Pierre Santandre is not what you may think he is to me."

He shrugged. "Lover or patron. What's the difference?"

"There's a big difference—and I had no choice in the matter."

"Like hell you didn't. Nina doesn't rule your life."

Raine's eyes flew up in surprise to meet his. "You knew all along that she had her hand in the business?"

"No, but it wasn't too hard to figure out. From what she's told me about her past, I gather that's the way Nina lived as a young dancer." Bran's eyes hardened. "But that doesn't mean you have to live the same way."

"The man's patronage is important to the Ballet du Monde," Raine answered smartly. "That's really what Nina's angling for, you know."

"So you have to compromise your own self-respect."

Raine flushed. "What are you saying?"

"I'm saying stand on your own two feet," he replied in a rough unequivocal tone. "This isn't 1910, Raine. You're no vaporous Edwardian lady. Be tough."

"Like Riva?" she snapped.

"Yes, now that you mention it."

A new thought crossed her mind. "You want us both, don't you? Riva on your stage and me...in your bed."

He laughed at her, and Raine recognized the familiar teasing. "Maybe it's the other way around."

"You're insufferable," she flung back heatedly, hoping to hide her jealousy, even though she knew he was just needling her—or was he? She busied herself dusting off the back of her tights, just as a burst of hearty laughter reached them across a thin canvas panel.

Margrit Blake stepped into sight, looking far more professional in a sober gray tailored suit than she had when Bran and Raine had encountered her at the flea market. But the dancing hazel eyes were the same. "Hello! So nice to see you both again," she called

out in delight. "I just had an interview with your for-
midable ballet mistress upstairs, and she corralled
Pierre into giving me the grand tour." As before, her
jaunty laughter was contagious.

Bran smiled. "Do you have second thoughts about
working for us after meeting Nina?"

"Not at all. I love a challenge!" She glanced back
briefly at Pierre, who had joined them, before resum-
ing her conversation with Bran. "I just have to get
used to the proportions of the theater. What are the
dimensions of this stage, anyway?"

As she and Bran paced off the area, Pierre's dark
eyes flickered in Raine's direction. "Sorry to inter-
rupt, Riva," he said coldly.

She shot him a wry smile. "Riva's upstairs rehearsing, Pierre."

He flushed. "You two are more alike than I
thought."

"What gives you that impression?" she rejoined,
her smile fading a little.

"Aren't you cozying up to all the right people?
Brandon—" he paused "—and my grandfather."

"I've been a friend to your grandfather, and in
turn Madame T hopes he'll be a friend to the Ballet
du Monde." Raine's self-defense was quick and
spirited, but Pierre seemed reluctant to believe her.

"Just don't cross him, and he'll come through,"
Pierre went on in the same harsh tone. "He reveres
loyalty."

"And you've been the disloyal grandson?" Raine
said more gently.

"I can be true to myself, or I can be true to him. I
can't be true to both."

"Why must it be one or the other?"

Pierre sighed in frustration. "Because he set the rules."

"Rules are meant to be broken," she persisted stubbornly.

"Now you sound like Bran."

Raine smiled impishly. "I don't know if that was meant as a compliment or an insult. Is there anything I can do to help heal the rift between you and your grandfather?"

Pierre's jaw set stubbornly. "He's made his decision."

"He's a lonely man," Raine countered in a persuasive voice, remembering Monsieur Santandre's bereft expression as he reminisced about his wife.

"So am I." His words revealed surprising conviction—and bitterness. "Riva encouraged me to break with him once and for all, but I couldn't do it. I could have had her, at least. Now I have nothing."

Raine was searching for something to say to ease his anguish, but their private conversation ended as Margrit broke in. "Say, Pierre, your work is marvelous," she commented cheerfully.

His eyes lighted up, his apple cheeks flushing with pleasure. "Nice words from a fellow artist."

Raine's gaze followed them as they strolled away before she turned back to Bran. "He's as bitter as his grandfather."

"That's what families are for—to wound one another," he replied broodingly.

"You don't really believe that," she insisted, troubled.

"I know it, Raine. Look at Pierre and Santandre. You and Riva—"

"You and your mother," she put in.

"That's long buried in the past," Bran informed her curtly.

Not for an instant did she believe that, but she wouldn't argue with him. "At least we can try to get Pierre and his grandfather together; it can't be too late for that." Her expression grew teasing. "You accused me once of using Santandre. Perhaps I can use our friendship to see him reconciled with his grandson."

"Forget it, Raine. It's not that simple. They're both driven stubborn men, and this thing's been simmering between them for ages—long before you came along." He spoke with the impartiality of a critic judging a performance.

"But don't you care?" she demanded.

"I care, but there's not a damn thing I can do."

"They have to come to terms with their differences eventually."

"Yes—in court," was his ironic reply.

"Now you sound like Riva."

"Maybe she was right," he conceded with a shrug. "Sentiment shouldn't cloud the issue."

"You frighten me sometimes, Bran," she whispered, her golden gaze washing over him, warm yet assessing. "You can be so cold."

He met her look, his own eyes hard. "I can't be any other way."

"No, you're wrong, Bran. I've known. . . I've felt the other you."

"A stage illusion."

Just then Margrit's laughter, abrim with life and enthusiasm, pierced the tension. Raine turned to follow the sound. "She's perfect for him," she observed with the decisiveness of a woman intent on playing matchmaker. "God only knows why he has to be so hung up on Riva. If anyone's destroyed his self-respect, she has."

Bran's laugh was almost a bark. " 'Love's a battle. . . .' " His brow lifted at a sardonic angle as he let the quotation trail off.

"What do you know about the subject, anyway?" Raine shot back tartly.

"Not much, thank God."

Leaving him where he stood, Raine turned abruptly and ran toward the stairs that led up to the workaday world of the studio. There, life was far safer and far more rational, she decided, than what she'd encountered here in the shadowed depths.

CHAPTER EIGHT

ALL THE GOSSIP and petty bickering, the Peyton Place intrigues that simmered beneath the ballet company's professional facade were momentarily forgotten in the days that followed. Auditioning for the tour was all that mattered now, and each dancer was concentrating on giving his or her best.

Raine had covertly begun to compare herself to the others, hating herself for doing it, yet unable to stop. Watching Riva especially, so serene and sure, drove her crazy. A belated attack of nerves had hit, because she knew now how badly she wanted to tour with the company. But she disciplined herself to drown the nervousness in fierce concentration. She wanted to prove to herself that she was capable. Even more than that, she wanted to prove it to Bran, to have his professional respect.

Bran and Nina had decided on a lively classic holiday repertoire that would guarantee the little company a packed house in each of the cities where it was to perform. Raine was especially excited about the Christmas Eve ballet, *Les Patineurs*, the ice skaters. There was, in fact, a small solo role in the dance that she felt would suit her perfectly. Confident that she could handle the light and graceful sequence, a young girl skating lovely patterns across a pond with her sweetheart, Raine was determined to have it for herself.

Later in the day, hugging that confidence to her like a security blanket, Raine found herself knocking softly on Bran's office door. Her calmness fled as she heard his low lazy baritone calling out, *"Entrez."*

His feet were propped up on the desk, his head bent over the papers in his lap. Raine saw that he'd already changed to casually tailored street clothes, the sleeves of his dark plaid wool shirt rolled up over his forearms. It had been quite a while since she'd seen him in something other than unitard and sweatpants, and unexpectedly reminded of the moments they'd shared together outside the company, Raine became a little unnerved.

Quelling the urge to flee before he looked up, Raine cleared her throat and spoke. "May I have a word with you?"

His blue eyes lifted slowly, narrowing just a bit when he saw who it was that had come to call. "Have a seat," he invited, those eyes flickering over her with a questioning look.

"No, thanks," Raine replied as she clasped her hands behind her back, suddenly aware of the less-than-professional image she presented with her stretched-out leg warmers straggling down her calves to the tops of her scruffy toe shoes. "I'm going up to work some more."

"What?" he came back softly. "No date with Pierre Santandre?"

Raine ignored that as she went to stand in front of the window, automatically drawn to the square of sunlight and warmth. She reached out to touch the spiky edge of a cactus flourishing on the sill. Still not looking at Bran, Raine took a deep breath and blurted out what she'd come to say. "I want to dance the sweethearts' sequence in *Les Patineurs*."

His chair swiveled around with a quick protesting squeal, and he brought his feet down at the same instant. "Don't you think that's a hell of a presumption on your part?"

Piqued by his tone, Raine shot him a defiant look. "No, I don't think I'm being presumptuous at all. Why shouldn't I ask for it?"

Bran stood up slowly, his eyes never leaving her as he tossed the forgotten papers onto the neat desk top. "I'm suspicious, I guess," he replied, lips twisted in a tight grin that did nothing to ease the intensity of his gaze. "Do you think one pleasant afternoon interlude is enough of a basis for you to start asking for special favors?"

Raine felt the color flooding up from her throat in a hot tide, but she fought to regain control. Her gaze swept around the room that was so different from Nina Tarsamova's office with its cozy clutter. There were no mementos here, no sentiment, no reminders of the past—nothing but the stripped-down implements of an uncompromising professional. Finally her eyes came back to settle on his face, the anger in their depths at once deriding and challenging his brittle manner.

"My body is a tool of personal expression, not a lure that I dangle for personal gain," Raine informed him slowly, her face gone white now as she bore the brunt of the insult he'd paid her. "I want that role because I think I can do it as well—no, make that better—than anyone else. And as for my personal reasons, damn it, I want the dance to be my test piece—to prove to myself that I can do it." She took a deep breath, before adding in a tone of gentle irony, "I didn't quite intend to bare my soul to you, Bran, but there it is."

Listening to her, Bran never allowed his expression to waver, except for a momentary flicker of his eyes as they followed the graceful impetus of her arm when she lifted it to brush an unruly strand of hair back from her forehead. Raine caught the look, but it was so fleeting that she might only have imagined the oddly angry, caressing light that touched her. Now as he came toward her, his expression was veiled again beneath the deep furrow of his brow.

She waited expectantly, hopefully, for his answer. But he said nothing immediately as he joined her before the window, his handsome profile presented to her.

At last he turned to fix her with a wintry gray blue stare. "I'm sorry to have to break it to you like this, but you can't have the part, Raine. Because you're not going on tour."

The precise words hit her like a blow.

"Why?" she finally demanded in a strangled voice.

"Because you're not strong enough."

"At least give me the chance to let me show you that I am!"

"I can't take that risk," he replied stubbornly. "You haven't shown me that you've got the stamina."

Raine stared at him in disbelief. "What do you

think I've been doing in the studio hour after hour, day after day, for all these weeks? If I haven't got the stamina then, damn it, no one does!''

Bran's gaze was forthright and deadly serious. "Maybe what I should have said is that you're lacking resilience. Look at Tracey or Mari, for instance. The one's working like crazy at the Folies, and the other's teaching a weekend dance class to neighborhood women. Even Riva gave up time over Easter to take a dance job with a Munich company.''

Raine's expression was stony as she listened to him go on. "I see what this is all about. You're punishing me because I have a patron and no one else does.''

"Don't twist my words around," Bran said in a flat emotionless voice. "All I'm saying is I still don't see a woman who can stand on her own two feet.''

Raine's eyes flashed. "I won't accept that.''

"It's too late. My mind's made up.'' His mouth tightened. "I don't owe you an explanation, Raine, so you can be damned thankful you got one at all. This is my company, run my way.''

"Tyrant.''

But he'd had enough. His hands shot out to imprison her arms. "Don't push me too far," he whispered in a voice so tense and strained that it grated on her. "You're lovely, Raine, but I won't let that blind me.''

Raine felt the pulse throbbing painfully in her temple, felt the stinging swell of tears behind her eyes as she stared up at him. Wrenching free, she ran blindly from the office.

That early November day was raw and blustery beneath a fading afternoon sun. A cold wind buffeted her back and crept down the neck of her jacket as she walked past the cheerfully lighted shops in the rue des Abbesses. But Raine was aware of none of that. She understood the truth now, a simple realization that left a painful void deep inside. Bran had excluded her not because he wished to punish her, but because he had no faith in her. The tears she'd held back began to fall, leaving a salty trail down her cheek.

IT WAS ANOTHER RAW AFTERNOON, much like the one three days earlier when she and Bran had argued in his office. She was sitting in a cozy café with mahogany walls and cut-glass windows, warming her hands around a cup of coffee. She'd invited Pierre Junot to join her, but she wasn't sure he'd show up. In his own way, the artist was very much like his grandfather, proud and stubborn, even if the old man tried to keep him down.

It was a relief for Raine to think of someone else's problems for a change. She'd sneaked away early from the studio, unable to bear any more of the tense atmosphere, the whispering excitement as the time drew near for the names of the chosen dancers to be posted. She'd told no one that for her, at least, the tension of waiting was over. In class she'd begun to dance as mechanically as a puppet, avoiding everyone's eyes. She had felt Bran's eyes boring into her more than once and knew that he was engaging her in a silent contest of wills. But she wouldn't ask anything of him again.

Raine looked up from her coffee as the café door swung open and Pierre breezed in, brown eyes bright, his cheeks ruddy above his trimmed beard. His open expression grew guarded as he caught sight of Raine at the corner window. She wanted to be friends with the talented artist despite the constraint that hovered between them, but it was growing more and more difficult. After all, she was not only Riva's twin, but also a friend of Pierre's grandfather.

She smiled as he came over to the table. "How do you manage to look so disgustingly healthy?" Raine teased him lightly. "I thought artists were supposed to be pale and starve in garrets."

Pierre bit his lip as he slid into the chair opposite her. "That isn't too far off the mark, believe me," he replied with a wry grimace. "But things are looking up. I'm having a showing of my paintings at the Tabor Gallery in the spring."

"Wonderful! May I come?"

He smiled at her enthusiasm. "Of course. I'd be honored."

"Getting ready for it won't conflict with your work on the new company sets, will it?"

"No. A big part of my life is there," he answered with unexpected force. She read the dark intensity in his eyes and knew that he was thinking of Riva again.

Hastily she sought to change the subject. "Will you invite your grandfather to your show?"

Pierre's answering laugh was bitter. "Are you kidding, Raine? You don't know him!"

"I suppose I know a different side of him," she countered softly.

But Pierre wasn't listening. His cheeks had puffed out in a little sigh of frustration. "He despises my career, not because it's art but because it is contrary to his wishes. That's why he cut me off. He thought

I'd come around and take over the business. He refuses to accept the fact that that life is meaningless to me.''

"The cold war has to end sometime," she remarked.

"No. It's only worsened since my Grandmother Sylvie died. She was always the mediator, trying to strike a compromise between two people incapable of it. Before she died, she took me aside and gave me money that she'd saved through the years without my grandfather's knowledge. I'll never forget what she said to me—her expression of love, her wish that I choose the life that would make me happy. The money was nothing compared to the gift of those words. And now she's dead.'' His eyes darkened with pain.

"There's no one else to intervene?" Raine asked, concerned.

His head snapped from left to right. "There's only us—the two Pierres. It seems I'm destined to be caught up with people who want me for their own reasons, not for myself. My grandfather...Riva.''

Raine bristled at that. "Don't blame her. You're a grown man. When you found out what she was like, that should have been the end of it.''

His lips twisted. "You can never have been in love, Raine—not if you talk like that.''

The words struck her forcibly. She'd accused Bran of coldness; now Pierre's words made her fear the same thing for herself.

A long silence fell between them, broken by Pierre's unexpected question. "What do you think of my grandfather?''

She looked up, startled. "He's irascible, hard-nosed, stubborn. But for all that I like him. He's a man of principle."

Pierre's eyes bored into her. "And me?"

Raine smiled impishly. "A man of principle, too. The problem with you two is that the principles aren't the same. You're true to a dream, while he's true to a hard-earned tradition. Not much common ground."

"Perhaps Riva and Bran were right, after all. I should have tried to make him see reason in court."

"No, you made the right decision. Riva worships power."

"And I have none?" Pierre riposted gloomily.

"You have the strength of your talent."

He shook his head. "That was never enough for her."

"If it's any consolation to you, I don't think she's ever been in love with any man. She loves herself."

For the first time Pierre produced a genuine smile. "I wish it were you who'd come to Paris first." Reaching across the table, he touched her hand. "Maybe it's not too late to start over again."

Gently she disengaged her hand. "I'm happy we're friends, Pierre."

He didn't miss the subtle emphasis. "You've already fallen under Bran's spell, haven't you, Raine? But since you've given me fair warning, I'll return the favor. Don't get involved with him."

Raine felt her face flooding with bright color, yet she had to ask, "Why not?"

"Because he's proud of his self-reliance. He's not interested in commitment."

"I'll remember that," she replied dryly as she slipped into her jacket.

Pierre's smile was world-weary, defeated. "No, you won't—not once you've fallen."

Raine tried to forget his parting words, but it was impossible. "Proud of his self-reliance." The phrase drummed itself into her mind. She remembered, too, Bran's accusation that she was unable to stand on her own two feet.

By the time she reached the apartment, Raine had made a decision. Without hesitation she reached for the telephone and dialed her patron's number.

RAINE SMILED WARMLY across the table at her companion. It seemed a little strange to have him there in her apartment that afternoon, because she'd grown so accustomed to Monsieur Santandre as her rotund genie of the night. She was playing truant from the studio that day. She had no desire to be present when the dancers were formally chosen for the tour.

Instead she'd invited the gentleman to lunch, a simple but tasty menu of fresh salad, crusty bread and pasta with shrimp and asparagus. She'd drawn the old card table up before the living-room window and draped it with a square of lace. The pink carnation in its Perrier bottle vase lent a festive mood to the occasion that made up for the mismatched crockery and silverware.

"I invited you here for a special reason, Monsieur Santandre," Raine began as she poured the red wine into a pair of squat tumblers. Gently she clinked her glass against his. "I wanted to thank you for your many kindnesses to me over the past weeks and—"

she faltered just a second before continuing "—and to tell you that I no longer need a patron."

His round dark eyes widened in surprise. "But my dear—"

Her own words interrupted his. "I hope we can continue to be friends, though I have to put one stipulation on that," she went on firmly, eyes twinkling. "No more gifts."

He regarded her with growing perplexity. "Why?"

"Because I want to be independent," Raine explained. "I've looked into the matter of part-time work. I can do private tutoring in English and earn quite a lot. You see, then I'll be indebted to no one."

He surprised her by chuckling. "Nina Tarsamova will not be happy. She worked long and hard to convince me to help you."

"I hope you'll still be a friend to the Ballet du Monde," Raine interjected hastily.

He waved his arm impatiently at that. "But you're like a granddaughter to me, child. I want to give—"

She interrupted him again. "Then you can give friendship. Besides, you have your grandson, Pierre."

Monsieur Santandre's chin quivered in mild indignation. "I thought it was understood, *mademoiselle*, that we would never bring up the boy's name."

But Raine shook her head stubbornly. "That was your stipulation when you were my patron. Now we're friends, I hope, and equals. I've come to care about Pierre. He's a fine man."

"He's a boy who can't admit he still needs my guidance," Pierre's grandfather blustered. "He's weak and dependent on his friends."

"But he's learning to be strong." Raine smiled. "You pushed him in that direction. You forced him to make a choice about his life. He has a lot to be grateful to you for."

Santandre looked disconcerted at that, but soon recovered. "And what do I have to be grateful for?" he went on in an aggrieved tone. "A grandson who abandoned me when I needed him most, after...after Sylvie died."

Raine was touched by this glimpse of his vulnerability, and her voice was gentle when she spoke. "That must have been a terrible loss for you, but it was for Pierre, too. From what he's told me, I think she must have been a very wise and compassionate woman."

"She was everything to me," he shot back, and Raine thought she understood his anger, anger because Sylvie was gone and because he regarded his loneliness as a sign of weakness. "I was ready to retire just before Sylvie died, but what could I do then but plunge back into the business? At least there I could have the solace of Pierre at my side—or so I thought."

Raine was silent for a long while. "Would your wife have wanted that?" Then, gathering up her courage, she went on, "She gave Pierre money before she died."

The man's eyes widened in shock. "I don't believe you."

"Pierre told me so himself. He loved his grandmother deeply, and she loved him." Raine paused. "She believed in him, *monsieur*."

But Santandre was shaking his head. "Then Sylvie betrayed me, too, by taking his side."

Frightened now that she had only worsened matters, Raine quickly tried to repair the damage. "No! You're so wrong. Don't you see that there are no sides, no right or wrong? All that's needed is a little compassion and compromise."

His expression was stony. "I've lived for seventy-five years without the need for either."

"It's never too late to learn." Tears threatened to spill from her eyes, and his attitude softened just a little.

"You are a sweet child, Raine, but you don't understand the harsh realities of life," he went on gruffly. "I think you Americans have an old saying: he has made his bed; now he must lie in it." With that he stood up from the table.

She smiled up at him a little shakily. "I just hope I haven't made matters worse. My only concern is the two of you."

He shook his head sorrowfully. "You remind me of my Sylvie. Too sweet, too soft, too easily swayed by emotion."

She rallied at that. "But practical, after all! She did all she could to prevent a permanent rift developing between you two. Her only womanly weakness was in caring deeply about you both. I do, too, *monsieur*. Please don't forget that."

He patted Raine's cheek, a little embarrassed by this simple display of affection. Then, turning abruptly, he left the apartment.

Riva returned home as Raine was clearing the dishes from the prettily decorated table. "Looks like a cozy afternoon," Riva observed as she unwound her Irish wool muffler from her throat and tossed it onto the easy chair.

"I had a few things to work out," Raine mumbled distractedly as she went back to the kitchen and slipped the piled dishes into the hot soapy water.

Riva positioned herself in the narrow doorway, arms crossed in front of her. "Well, it won't do you a damn bit of good. It's too late," she observed coolly, although her eyes shone with a curious brightness. "The notice was posted today. You're out, Raine. You're not going on tour. And there's nothing Pierre Santandre can do about that."

Raine glanced over at her with a rueful smile. "That's not what I meant when I said I had a few things to work out. I knew I wasn't going even before Bran posted the notice."

"How could you have known?" Riva demanded peevishly, not certain whether she should believe her or not. Raine ignored her. She was in no mood for more verbal sparring.

By the time she'd finished the washing up and the other chores she had to do, it had already begun to grow dark outside. Riva looked up in surprise, her brush poised over her peach-colored nails, as Raine grabbed her coat from the hall closet and left the apartment without a word.

Hands thrust deep into her pockets against the growing cold, Raine stared up at the ballet theater from where she stood in the deserted courtyard. Every light was extinguished but for the one in Madame Tarsamova's office. Raine slipped inside the building and swiftly made her way up the stairs.

"I'm sorry, Raine," the ballet mistress began without preamble as she looked up to see her young dancer in the doorway. "But there will be other tours."

Raine shrugged as she came forward, past the table laden with keepsakes of the elderly woman's past. "It's a disappointment, but I'll survive." She sat down on the floral-print chaise next to the desk and unbuttoned her jacket. "I invited Pierre Santandre to lunch today," she began.

Madame's head tilted, birdlike, watchful. "And?" she prompted.

"I told him I no longer needed a patron, only a friend," Raine answered, her chin lifted proudly.

The Russian woman's thin expressive brows rose so swiftly and so high that the effect was almost comical. That cool pronouncement was obviously not what she had expected. "I thought I had explained well enough how important the man's patronage is, not only to you but to the company," *madame* replied with some asperity.

"I'm sure he'll want to continue supporting the Ballet du Monde," Raine replied with a confidence she was far from feeling. "Besides, that has nothing to do with me."

The older woman's lips tightened in a thin line. "May I ask what prompted this decision?"

"No."

"I see." Her quick black eyes darted over Raine's face. "And I suppose Brandon had nothing to do with all this?"

Raine shot her a startled, almost angry look. "Why bring him into the discussion?"

"Why?" the ballet mistress repeated. "Because I'm not blind, my dear. I've noticed the increasing edginess between the two of you. Have you slept with him?''

Raine was aghast at her directness. "No," she blurted out in confusion.

"Good," *madame* replied with a satisfied air, before she went on in a more ruminative strain. "I've noticed the transformation in your dancing, *chérie*. I was right to pair you with him. I see far less of the innocent child; he's brought out the woman in you." She paused again, eyes sharp as obsidian as they played over Raine's lovely composed features. "But don't mistake that for love."

The crisp words were like a slap in the face. Raine felt her composure crumple, felt something snap inside her. She shot her wise and cynical mentor a defiant look. "And what if I say I've fallen in love with him?" Raine countered, her manner at once calm yet oddly breathless. The thought had tugged at her, like an exciting thread of melody, from the very beginning. It was a heady relief now to suggest it aloud.

Madame Tarsamova surprised her by chuckling softly. "And every dancer who's ever joined the company has done the same at one time or another. Brandon does tend to have that effect on women."

Raine regarded her distantly. "And he's fallen in love with every one of them in turn?" she rejoined.

The other woman laughed again. "Perhaps. What difference does it make? Love doesn't last. Only our art endures."

Raine shook her head in angry denial, remembering all the stories that had circulated through the company about the string of lovers Nina Tarsamova had taken and discarded in her lifetime. "That's your credo, not mine."

The ballet mistress's eyes sharpened again. "It's Brandon's credo, too."

But Raine couldn't accept that. She stood up and bade the woman a curt good-night.

Outside once again, she turned around to stare up at the single lighted window whose brightness spilled over into the dark courtyard. The old woman would work far into the night, satisfied with only that.

As she walked back up the hill to the apartment, Raine tried to shut out the echo in her mind. But it was there all the same, reinforcing Pierre's earlier warning: "It's Bran's credo, too."

It was a rainy Friday afternoon, gloomy and gray. The electric fire had been lit. Raine stood before the window, staring out unseeingly beyond the misted pane. She drew the deep collar of her white terry robe closer around her throat.

Suddenly the apartment seemed so empty, though less than an hour ago she had thought Riva would never finish her packing and leave. The inevitable bustle of choosing what to pack, of checking and rechecking tickets and visas only served to prolong Raine's private agony of being left behind.

The company's timetable was etched indelibly in her brain. There were to be three performances in each city: Brussels, Amsterdam, Munich, Bern and Florence. Her thoughts went skidding back to the long lonely months of her recuperation in Pennsylvania, when Riva's postcards would arrive with clockwork regularity to taunt and tease her.

Yet so much had changed since then. Raine was a different person, stronger. She had to believe that, even if Bran refused to.

With a sigh she crossed back to the fireplace and retrieved her mug of hot tea from the mantel. She took a big gulp, not caring that it scalded her throat. She was about to curl up in the easy chair, when there came a sharp insistent rap on the front door. Startled, she took a step forward and called, "Come in."

The door was flung open, and Bran stood there. She stared at him, bemused, perplexed, believing for an instant that her own thoughts had conjured him up. Raine noticed then the dampness across the wide shoulders of his overcoat and the wet tousle of his hair. He'd brought the wind and rain and out of doors in with him. There was a freshness and vitality about him that made her blood automatically quicken in response.

His eyes were busy, sweeping over the cozy outline of her terry-wrapped figure and the abandoned tumble of chestnut curls down her back. "Get dressed," he said at last in a clipped tone.

Raine's hands came up to her hips. "What right do you have to barge in here and start giving orders?"

"The train leaves in less than a hour," Bran informed her in the same flat tone. "You're coming on tour."

Her mind was reeling. Her gold-bright eyes flashed a thousand questions at him. But she asked only one. "You've changed your mind about me?"

He breathed a swift muffled sigh of frustration. "Violette fell and broke her ankle on her way home from the studio this morning." A shadow of a grin touched his lips as his gaze met Raine's. "You win by default again."

She bit her lip, the jeweled brightness of her eyes suddenly extinguished. "A very unsatisfactory victory," she retorted acerbically.

"Will it cheer you up to remember the role she was to dance?" Bran countered wryly.

Raine drew in her breath. "The young girl in *Les Patineurs*."

"It's yours now."

She hesitated, not quite ready to believe the sudden change in her fortune. But Bran's impatient voice jogged her into action. "Damn it, get a move on and pack. The taxi's waiting."

CHAPTER NINE

THE TAXI moved into the stream of traffic on the dark wet boulevard. Bringing the collar of her jacket up protectively against her face, Raine didn't look at her companion. She stared straight ahead, eyes fixed on the rhythmic swish of the windshield wipers. Bran sat lost in thought, his gaze turned to the dreariness beyond the window. Even the cabdriver seemed affected by the subtle tension as his eyes darted curiously between them in the rearview mirror.

Unable to contain her restless curiosity any longer, Raine turned to look squarely at Bran. "Why me?" she asked at last, speaking in rapid English to shield their very private conversation from the cabbie's ears, "when you had three others left to choose from?"

Although he shrugged, Bran's eyes glinted teasingly. "Maybe I couldn't stand the thought of leaving you alone for six weeks."

"Damn you, I want to be taken seriously!"

"You're here now," he replied. "Isn't that enough?"

Her bright gaze swept over him. "Not quite. I'd hoped to be something more than a replacement part," she said sarcastically.

"Some women can never be satisfied," he scoffed. "I thought you'd be ecstatic."

"All I can remember is my having to beg," she retorted disdainfully. "I had to sacrifice a lot of pride to come to you."

"Begging!" He laughed. "Is that what you call barging into my office and demanding a particular role?" Her face flushing, Raine turned away again to stare out the window. But he hadn't done with her. His low voice, its tone a curious blend of irony and grudging respect, cut into her churning thoughts. "Maybe I reconsidered because you didn't try to have Nina or Santandre pressure me into changing my mind."

Her head snapped around at that. "I no longer have a patron."

Bran couldn't resist teasing her. "It's a little late to try to please me, don't you think?"

"What I did, I did for myself."

"But you dance for me," he told her slowly, ignoring the fury in her eyes. The curiously possessive words sent a flutter of warmth along her limbs.

Had they been a reminder, a warning? Raine remembered the way he'd laughed in the intimate darkness of the theater when she'd accused him of wanting Riva on his stage and her in his bed. Again she felt the sweet ineluctable force of his desire, which drew her like a moth to a flame. But now that desire frightened and half angered her, because she wasn't certain what she wanted from him.

Silence fell between them as the taxi completed the journey to the station. Outside there was mild pandemonium as travelers rushed to escape the downpour and deposit their baggage with harried porters. Bran motioned for Raine to go on ahead, and she did so gratefully.

She climbed up the narrow iron steps of the Brussels-bound train and made her way along the aisle between the old-fashioned, second-class sitting compartments. She had stopped to study the ticket Bran had given her, when a familiar voice caused her to look up at once. Riva stood facing her in the aisle, her hair caught back with a stylish designer scarf and a French fashion magazine tucked beneath the arm of her lamb's-wool jacket.

Riva's smile of greeting was not at all pleasant. "So Santandre came through after all."

Raine returned the look evenly. "Pierre Santandre had nothing to do with it. Violette broke her ankle. Or do you think the old man hired a thug to break it for her, just so I could come along instead?"

Her sarcasm wasn't lost on Riva, who only grew angrier. "Just don't get it into your head that you made it this far on talent. Do you think I'm blind to the way Bran looks at you?" she flung back, lowering her voice to a whisper as an old couple brushed past them in the aisle. "But he'll get tired of you. And when he does I'll be waiting in the wings."

"You've been waiting awfully long as it is, haven't you?" Raine countered sweetly, eyes ablaze at her sister's implications, yet wanting to hurt in turn.

But Riva had a parting shot. "Bran may *want* you, but it's me that he respects!"

THE THEATER where the company was to give its first performance was tucked behind the flag-bedecked Guild Halls on Brussels's central square. It was little more than a drafty barn with uneven floors, but for Raine it symbolized the heady magic of performing again.

After a quick but pleasant breakfast of rolls and cheese in the tiny hotel dining room, Raine walked the two blocks to the theater. She was so busy going over the steps of her solo role in her mind that she paid scant attention to the twisting medieval lanes of Brueghel's world.

She had just two days to hone her role to perfection. She wanted to practice alone for an hour before Paul and Michel, the danseurs who would be alternating as her partners in the sequence, arrived for rehearsal. The practice area that had been assigned to her was a cold windowless rectangle in the theater basement, but that didn't bother her. She was too keyed up over the role to think of anything else....

Raine and Paul were hard at work when Bran silently entered the studio. Straddling a chair in the corner of the room, he dropped his chin to his forearms and watched them with attentive eyes. A short while later he stood up again, dismissing Paul.

Raine lifted the ever-present hand towel to her upper lip, watching Bran approach. Though he wore street attire, it did little to hide his athletic body as he moved so sinuously. And as always when she looked at Bran, something within her leaped to meet him.

"You're trying too hard," he said quietly after Paul had gone. "Just let it come."

Her luminescent eyes played over his features. Then she lifted her hand to his and invited, "Show me."

As Bran walked through the danseur's role with

her, Raine did begin to relax. Now she danced to her own rhythm rather than to Paul's hard competitive propulsion, and the subtle playfulness of her nature emerged, until she felt as alive and mischievously vital as a yearling feeling its oats.

Eyes flashing like newly minted gold, she glanced over her shoulder at Bran. "Dance it with me," she urged.

"I'm not dressed for the part," he protested with a laugh, tugging at the shirt collar above his blue gray cashmere sweater.

She whirled on pointe to face him. "I mean in Amsterdam. Dance it with me on stage."

His brow dipped in a slight frown. "That wouldn't be fair to Paul or Michel."

But Raine wasn't buying his excuses. "They idolize you, Bran. In fact, they probably wonder themselves why you don't dance, but they're too timid to ask."

"Don't push me, Raine," he warned her softly. "You want too much."

Her eyes flashed golden light, teasing. "No. I want it all." The music swelled around her again, and before he could reply she moved away in a quick graceful glissade, evocative of a skater on an icy pond.

He followed her across the room, put off guard by this new puckish mood. "I want a woman, not a dancer," he growled suddenly.

She laughed and twirled. "I don't want a man; I want a partner."

Annoyed, he grabbed her arm and pulled her down off pointe. "Come to dinner with me tonight after the performance," he said in a curiously tense voice.

The mood had changed in a twinkling, and her luminous eyes darkened in response. "I'm sorry. I don't think I should."

"Why not?"

Raine gave the first excuse that popped into her head. "I'll be too busy rehearsing."

"I'm the one who gives the orders as to rehearsal hours," Bran retorted with growing impatience.

"Are you going to order me to come to dinner with you, too?" she flung back. Her eyes were hard, protecting the fragility underneath. She hadn't forgotten Madame Tarsamova's words.

"My mistake." Bran's own eyes bored into hers like cutting sapphires. "I thought it was something you would have enjoyed."

Though his expression was angry, Raine caught a fleeting trace of the vulnerability she'd sensed once before. But before she could take back her words, he'd dropped her arm and stalked out of the studio. With a sigh she picked up the thread of music, dancing alone.

AMSTERDAM WAS a rehash of Brussels—train chugging into the station at dusk; the quick taxi trip across town past blurred boulevard lights to their modest hotel.

Sitting alone in the back of the taxi, Raine went over in her mind the troupe's three performances in the Belgian capital. Madame Tarsamova had arranged the schedule so that not every dance was performed in every city, and her principal dancers would not exhaust themselves. Still, the schedule itself was exhausting enough—two evening performances in each city with a matinee sandwiched in between. Raine understood now Bran's emphasis on the need for strength in his dancers.

Raine was grateful that *Les Patineurs* was scheduled for their second stop. In Brussels, she'd had the chance to be on stage again without yet facing the tremendous tension of performing a solo role. That test still lay ahead....

The Municipal Theater in Leidse Square was an attractive building, though its dressing rooms were as cramped and crowded as any. Raine jostled with the two dancers to either side of her as she reached up to pin her hair more tightly. Her made-up eyes stared back at her enormously from the small mirror.

There had been some comfort at least in the familiar routine, in the faint greasy smell of the makeup that reminded her of wax candles. She'd deftly applied the black pencil to her eyes, remembering the basic rule of stage makeup—to enlarge and extend. One line followed the crease of her eyelid, while the other she drew below the eye, so that it seemed to grow outward from the lashes.

That done, Raine had an attack of nerves. The room was hot from too many bodies. She stood up swiftly and fought her way through the tangle of legs and tote bags to the wardrobe room.

Her costume was of a gossamer silk that delineated yet subtly veiled the beautiful contours of her dancer's form. Ruffs of white fur at the collar and cuffs lent the illusion of an elegant winter jacket. After dressing, she picked up her brand-new white toe shoes with slightly shaking fingers and began to bang them rather fiercely, one against the other, to break down the pointes and make them more pliable.

Nervousness made her fingers clumsy, but she managed to sew on the satin ribbons at last, only to give way to a new wave of panic as she slipped into the shoes and found they were a touch too large at the heels. She raced down the hall to the bathroom and turned on the water faucet. Gracefully she swung her leg up and slid her foot into the sink, wetting the back of the shoe so that it would shrink a little to fit more snugly against her heel.

The door swung inward again, and she looked up to see Tracey come in, her blond hair standing straight up and only half of her stage eyes done.

"God—" Tracey giggled as she looked at her friend "—if the audience could only see us now." Raine laughed, too, and the sound helped ease some of the tension that was cramping her stomach into a hard cold ball of fear.

More slowly now, she made her way to the theater wings, pausing to glance out into the darkened abyss of the filled auditorium. She was just grinding her heel into the box of rosin crystals when Paul materialized beside her.

She looked up at him with her enormous eyes. "That floor looks murderously slippery," she whispered. "I don't think the rosin's going to be enough. Wish we had a little soda to coat the bottom of our shoes."

"Will you relax?" he shot back. "The stage is no problem." Paul could afford to be expansive, since he'd danced all three Brussels performances and was an old hand by now. Still he betrayed his own nervousness by asking, "Do you mind if we rehearse that balance just one more time?"

Raine complied at once, grateful to have something to concentrate on besides her own paralyzing fears. They executed the movement perfectly. Paul seemed satisfied and released her.

She had just taken hold of a discarded prop to balance on, bending her knees in a slow easy stretch, when she heard the gliding crescendo of chords announcing their role. Raine straightened to find Bran standing beside her.

He must have sensed the fear and blind panic gripping her, because he reached out to take her chin lightly between his thumb and forefinger. *"Merde,"* he whispered, his shadowed eyes almost gentle as they regarded her. The rude oath was balletic slang for "good luck."

"Thank you," she whispered in return, managing a small tight smile. His presence had given her heart, even though fear stabbed at her again as Paul grabbed her hand and propelled her onto the brightly lighted stage.

Miraculously, the mind-numbing panic evaporated as the music washed over her in a warm enveloping wave, and she began to move with it, all the time remembering the advice Bran had given her in rehearsal.

And as Raine danced she pretended it was he who was her partner. She resisted the impetus of Paul's movements, responding instead to her own inner rhythm, a rhythm matched by the slow dynamic strength of Bran's body. She felt pain in her leg, but it was secondary now to the joy and wonder of performing.

Long afterward, the dressing room was empty but for Raine; she was the straggler. Her calf had been aching ever since the company had arrived in the northerly port city, and she knew it was the combination of coldness and moist sea air that made it hurt. Still taking no chances, she bound it tightly with an Ace bandage before slipping into a pair of heavy wool ski socks. That done, she pulled on her slim black cords and heathery-soft coral pullover and woolen jacket, ready for the trek back to her hotel.

When she pushed open the rear stage door, Raine was stunned to see Bran leaning on the iron railing, his dark profile illuminated by the cigarette he held meditatively between his fingers. Lazily he turned to face her. "What took you so long?" he teased. "Couldn't tear yourself away from the roars and applause?"

Her bright eyes swooped up to meet his head on. "I have to admit it felt wonderful to be on stage again."

A fleeting grin touched his lips. "Aren't you going to ask me if I thought you did a good job?"

"I don't have to ask," she retorted, her chin tilting upward. "I felt it inside."

"We'll have dinner, then, to celebrate."

She shook her head. "No, Bran. I'm tired."

The boyishly crooked grin was in place again. "A thick juicy cut of filet mignon is just what the doctor ordered."

Despite her resolve, Raine's mouth began to water. The dancers' spending allowance was a meager one that allowed them little beyond starchy hotel fare and the apples and yogurt they could pick up cheaply in corner markets.

Suddenly Raine found herself resenting Bran's apparent wealth. "You won't think I'm weak if I accept a dinner invitation from a man of influence?" she needled, all too quick to remind him of his stubborn stand on her friendship with Monsieur Santandre.

His grin grew broader. "Not if the man's me."

But she was equally stubborn. "Sorry."

"Raine, stop being such a hellion," he retorted with feigned weariness as he flicked the cigarette over the rail with an impatient gesture, though his eyes still held a glint of amusement. "I'm not used to being the pursuer. You're wearing me out."

"I didn't realize I was being pursued," she retorted tartly, racing down the stage-door steps without waiting for his reply. But he caught up with her easily.

The restaurant he chose was intimate, quiet, expensive. She dug into her poached salmon with undisguised relish, amused that Bran allowed her only a scant half glass of the exquisite Montrachet wine he'd ordered to accompany their meal. When the waiter presented her with the dessert menu, Bran whisked it out of her hand.

"*Neen,*" he said firmly in Dutch to the amused waiter. "The lady's in training."

Raine regarded him in false dismay. "You know, ever since you bought those meringues in the rain I've had a horrible sweet tooth."

Bran shook his head slowly, his cut-sapphire eyes playing over her features in a deliciously intimate way before settling on her full gentle mouth. "Sweet mouth and sweet lips."

Warmed by the wine and the excellent meal, they strolled slowly along the narrow canals past Dam Square. A fog had blown in from the sea, swirling around the bases of the tall gabled mansions and obscuring the lamplights until they resembled free-floating moons above the black water.

They were alone in a world that seemed expressly created for them.

Raine half tilted her head to glance up at him, only to find his eyes fixed on her in that broodingly caressing way that had set her nerve endings afire in the restaurant.

"Ready to turn back yet?" he asked.

"No, not yet," she murmured, her voice a whisper that seemed to warm the air around him. The fog and city silence bound them in a curiously intimate way, making her breath catch in her throat.

Bran must have felt this, too, because he stopped and his hands came up to pull her to him. Raine went willingly, forgetting all else in that instant as his arms swept around her, and his fingers moved hungrily along the supple smoothness of her back. She clung to him, hungering, too, as she savored the hard muscular body molded to her, the pressure of his powerful thighs against her own and the pounding of his heart that spurred hers to a matching rhythmic intensity.

She lifted her head then to meet his in the darkness, and their gazes burned into each other before he lowered his head. She felt the cold tip of his nose against her cheek, the trailing warmth of his mouth as his lips grazed one lobe, and he murmured her name over and over against the soft shell of her ear.

She shuddered as those same teasing lips and teeth moved down to trace the line of her jaw and nip her chin. His parted lips brushed the valley between chin and waiting mouth, teasing and inflaming the sensitive contour of her lower lip until she moaned, a soft demand that the promise of a kiss be fulfilled.

But he hadn't yet finished with his teasing. His slow wicked mouth explored the moist corners of her lips, his tongue flicking gently to taste the last vestige of wine and the salt tang the night air had left. Now their lips brushed back and forth together in a slow silken haze, the pressure building until his hand came up to cup her nape and their tongues met in a sweet hot explosion of fulfillment.

The sensual thrust and parry was at once tender and fierce, an intimate duel to which they both succumbed. Still his questing mouth advanced and tantalized, until she arched away from his encircling arm and felt the tumescent need of his loins against her own.

"God, how I want you," he said in a rough shaky voice, the words grating and tearing across the crushed sweetness of her vulnerable lips.

Her eyes flew open, then narrowed again to golden catlike slits. How many times had he made that bald proclamation of desire, and how many women had succumbed? Bran sensed her stiffening and reluctantly raised his head, the blue black depths of his eyes raking her with unspoken questions.

Raine steeled herself against those hot caressing depths that could so inflame her. Drawing a ragged breath, she composed herself enough to whisper up at him, "Bran, we're going to be thrown together for the next five weeks while we're touring. Everyone lives in such enforced intimacy that you know the gossip would spread. I had to face that already with Pierre Santandre. I couldn't bear to be accused of using you."

"I think my dancers know me better than that."

She regarded him curiously. "Maybe they do." Her voice was soft, hesitant. "Maybe that's why I'm so reluctant. I sometimes feel I don't know you at all."

"Whose fault is that?" he grated.

"I don't know!" she cried in weary exasperation, her dark lashes dropping against her cheeks. "Look, don't you think we should be getting back? We've got early rehearsals tomorrow."

"That's right," he ground out. "Don't ever forget for even a minute that your life's geared for the stage, Raine."

"No, I can't," she answered him in a flat voice. "Not just yet I can't." Her eyes begged him to understand, but he said nothing, and they made their way back to the hotel in tense silence.

In Munich Raine was assigned to share a room with Riva. They were lodged on the fourth floor of a quaint, narrowly built guesthouse that caused Riva to complain spiritedly. Raine was wishing for an elevator herself, but she said nothing.

Inside the room, Raine unpacked her makeup bag and bathrobe, then eased down into one of the armchairs and swung her legs onto the soft bed. Riva shrugged out of her jacket and tossed it on the puffy goosedown quilt covering her own bed.

"Some of us are going out to Schwabing to do a little café hopping," Riva said as she kicked off her shoes. "Tracey said to invite you along."

Raine stretched and yawned. "No, thanks. I'm beat."

"I heard you got back to your room in Amsterdam late last night," Riva remarked. "That was foolish. You know the city has a crime problem now."

Raine was in no mood to tolerate her sister's condescension, no matter how well-meaning. "I wasn't alone," she said, waiting for the inevitable comeback.

"A tryst with Pierre Santandre?" Riva needled.

"No," Raine answered. "I had dinner with Bran."

Riva's shoulders lifted with pretended indifference, though her narrowed eyes revealed her jealous curiosity. Pride forbade her asking any questions. She shrugged out of her clothes and reached for the terry robe Raine had unpacked.

Raine's hand shot out to grab the hem. "You're always borrowing mine," she teased, perversely lighthearted in the face of her sister's annoyance. "Why don't you buy something more practical instead of that flimsy thing you wear?"

Riva gave a sharp tug and pulled the terry robe to her. "Oh, don't be so damned selfish," Riva retorted, ignoring the logic of Raine's remark.

IT WAS MIDAFTERNOON. Raine sat on the top step of the theater stairs, resting her leg and watching the others at work. Again and again her eyes were drawn to Bran, to the controlled power in his torso and limbs as he demonstrated and corrected. He was the company's vital core, the man who gave it dynamic impetus and meaning.

As she watched him, Raine remembered the invasive power of his kiss and her own kindled desire. Excitement rushed along her limbs because she knew she had her own measure of power over him, too. But her pleasure at the thought dimmed as she recalled the words Riva had flung at her in the train corridor before they'd left Paris: "He respects me!" Raine shook off the unsettling implications and watched Riva take center stage.

Her lips twitched in amusement when she saw that her twin was dancing with far more fire than brilliance this afternoon. Raine guessed she was still seething over her own admitted dinner date.

Brandon crossed the floor now toward the wildly spinning Ballerina. "What's gotten into you?" he demanded irritably.

"Oh, nothing," Riva answered in a petulant breathless voice. "Danny's too slow."

Raine smiled again to herself, knowing Riva was right about that. Built like a Clydesdale horse, the tall Swiss possessed great strength, but he would never be a great danseur. Still he would be a nice foil for the Ballerina's quicksilver talent, and with a dark wig and makeup he'd be a credible Moor on stage.

But Bran might have agreed with Riva's assessment, too, because he motioned for Danny to take a break and held out his hand to the waiting Ballerina. "Shall I go through it with you?"

"Yes, please," Riva replied in a soft, sweet-tempered voice that amazed her sister.

From her shadowy stair perch Raine watched narrowly, her back straightening in a tense line as she followed the two dancers across the empty stage. Riva wasn't dancing full out as she usually did. Her movements were controlled, contained. And she kept glancing back at Bran, making the spark of connection time and again. It was a far cry from the same pas de deux she'd danced with Danny, when her haughty bravado had propelled her across the floor in total disregard of her partner.

With increased misgivings Raine observed the way Riva's breast grazed Bran's arm as she dipped in supported arabesque, the way his dark hands caught Riva's small waist. And always the dancer kept that vital connection with her partner, until Raine realized that her twin was dancing more like.... "Like me," she whispered to herself in puzzled astonishment.

The music stopped, and the man and woman on stage regarded each other for a moment. "You should always dance like that," Bran said finally.

Riva's head tilted back to look at him. She smiled slowly. "Is this lesson number one?"

Raine should have been gloating that Riva, the technical purist and *virtuosa suprema*, had taken a few lessons from her in balletic expression. Instead she was rocked by jealousy and anger. She had grossly underestimated her clever sister!

Raine came down the stairs in a rush and grabbed her jeans and sweater from the chair where she'd laid them. She was just straightening the soft wool over her leotard when Bran came up to her.

"Where are you going?" he asked as he toweled the fine sheen of perspiration from his face.

"I haven't seen daylight in a week," she replied shortly. "I'm going for a walk."

"Good," Bran answered her with a negligent shrug of agreement. "It'll probably do you more good than burning out in practice."

His equanimity enraged her. She could only think that he wanted the opportunity to be alone with Riva. Her jealousy was barely containable now, mixed as it was with all her fears and uncertainties. Never had she been more aware of how much she wanted and needed him, how little she could bear seeing him hold Riva in his arms.

Bran sensed that something was bothering her. "Maybe I'd better come along," he said quietly. "You look like you could use some company. Besides," he added, glancing back with satisfaction at the dancers who were rehearsing on stage, "everyone's primed as it is."

Her eyes snapped and glinted like a winter aurora. "And all you have to do is set a match beneath them, right?" she said tartly.

His eyes slid over her curiously, and the thought flashed through his mind that he'd love to have her on stage in just that mood, with the fire simmering beneath the surface and the unreadable depths of pain in her eyes that lent such character and strength to her fragile features. Yet, perversely, he longed to spark the fire, erase the pain. . . .

"What are you staring at?" she demanded.

He chuckled self-deprecatingly. "Nothing."

She found his laughter irked her as much as his equanimity.

They strolled along the pedestrian promenades of

Neuhauserstrasse in the half light of a cold autumn afternoon. The wind buffeted them and caught the ends of faded tattered streamers billowing above the walkways.

Rounding the corner that led to the open market, they took refuge before a tiny kiosk selling fat, cinnamon-sugared waffles. Bran leaned back against the wall, shoving his hands deeper into the pockets of his trousers. "I've been thinking, Raine, ever since you and Riva played that farce in the *Petroushka* rehearsal," he began, the ghost of a wicked smile on his lips. "I'd like to see the two of you on stage together. The effect might be amusing."

Her eyes were like pools of frozen amber. "Never!" she replied with quiet vehemence.

He studied her for a long moment. "You're still afraid, aren't you?"

"No, I'm not. I just don't want to be manipulated. I don't want to be one of your dancing pawns."

"That's a lie." His voice cut into her like a cold steel blade. "You're afraid she'll beat you. She's been doing that all your lives, hasn't she?"

"That's none of your business," she responded heatedly.

"You're a woman. For God's sake, grow up," he muttered, his voice harsh. "You talk about your pride and self-respect, but it's all a sham. You can't even stand up to Riva."

"What do you know about it?" she snapped. "You admitted yourself that we're strangers to each other."

"I've seen the way you watch Riva in class, on stage. You want everything she has."

"I don't!"

"Quit lying to me," he went on relentlessly. "You've never been able to stand up to Riva, and you never will be until—"

Raine refused to listen to any more. "Go back to the studio," she rasped at him. "You're wanted there."

"But not here, is that it?" His eyes were hard above the angry flush of his cheeks.

Without answering him, Raine turned and hurried away into the gathering darkness.

RIVA STOOD before the mirror in the tiny hotel bathroom, the collar of her sister's white terry robe drawn up defiantly against her cheek. She'd gathered her hair back in a tight ponytail and scrubbed her face clean. It was part of the ritual of getting ready for performance. Pulling the rubber band from her hair now, she was just dragging a brush through the strands with long punishing strokes when she heard a sharp rap on the door.

She moved barefoot across the room to answer it, her eyes widening in surprise at seeing Bran there. He leaned against the door frame. "Raine, I have to talk to you," he began, his deep attractive voice edged with anger and a fleeting echo of apology.

Even as her devious mind whirled, Riva smiled up at him with feline softness and threw open the door invitingly. When he stepped inside and closed the door behind him, her smile widened in triumphant delight.

RAINE WANDERED along past the hubbub of people and traffic in the Karlsplatz, oblivious to the clangor of trolleys and the choking diesel fumes mingling with

the odor of sizzling bratwurst. She was still tightly
wound up after her argument with Bran and could
think only of that.

Gradually her sense of injured pride gave way to
the reluctant realization that he might have been
right. But, damn it, that gave him no right to bully
her!

She found that her steps had led her back to the
open market again, but the waffle-seller's kiosk was
deserted. Raine stopped to watch a plump hausfrau,
whose eyes were fixed watchfully on the sauerkraut-
vendor's scale after he'd dipped out a hefty ladle
from his wooden barrel. She smiled in amusement at
the homey sight, her sense of humor returning as her
anger drained away. Perhaps she'd judged Bran too
harshly, after all. Perhaps his uncompromising
toughness was motivated by wanting what was best
for her. Cheered by that thought, Raine walked
swiftly in the direction of the hotel to get ready for
the evening's performance.

Climbing the four narrow flights briskly, she
opened the door to her room. Her hand tightened in
shock at the scene that greeted her. Her softened attitude toward Bran changed into cold hard fury as she
stared at him in disbelief, her gaze taking in his lazily
intimate hand on Riva's thigh beneath *her* robe. She
felt the hot flush of anger and mortification creeping
up into her cheeks.

Her eyes glittered, but when she spoke her voice
was astonishingly cool and sarcastic. "Wouldn't you
be more comfortable in the bedroom?"

"That's none of your business, Riva," Bran
replied in curt English.

"You're wrong on both counts. It *is* my business, and my name isn't Riva." She tried to force her lips into a sardonic smile, but to her chagrin they trembled in hurt betrayal.

Bran's eyes raked her, puzzled and disbelieving, before coming to rest again on the familiar outline of the trembling mouth that his own had teased, caressed, invaded. Raine stared back at him. Her whole body was tense with anger and jealousy, though she wasn't quite certain whether Riva or Bran was to blame.

Now Bran's gaze moved confusedly between the two women. In an uncoiling rush he got up, dumping Riva in a tangle of arms and legs onto the chair. He looked at her with a mingled look of anger and wry amusement as she laughed mockingly up at him.

"What's the matter, Bran?" Riva cracked. "Can't handle twins?"

He replied as easily as if he'd been extricating himself from ridiculous Oscar Wilde farces every day of his life. "I can never handle duplicitous women," he retorted with a wry grin. "Besides, a ménage à trois isn't quite what I had in mind."

His easy acceptance of the situation grated on Raine, and she cocked her head defiantly. "But you wouldn't object to it on stage, is that it?" she interposed from the doorway. "As long as it suits your purposes."

Bran sauntered toward her, his fingers coming up to grasp her chin lightly. "Always have to have the last word, Mademoiselle Cameron, don't you?"

He spoke in French now, hoping to establish a link with her separate from Riva. But she resisted, jerking her head away and stepping back. "Now will you please get out, du Rivage?'' she said, still seething. ''We've got to get ready for tonight's performance.''

''Bran!'' Riva called after him pettishly as his back disappeared through the door, and she realized she'd been forgotten.

After she'd shut the door, Raine turned back to her sister. ''Now will you give me back my robe? You've caused enough mischief, damn it.''

Riva laughed slyly. ''It was worth it.''

Raine turned away in annoyance, her back tense as she began to undress.

Riva watched her assessingly. ''You're jealous.''

Raine turned her head swiftly to regard her twin with angry eyes. ''Don't be ridiculous. I don't care a thing about him.''

Riva's sharp laughter burst out again. ''Oh, you're such a miserable liar!''

CHAPTER TEN

THE DAYS MERGED one into another, time bound by endless railway tracks.

As the tour progressed, the dancers began to think of it as something of a lark—all except for Raine. While they went out after morning class to sightsee and shop, she stayed to practice alone, working resolutely in one drafty old theater after another. Her schedule became practice by day and performance by night with no energy left for anything else.

Not that there was anything else. Since the episode in that Munich hotel room, Brandon had kept his distance from both women. Raine, too, had been left in a bemused unsettled mood by the incident.

Even though she knew Bran's confusion had been all too real, that didn't make it any more understandable or forgivable in her mind. Had she deceived herself into believing that she was special enough to him that the taste and contour of her mouth should have been as familiar to him as his own?

She also had to contend with the old familiar pangs of jealousy. Bran was the one thing Riva hadn't won from her. Then to have seen him wrapped in Riva's arms, no matter how false the pretenses, was difficult to handle.

They collided only once, shortly after that disastrous episode. She'd come up to him after a stage rehearsal. Everyone else had gone. The lights had been dimmed for the evening performance.

"You've been avoiding Riva and me like the plague, Bran," she accused, the words softened by the hint of regret in her voice. "Not that I blame you entirely."

His dark brows came together in a scowl. "You're lucky you both have talent; otherwise, I'd have sent the two of you bouncing—skating, in your case—out of the company on your ears. I don't like cheap stunts."

"On the contrary," Raine answered, annoyed. "I got the impression you enjoyed the whole thing."

A reluctant grin touched the corners of his mouth. "I'll admit I was enjoying it until you walked in to confuse things."

"How could you practically make love to a woman and not recognize her?" Raine bristled.

Bran sighed in frustration. "All I noticed was the white robe, the same one you were wearing that rainy afternoon I came to find you."

But she refused to be mollified. "I suppose at heart it didn't matter which one of us was wearing it."

His eyes narrowed. "Why the hell am I on trial all of a sudden?"

Realizing how jealously possessive she must have sounded, Raine retreated. "Look, Bran, I didn't come up here to argue with you," she went on. "I came to apologize—for Riva's behavior. I'm guessing she won't do it for herself. But maybe you already know that—" she couldn't resist needling him "—since you seem to have gotten on such intimate terms with her."

He laughed at that bit of spite. "Now who's quick to jump to conclusions?" he retorted. "Maybe now you see why I've worked so hard to avoid commitments in the company? Otherwise, first thing you know you have women scratching one another's eyes out."

"You conceited bastard! That's just a cheap excuse. What you really want is a dozen women just a little in love with you, so that they'll give full measure whenever they're asked—onstage or off."

He stared down at her angrily, not admitting to her accusation but not denying it, either.

THE LAST CITY on the company's whistle-stop tour was Florence. The train wound south through umber fields, past hilltops crowned by the red-tiled roofs of slumbering villages. Florence itself had the richly burnished patina of great age, a city of wind-stirred light and stately Renaissance magnificence.

The dancers were in a festive mood, fueled by Bran's announcement that a friend had opened his luxurious hilltop villa to the troupe. No more quaint but rudimentary hotels; they would be the guests of Massimo Chiari.

From the train station, they were taken directly to the Teatro Comunale for a matinee performance. Raine's fear of performing had gradually dissipated in the preceding weeks. Now she felt only a slight but pleasurable tension before going on. The weeks of hard work and discipline were paying off. She sensed the new maturity in her dancing, the strength and the confidence that had begun to flow back into her bit by bit.

She listened distractedly to the banter of the other dancers in the dressing room as they made reference to their approaching "kiddie-time" show. But Raine was happy to be dancing before an audience of children. Perhaps she'd inspire a young girl to choose that magical world for her own. . . .

The disappointments, the heartaches would come later. Raine's shadowed eyes stared back at her from the mirror as she fluffed loose powder over her features with a sable brush. She refused to let herself think of Bran, to torture herself with the question of where they'd gone wrong when the chemistry between them was so right.

After the performance, a white van was waiting to transport them to the villa-studded hilltop of Fiesole, outside the city. The brilliant Florentine light had already begun to fade into dusk as the dancers emerged from the theater.

Raine was the last to board, late again because she'd taken the extra time to wrap and bind her troublesome calf. Her eyes swept the crowded van before coming to rest on Bran where he sat in the double seat directly behind the driver. Since the place beside him was the only vacant spot left, she was forced to take it. He was sprawled lazily, head turned to the window, but Raine sensed his awareness of her as she sat down.

She leaned forward to rearrange the elastic bandage beneath her pant leg, and he spoke in her ear. "How's the leg, granny?" he teased softly.

Her answering look was wry. "Fine, I guess. It twinges now and then, so I'm not taking any chances." Raine glanced past him, outside the window. What she didn't admit to aloud was her dread of returning to Paris and the winter cold that would play havoc with her newly won strength.

But he must have read the faint anxiety in her eyes. "You've gotten over the worst part, Raine—the fear. Nothing'll be that bad again, I promise you."

She sighed and shook her head as she ran impatient fingers down the soft nap of her cords. "How can you be so confident, Bran?"

"You've still got my lilies, haven't you?" he answered with a laugh. "They were supposed to be your talisman." His teasing was a net of warmth that enveloped them both.

"I still have them." Her smile was faintly conspiratorial, as if they were sharing an old and well-loved joke. Resisting the urge to reach out and touch him, Raine marveled again at the unexpected feelings he could engender in her—and at that mood of easy intimacy that should have belonged to lifelong lovers alone.

"Besides," he went on in a more serious tone, "I've watched you these past six weeks—"

"Six weeks," she repeated musingly, not allowing him to finish. "I feel like I've seen Europe only in snatches at night—like a dream. All those brightly lighted cafés and the Dutch canals in the mist—" She broke off suddenly, flushing as she remembered the rare evening they'd shared in Amsterdam and the way she'd clung to him in sweet abandonment with the fog swirling around them.

Raine felt his eyes on her for a long moment before he finally replied. "I'm glad you've remembered the good along with the bad."

She looked up swiftly to meet his gaze. "None of it's been bad."

His brow lifted at that, and a cynical grin touched his lips. "Not even having to put up with Riva's antics?"

"She's always done what she wanted, and the devil take the hindmost. It was rarely directed at me, until now." Raine paused, her look thoughtful. "I suppose I should feel flattered in a way. She's finally considering me a serious rival, and I intend to show her just how serious I can be." Although she spoke lightly, there was no mistaking the determination in her eyes.

"Merde," Bran swore beneath his breath. But she couldn't be certain if he were wishing her luck or cursing his own ill fortune at being a player in their private drama.

THE OCHER WALLS of Villa Chiari loomed in the golden dust of a Florentine sunset. The elegant loggia was already bathed in shadow. The villa's windows sparkled in the dying light. Awaiting them in the fountain-graced atrium was the villa's majordomo, flanked by a retinue of smiling maids.

Riva caught up with her sister as they were being led along the second-floor gallery to their rooms. "Now this is more like it," she breathed in delight. "I could see myself spending a lifetime here."

Raine shot her an impish grin. "This place is more suited to a patroness of the arts than to us lowly artists."

"Speak for yourself," Riva sniffed.

Actually Raine was delighted by the villa, too,

though her pleasure was motivated by the more mundane luxury of having a room all to herself. Once inside, she shut the door and executed a playful extended leap across the soft rug that graced the wide expanse of marble-tiled floor, stopping short to examine the velvet draperies at the window and the carved walnut furnishings.

An hour later she returned downstairs, refreshed and smiling. Raine had freed her hair from its tight chignon to let it frame her face in a soft chestnut cloud. Accenting her coloring and her lithe figure was a simple matte jersey gown in a rich hunter green with long sleeves and a neck scooped low toward a row of tiny buttons bisecting the bodice.

She followed the baritone rumble of voices and found herself in the entryway of a large, richly appointed drawing room. Her eyes were drawn to the pilastered walls, covered alternately with inlaid fresco panels and shimmering expanses of damask that set off museum-quality paintings. Raine saw Bran at once as she came inside. He was deep in conversation with a short, barrel-chested man whose back was to Raine. At that moment, Bran lifted his gaze to her, and his companion turned around at once.

"Ah, the Ballerina!" their host cried, a smile of welcome illuminating his deeply lined face as he stepped forward to greet Raine in faultless English. "Good evening. I admired your performance greatly in *Petroushka*."

Before Raine could correct him, Bran interposed with a low rueful laugh. "I'd better warn you, Massimo. You're going to be seeing double all evening."

Raine's soft laughter echoed his. "I'm afraid Bran's right, Signor Chiari. That was my twin sister you admired. I danced in *Les Patineurs*."

"Ah," he replied as he took her hand, his smiling brown eyes frank in their admiration. "That explains the intriguing variation in styles." Chiari turned back to Bran. "How lucky you are, du Rivage, to have two such dancers under one company roof."

Bran grinned. "Lucky?" he replied lightly. "It's like working in the hall of mirrors at a fun house. You never know who's going to jump out at you."

Raine shot him a playful glance of her own past their host's shoulder. "It's just that you scare too easily, Bran," she couldn't resist observing.

"Watch it, Raine," he riposted, eyes agleam as they swept down to caress the revealing outline of her breasts in the soft jersey. "Or I'll call your bluff on that one."

"Just try," she replied softly, oblivious to everything but the blue gaze pinning hers and the disturbing rush of sensation the man ignited deep inside her.

The spell was broken as Chiari's voice rang out between them, and they forced themselves to focus on what he was saying. "Ah, here's the other half of the beautiful team!"

Raine turned to watch Riva approach, elegant in black silk trousers and a bare-cut chemise peeping from beneath the soft ivory of her jacket.

"It's an honor, *signorina*," Massimo greeted the newcomer, bending low over her hand to brush it with his lips. Riva blossomed like a tropical flower in response to the Italian's courtly greeting, and the two were soon deep in conversation.

Quickly then the drawing room filled up as the rest of the corps found their way downstairs. Bran had drifted away to join Paul at the bar, and Raine found herself in the midst of a lively three-way exchange with Danny and Tracey, who persisted in teasing the blushing Swiss danseur unmercifully about his role as the Moor.

The mood for the evening had been set. Like unruly kids set free at the end of a long school year, the dancers carried on outrageously. Tracey, as usual, was the ringleader, breaking off her laughing badinage to erupt in a gleefully self-mocking rendition of her Folies routine. Everyone automatically looked around for Riva to jump in and take over center floor from the blond imp, but the ballerina seemed oblivious to the others, her attention focused exclusively on Massimo Chiari.

Though Raine joined in the fun, she was constantly aware of Bran's presence. Now and again their eyes would meet across the room as if, despite the crowd that separated them, they were still carrying on their own teasing and quite private tête-à-tête.

The lively party mood wasn't dampened even when the majordomo interrupted the cocktail hour to announce in rather sepulchral tones that dinner was served. The dancers, however, did pay due homage to the exquisite meal, which began with a fragrant consommé, followed by a fish course, a palate-cleansing sherbet, and finally roast pheasant on a bed of wild rice. Glancing down the long table, Raine was amused to see that only Riva and Massimo, still engrossed in each other, were oblivious to the culinary tour de force on the plates in front of them. For the first time Raine wondered what on earth they could have to talk about.

Coffee and brandy were served in the drawing room, accompanied by appropriately mellow conversation. The restful tone vanished, however, as soon as Tracey wandered over toward the French doors. "Hey, gang, it's snowing!" she exclaimed.

Someone switched on the outside lights, illuminating the tumble of enormous flakes that had already left a spun-sugar dusting on the marble terrace. A blast of cold air whooshed into the room as Tracey flung open the doors and went out to make tracks in the unexpected wintry carpet. The other dancers followed in delight.

All except for Raine, who stood back in the shadows watching them. She shivered uncontrollably against the cold wetness and the old lingering fears it brought to mind.

She started a moment later as she felt a pair of hands encircling her upper arms and warm breath against her cool temple. She knew at once that it was Bran. The connection between them had been strong all evening; he must have sensed her fears. With a little sigh she leaned back against him, savoring his warmth and strength.

"You need a winter's fire, not this," he murmured against her hair. "Come on. I'll pour you a brandy."

She went with him unprotestingly as he led her out of the drawing room and up the staircase with its curving rail. They walked the length of the gallery, finally stopping before a pair of ornate carved doors. As they stepped inside, Raine saw that he had an entire suite to himself. A fire burned in the wrought-iron grate, sending flickering shadows up along the pale-veined marble front.

She sat down gratefully on the ottoman before the fire, her gaze drawn to the warmth and light of the crackling cedar logs. She looked up, startled, when Bran knelt beside her. Then surprise gave way to a little shock of pleasure as she felt his hands gently reaching for the carefully bound leg beneath the skirt of her gown.

"Let me help you, granny," he couldn't resist teasing again as his fingers unfastened the tight elastic.

She laughed down at him, a soft retort ready on her lips. "Look who's talking, old man! I'm surprised Paul and the others don't call you papa." As she said that, Raine reached out to finger the streak of gray where his hair curled at the nape.

Bran turned his head and pressed his lips to her wrist, then let his tongue explore the ridge of tendon that vanished under the sensitive surface of her inner arm. Her pulse quickened and throbbed as pinpoints of sensation rushed along her shoulder to her throat, setting that pulse afire, as well.

It was he who reluctantly withdrew, focusing his attention once more on her exposed length of leg. Her eyes followed the manipulation of his fingers, supple and dark against the pale bare silkiness of her skin. Warmth and a nascent excitement flooded every inch of her, mocking and spurning the silent snowfall outside the window.

"That's the most I can do," he said finally, his fingers still moving in a feathery-light stroke against the tender hollow of her knee. "I think you'd better soak it in the whirlpool."

Her eyes flickered open with the lazy awareness of a cat's. "Whirlpool?" she repeated.

For answer, he got up and went to a narrow door at the opposite end of the room. Opening it, he gestured inside. Raine stared past him at the mist rising from a free-form tub set into green marble tiles and banks of delicate maidenhair ferns. Her gaze shifted back to Bran. "You've got to be kidding me!" she laughed, her voice gentle and warm.

He grinned. "Go on in while I get the brandy."

The green-tiled room was a steamy jungle whose only illumination came from the cold night sky beyond the arched window. Pulling her dress up over her knees, Raine sat on the edge of the tub and dangled her legs in the hot swirling water.

The whirlpool jets felt wonderful on her tight calf muscles, and she threw her head back with an utterly relaxed sigh. With trailing fingers she reached up to brush her hair back, her eyes roving to the window and the misted blackness that fell away to a river valley far below.

When the door opened behind her, she glanced languidly around; her eyes flicked upward in surprise. Though his face was shadowed, the spilled lamplight from the other room outlined the hard sculptured contours of Bran's bare shoulders and limbs as he stood in the doorway. He'd changed into a pair of very brief swimming trunks, and in his hands were two small snifters of brandy. The unexpected sight of his nearly naked body sent a tremble of excitement through her, and it was with slightly shaking fingers that she accepted the proffered drink.

Bran eased down beside her on the tub's edge and

reached across to clink his glass against hers. "Here's to your success, Ballerina," he murmured. "You danced better today than I've ever seen you dance, Raine. You've come a long way."

"Thanks," she murmured huskily in reply. The praise was sweet and heady, yet she was disturbed by a fleeting look in his eyes that she couldn't quite fathom...sadness, perhaps, or a sense of loss. Somehow that look emboldened her. "But I still wish you were partnering me, instead of Paul."

Bran shook his head in disbelief as he eased into the tub and sat on the submerged ledge. "God, you're a stubborn woman. What am I going to do with you?"

"Simple." She grinned. "Dance with me."

Silence fell between them, and Raine lifted her glass to her lips, savoring the warmth that suffused her. The velvet darkness surrounding them seemed to invite confidences, and after a while Bran spoke again, his voice low and bemused. "Life can be strange, Raine. I asked myself a thousand times why it had to be ballet. I love it; it's my life. But sometimes I get the feeling that I betrayed my father all over again. It was like a slap in the face, an all-too-painful reminder of Lucille."

Raine was quick to notice the tensing of his neck muscles as he said the name, and automatically she reached out to rub her fingers gently upward over his nape to where his hair just curled over it. "Lucille?" she repeated.

"My mother." The reply was curt, and Raine felt the tension radiating downward over his broad shoulders.

"She must be very proud of what you've achieved," Raine observed softly, at the same time pressing her fingertips in a circular massaging pattern across his bare sinewed flesh.

"Maybe she is...I don't know," he replied in a distant tone that held a note of sarcasm.

"Don't you want to talk about her, Bran?" Raine asked gently. "I have a feeling she's part of the reason why you've stopped dancing. You're punishing her and yourself at the same time." As she said it, Raine felt the muscles of his neck go rigid.

For a long while he was silent. When he spoke again, his tone was still reflective, but angry. "I never saw her much after their divorce—only when she breezed through town. She'd let me sit in the wings while she performed. I was enthralled, but I hated her, too. Dance got in my blood, much to my father's sorrow."

"So you tried to give it up," Raine whispered sympathetically.

Bran nodded curtly. "It didn't work. I had to dance. I had no choice but to return."

"And you're happy?"

His shoulders lifted slightly. "As happy as most people."

She laughed, the sound washing down over him in a caressing wave. "You're not most people."

Bran reached up to trap Raine's hand against his skin as he half turned to glance up at her. "And what am I?" he growled.

"Hard, driving, practical," she replied, her tone teasing and rueful. "That's why you admire Riva so. You have some of the same qualities."

"You despise me for that?"

"No," she whispered. Her hands lay still and warm against his neck. "I could never despise you."

When he spoke again his voice was low and fluid, the voice she loved. "Don't stop," he murmured in English as he pressed her fingers against his flesh. "I love your touch."

The words excited her, and again she felt the electric intimacy that could so easily bind them to one another. Leaning forward, she scooped up a handful of water and dribbled it over his shoulders, following the trail of droplets with two fingertips toward the dark hollow at the base of his throat. Bran caught her hand and drew it up to his face, using his tongue with an exquisitely slow lingering pressure to lap the wetness from her palm.

Seeing the rush of warmth that suffused her in response to the heady sensuality of his touch, Bran turned in the water and knelt on the submerged ledge between her uncovered legs. Raine sucked in her breath as his hands, warm and wet and strong, came up to caress the lithe contours of her thighs before reaching even higher to her bodice, where his fingers deftly unfastened the row of tiny buttons. The dress fell back from her shoulders to reveal the soft outline of her breasts and waist in a lace-fronted silken teddy that was the color of fresh apricots.

His hands grasped her waist as he drew her to her feet on the ledge and the dress dropped to her ankles. "Raine, do you have any idea how your dancer's grace enthralls me?" he whispered huskily as his eyes raked upward with naked desire. "You *are* a sorceress."

His gaze ignited an answering fire within her. Never before had she glimpsed the very depths of his emotional intensity, never until now. He had been so careful to keep himself in check.

Bran lifted her free of the ledge and the folds of her dress, and she twined her legs around his waist, savoring the intimate feel of his torso against the softness of her inner thighs. He swung her around in a spiral that brought them lower and lower toward the surface of the roiling water. Raine lifted her face to his, and their lips met in a slow smoldering explosion of passion. Hungrily, unashamedly their kisses devoured as their limbs slid wetly past one another in intoxicating collision. They submerged for an instant, and Bran relaxed his firm hold so that his fingers could gently caress and probe beneath the gossamer edge of lace.

As they resurfaced, Raine's quickened breathing became a mingled gasp and moan as she felt the wet brushstroke of his hair-matted thighs against the silken smoothness of her own. They were on the far side of the tub now, and Bran reached outside the pool past her shoulder to flick a switch. Instantly the water was bathed in a soft green blue light that banished the protective mantle of darkness.

Her legs now twined around his in wicked intimacy, Raine found herself half reclining on the tub ledge. Dimly she realized that the whirlpool timer had clicked off, leaving them in a still lagoon, where every sound and movement was suddenly magnified. The ragged harshness of her breathing caused her breasts to rise and fall in a delicious flutter that drew Bran's gaze downward. She followed the slow raking intensity of his eyes over the wet silk, and trembled now as if his eyelashes had actually brushed the coral tips of her nipples. But his glance only touched there for an instant before sliding down to linger on the dark furred softness springing against the sheer lace.

Slowly Bran leaned forward, his mouth covering hers even as his fingers dipped beneath the lace to stroke and explore her tendriled femininity. She moaned against his lips, opening a sweet passageway for the gentle uncurling thrust of his tongue. The kiss was long and deep, intimately probing along with the deft sensuality of his fingertips, until Raine felt her hips arching shamelessly against the sweet agonizing pressure of his touch.

His head drew slowly back from hers, and Raine's breath escaped in a soft exhalation of mounting desire. Bran lifted her out of the hot still water.

"Let's get out of here," he whispered as his eyes roamed over her with hungry impatience. "We'll dry off by the fire."

"Afraid I'll melt again?" she teased against his ear.

His low laughter was as soft and hypnotic as his caresses. "You won't get away from me that easily."

Minutes later they lay side by side on two thick black Turkish towels, their eyes feasting on the flicker of light and shadow as it played over their recumbent forms. Bran reached out to touch the last gleaming vestige of wetness on her skin, his fingertips moving in a lazy curve up and down the length of her leg.

"Bran, don't. I can't think straight when you're touching me," she scolded in a soft voice, her anger belied by the soft tremble of excitement in her voice.

"Don't you like it?" he asked ingenuously, his fingers continuing their sensuous discovery, sending fire racing along every nerve in her body.

Raine's gaze swooped up to meet the pretended innocence in his, and unexpectedly she laughed. The rich sound distracted him from the pain reflected in her eyes. Now she looked at him in a lingering way, a way that made his heart pound with growing excitement. "You're the sorcerer, not I," she whispered up at him, the words as gently caressing as her eyes. Lifting her face to the warm shield of his chest, she parted her lips to nuzzle the moist cloud of hair in a slow back-and-forth motion.

The sweet sensuality of her touch brought a muffled groan to his lips. "Raine," he muttered hoarsely, "let me make love to you now."

Again he felt the gentle back-and-forth motion of her face against his hungry flesh, but this time it was a gesture of denial. "Not here, Bran," she murmured almost inaudibly. "Not now."

"No one will know," he countered, impatient.

She reached up with gently inquisitive fingers to trace the etched outline of his mouth. "I'll know."

"You're damned right you'll know," he growled, his voice tense with an urgency that threatened to inflame her own smoldering passions, but she managed to hold herself in check.

"Bran, please! What I meant," she went on more softly still, "is if we do this now, I'll never be sure that what I've achieved was on my own or because you willed it. And I'll never know if I stayed on stage because I was a good dancer—or a good lover."

"And once you've made it, then what?" he retorted with scarcely veiled anger, his hand tightening at her waist.

Raine lifted her shoulders in a helpless shrug. "Do we have to answer that now?"

His reply was harsh, quick. "I'm sure as hell not going to wait for tomorrow."

"I'm sorry, Bran."

Raine ached inside from wanting him, yet she knew she had no choice. *Why,* she asked herself as she made her way down the long empty gallery to her own room. *Why do I have to punish us both?*

CHAPTER ELEVEN

A NORTHERLY WIND slammed across the terrace fronting the hilltop basilica of Sacré-Coeur, causing Raine to push her gloved hands more deeply into the pockets of her jacket. She hated the cold, but she hated even more the thought of being cooped up in the apartment. Weeks of crowded trains, dim auditoriums and cramped hotel rooms had made her claustrophobic. She was relieved to have these two days to unpack and unwind, to wander through the city that she'd come to regard as her home.

As she climbed the steps toward the cathedral doors, Raine glanced up in surprise to see a small familiar figure emerge. Nina Tarsamova was clad in black from her felt beret to her low-heeled shoes, except for the burgundy muffler wound around her throat. Raine smiled at the image that rose mischievously to mind—that of an elegant black widow spider spinning and weaving with a single grand design in mind.

The two women met at the top of the stairs.

"It's not Russian Orthodox," the old ballet mistress began without preamble as she glanced back over her shoulder at the white marble facade of the basilica, "but at my age one can't be choosy."

Raine laughed as she leaned across to brush the

woman's cheek with her lips. "A practical philosophy if I ever heard one. How are you, Madame T?"

"Six weeks haven't changed me," the Russian replied with a little snort of impatience as her eyes fixed sharply on Raine. "Now, how was the tour?"

"Challenging."

"I hear that you are dancing well."

"Not quite well enough."

Madame nodded, satisfied. "A perfectionist, I see. I like your stubbornness. I was the same at your age."

"I meant that the cold has begun to bother my leg," Raine clarified, curiously unwilling to have the wily old woman identify with her in any way. She'd had enough of *madame*'s intrigues.

"Ah," *madame* answered simply. "If that's all that bothers you, then I have a pleasant surprise in store. I haven't told anyone, so you'll be the first to know. The company is going to Provence for the month of January. I've had the offer of a studio in Stes-Maries-de-la-Mer."

"But why are we leaving Paris again?"

For the first time the ballet mistress smiled. "My bones are suffering from old war injuries, too. Besides," she added crisply, "a Canadian dance troupe has offered a small fortune for the use of our studio, so the Ballet du Monde will come out well ahead on the account ledger."

Raine was amused. "You've discussed your plan with Bran?"

Madame shrugged airily. "Why bother him with

details when he's just got back? Especially when I know he would have opposed me on this."

"Why?"

"Let's just say the south of France does not hold particularly happy memories for him."

"It has to do with his mother."

Raine's reply was more an observation than a question, causing *madame* to study her sharply. "He has told you?"

"A little. I just find it ironic that a mother and son with so much in common should be like strangers."

Madame Tarsamova's black eyes gleamed. "They are too much alike."

Raine bit her lip at that. "And he suspects other women of being like her."

The older woman regarded her with a shrewd look as she burrowed more deeply into her collar. "You are growing very wise, my dear." She shook her head with an air of impatience. "Now I must get back to the studio. There are mountains of paperwork to get through before the company leaves."

Raine's chance meeting with Madame T had forced her thoughts back to Bran, though she hadn't wanted to think of him at all. It was still too painful to remember the curious look of betrayal and anger in his eyes when she'd turned away from him in the villa.

Unable to withstand the biting wind any longer, Raine retraced her steps back down the hill to the apartment and quietly let herself in. She could only gape in astonishment at the man who sat on the sofa, a glass of sherry in hand as he leafed through Riva's bulging scrapbook.

Recovering at once, Raine crossed to him with a smile. "Signor Chiari, I had no idea you were coming to Paris!"

He stood up and took her hand. "Signorina Raine, a delight to see you again. It was your sister who so kindly invited me to come." As he offered this explanation, Riva stepped out of the bedroom, dressed stylishly for an afternoon out. Raine shot her twin a glance before agreeing smoothly with their guest's observation. "Yes, she is kind, isn't she?"

Riva studiously ignored the mingled look of mischief and irony in Raine's eyes. "Shall we be off, Massimo?" As she retrieved her jacket from the closet, Riva explained, "We're going to a new Picasso exhibit at the Centre Culturel. Massimo is hoping to talk the artist's widow out of a lithograph or two for his villa."

Ignoring this none-too-subtle reference to Massimo Chiari's wealth, Raine smiled warmly at the Italian and asked with an air of innocent inquiry, "How long are you in town for?"

He inclined his head, charmingly, apologetically. "Just the one day, I'm afraid. Business compels me to return to Italy, but I hope to visit Paris with much greater frequency in the future."

Riva slipped her arm through his and smiled. "Massimo's taking me to Chez Martinique tonight for dinner." Before he could extend the invitation to include Raine, Riva steered him deftly toward the front door, and they were gone.

Raine stared after them bemusedly, her lips curved in a wry smile. Once Riva knew what she wanted, she made no bones about it—especially if the patron she had chosen was vastly more wealthy than Monsieur Santandre. Nina Tarsamova wouldn't be displeased, either.

Her train of thought was interrupted by a light rap on the front door. Thinking Riva or Massimo had forgotten something, she moved to open it just as Margrit Blake popped her head around. "Hello, Raine. I ran into your sister on the steps, and she said you were up here. I just came by to chat and see how your road trip went."

Sometime later, after they'd caught up on news and gossip, Margrit reached out to take the cup of tea that Raine had made for her, stirring it meditatively. "Who's Riva's new flame?" she asked with a pretense of casualness. "He looks as though he's got pots of money."

Raine laughed. "Oh, he does. He inherited a Tuscan wine empire. Massimo's the owner of that fabulous villa I was describing. He and Riva were inseparable at his dinner party. Tonight he's going to wine and dine her at Chez Martinique."

Margrit glanced up sharply. "The lovely Riva didn't waste a minute."

"Listen, that's my sister you're talking about!" Raine retorted in feigned reproof, still laughing.

But Margrit didn't see the humor. "Sorry, ducks," she replied, slamming her cup back down on the low table without even tasting the tea. "But it infuriates me the way she hurts Pierre, blithely dangling him along until she's found someone more...suitable."

Raine looked at her red-haired friend with mingled sympathy and amusement. It was apparent that Margrit was growing very fond of her fellow artist, even if he didn't reciprocate the feeling. "If Pierre's still being hurt, it's because he wants to be," Raine said quietly. "You know that old saying about love being blind."

Margrit looked up at that, her hazel eyes dancing with new brightness. "Yes, well, perhaps we should open Pierre's eyes a little."

"What do you mean?"

Margrit leaned back in the armchair and smiled innocently. "Perhaps we could *all* use a spot of fancy dining."

THE ANCIENT GRAY MORRIS skated along the crowded boulevards with the panache of a Mercedes. Behind the wheel, Margrit seemed oblivious to the utter madness of night-time Parisian traffic, and Raine marveled at the Englishwoman's sangfroid.

In other respects the impetuous redheaded artist was rather less restrained. Raine shifted uncomfortably on top of the springs poking through the worn leather of the passenger seat, half wishing now that she hadn't let Margrit talk her into the bit of devilry they were about to embark on. She had a suspicion, too, that Margrit hadn't told her everything when she'd called her that evening after leaving Raine's apartment in a tearing rush.

The parking attendant looked askance at the battered automobile when it drew to a halt beneath the covered portico in front of Chez Martinique. But Margrit was oblivious to his snobbery as she jauntily handed him the key and went to join her friend on the curb.

Raine's misgivings grew as they approached the entrance of the exclusive restaurant. "Margrit, I thought the British were aboveboard and honorable and all that. But this doesn't seem exactly cricket to me," she said with an accusing laugh.

The redhead waved her arm as she had at the valet. "Never mind! Just think of poor Pierre."

"Where *is* our poor Pierre?" Raine inquired. "He was supposed to meet us out front."

Once inside the doors, the women found themselves in an exotic other world. Plants grew down in lush profusion from a high cane ceiling, where several fans whirred as languidly as if the locale were the French Antilles rather than winterbound Paris. Through the dining-room entrance they caught glimpses of dark-skinned waiters in bright calypso costume, who called to one another in an indecipherable Creole patois. The sounds of a lively marimba band wafted out from the bar, which was wall-to-wall people.

Slowly they made their way through the crowd, with Margrit in the lead, rising on tiptoe from time to time to get her bearings. "There they are!" she cried at last in satisfaction.

Raine had no time to speculate on what she meant by "they," because the two women suddenly found themselves wedged up against the long curving bar directly in front of Pierre, who was nursing a beer and conversing desultorily with someone next to him.

"Hello, there!" Margrit greeted him brightly.

His head swiveled around, and he grinned at her as he stood up. "Typical artist," Pierre teased. "No concept of time at all. We've been waiting a half hour."

But Raine wasn't paying any attention to their good-natured raillery. Her eyes were fixed on the hard familiar profile beyond Pierre. Bran stubbed out his half-smoked cigarette in the ashtray and turned around, his own gaze narrowing sharply when he saw Margrit's companion.

The redhead's eyes danced between them, and it was apparent that she was enjoying this additional little twist of mischief she'd stamped on the evening. Raine shot her a daggered look that Margrit blithely ignored as she explained, "Bran was so pleased with the costuming work I'd done while the company was gone that he promised me a special treat of my choosing. Wasn't this a marvelous idea?"

From the dark look on Bran's face, Raine guessed he was even less enthused than she was. Nevertheless, he stood up and began to play the role of gracious host. "Shall we go on into the dining room, then? They're holding our table."

Margrit slipped her arm through Pierre's, leaving Raine no option but to fall into step beside Bran. She was grateful for the noise and bustle that precluded any conversation between them; still, she couldn't help but be aware of his proximity as they threaded their way through the lively crowd. Glancing up, she found his gaze focused on the rich green sleeves of her jersey gown. It was the same dress she'd worn to Massimo's dinner party. Recalling that evening, she flushed and wondered if Bran was remembering the same thing.

She was grateful when the maître d' sat them side by side rather than across the table. At least she might be spared the assessment of those cutting blue eyes all evening! Raine sensed that the argument they'd left unfinished in his suite at the villa still simmered between them. But she had no wish to conclude it, because she knew who would win. The thought of succumbing in his arms was a burning temptation that haunted her every minute.

Margrit's bobbing red head distracted Raine from her troubled thoughts, and she observed the woman's actions with a smile. Margrit craned and twisted her neck as she pretended to study the restaurant decor and watch the dance band. Raine leaned forward, her chin cupped in hand, waiting for the inevitable pronouncement, which wasn't long in coming.

"I say!" Margrit cried with slyly innocent enthusiasm as she shot Raine a quick wink. "Isn't that your sister across the room?"

But Raine's eyes were fixed on Pierre, and she bit her lip at the pitifully swift way his head shot up in response to Margrit's words. His brown eyes clouded over with mingled pain and anger as he stared past Raine's shoulder. Reluctantly she turned around, not too terribly surprised to see Riva and Massimo with their heads close together at a small table near the band.

Finally Bran turned to glance across the crowded dining room. When he turned around again, he fixed his gaze directly on Raine. "Shall we dance?" he suggested with an abruptness that startled her. Before she could reply, his hand had closed around her arm, and she was being pulled none too gently to her feet.

Bran's arms slipped around her waist, and as the couple moved to the syncopated West Indian beat, Raine couldn't help but savor the novel sensation of dancing like this with him. He moved as easily on the ballroom floor as he did on stage or in the studio. Whenever they were together, he had that curious power over her, the ability to bring her body so in tune with his that their mutual awareness became an exquisite rhythm. Their legs slid against one another's in a slow sensuous brush that made them oblivious to the rest of the couples on the crowded floor. Raine fought the urge to lay her head against his chest and twine her arms around his neck.

It was Bran who broke the mood of drifting intimacy. His hands tightened on Raine's waist as he pushed her away slightly and looked down at her. "Now," he began, "do you mind telling me what the hell's going on? I don't think it's coincidence that we all wound up so cozily in the same Parisian night spot."

She resented his harshness. "Why don't you ask Margrit?" she retorted.

His fingers dug insistently into her ribs. "I'm asking you. Is this your clever way of insuring that I know what Riva is up to? You want to make sure I see that Riva has a patron, too, is that it? You and Riva have been involved in a bloody game of one-upmanship ever since you arrived in Paris."

Raine's eyes darkened. "I told you before, Bran. I'm not interested in games."

"You may have told me, but I'm not convinced."

She breathed a sigh of vexation. "Look, Margrit engineered this little outing because she's had it with Pierre's puppy-dog adoration of Riva. She hoped the jolt of seeing Riva with another man would bring him back to earth."

"But why the devil involve me?" Bran scowled in annoyance.

Raine's shoulders lifted in a subtle shrug. "Because she knows you're Pierre's friend, I suppose, and she assumed you'd want to help. I'm surprised you haven't tried to intervene yourself long before this. You knew what Riva was like. Surely you never wanted to see him hurt so badly."

"I tried to intervene once." Bran laughed, though the sound was curiously lacking in warmth. "He accused me of wanting Riva for myself."

Raine's eyes were vaguely troubled as they played over his features. "Does he still believe that?"

Bran's low laughter drifted over her again. "Not now. Pierre and I understand each other far better. In fact, we tend to commiserate over our...mutual weaknesses." As he said that, Brandon slowly relaxed his fingers. The tips were almost caressing against the soft thin fabric of her gown.

Raine flushed as the subtle meaning of his words overtook her. "Please take me back to the table," she requested rather sharply, trying to ignore the hot pleasure his touch aroused in her.

But he only laughed again. "The music isn't over."

They continued to move in delicious harmony across the floor, yet now Raine sensed that each glance, each casual touch of his was meant to subtly taunt her.

Inevitably the music did end. Though Bran's arms relinquished Raine's waist, his hand took firm possession of hers as he led her toward Massimo and Riva's band-side table. Seeing Bran, the Italian stood up and smiled cordially at his friend, inviting them both for a drink.

"Thanks, Massimo, but we're having dinner with friends at another table. Why don't the two of you stop over there instead?"

As the men exchanged pleasantries, the twins exchanged assessing glances. Riva's smug, cat-that-got-the-cream look sagged a little as her watchful eyes took in Bran's and Raine's twined hands. Aggravated, Raine couldn't help wondering what more her sister could possibly want.

As the foursome crossed the room, Pierre Junot's bearded countenance seemed to hover like a forlorn beacon. Raine's heart twisted a little at the expression in his eyes when he saw Massimo's hand on her sister's waist and the way Riva fitted herself so closely into the curve of his arm. Once at the table, Riva greeted Pierre with the indifference of a stranger. The ballerina's attention was reserved for Massimo and Bran, as if she hoped to elicit some smoldering spark of jealousy from both men—particularly from that cold blue stare.

Pierre turned away stiffly and looked over at Margrit. "Care to dance?" he suggested curtly, ignoring the others.

Sympathy, amusement and not a little anger warred in Margrit's expressive hazel eyes, but she made herself smile. "I thought you'd never ask," she chided him gently. As the two artists stood up from the table, Pierre shot one last look in Riva's direction before turning away without a word.

That set the tone for the evening. Eventually, signaling her defeat in the battle if not the war, Riva suggested she and Massimo return to their table. The foursome continued to eat, drink and dance.

Finally, when Raine thought she couldn't bear Bran's nearness for another second, Margrit suggested they call it a night. With unseemly haste she slyly whisked Pierre off in the Morris, leaving Raine alone with Bran. She had no choice but to accept his offer of a ride back to her apartment. Had that been more of the Englishwoman's clever planning, she wondered.

Her lips curved in a smile as she slid onto the cold black leather of the bucket seat. She had been so eager to play matchmaker for the sympathetic artists, not knowing that Margrit must have planned all along to give her a double dose of her own medicine!

Bran shot her a questioning look as he slid behind the wheel of his Spider. "Do I get to share the joke?"

Raine shrugged. "It's nothing, really. I was just thinking that the older I get, the more ironies life has to fling at me."

"You think too much." His voice echoed accusingly between them in the cold trapped air, and they drove in silence for a long while.

When she finally replied, her own voice sounded small and fragile. "It's safer than feeling too much."

"Your feeling is what's going to make you a great dancer," he countered roughly.

"No. What's going to make me a great dancer is hard work and discipline," she replied in a flat voice, as if she were reciting a catechism lesson. Raine stared ahead of her, her eyes following the dark curving lane they were traveling on.

Bran wheeled into the quiet square and braked

abruptly. His hand reached across and closed on hers as she fumbled for the door latch. "You're wrong."

"Damn it, what else is there?" she nearly shouted at him.

"There's this." Even as he grated out the words in a harsh whisper, his mouth closed on hers with forceful intensity, pushing her head back against the seat. The kiss was angry, invasive, an expression of feeling that was all too raw and powerful. Against her will she felt her own savage need rising to meet it. Their cold lips chafed and clung, the heat of their sudden collision setting off a firestorm that raged between them.

In that instant she opened herself completely to him. His tongue probed and tasted until she was incapable of thought, and still she moved her head, wanting more. She returned the naked burning kiss, measure for measure, her tongue thrusting unashamedly to meet his in desire that surged dangerously close to ecstasy.

Suddenly Raine dragged herself back from the brink, twisting her face from his as she pulled up on the latch. "Damn you!" she swore, her breath coming in short agonized pants.

But his hand closed around hers to prevent her escape. "You're a woman," he muttered, his own breath coming in harsh gasps. "You can't hide your feelings. You can't hold them back in a kiss anymore than you can in dance."

"I don't need to be told that by you!" she stormed.

Raine shook off his touch and stumbled from the car as passion and fury warred within her. Everything he'd said was true, but she couldn't face that. She was furious at how easily his drugging kisses could arouse her, furious that he had made her life so impossibly difficult at a time when the choice should have been simple and direct.

Without looking back, she ran for the stairs that led to the dark apartment.

CHAPTER TWELVE

RAINE SWUNG HER VALISE onto the metal rack high overhead, her knees digging into the worn velour of the second-class compartment seat. When she turned around again, she gave a little start of surprise to see Bran standing there. A slow blush rose in her cheeks as she remembered the wildly passionate kiss they'd exchanged in his car and the awkward constraint that had come between them later. But he didn't seem to notice her heightened color. He was staring at her hair.

Raine reached up with nervous fingers to touch the coronet of small lilies that she'd tucked into the top of her simple chignon. "They're the last three," she explained softly. "All the other blooms have already faded and died. I...I decided to take these few remaining ones with me while they were still fresh."

"You won't need them in the south. Provence usually manages to hold winter at bay." A smile touched his lips, it didn't quite reach his eyes.

Raine met his gaze unflinchingly. "You're sorry we're going, aren't you?"

He shrugged. "Paris is home."

"I've got only one home—the Ballet du Monde."

The wistfulness and determination blending in her soft voice caused Bran to smile again in that ambivalent way. "You should have been Nina's daughter; you're very much alike."

"That's not true!" Raine shook her head vigorously, and as she did so one of the lilies worked loose and fell from her hair.

Other travelers began to jostle Bran, filing into the compartment. He tossed his canvas duffel bag into the window seat opposite Raine's, then turned and disappeared down the aisle.

The train rocked forward and gradually picked up speed. Within minutes the last straggling suburbs were behind them and they were cleaving a path through the great forest of Fontainebleau with its wild stags and gigantic rock outcroppings.

As the train raced southward, Raine's thoughts inevitably turned to Bran. She wrestled with the puzzle of his refusal to dance, when such a decision could only cause him pain. She longed to reach out to him, but he didn't trust her enough to let her.

She stared pensively out the window. Soon the rhythmic motion of the train lulled her senses and she dozed, stirring from time to time to glance out the compartment window past the wooded hills and neat vineyards of the Burgundian countryside.

Much later she awakened. The lily that had fallen from her hair hours earlier had begun to droop where it lay on the narrow table beneath the train window. The sight of it made her unaccountably sad, and she forced her gaze upward to the picturesque landscape sliding past. The hustle and bustle of modern Lyon was far behind them. Now the Rhône valley opened onto rural farmland dotted with ancient châteaus and abbeys. Westward, the winter sun had already begun its descent over the rugged peaks of the Cévennes.

It was dark by the time the train chugged into the station at Avignon, so that Raine had only the vaguest impression of medieval ramparts whose battlements and towers brooded over the ancient city of the popes. Again a vague feeling of discontent swept over her. She was reminded of the hectic company tour, when so much of her time had been lived in the shadows of a theater. Where was the Provençal sunshine Madame T had promised?

THE OTHER DANCERS were already lined up on the theater stage, ready to begin practice, when Raine arrived. Hastily she tossed her jacket onto one of the front-row seats and hurried to join them.

She was late because she hadn't been able to resist a little early-morning exploration of the seaside town, Stes-Maries-de-la-Mer. Waves had lapped toward her on the deserted beach as she'd stared in delight across the Mediterranean. A wind blew steadily, chasing the light across the sea. There was a faint warmth to the air, as if it bore secrets from the distant North African shore, and she had been reluctant to leave it.

Raine's attention was recalled to the business at hand when Bran emerged from the upstage wing and plunked a chair on the stage. She was surprised to see that he'd forgone the customary unitard for a pair of comfortable jeans and a nubby sweater. He resembled one of the local fishermen, but there was no mistaking his business-as-usual attitude as he straddled the chair in his familiar manner and lifted the clipboard in his hand to rest it on the wooden back.

Strains of Tchaikovsky's lyrical music wafted out from the portable stereo in the corner as the dancers took their places, titters of excitement ruffling their professional demeanors, so that for a second they really resembled the cygnets they would portray in *Swan Lake*. Bran had purposefully fanned the excitement by announcing that the principal solo role—the dual part of Odette-Odile—was wide open. He intended to give each dancer a fair shot at it.

A few hours later the building tension of competition was diffused by laughter. In the midst of her solo audition, Tracey threw herself into the demanding character of Odile with a harum-scarum bravado that proved to be her undoing. Somehow her legs got tangled up in the *fouettés*, so that what should have been a dramatic evocation of evil whirling fury ended in an undignified sprawl midstage.

She gathered herself in a hilarious parody of injured dignity and made her unruffled way offstage. Even Bran's scowl of concentration gave way to a reluctant grin as he called out, "Next!"

Tracey sauntered up to Raine, who was last in line to audition. "Quite a show, wouldn't you say?" she demanded coquettishly of her friend.

Raine laughed her agreement. "Quite!"

"But you know, I don't even care!"

The American dancer bit her lip. "You'll be going home soon, won't you, Tracey?"

She nodded, eyes shining. "By winter's end, I think. That'll be the end of summer back home, and I've always sort of fancied an autumn wedding."

A fleeting pang of envy for the Australian woman's happiness touched Raine, but she was drawn back to the matter at hand as her name was called out.

Moving slowly toward center stage, Raine reviewed the tragic story line of the century-old fairy-tale ballet. On a moonlight hunt, Prince Siegfried observes a flock of swans alighting on a lake. One of them is a maiden who can only take on her true form in the midnight hours, because the evil Von Rothbart has put a curse on her. This is Odette, the soft lyrical creature the prince falls in love with. Raine danced the role with a delicate intensity that far outshone the other dancers.

Odette's alter ego, Odile, is a beautiful but conniving lookalike who is actually the daughter of the black magician, Von Rothbart. Odile's allure is dangerous, a cruel cunning fed by lightning sharpness.

Raine gamely danced the alternate role, putting everything she had into it. Her balletic climax didn't end in comic failure as Tracey's had, but neither was it a tour de force. Her performance didn't quite attain Riva's razzle-dazzle, the technical perfection that lent such colorful brilliance to the depiction. As she left the stage it struck Raine that as dancers, she and Riva formed an intriguingly tenuous balance, much like the mythical Odette-Odile.

When rehearsal ended, all the dancers were dismissed except for the Cameron women. Two pairs of lovely topaz eyes fixed curiously on Bran as he crossed the stage toward them.

He surveyed them both with a slow measuring gaze. Purely by chance, they'd worn the same practice outfits that morning: sleeveless black leotards over pale pink tights, the dancer's classic apparel. When he finally spoke, Bran's voice had the same measured equanimity expressed in his eyes. "I just wanted you two to know that I've already made my decision."

Raine swallowed nervously, her mouth dry as sand when Bran turned toward Riva and told her, "You'll dance Odile." But the ballerina's smug triumphant smile was short-lived, because Bran had turned back to Raine, and in the same voice announced, "You'll be Odette."

Both dancers stared at him with an expression of shocked disbelief, only to chorus together an instant later, "But that just isn't done!"

A glint of humor lightened the brooding shadows in his eyes. "That's precisely why I'm doing it—because it'll add an element of surprise and fun to an old overworked classic."

Riva brought her chin up at an imperious angle. "Odette-Odile belongs to one ballerina...." Though she didn't say it aloud, the word "me" hung arrogantly in the air.

Bran's expression was uncompromising. "And I say the dance will have a more interesting dimension this way."

"You're making a terrible mistake, Bran," Riva bristled. "I swear you are."

His gaze narrowed in response to her growing fury. "Is that a threat, Riva?"

Not bothering to answer him, the outraged ballerina turned on her heel and stormed off toward the wings.

Arms crossed casually in front of her, Raine had

observed this interchange with a troubled expression. Bran turned back to her, his brow drawn into a scowl of annoyance that made Raine want to lift her hand and gently smooth it away. He must have sensed her sympathy, because his tightly held mouth began to relax in an engaging wisp of a grin.

The quiet moment between them was unexpectedly shattered as Nina Tarsamova's voice called out from the darkened auditorium.

"Bran," the old ballet mistress called again with growing impatience. "May I speak to you one moment, please?"

He leaped agilely to the auditorium floor, then surprised Raine by turning back and offering with upraised arms to lift her down beside him. She went without hesitation, her pulse quickening when she realized that he was oddly reluctant to leave her.

They moved together up the wide center aisle toward the back row of the theater. As they came closer, Raine noticed with interest that Madame Tarsamova wasn't alone. There was another woman with her, in her fifties and still quite attractive. As the newcomer stood up, Raine sensed from her graceful bearing that she must have been a dancer at one time, too.

Bran's long easy gait slowed as he saw the second woman, and Raine's curious gaze darted between them. Her heart did a little flip-flop of nervousness when she noted the similarity in the two profiles. She made the connection at once, shaking her head a little at Madame Tarsamova's audacity. It was obvious she had invited Bran's mother to Stes-Maries!

"Bran, I've a surprise for you," *madame* said in

her austere way, though the pronouncement was wholly unnecessary, judging from the tension that already charged the air.

Raine stood back, wide eyes observant as she watched mother and son together. He brushed the woman's cheeks with his lips, yet Raine sensed the greeting was a formality that held little warmth. Both of them seemed curiously withdrawn.

"How are you, Lucille?"

"Very well, thank you, Brandon," the woman replied automatically, her American accent softened from years of living abroad. "Nina invited me here today. I've so rarely seen your stage work, you know."

"It's a little late, isn't it?" he answered with a curtness that bordered on rudeness. "I don't dance anymore."

"I'm sorry to hear that, Bran," she responded quietly. "Nina tells me you have a great talent."

"Inherited, no doubt." There was just a hint of sarcasm in his reply.

Lucille inclined her head stiffly. "I'll take that as a compliment."

"Take it any way you want to."

Lucille stiffened a little, but she met her son's gaze steadily.

Even *madame*'s iron-clad calm was affected by the hostility in the air, and she seized gratefully on the nearest diversion. "Raine, why are you lurking in the shadows? I want you to meet an old and dear friend of mine, Lucie Martina."

The woman's cool palm pressed Raine's for a moment, her smile pretty but distant. "Actually, it's Lucille Martin. My stage name was romanticized, because that's what audiences seemed to want thirty years ago.'' She paused, and the blue eyes that were so like Bran's swept down her figure. "I greatly admire your dancing, Miss Cameron. You'll make a fabulous Odile. One rarely sees such single-minded dedication these days.''

Madame Tarsamova interposed at that. "Lucie, I'm afraid you're confusing Raine with her sister, Riva.''

Bran's sharp laughter cut between them. "The sisters are more alike than you might think.'' Raine slanted him a questioning, half-angry look, wondering why he should suddenly wish to hurt her.

Nina ignored that sally. "Bran, you know you promised to have tea with me today,'' she began, injecting her voice with a command that he totally ignored.

"I'll see what I can do, but Paul's fighting a bout of bronchitis, and I promised to pick up something for him from the druggist.'' He paused a second before going on. "You know me, Nina. My duty is first and foremost to the company.'' There was a barbed edge to his words that made the two older women exchange quick glances, but Bran had already disappeared through the rear door of the theater with a curt, "See you later.''

Swallowing her annoyance as best she could, Nina fixed a gimlet eye on her young protégée. "Raine, why don't you come along with us, then?''

MADAME T'S APARTMENT was on the second floor of a converted church rectory that overlooked a forlorn graveyard overgrown with harebells and wild thyme.

Raine smiled when she saw that her employer had brought her silver-framed photographs and beloved samovar from Paris, so that the rustic apartment with its stone mantel and chintz curtains took on the semblance of her home office.

A strong pot of tea, sweet biscuits and a tray of sandwiches were served without ceremony. Raine had readily accepted the woman's invitation, because she was curious to learn more about Lucille Martin and her relationship with her son. But whether it was done subconsciously or otherwise, the two older women effectively blocked her participation in the conversation by steering it to a distant past of dancers and intrigues that had no meaning at all for Raine.

Lucille glanced in the young ballerina's direction from time to time, and she must have sensed the questions lurking in the other woman's eyes; her own expression grew steadily more unrevealing.

Each time a door slammed or a dog barked in the distance, the three women looked up, the same unspoken question hovering in the air: would Bran put in an appearance? Two hours had passed, and it was apparent that Lucille had given up. She was just pushing her chair back from the table when there came a sharp rap on the door and he breezed in. Though he'd pulled a sports coat on over his jeans and sweater, his black hair was tousled. He brought the scent of the sea in with him.

"Sorry I'm late," he said indifferently, "but I didn't think I'd be missed. With three generations of ballerinas in one room, I thought you'd have plenty to discuss."

Nina regarded him with undisguised annoyance, fuming that he'd refused to fall in with her carefully laid plans. "Your mother was just about to leave," she chastised him. "Perhaps you'd care to walk her down to her car."

Bran nodded, not looking at Lucille. "Are you ready too, Raine?"

Madame shot the young dancer a warning look, which Raine also pointedly ignored. "Sure," she replied, standing at once.

The three descended the stairs in a silence that wasn't broken until Bran pulled open the door of his mother's gray Citroën. Lucille paused as she was about to climb inside, resting her hands lightly on top of the door as her eyes played over her son's features. "I've been teaching dance these past several years in my own studio," she said, almost as if pretending to herself that Bran had actually asked the question. "I...you might enjoy seeing a class sometime," she went on tentatively.

Bran nodded curtly. "Thanks for the invitation, but you know what preproduction schedules are like."

"Yes, I suppose I do." Lucille pursed her lips. "Look, Bran. I know I haven't been the ideal mother through the years, but don't you think we could begin to behave like something more than strangers?"

"We are strangers, aren't we?"

"We all make our choices in life," she returned quietly. "Looking back now, I suppose I made a few bad ones. But I can't go on apologizing forever. Don't be like your father, Bran. Don't be that harsh and unforgiving. I was hoping we could get to know each other again.''

He looked at her for a long moment. "You're asking a lot from me, Lucille. Old wounds take a long time to heal."

"I suppose they do." Lucille studied him with thoughtful eyes that held just a hint of pain. But when she glanced back at Raine, the smile she flashed was poised and professional. "Goodbye, Miss Cameron. By the way, that invitation to visit my villa includes you, too."

"Thanks, Mrs.—Miss Martin," Raine answered. "I'd like that."

Stepping back then as she slid behind the wheel, Bran and Raine watched in silence until the car had disappeared along a bend in the road that would take Lucille to Marseille. Raine turned her gaze toward Bran, observing him from beneath her lashes. Her heart twisted a little at the hurt that was revealed for an instant in his usually hard features. She longed to question him and somehow ease his pain but wisely sensed that any intrusion into the privacy of his thoughts would be resented.

Instead she turned to him with a smile and asked casually, "Do you feel like walking some more?"

He glanced down at her with a distracted air before finally replying, "Sure. Why not?"

They headed toward the deserted beach at the edge of town, where several weatherbeaten fishing caiques were pulled up in a neat row on the sand. Beyond was a tumble of high rocks that they clambered over unhesitatingly. The wind was high but not biting, its sharpness blunted by the soft Provençal light that glimmered and danced on the waves as they broke on the shore.

Walking on, they came to a small cove entirely sheltered from the wind. Sea flowers and lemon balm fought the salt air to grow in delightful profusion from the rocky nooks and crannies. Bran and Raine sat down with their backs to the warm granite and stared out to sea.

It was she who finally spoke. "I haven't thanked you yet for giving me such a plum role."

A crooked grin touched his lips. "What? You're not griping because it's only half a plum?"

She eyed him warily. "Why *did* you divide the role? It's pretty unorthodox."

"I'm an unorthodox man," he teased.

Raine turned to face him, her eyes shadowed with troubled speculation. "I can't help thinking you did it because you couldn't resist bringing Riva down a notch or two."

Bran arched his head back to stare at the empty sky. Then, reaching out to break off a stalk of lemon balm, he brushed it meditatively along the length of her jawline, the bittersweet aroma mingling with salt tang. "So you think my motivation was to punish Riva instead of reward you, is that it?" His laughter was brusque, harsh.

Though she flushed, Raine was still determined to have her answer. "Why *did* you give me Odette?"

Bran caught his lower lip between his teeth, his sea-colored eyes pinning her with a look that was half taunt, half caress. "Why do you want to know?" he countered. "Are you worried that I gave it to you out of love, instead of merit?"

Her heart quickened dangerously at the unexpected words, until she found the subtle sarcasm underlying them. She understood now that he was mocking her with the conversation they'd exchanged in his bedroom at Massimo's villa. She'd been afraid to give herself to him for fear of not being able to trust his objectivity in the studio afterward. How silly and futile her overweening pride seemed to her now!

Raine's lips curved as she met his eyes. "I suppose I deserved that crack."

"Yes, you did." His grin dispelled a little of the brooding undercurrent that rippled just below the surface.

They were both quiet then as they stared out to sea. Somehow in that protected cove, an easy intimacy had caught them both and held them. Raine wanted to prolong it, to talk to him about everything she thought and feared and wanted. But she was afraid to speak and disturb the mood.

It was Bran who stirred first, standing and pulling her to her feet beside him. "Come on, we'd better get back. The sea air's pretty bracing, and I wouldn't want to see you get sick."

She smiled at his concern. "Don't worry. If I do, you know that Riva will have understudied my role to perfection," she teased him.

"No one's going to take that role from you," Bran growled. "You worked for it; you deserve it."

Raine should have been thrilled to hear that from his lips. The words were a tremendous accolade. Yet she sensed the lack of real warmth behind them. They'd been spoken as one professional to another. Raine's heart contracted in sudden fear as she wondered how much she'd given up in exchange for the achievement of her goals.

They walked back to town without a word, but her mood of quiet despair was broken unexpectedly when Bran stopped in front of the theater and turned to her. "I'm running up to Avignon tomorrow to have a look around. Do you have any interest in the place?"

The look of tension around her eyes eased at once. "That's the city with the dark battlements where we stopped last night, isn't it?" He nodded, waiting. "I'd love to go," she said softly.

His own expression grew subtly less guarded and watchful. "Good," he replied with a quick grin. "We'll take off after one o'clock practice tomorrow."

Buoyed up by the prospect, Raine needed no music at all to sail through afternoon rehearsal. Tomorrow gleamed brightly in her thoughts.

CHAPTER THIRTEEN

THE EARLY AFTERNOON was fine and warm, like a window into spring. As he'd promised, Bran came by for Raine directly after rehearsal, but she was almost late, reluctant to tear herself away from the theater. Raine felt a keen responsibility toward the solo role she'd been given. She didn't want to let Bran or the company down.

But now the ballet was forgotten as she rolled down the window of the gray Simca Bran had rented and stared out past the hundreds of mirrored ponds dotting the marshy landscape inland from Stes-Maries-de-la-Mer. The Camargue, Bran had told her the region was called, was a land of French fighting bulls and sturdy ponies. They drove along the country highway for miles, occasionally passing rutted lanes leading to whitewashed farmhouses with straw roofs.

Raine leaned back against the headrest, content to feel the mild wind rushing past her. They spoke very little, and that gentle silence somehow fed her contentment, too. She glanced over at him finally, observing his dark hands on the wheel and the easy way he controlled the car.

"You know," she began, "I think Nina's idea was a good one—to come south."

He glanced over at her questioningly. "Why?"

She shrugged, trying to find the words to explain. "Everything seems fresh all of a sudden, as though I'm seeing things in a new perspective."

She half expected him to ask her to elaborate, but he said nothing. Perhaps he understood.

As the highway climbed toward Arles, the sun emerged in full splendor. Gone was the eerie gray uniformity of the Camargue. Here the landscape began to unfurl in a blaze of warm color. The earth itself was a deep carnelian, contrasting with the melon-colored stone of the villas nestling amid forests of cypress and fields of lavender.

They stopped in a small village and divided up the task of shopping for their picnic. While Bran headed across the street toward a wine shop, Raine entered the local market. The atmosphere inside the dark store was rich and warm. Curing hams hung from the beamed ceiling, and local deli items were displayed in pretty faience crockery. With the help of the mustachioed proprietor, Raine selected a fresh sourdough loaf, a small round of cheese, a sampling of Provençal olives and a regional pâté that he called *poutargue Martigues*—made, he explained, from eggs and caviar. They laughed and joked their way through the selection, so that when Raine finally reemerged into the sunshine with her bulging string bag, she was in high spirits.

Her lips curved in a smile when she saw Bran in the middle of the dusty, blindingly white street, engaged in an impromptu soccer match with a group of schoolboys home for lunch. Coming around the car, she leaned against the door on the driver's side, following the action with dancing eyes. There was a lean vitality to him that never failed to quicken her blood, a sense of the male animal in his prime, which called to her own instincts in a deeply exciting way.

He broke off the match at last, leaving the boys to their high-spirited play, and sauntered back to her. Grinning, he brushed off the sleeves of the navy pullover tucked into his low-slung cream-colored cords.

"Judging from the laughter in the shop, you must have made quite a hit with the proprietor," Bran teased her. "I figured you'd be a while."

"Looks like you made a hit, too," she replied, her nose crinkling in laughter. "I would have loved to have seen you in your heyday. I'll bet you were quite a hotshot."

"Still am," he countered, his eyes raking her teasingly as he reached behind her to open the door.

"Bran, let me drive!" she said impetuously. "I haven't been behind the wheel of a car since I left the States."

Grinning still, he dug the keys out of his pocket. "Lead on, *mademoiselle*."

Raine shifted a little jerkily into first, and the well-mannered Simca left the curb at a sedate pace. At a fork in the road beyond the village, Raine struck off toward the northwest past a battered road that indicated, Les Baux 10 km. Whistling now under her breath, she pressed the accelerator, enjoying the feeling of control as she drove along the narrow twisting road.

At the crest she drew to a halt and stared in delight

at the ruins of the medieval village of Les Baux-en-Provence, huddled beneath two enormous gray outcroppings of rock. She parked the car in front of one of the restored Renaissance homes in the lower village, and they set out on foot. Beyond the magnificent remains of a castle, the landscape opened onto a wide valley.

Raine eased down gratefully beside a dry stone wall shaded by a gnarled cypress tree. After pulling her gray sweater over her head, she shook out her hair and pushed the green charmeuse blouse into the waistband of her softly gathered skirt. Glancing over her shoulder, she was startled to find that Bran, from his casual perch on the wall, was observing her every movement. Unwilling to tear her own gaze away, Raine stared up into eyes that seemed to reflect the vivid winter sky overhead.

Finally they both looked away, and feeling confused and strangely unsettled, Raine made a busy show of poking through the wrapped parcels they'd carried up the hill. She exclaimed in surprise when she pulled out the heavy green bottle Bran had obtained from the wine shop. "Champagne!" she cried. "What are we celebrating?"

"Typical American attitude," Bran growled in mock reproof as he slid down beside her on the warm ground and propped himself up on one elbow. "The best reason to drink champagne is no reason at all."

But Raine was only half listening to him as she tore off the wire and lead wrapping from the neck of the bottle and slowly began to work the cork loose. It sprang free with a little pop and the champagne gushed out in a golden stream, filling the air with a dry flinty aroma that reminded Raine of a wheat field in summer. Bran hastily held up two paper cups to catch the overflow, and they toasted each other with laughing eyes.

After they'd eaten the simple but delicious alfresco meal, Raine leaned her head back against the rough stones and stared up in contentment at the wide sky. The air had a mellow crispness to it, faintly redolent of the sweet herbs that would blossom come summer in the Provençal highland. Far below them, gray woodsmoke wafted over the slate rooftops of the village.

For no reason at all, Raine began to talk about her childhood. "I can't remember if it was Riva or me who first decided she had to dance. Before the age of fifteen our lives and our memories sort of mingle and merge. All I know is that I've always loved movement—turning around and around on the grass until the sky started tumbling like crazy over my head, and I was dizzy. But even then I knew dance made me feel alive. Riva was always the competitive one, *always* having to do it better than anyone else." Raine broke off with a frustrated sigh and reached forward to pull a clump of dry grass out by the roots. She turned suddenly to look at Bran. "Riva's madder than hell at both of us, you know. She feels she's been robbed."

He cast a lazy look in her direction. "Quit looking for something to worry about."

"I know her," Raine persisted with the same intensity.

He shifted position so that his face was just inches from her own, but so caught up was she in her thoughts that she was hardly aware of him. After studying her for a long moment, he matter-of-factly changed the subject. "I'm choreographing a new dance."

Raine's troubled expression cleared a little, and her eyes brightened with interest. "When I was on break this morning I saw you working alone in the small studio. What are you doing," she asked, striving for a lighter tone, "a solo number for yourself?"

He grinned. "No. A pas de deux."

"Is it done yet?"

"Not quite. I'm waiting for inspiration." He stared off down the hill, but when he turned back he purposely kept his tone teasing. "You've got four freckles on your nose," he remarked, apropos of nothing.

"Who ever heard of a Swan Princess with freckles? Disgusting!" Raine answered with a laugh.

"Downright ordinary," Bran commiserated with her, his baritone chuckle like a warm breeze caressing her face. "And I'll bet you're not the type who's sensitive to a pea hidden underneath twenty mattresses," he went on in the same vein. "Not the way you snoozed in the train seat all the way down from Paris."

That silly needling line set off a whole chain of remembrances in her mind, and Raine suddenly felt her cheeks flooding with color. Again she stared off in confusion down the hill, at once afraid yet breathlessly eager to see where the easy intimate give-and-take of their afternoon was carrying them. When she turned around to face him again, Raine found that his eyes had never left her face. "You were right about my not needing the lilies anymore, Bran,'' she said softly.

It was he, not his gift, that was her talisman. Even as she thought that, an ineffable tenderness crept over her, and Raine reached out with gentle tentative fingers to smooth the dark thickness of his hair. He caught her hand before she could withdraw it and brushed the palm with his warm lips, a gesture that caused her heart to pound in sweetly reckless rhythm.

But he seemed determined to keep the mood playful and light. Releasing her hand, he reached out beside him to pluck a renegade clover from a crack in the warm stone wall and tucked it behind her ear. Standing up then, he pulled her to her feet. "Come on. I want you to see Avignon before it's dark. I'll drive this time. I'd like to get there before morning."

Their badinage carried over to Avignon, where they explored the massive palace of the popes and wandered along the narrow lanes that wrapped around the base of the palace like a tangled necklace. They watched an old woman in a black beribboned straw hat selling spiky handfuls of sea urchins from her basket. From another street vendor they bought two thick slices of *pissaladière*, a thick Provençal pizza filled with olives and onions and sprinkled with locally grown basil. Later they rested their feet at a sleepy café overlooking the bridge of St-Bénézet and sipped a refreshing anise-flavored aperitif, *pastis*, that was a favorite of the locals.

A chill wind sprang up in the late afternoon as they drove southward out of the city. The winding secondary road led past another chain of hilltop villages, each more picturesque than the last. Beyond the curve of one particularly steep narrow hill, the road opened out near a squat windmill adjoining a tiny Provençal house, all harsh angles and severe lines. There was something whimsical about the unexpected juxtaposition that made them both laugh, and on impulse Bran turned off into the dusty drive.

As they got out of the car to have a look around, Raine noticed the creaking sign above the door that indicated the home was now a pension and tavern. Ma Mère L'Oye, the proprietor had christened the hilltop retreat, and Raine smiled as she translated into English: Mother Goose. More whimsy to match the windmill.

After exploring the exterior of the whitewashed mill, she joined Bran where he stood at the bottom of the hill, gazing back over the countryside they'd just passed through. The hillsides were a checkerboard of silvery-leafed olive trees and neat winter-garden patches planted with rows of artichokes and peas. A pastel sunset streaked the sky overhead, a soft pink mingling with the deep glowering purple of storm clouds billowing northward. Raine was standing so close to Bran that her shoulder brushed his sleeve, and she longed to be taken into the safe harbor of his arms. But a vestige of restraint still lingered between them, so that their eyes didn't quite meet. Each was reluctant to make the first move.

The still moment was broken by the swift heavy tread of footsteps on the gravel path leading down from the cottage. They turned to see a rotund woman approaching them, her girth swathed in a billowy print skirt. A short fringe of blond curls peeked out from beneath her matching bandanna, tied Gypsy fashion at the nape of her neck, and her dimples twinkled deeply in her round cheeks as she smiled at the surprise visitors. Observing her, Raine realized that the woman must have been quite lovely at one time, and her words proved that her charm hadn't diminished with the years.

"Bonsoir, mes amis!" she greeted Bran and Raine jovially, her periwinkle eyes dancing a merry welcome of their own. "I don't get too many visitors during the winter, so I'm happy indeed to see the two of you. Why don't you stop in awhile out of the evening chill? With any luck at all the storm will pass us right by, and you can be on your way again in safety!"

Madame Mirardeu's friendly patter accompanied them as she led the way to her small restaurant-tavern. Passing through the quaint entryway, complete with a staircase curving around a central well, they found a cheerful and airy cottage.

"We're celebrating the feast day of Saint Crillon up in the village tomorrow, and my contribution is to be a great pot of cassoulet. But a few ladlefuls will never be missed. Now sit down!" she urged happily. "Sit down."

The fragrant stew of haricot beans, sliced sausage and tender morsels of duck was preceded by a whole artichoke with drawn butter that the woman must have intended for her own supper. But when Raine attempted to protest, Madame Mirardeu would hear none of it. She disappeared briefly, only to bustle back with a bottle of Châteauneuf-du-Pape from a local vintner. The tavernkeeper seemed eager to have them join her, and it was obvious that for all her joviality, she was quite a lonely woman.

As they ate the simple but delicious fare, *madame* told them about her life. She'd been a dancer in Paris before the war, a chorus girl, in fact. With the money she'd saved, she'd returned to Provence and married Monsieur Mirardeu, a farmer. After his death in the war, she'd kept up the fields and her home, and with no children to occupy her, turned to cooking as a hobby, converting her home into an inn for the tourist trade. She informed them proudly that she had finally achieved her goal, receiving a star rating in the famous Michelin Guide.

A sharp crack of lightning beyond the curtained window caused them all to glance up in surprise, and Madame Mirardeu broke off her monologue to ask a few questions of her guests. When she found out they were associated with the ballet, the Frenchwoman was overwhelmed.

"Most people think I named my inn after the old fairy-tale goose—*mais non!*" she exclaimed with a delighted chuckle. "It was the music that inspired me." As she rose and moved toward the old phonograph in the corner, Raine and Bran exchanged amused glances.

The dreamy orchestral music of Ravel's *Ma Mère L'Oye* drifted up into the dark wood rafters of the hilltop cottage, drowning out the ominous rumble of thunder outdoors and the wind-driven rain that had begun to lash against the windowpanes.

The stormy night had crept up on them unaware, leaving the wide room in shadowy half darkness, the only light emanating from the small fire in the corner chimney and the flickering hurricane lamps on the long plank table. Inspired perhaps by the darkness and the beloved music, Madame Mirardeu took a few practice steps and then, incredibly, began to dance.

Raine bit her lip at the funny-sad sight. Belatedly the old woman must have grown embarrassed by her actions, because her steps faltered even as the music swelled around her. *"Mais non,"* she sighed. "I am being too silly."

Not knowing what to say, Raine dropped her eyes and kept them riveted on the table. She looked up quickly a moment later as Bran's chair scraped back against the floorboards and he stood up. Her confusion turned to wonder as he crossed to the center of the room and gently slipped his arm around Madame Mirardeu's vast waist. No less surprised, the proprietress raised her eyes and stared up into Bran's face.

They began to dance, a soft glide together across the polished flagstones. Watching them, Raine found it difficult to swallow past the lump in her throat. She caught a glimpse of Bran's expression, admiring yet faintly teasing, as he looked down at his companion. The glance held nothing of condescension or pity, and the Frenchwoman realized it. For all her great bulk, the tavernkeeper's steps took on a grace and lightness. Once again she was that lively chorus girl in a Parisian cabaret, desirable and pretty, her whole life stretched ahead of her.

When Bran caught her eye, Raine tried to smile but found it impossible. Tears had begun to well up in her eyes, blurring the image of the shadowy incongruous forms twirling across the room.

It was Madame Mirardeu who brought the duet to a graceful halt. They stopped before the table where Raine sat alone, and the old woman stared down at the younger woman with shining eyes. "Don't cry for me," she gently commanded. "It was enough to relive those years for a moment, when I never expected to find them again. Now I ask only one more thing. Will you dance for me, *mademoiselle*—with *monsieur*? It has been forty-two years since I left Paris, that long since I've seen something beyond my cooking pots and green fields. Show me a ballet."

As Bran held out his hand to Raine, she saw that underlying his cool devilry was a fleeting expression of tenderness. But she didn't know if the look of gentle caring had been meant for her or for their lonely hostess.

Feeling as vulnerable as a child, Raine kicked her walking shoes off beneath the table and stepped across the cold stone floor in her gray stockings. Then Bran slipped his arm around her waist, and they began to dance an improvised sequence that seemed to draw a little from every ballet the company had rehearsed in the preceding months. They drew apart and came together again, the beauty of their improvisational performance not in the steps that were laughingly made up as they went along, but in the lithe strength and charged connection between their bodies. As always, there was that electrical awareness between them that brought fire to Raine's cheeks and made her so breathlessly aware of her own femininity.

Once the music had died away into the darkness, the storm outside seemed to redouble its fury.

Madame Mirardeu glanced out the windows before turning to her guests. "The road at the bottom of the hill will be a quagmire now. If you tried to use it, the car would be stuck." As she spoke she reached for another bottle of the exquisite Châteauneuf-du-Pape and uncorked it easily. "So sit down again." Raine stared at the innkeeper as if she had willed the rain and the lightning to isolate them on this hilltop. And perhaps *madame* read her thoughts, because she began to chuckle.

Realizing that they were marooned and had no choice in the matter, Bran and Raine sat down again with their genial hostess. Three glasses were lifted in a toast.

Two hours later they'd polished off not only that bottle but another, and Raine's face was streaming with tears—this time prompted by laughter rather than sadness. Bran was in rare form that evening, teasing both women and telling one outrageous joke after another until it hurt for them to laugh anymore. A light insistent rain was still falling when Madame Mirardeu pulled out the bottle of fiery peppermint schnapps that a well-satisfied German gourmand had sent her. Now she poured a final round of nightcaps.

Raine was dismayed by the unsteadiness of her limbs when she finally stood up from the table. "I think we should be going," she mumbled softly.

Their hostess clucked and shook her head. "Stubborn thing. You and Monsieur du Rivage will be safe and warm here for the night; I'll give you a room upstairs." She winked with sly good humor, her look conveying her certainty that, judging by the way the handsome couple had danced together, they were already the most passionate of lovers.

"You're being silly," Raine protested.

"No, you're the silly one," Madame Mirardeu returned with sudden seriousness. "You're young once only in this life, and if you are very very lucky you will find one great love. It would be foolish to waste either. Now go up to bed." The innkeeper stood up when that little speech was done, and after bowing to them both with the regal grace of a duchess, she sailed out of the room.

Raine glanced down at Bran with a little smile on her lips, wondering what he was thinking. But the candle had guttered out and it was impossible to read his expression in the darkness. "I... I think I might need a hand on those stairs," she finally observed.

Bran's laughter sounded in her ears as he stood up. "Yes," he agreed. "I can see that."

Rather to her dismay, Raine felt herself being lifted easily into his arms. "This isn't what I had in mind," she protested, raising her head until her lips almost touched his neck. "You know how I feel about being carried up a staircase."

"Stop complaining, will you?" he murmured gruffly against her hair. "Or our hostess will come running to find out what the lovers' tiff is all about."

Raine's soft laughter rang out even as she nestled her head more closely against his chest. "You're right, you know."

Their destination was heralded by the bedside lamp Madame Mirardeu had left burning. Pushing open the bedroom door with his foot, Bran eased her gent-

ly to the ground. A heap of embers still smoldered in
the fireplace grate, and reluctant to relinquish their
delightful closeness, Raine let her hands slide around
to lightly encircle his waist as she looked up at him.
"Bran, I just want to tell you one thing," she
whispered. "What you did for Madame Mirardeu
tonight was extraordinarily kind and beautiful."

He shook his head. "Any man would have done
the same."

"No, they wouldn't have. They'd have been uncomfortable. You were the one sensitive enough to
give her a little of what she so desperately needed."

As he listened to her, Bran brought his hands up to
imprison her face. Idly his thumbs traced the spots
where her tears might have fallen, the rivulets of
sadness and laughter all but dried on her cheeks. He
followed their imaginary path from beneath her eye
to the corner of her mouth, and Raine turned her
head slightly to press her lips to his thumb, tasting
with her tongue the salty vestige of her tears on his
skin. Her pulse quickened as she tilted her head farther back, inviting his own lips to move over hers in
an intimate kiss.

But he took his hands from her face and used them
to gently remove her arms from around his waist. "I
think you'd better go to bed, Raine. You're drunk
and you're maudlin," he accused in a low voice that
mingled amusement with regret.

Her half-closed eyes shot open to regard him in
disbelief. "I'm neither, damn it!" But even as she
denied it, her eyelids drooped a little, giving some
credence to his words.

Gently he lifted her again and laid her down on the

soft blue counterpane that covered the high four-poster bed. She closed her eyes, unable to fight off the warm lassitude any longer. Vaguely she was aware of Bran as he moved around the small room, adding several split logs to the grate and filling the carafe on the bedside table with water. Then she drifted off.

When next she opened her eyes the room was in utter darkness. Even the blazing fire in the chimney had burned down to gray ash. The bed creaked a little as she shifted position, and she was startled to hear a low groan.

Bran was lying down beside her. He'd fallen asleep in his cords. A gentle smile touched the corners of her lips as she watched him, but she resisted the impulse to lean down and brush them against his. He would only mistake her tenderness for lightheadedness, she thought ruefully. Perhaps she deserved that, after all. She had kept him at arm's length for so long. Why should he suddenly believe she'd changed?

Feeling restless and warm, Raine got up from the bed as quietly as she could and slipped out of her skirt, blouse and stockings. But even in her brief white camisole and slip, she felt too warm. Using the high wooden posts at the foot of the bed as a guide, she felt her way across the room. Unlatching the casement window, she set it slightly ajar and breathed in the night air.

Outside, the last tattered storm clouds scudded across a sky that gleamed with the chased-silver brilliance of countless stars. Goosebumps had begun to rise on her arms and shoulders from the cold rain-washed air that slipped into the room, but she was reluctant to close the window again. She felt like Sleeping Beauty in reverse, the princess prematurely awakened while the rest of the world slumbered at her feet. The ridiculous thought made her laugh softly.

Perhaps her laughter had awakened Bran, because the bed creaked again, and when she turned around he was leaning on one elbow, running his fingers distractedly through his hair. "What are you doing padding around in the dark?" he asked, his voice husky and warm with sleep. "Casting a spell on the night?"

Her lips curved at that, a slow smile that illuminated her face and made her eyes gleam like beaten gold. "Just the opposite, as a matter of fact. The night's cast its spell on me."

Bran stared up at her for a long moment. Now that his eyes had adjusted to the darkness enveloping the room, he took in the details of her with a slow savoring look: the filmy white silk of her undergarments that at once veiled and subtly delineated the darker satin of her woman's body, the softly mussed hair, the cheeks flushed from sleep.

Raine closed the casement and came to perch on the corner of the bed beside him. She poured a glass of water from the carafe and took a long drink. Sensing his eyes on her, Raine looked over at him and smiled, holding out the glass. "Want some?"

He ignored the proffered glass, irritated that his growing desire was bound by an uncertainty that made him feel as awkward as a schoolboy. He took refuge in a reprimand. "That thirst of yours is the aftereffect of too much wine," he began. "You—"

But she silenced him by placing two fingers across his chiding lips. "Shhh...no more," she whispered. "It isn't true now, and it wasn't true before." Raine smiled, a teasing smile that mocked his scowl. "I'm as sober as a judge."

"You can't convince me," he growled, though she saw that his eyes, too, had begun to glint with amusement.

"Look," she insisted with a laugh, "you can feel how steady my hand is." And with that she laid it gently, provocatively, along his thigh.

Her touch burned him like a brand, and his own hand shot out to close around her fingers with an almost angry intensity that startled her. Gone was the playfully upbraiding mood of a moment earlier. The very air between them had become charged, tense, electric with expectation. Bran's eyes, dark as midnight in the shadowed room, bored into hers. "This is a dangerous game you're playing, Raine."

She shook her head slowly, aware of the reckless heat flooding upward from her loins. "It's no game, Bran. I want you." For all the gentleness of the words, a wildness lurked beneath them and was echoed in her glimmering, fire-bright eyes.

He fought the hungering urge to reach out and pull her to him. "What made you change?" he demanded thickly.

Raine's eyes never left his. "*Madame*'s words."

"Madame T?" he taunted. "Gather your lovers while ye may?"

"You know that's not who I meant," she replied softly. "I...I don't want to take the chance of throwing away a great—" Raine faltered again, unable to say the simple word but still needing to finish what she'd begun. "Nothing would be worth losing that for," she murmured in a soft rush.

Then, before he could reply, Raine leaned forward and brushed her lips against his, tasting the hot peppermint sweetness that still lingered there. As she did so, the thin straps of her camisole fell down over her upper arms to reveal the swelling ridge of her breasts. Bran had to respond to her closeness then, reaching up with lazy but circumspect fingers to trace the silk edging them and dip down for one long tremulous instant into the shadowed enticing valley between them.

Raine sensed his unexpected shyness. Amused, she became the aggressor—taking without asking. Like a precocious kitten she nipped and bit at the corners of his mouth. Her tongue enticed, coaxing some reply from his own.

His eyes, though smoky with desire, shone with answering amusement, and she read in their depths a challenge to play out her game of seduction. Spurred on by her own mischievous mood, she accepted the challenge, climbing onto the bed and straddling his lap.

He grinned at her boldness, waiting.

Slanting him a reckless gaze through her lowered lashes, she allowed her hands to slide lingeringly over his stomach and the dark matted shield of his chest. Her heart beating madly, Raine lay forward, using her parted mouth to explore the thin line of hairs that bisected upward from his stomach. And still her hands caressed and teased, kneading the hard muscles of his pectorals and the hollow where they dipped into the sinewed breadth of his shoulders.

She grew more and more deliciously aware of him beneath her, of the powerful thighs that chafed enticingly against her own. With growing excitement Raine sensed his mounting desire, felt his arms encircling her.

His hands slid down with reckless impatience to cup the tender womanly curve of her derriere, allowing his palms to glide across the slippery silk and his fingers to touch every hollow and gentle swell until Raine cried out with pleasure.

The net of excitement had caught them both now, yet she kept her own movements deliberately slow and languorous, a banked fire that burned with ever hotter and more potentially explosive intensity. Crossing her arms at her waist, she grasped the hem of her camisole between her fingers and pulled it in one long, slow, smooth movement up over her head. Her breasts shone pale and firm in the diffused starlight, casting two crescent-moon shadows onto her torso.

And it was those curving shadows that Bran's fingers traced, as if he couldn't quite believe that the lovely image before him was something more than a will-o'-the-wisp that would vanish if disturbed. Yet what his fingers found was warm, violet-scented skin, desirable and yielding. With a muffled groan, he gripped her tightly and drew her down to him.

Raine let her head fall back in exultation as she felt his lips pressing feverishly along her jaw and throat... before he pulled her closer so that he could make a moist teasing ring around her breasts. His mouth closed gently in turn around each tip, his tongue a deliciously wicked loop that clung and circled like a summer vine. Raine moaned softly, imagining herself atumble in a moonlighted field—every part of her ripe and warm and waiting.

Once his mouth had relinquished its hold on the dark strawberry sweetness of her engorged nipples, Bran's tongue traced a succulent path downward to her shadowed navel. Each dropped kiss was a maddening caress that sent out a spindrift of licking effervescence into every part of her fevered body.

She knew nothing then, was aware of nothing but the two of them drawn together into a hot spinning vortex of mounting ecstasy and mutual need. Breathlessly she reveled in the almost unbearable sensitivity of her uncovered skin. The slip had bunched and twisted until it was but a silken rope girdling the smooth ivory of her hips.

Still Bran's mouth traveled downward in a gentle imitation of her own wanton aggression, inflaming her senses beyond all reason as his lips parted to gently caress the triangle of silk spanning her hips. Impatient then with that final barrier between them, he dragged her delicate panties downward, allowing his knuckles to tease the bared flesh of her hips. Still astride him, Raine was exquisitely aware of her nakedness beneath the slip.

She bit back the cry of wild delight and unsatisfied yearning that rose in her throat as he eased her gently down beside him on the bed. Half lying across him, she reached with impatient fingers to open the belt at his waist. But he was more impatient and rolled away from her. Sprawled naked on her stomach, Raine followed him with her eyes, her breath drawn in on a sharp intake of delight as he slipped with catlike grace out of his clothing and lay down beside her.

Now she closed her eyes, savoring the exquisite opposition of their bodies—his taut thigh muscles and corded sinews against the lithe contour of her silken flesh. His coarse chest hairs raised little pinpricks on her back as he leaned across to lift her hair from her neck and kiss the nape. Then he kissed the gentle slope of her shoulders and ran his teeth lightly along the ridge of her shoulder blades, trailing down her spine to the small of her back.

In just that way he kissed every inch of her, his mouth caressing her legs and his tongue dipping into her inner thighs, the ticklish hollow at the backs of her knees, his teeth gently circling her ankle in a playful bite. Sensing that he took as much pleasure in the womanly taste and texture of her body as he gave with his own male sensuality, Raine felt herself unfolding to him like a richly fragrant tropical flower. And even as he nudged her gently over onto her back, Raine's hips rose instinctively, demanding the full length of him. The slow circular thrust of their loins sent shudders of agonized delight through them both, until their joined lovemaking quickened in breathless tempo and propelled them, reeling, toward an erotic explosion so intense and so sudden that they fell back spent, like soaring birds shot down in flight. . . .

They were lying on their sides now, Bran's arm hooked over her waist from behind, Raine marveling at how the curve of her hips molded so naturally to him. For all her joyful satiation, a tiny shiver of delight breathed through her as Bran lowered his head to kiss the side of her throat and gently catch her lobe with his teeth. "Raine," he whispered against her ear, "was it over too quickly for you?"

She turned to stare up at him, her golden eyes extraordinarily tender yet glimmering still with reminiscent ardor. "Bran," she whispered softly in turn, "the fury of it caught us both. I've...I've never experienced anything quite like it in my life!" Though she laughed, Raine lowered her lashes protectively against her cheek.

"Maybe we should send down to Madame Mirardeu for a bottle of champagne," he teased.

Raine's eyes flew open. "My God! Do you think we might have woken her up?"

"If we did, her dreams'll be all the sweeter when she does sleep again," Bran growled with laughter.

"Wretch!" Raine exclaimed as she pulled away from him and got up on her knees to reach for the glass of water on the table. "Besides, if we had champagne you'd only accuse me of drinking too much again." She turned to glance back playfully at him, only to draw in her breath at the way his eyes devoured her. Like hot blue flames they licked at the contours of her naked haunches and the ripeness of her small rounded breasts, revealed in tantalizing half shadow against her arm as she braced herself with her palms on the bed. She was the classical enchantress, half woman and half mystic creature, working her magic on all-too-mortal man.

In a rush of womanly instinct, Raine felt the depth of her power over him, a power that was both frightening and exciting. She lowered her lashes in a gesture at once shy and seductive as she continued to gaze back at him, Bran's fevered need coiling her toward him though she hadn't moved.

Now her own renewed desire danced through her veins in a headlong rush that seemed to tinge her whole body with the flush of passion. Raine quivered as his hands came up to grasp her hips and his thumbs gently kneaded the smooth white skin and bone. Drawing himself up slowly behind her, he tightened his grip as he felt the shudder that racked her and heard the low moan that begged him not to wait. Spurred by an age-old instinct that sent his blood racing in hot excitement, he inched closer to her and breached the depths of her femininity.

Again they shared a slowly building ecstasy of hips in opposition, yet united in a circular rhythm that brought Bran even deeper and deeper, until she emitted a low feral cry. Hungering for the closeness of all of her, Bran gripped Raine's waist and drew her up gently, so that her palms lifted free of the bed and her naked back nestled against his perspiration-slicked chest. Now his arms closed around her, one hand caressing her upthrust breast, while the other slid down to furred darkness, where her pleasure mounted and quivered on the brink of explosion.

The maddening pleasure of his touch and his masculine strength inside her unleashed something wild within Raine. Her senses responded with a joyous blending of feeling that was pure unrestrained ecstasy. She felt the heat of their joined bodies and the gentle rasp of his hands against the length of her; she breathed in the sexual musk of their lovemaking and the dark male scent that was Bran's alone. Arching her back slightly, Raine threw her arm backward to encircle his neck, twisting her head so that her eager mouth could find his. Their tongues met and clung in a loving duel, an intimate fevered thrusting that was an echo of the sustained rhythm of their lovemaking.

Still the raging tide of their passion carried them higher, like a mounting wave on a tropical sea that slowly builds and crests until it crashes on the shore in a great shower of spray. So their lovemaking flowed in a slow cresting wave that submerged them both.

They came down gently like gulls adrift above a windless sea. Raine opened her eyes reluctantly, only to notice with a sense of shocked surprise that the gray light of dawn had already begun to lighten the sky beyond their window. Bran released her with the same slow reluctance, planting one last lingering kiss in the hollow of her shoulder before pulling her down beside him on the well-used bed.

Though the fire had died down hours before and an early-morning chill had crept into the room, their bodies were slick with perspiration. Long moments later, Raine sat up against the headboard, pushing the damp hair back from her forehead. "I'm so hot," she said with a soft laugh, fanning herself coyly with one hand.

Bran eyed her lazily. "Women are never satisfied," he grumbled in mock reproof. "When she's in Paris she complains about the cold; now in mid-winter she claims it's too hot."

Laughing, Raine reached out and surreptitiously dipped her fingers into the glass of water on the table. Then, as Bran closed his eyes and shook his head, she pelted him with the icy droplets.

His response was instantaneous. Pinning her down to the bed with one arm, he reached across her and picked up the water glass itself, pouring a slow trickle down her torso. Her smothered squeal of protest against the cold gave way to little moans of pleasure and helpless giggles as he bent his head and licked the drops from her skin in a way that was at once teasing and tantalizing. She was still giggling when he brought his mouth up to silence her with a deep kiss.

Raine's fingers dug into his muscular upper arms as they drew unwillingly apart, her eyes wide and giving. "I've never had a night like this before in my life," she whispered, her lips trembling and still warm from his kisses.

His hands moved meditatively down the lovely naked length of her. "I'll cherish the memory, too," Bran murmured in a husky voice. But a moment later he looked away. His gaze, at once shadowed and darkly gleaming, was fixed on some distant point beyond the window.

She reached up to cup his face tenderly with her hands and force him to look at her again. "It was more than that," she persisted, her voice at once stubborn and gentle. "Bran, I love you."

Raine waited with heart pounding, not quite believing she'd made the admission that she'd held inside, even denied to herself, for so long.

He brushed her damp forehead with lips gone cool. "What we had was beautiful, Raine, an incredible shared experience. If that's what love is, then yes, I loved you, too."

"Loved?" she repeated in a taut voice. "Somehow I don't think we're saying the same thing."

Bran rolled over and sat up on the edge of the bed, his back, broad and tense, turned to her. He looked up at the ceiling, his breath escaping in a low impatient sigh. "We shared our love for the moment. Why do women always want more than that?"

Sitting up abruptly, Raine pulled the sheet up protectively around her nakedness. "Because I'm not other women!" she cried. "I thought you cared for me."

"I do care." He glanced back over his shoulder, his blue eyes still midnight dark with passion and some vestige of pain.

"But not deeply enough for commitment, is that it?" she asked at last in a voice that accused herself as much as him.

"I don't know what the hell the word means."

"Madame T told me that about you, but I didn't want to believe her," she whispered in a voice that trembled on the brink of desolation.

"You should have," he said a little more gently. "It would have saved us both a lot of hurt." Bran shook his head. "I'm sorry, Raine."

Unmindful of the cold that seemed to invade her limbs at his words, she watched in numb silence as he pulled on his clothes and finally left her alone in the bedroom.

Raine had given him the ultimate gift—herself. And after taking it, he had spurned her as if she'd had no right to ask for commitment. She remembered then all the old tales Madame Tarsamova had told her—about Bran being loved by every ballerina and his loving them each in turn—a little—as it suited his purposes.

Feeling empty and almost sick, Raine pulled herself from the bed and dressed in the shadowy half light. She knew that what she'd felt between them was real, compelling, deep. Why had he chosen to deny it?

CHAPTER FOURTEEN

As RAINE HAD FOUND in the past, work was a refuge in which she could safely lose herself. The rest she would try to forget, would try to convince herself that the magical night at Ma Mère L'Oye had meant nothing. She paid no attention to the gossip that had blossomed in the wake of their overnight absence from Stes-Maries, and everyone was left to speculate wildly on the couple's coolness toward each other during rehearsal—a clever facade meant to fool them all?

Raine practiced the Odette sequences over and over again, until each step was second nature and she was free to concentrate on the far more subtle evocations of gesture and character. Though she moved with lissome grace, there was a fleeting overlay of pain to her expression that lent added weight and gravity to her depiction. Now there was no mistaking a ballerina in her prime.

Not wanting to mingle during break, Raine filled a paper cup at the cooler and wandered down the long corridors of the old mansion that had been converted into a successful summer theater. From the far studio where she'd seen Bran working alone the previous week came the lush notes of a Ravel suite, and her heart turned over. When had he decided on Ravel for the dance he was creating? She couldn't remember having heard it before.

As though her feet had a will of their own, they carried her slowly forward toward the music that grew louder and more definitive the closer she came. Raine stood back in the shadows at the doorway, her eyes following the sweep of movement in the cold sunlighted room. Bran wasn't dancing alone. Riva was with him.

And as she watched them, curiosity overcame the festering anger and raw hunger that had gnawed at her ever since they'd parted as strangers. This new piece of Bran's was no showcase for a ballerina. It was an incredibly poignant coming together of a man and a woman, an intimate drama of supercharged emotion that was meant to glimmer far below the surface. With her sensitivity, Raine understood that at once.

Her eyes narrowed critically as she observed her sister's performance. The movements were all wrong! Too quick, too blatant, when the piece called for a slow building of tension. Bran knew it, too, because in mid-sequence he stopped abruptly and moved to switch off the music. "It's not working, Riva," he told her with aggrieved impatience. "You're supposed to be a woman in love, not a god-damned martinet. Do you understand the difference?" His sarcasm was cutting and fired Riva's own ready temper.

"Love!" she flung back heatedly. "You're a fine one to talk, Bran. You've been blinded by it yourself. You stole Odette from me, stole half of the one piece that could show the full range of my abilities. You had to give it to dear little Raine. Well, I hope she's paid you well for it...."

Riva's ugly accusation stung like a lash across the face, and Raine backed hurriedly from the doorway, afraid she might be noticed. Inside her feelings raged in turmoil. She felt like crying and laughing bitterly at the same time.

Attempting to get hold of herself, she turned her thoughts back to Odette. But it wasn't Tchaikovsky that she moved to now. In her mind she was hearing the strains of Ravel and wondering what Bran would call the beautiful new dance he was creating. Her concentration was completely shattered as a slamming door echoed down the corridor, and she guessed that Riva had stormed out—Raine had seen her do it all too often in New York.

Thoughtful and tense, Raine stood in the center of the room trying to compose herself enough to resume practice, when Bran suddenly materialized in the studio doorway. His face was a hard angry mask, so different from the man she'd made love to in a Provençal cottage. She lifted her chin.

"Raine, I need you." The words were simple, curt, but just for an instant their eyes collided, an emotional undercurrent rocking them both. She bit her lip, heart pounding in expectation. But the look was gone from his eyes as swiftly as it had appeared. When he turned to go back to his own studio, she reluctantly followed.

The words he'd spoken in the doorway were the last even remotely personal thing he said to her. They began to work, and Raine submerged her feelings in the dance, knowing instinctively that it was right for her. Bran had reverted to form—push, push, push. On the surface Raine complied as they kept their eyes averted, while inwardly she screamed at the hard unfeeling shell he'd donned.

Over and over again he ran her through the steps, correcting her position and partnering her only when it was strictly necessary. But now his touch was so cold and indifferent that Raine almost began to dread it. All the love and joy they'd shared at Ma Mère L'Oye faded as she felt herself being treated more and more as an object.

For three hours and more they worked. Bran was so wrapped up in the creative process that Raine knew he no longer saw her as a woman. Like all his other dancers, she was an instrument, and the realization stung her to the quick.

Finally, during one particularly tender sequence when all he could do was criticize her positioning in relationship to their hypothetical audience, Raine rebelled. "All you've talked about today is steps until I'm sick of it. Not once—not for one bloody second—have you mentioned emotion!" Her eyes glittered with an anger that encompassed more than the current argument. "I'd just like to know what kind of ice flows through your veins," she needled him.

His eyes lost their look of fierce concentration, and Raine felt a fleeting bitter triumph to see that she'd aroused some feeling in him at last, even if it was fury.

"I'll show you how cold I am," he answered slowly, the words bitten out between clenched teeth. His hand came up to grip her chin, and he forced her head back. Then his mouth swooped down to take possession of hers in a kiss that was so intimate, yet at once so coldly furious, that Raine felt as if she'd been emotionally raped. There'd been no tenderness, no sharing, nothing but the arrogant stamping of his will on hers.

In that instant she hated him. She willed back the hot flood of tears that threatened to blur her vision, desperate to prove that she could be every bit as ruthless as he was.

Taking refuge in her mantle of brittle hauteur, Raine said icily, "I've had it with you. I'm tired of being pushed and harried—and bullied."

"As a dancer you'll put up with that and more," he responded with a trace of his former impatience.

"As a dancer, maybe. But not as a woman. I'm through with practice for now." The words were a challenge, but he chose to ignore them.

"Get out, then," he replied, anger and weariness blending in his voice.

Raine showered hurriedly and changed into a knit dress of cranberry wool, all the time debating whether she should take a bus into Marseille or grab her jeans and go back into the Camargue country. The only thing she was certain of was that she had to get out of Stes-Maries for a while to preserve her sanity.

Two men were lounging in the hall in front of the doorway, and Raine recognized Bran at once. The other was a stranger to her. She was about to rush past them both, when Bran's sandy-haired companion addressed her obliquely in a lilting Irish brogue. "Will this be one of your lovely ballerinas, du Rivage? If she is, then I envy you, man."

Raine found herself smiling despite herself. After the afternoon session with Bran, her ego was dragging on the floor, and this man's flattery and admiring eyes were a pleasant antidote. She smiled as she extended her hand to him. "Hi, I'm Raine Cameron, and you're only half right. I'm a soloist with the company, but not quite a ballerina."

He grinned in turn. "Michael O'Donovan's the name, and Bran's a bigger fool than I thought if he hasn't made you his star by now."

Bran listened expressionlessly to this exchange. "I see your line's as smooth as ever, O'Donovan," he commented.

The Irishman winked at his friend. "That's because I keep it well polished." Then without missing a beat, he turned back to focus his attention on Raine. "An old soccer buddy crosses the Channel to see him, and the bloke tells me he's tied up in rehearsals. But you look free as a bird. Care to run into Marseille with me for the evening? They tell me it's a grand wicked place."

"I'd love to, Mr. O'Donovan." Raine laughed up at him teasingly, ignoring the scowl that darkened Bran's features.

"Call me Michael, now, please."

"Michael, then," she agreed. "You know the old adage about all work and no play...."

He winked as he reached to take her arm. "Now do I ever!"

Bran followed the pair with his eyes as they walked outside. Raine was aware of that hard relentless gaze as she got into Michael's car, but she willed herself to ignore it.

As it turned out, the most wicked thing in Marseille was Michael O'Donovan himself, and long before the evening was over Raine was regretting her impulsive decision to go out with the man. *I deserve to suffer,* she told herself with a smile, knowing she'd accepted his invitation primarily to get back at Bran for his cruelty.

Not that Michael wasn't a charming enough man and willing to please. He treated her to a wonderful meal of saffron-spiced bouillabaisse at the prestigious Michel Brasserie des Catalans, and later they'd gone to an equally exclusive nightclub. But the man was a born hunter where women were concerned. He told Raine that he was divorced—and she could understand why. She doubted if marriage had stayed his roving eyes and hands for long! She fended him off as gracefully as she could all evening, but he took her refusals as coyness, which whetted his appetite all the more. It was with a great deal of relief that she accepted his suggestion that they return to Stes-Maries. At least he'd be forced to behave while driving and keep his blasted hands on the wheel.

As they headed northwest out of the city, Raine's eye was drawn by the lighted villas set back in the hills overlooking the bay. She thought of Lucille Martin then and made a silent vow to go visit the woman, alone if she had to, before the Ballet du Monde left Provence. For all the distance between herself and Bran after those fateful twenty-four hours they'd spent together, Raine still loved him. She felt the need to touch some connection with him and was curious to know why mother and son were still estranged, why it angered Bran even to say her name.

After another inevitable tussle with Michael in the front seat of his car, Raine extricated herself with an abrupt good-night and a few acid remarks that obviously didn't faze Michael in the least. Then she made her way swiftly toward the door of the small pension where she was lodging. On the dark porch she nearly collided with someone.

"Oh, Riva, you startled me," she said breathlessly.

The ballerina's eyes glimmered coldly. The woolly collar of her jacket was drawn up against her throat, and it was apparent she'd been out walking. "Who's the new beau?" she asked with a pretense of casualness.

Raine brushed back the hair from her cheek. "A friend of Bran's, actually. Michael dropped into town to see him."

"And you volunteered to show him the sights. How cozy."

Raine flushed, wondering how much her twin had seen of their awkward parting. "We had dinner in Marseille—period," she replied stiffly.

Riva's brows arched in mock disbelief. "Faithless little thing, aren't you?"

Raine regarded her with a level stare. "Do you have anything else to say, Riva? Otherwise I'm going up to bed. Good night."

"Wait a sec," Riva said abruptly as she pulled a pack of Gitanes from her pocket and sat down on the rush-bottomed bench against the porch railing. Shoving her hands deeper into the pockets of her jacket, Raine waited, observing the gray smoke that wafted around Riva's head as she lighted a cigarette. Then

Riva leaned back and stared up at her for a long moment. "I hear you conveniently stepped in for me this afternoon."

Raine lifted her shoulders in an impatient shrug. "What else could you expect—after the way you stormed out in such a huff?"

"Yes, but why you?" Riva countered, her penetrating topaz stare not wavering for an instant. "First you got Odette away from me, and now you're angling for *Sweet Seduction*, too. How far are you going to go to dislodge me?"

Raine laughed suddenly and eased down beside Riva on the bench. "Dethrone—isn't that what you meant to say? In your book, there was never enough room for more than one queen, was there?"

Riva reached around to stub out her cigarette on the rail, ignoring her sister's gibe. "You warned me when you first got to Paris, but I didn't believe you, Raine."

"I'm not the same woman I was six months ago."

"No, you're not. I suppose you consider yourself Bran's woman now," she said, the words sarcastic and biting. "Even if you are dating his old friend."

"That's none of your business."

Riva stood up, her eyes agleam with dark amusement. "Well, you may have changed, Raine, but I haven't—and you know I play to win."

With that she was gone, and Raine was left alone on the dark, salt-misted porch. It was cold but she was in no rush to go in. As she played back the acrimonious conversation in her mind, the one thing that stood out was the name of Bran's new ballet: *Sweet Seduction*. And for the first time she smiled.

The title could just as easily have fitted the enchanted interlude they'd spent in the old-fashioned bed at Madame Mirardeu's inn.

THE NEXT FEW DAYS were frantic for Raine, her time divided among company class, group and private rehearsals. Raine hadn't seen Michael since their evening out, which was just as well. She continued to work privately with Bran on *Sweet Seduction*, but for all the enforced closeness of their professional association, an impenetrable wall still separated them. Their harsh words, the even harsher kiss were never mentioned again, but the residue lingered. They were no longer comfortable together.

Later that week, after her customary morning walk on the beach, Raine crossed to the studio and met Michael O'Donovan coming down the steps. Before she could stop him, the grinning Irishman had thrown his arm around her waist and drawn her close, planting a lingering kiss on her mouth that she broke off with an angry shake of her head. Didn't the man ever give up?

"What's the matter, luv?" He glowered in exaggerated fashion. "Why so standoffish all of a sudden?"

Raine, backing up a safe distance from the unrepentant wolf, regarded him in disbelief. "All of a sudden!" she repeated.

He winked and leered as if they shared some very private joke. "Just as you say, luv." He lifted his hands in jest to show he wouldn't touch her there on the theater steps, though his look said all too clearly what he might do in the after hours.

By turns outraged, amused and perplexed, Raine went into the building and made her way to Bran's studio. He was already there, pacing and fuming like a caged animal. Raine glanced down at her watch defensively, knowing she wasn't late.

He turned when he saw her in the doorway, and his already brooding eyes darkened like storm clouds amassing threateningly on the horizon. "Michael's just left."

"Yes, I know," she answered a little uncertainly. "I just ran into him outside."

As she said that the young pianist Bran had hired, a fresh-faced boy on leave from the university, sauntered up to join Raine in the doorway. *"Bonjour, mademoiselle, monsieur,"* he greeted them both with a cheerful grin.

Bran shifted his gaze to the boy. "Get out!" he growled menacingly.

A stricken look on his face, the pianist retreated in hasty confusion. But Raine wasn't so easily bullied. She crossed the room as if she owned it and stopped directly in front of Bran. "What on earth is the matter with you?" she demanded quietly. "You scared that poor kid half to death with your crazed-bear act."

His darkened eyes raked her slowly, ruthlessly until every nerve in her body quivered with mingled resentment and expectation. Never had she seen him in such a dark mood. "How do you expect me to act?" he countered harshly. "After I had to stand here for fifteen minutes and listen to an old friend describe in leering detail how he made love to you, how his hands and lips caressed and aroused your naked body and how yours did the same to him, until I wanted to knock his teeth down his throat. But I couldn't, because he'd made it apparent that you were an all-too-willing partner.''

Raine's face flamed scarlet, then went chalk white as she listened to his deliberate recital. She felt the tension like a coiled spring inside him. His whole body exuded fury, betrayal.

With an effort she kept her voice steady, low, reasonable when she finally replied, "He's lying."

Bran never took his eyes from her face. "Like hell he is. Michael may be a spendthrift and a charming reprobate. But he's no liar."

"Bran, you're so wrong about me." Her voice was little more than a husky whisper now. "How could you take his word over mine?"

"Because he has no reason to lie," he ground out, fury still eating at him.

"And I suppose I do?" she countered softly.

They looked at each other, both remembering the kiss he'd inflicted on her. But she shook her head again. "You're wrong," she insisted, and even as she did a tiny suspicion nudged at the back of her mind.

Not wanting to prolong the useless argument, Raine turned on her heel and hurried from the room, her own anger fomenting as she realized who was to blame for this latest ugly little farce.

A cool, sea-misted wind buffeted her when she reappeared on the theater steps, but Raine knew she wouldn't have to wait long. Finally she saw the familiar figure approaching across the square from the pension, her lamb's-wool jacket draped with casual elegance over her shoulders. Riva's expression was veiled as she looked up to see her sister waiting at the top of the steps. She climbed them slowly, her eyes watchful.

Raine didn't keep her in suspense for long. "You've been busy, haven't you?"

They stood eye to eye now just outside the doors, as tense and bristling as a pair of feuding cats. "What of it?" Riva flung back carelessly.

"Shall I put it more bluntly? You slept with Michael O'Donovan."

"That, dear sister, as you reminded me earlier in the week, is none of your business!"

Raine stared at her, shocked, realizing that Riva was actually enjoying their confrontation—had in fact been looking forward to it. She tried to keep her tone even but wasn't too successful. "It's my business when you try to pass yourself off as me."

Riva grinned. "He cornered me at the Hippocampe last night after dinner and suggested we have drinks. Why should I have refused?" Her shrug spoke volumes.

Raine let out her breath in a long sigh of exasperation. "You miserable little witch! Just how far will you go?"

Now the other members of the troupe had begun to arrive in twos and threes for rehearsal and were staring curiously at the identical profiles almost nose to nose.

"Will you lower your voice?" Riva hissed. "Do you want everyone to hear us?"

Raine shook her head. "No. . . not everyone. Come on. We're going in to have a word with Bran."

It was Riva's turn to eye her twin in disbelief. "Like hell we are!"

"This is one destructive game too many, Riva. We've always been rivals, but we've never deliberately hurt one another before."

"Aren't you exaggerating a little?" Riva countered, her tone impatient.

"I meant every word. Bran's respect means the world to me." Raine paused. "Michael was bragging to him about his latest sexual conquest. How do you think that made me feel?"

Riva had the grace to look embarrassed. "All right," she conceded, frowning. "I'll tell him . . . but you owe me one, Raine."

Bran looked up in surprise from the piano where he stood, idly striking a series of discordant notes, and watched the two dancers approach him from the doorway. How alike yet how different they were!

He listened in silence to Riva's grudging admission without a flicker of expression on his face. When she was done his gaze shifted from one to the other, as if debating. Neither was prepared for what he finally said. "I warned you Camerons once before that I wouldn't put up with these games. You're both fired." With that he turned back imperturbably to the musical score he'd spread out on the piano ledge.

The women stared at him in shocked disbelief for a minute. Riva broke out angrily, "Brandon, that's not fair! You can't do that!"

He looked up again as if surprised to see them still standing there. "I've already done it," he said tautly.

Riva was set to go at it with him full tilt, but Raine refused either to argue or to beg. For the second time that morning she turned her back on him and left the studio. She had no intention of standing around until he cooled off.

LUCILLE MARTIN and her guest sat facing one another over cups of coffee and egg-salad sandwiches. For all her European veneer, the retired dancer was still very much an American at heart.

She had listened with a bemused expression to the younger woman's story, her manner at once detached yet sympathetic. Again Raine found herself wondering why she'd come to visit the woman. It was all a little pointless, especially since she hadn't even dared to broach the subject of Lucille's estrangement from her son.

Lucille set down the spoon she'd been idly toying with and shook her head at the silly imbroglio that had got the twins fired. When she smiled, her expression was so like Bran's that Raine's heart twisted a little. "It's reassuring to know human nature hasn't changed all that much in forty years," the woman began. "The same or similar things went on in every company I danced with. It's only a shame that your rival happens to be your sister, too. That love/hate kind of situation can be so difficult to deal with."

With a little sigh Lucille broke off and stared out to the distant Mediterranean. As the conversation lulled, Raine found she had calmed down enough to take in her surroundings. She couldn't help noticing how cleverly the villa had been situated, so that all the oil refineries of Martigues to the west and the highrise-dotted cityscape of Marseille to the southeast were out of the picture. The setting might have been the Côte d'Azur of another era, when there were nothing but sleepy fishing villages, lemon groves and stony hills bordering the winding coastal highway.

Raine glanced back at her hostess and studied her lovely, remarkably unlined face. Lucille had created a perfect isolated little world for herself that needed no stimulation from the outside. Thinking of Bran's penchant for withdrawing from emotional situations, Raine grew angry, so that when she spoke her voice had a slight edge to it. "Ballet has been your life for forty years, then?" she asked.

Lucille turned at that, regarding the younger woman levelly. "Yes, it has, and I suppose it's true that I've regretted my decision at times. It was hard traipsing around Europe with various companies. But you see, I found the only way I could give was through my art. Some people might regard that as selfish—" a glimmer of some old defiance shone in her cool blue gaze "—but I never had the strength or the will—or whatever you might call it—to give fully in more than one direction. Can you understand that, Raine?" The words were almost a plea, and Raine sensed how awkward Bran's mother felt, how unused she was to expressing emotion.

"I don't know," Raine answered quietly. "I don't have a husband or a son."

Lucille considered her guest with a saddened gaze that made her seem more vulnerable. "Don't judge me too harshly, Raine. I've had enough of that from my family—and many so-called friends. It wasn't all one-sided. These things never are, you know."

Raine looked down at her hands. "I'm sorry."

"No," Lucille sighed. "Perhaps you have a right

to know. I . . . I was deeply in love with Giscard." The words came slowly, as if she'd never voiced her feelings aloud in all the long empty years. "But he was very much the old-style European. He couldn't stand the thought that his wife might have a career and life apart from marriage. My refusal to give up dance ate away at him like a cancer, until eventually it destroyed our marriage."

"But didn't you think of Bran?" Raine interposed.

The older woman's smile was sad. "How passionately you leap to his defense." She sighed before going on. "But of course I thought about Bran. I thought of nothing else! Giscard's corrosive possessiveness destroyed whatever feeling there had once been between us as man and wife. But Bran was the light of my life."

"You abandoned him," Raine murmured in a tone of quiet accusation that caused Lucille to flush deeply.

"Did he tell you that?" she asked hurriedly. "It's not true. I desperately wanted to have custody of him, but Giscard never would agree to that. And eventually I reluctantly had to agree that my husband's logic was infallible." Her voice grew dry and bitter. "What kind of life could I have given a five-year-old boy, traveling with a ballet company? Giscard was able to give him everything I couldn't—stability, fine schools, the best clothes, toys, books—everything."

"Everything except a mother's love." There was no accusation in Raine's voice now, only sympathy.

"I tried to make it up to him in my visits to Paris,

but he had already begun to withdraw from me. The more I feared losing him, the more I turned to dance. My art kept me sane."

"Lucille, his turning away was a facade to hide his hurt."

The woman's eyes were anguished. "I was so young then. I didn't see it. And as the years went by, it somehow became easier not to feel."

"Even knowing as little about you as I do, I can't believe that," Raine said firmly, her eyes roaming to the bare hills beyond the terrace. "In Bran's case, the hardness has become less of a facade, more real." Her voice reflected much of the hurt she herself had been experiencing.

Lucille looked at the young dancer in sudden understanding. "You're in love with my son, aren't you?"

Raine started to shrug evasively, only to realize the pointlessness of any denial. "Yes," she said in a clear voice. "Yes, I am."

"I don't know if it could ever work."

"Why not?" Raine demanded.

Lucille stood up from the table and glanced around her with an impatient, almost trapped air. "I hurt him so badly that he's shied away from any serious relationship with a woman, as far as I can tell. Who's to say he'll see you any differently?"

"I'll make him. I have so much to give."

The older woman smiled at that. "I admire your willingness to go after what you want."

"Bran's worth it. He's a fine man." Raine's eyes shone with the intensity of her feelings.

"I'm sure he is. How I wish he would just give me

another chance," Lucille murmured, shaking her head to hide the gleam of tears in her eyes. But she recovered her rigid control at once, making her voice serene and low as she added, "Perhaps you'll come again to talk. This visit has meant a lot to me. I've never really discussed Bran with anyone. But if you will excuse me, it's getting very late."

And as Lucille escorted her out of the villa, Raine reflected a little guiltily that the emotion-charged visit seemed to have drained Bran's mother. Yet if she ever hoped to get close to her son, both of them would have to be more willing to break down the barriers of pride and fear that stood between them.

As she drove back alone in her rented car toward Stes-Maries, Raine felt a curious sense of emptiness and loss. She remembered what Lucille had said about the two sisters' rivalry: "That love/hate kind of situation can be so difficult to deal with." But more than the words, Raine recalled the woman's tone of voice. There had been so much suppressed feeling in it.

Raine wasn't blind. It was painfully apparent to her that Bran had just that sort of relationship with Lucille. But Raine's new understanding did nothing to lessen the uncertainty of her future with Bran. If anything the women's talk had only underscored the difficulties lying ahead.

CHAPTER FIFTEEN

EVENING WAS JUST FALLING over the deserted seaside resort as Raine drew her car to a stop in front of the green-shuttered pension. From the top step she turned around to look back along the beach. There was a lone figure moving with a long easy gait that she recognized at once, and her pulse quickened. But Bran didn't see her. Raine smothered the impulse to follow him, afraid that once they met there would be nothing more to say but cool goodbyes.

She climbed the stairs to her room and was surprised to see lamplight spilling out from beneath the door. Her surprise only increased when she opened it to find Nina Tarsamova seated in the armchair, placidly reading.

The ballet mistress looked up over the tops of her glasses as Raine stepped into the room. "I believe you have the *Swan Lake* musical score that you were supposed to return to me days ago."

Raine perched on the foot of her bed opposite the waiting woman and rummaged through her bag. "Here it is. I guess I won't be needing it anymore," she replied with a wry smile as she handed it over. "Has Riva already left Stes-Maries?"

Madame slowly removed her glasses. "No one is going anywhere except back to work tomorrow morning. There's been enough foolishness as it is,'' she announced decisively.

Raine let out a long sigh, feeling more relief than surprise at the ballet mistress's words. Madame T wasn't about to let petty feuds interfere with her ballet company. "Bran was awfully angry," Raine observed at last. "How'd you convince him?"

"The man is arrogant, but he's no fool. He knows he can't dispense with his two finest dancers in mid-season and think he still has a viable company."

Raine's eyes brightened with pleasure at the woman's compliment. "Thank you," she told her softly.

But the ballet mistress had misunderstood. "Don't thank me. Thank Riva."

Raine's head shot up at that. "What did she do?"

"Riva is no fool, either. Your sister knows how to play her cards."

Though Raine laughed at that, her eyes narrowed a little in speculation. "What has she talked you into?"

For the first time the Russian woman smiled, and Raine recognized in her eyes the self-satisfied glint that spoke of a deal cleverly arranged. "You know me, Raine. I work things out in the most practical way."

"Meaning money?"

"Meaning I cannot run a ballet on thin air."

Raine's suspicion was confirmed. "What did Riva guarantee you—that Massimo Chiari would come through for the ballet if she asks him to?"

Madame smiled thinly. "As I said, we are all practical women. The only difference is that I *always* put the company first, no matter who might get hurt. You understand that, don't you?'' Her gimlet eyes bored into Raine's for an instant as she stood up. Then she was gone before the younger woman even had a chance to murmur good-night.

Raine sensed some hidden meaning in that last remark, but she was far too emotionally wrung out from her long day to let herself dwell on vague innuendos. The news *madame* had brought should have relaxed her, but she only felt more restless and tense. Feeling the need for some activity, she slipped into a pair of jeans and went out again, heading automatically in the direction she'd seen Bran walking fifteen minutes earlier.

Her presence was announced by a clatter of pebbles as she slid down the rocky incline to the beach with the quick grace of a twelve-year-old tomboy. Bran had been idly skipping stones across the still water in the cove, but he turned at the noise and watched her.

''I suppose you've come after an apology,'' he said as she came up to him. Though his tone was gruff, Raine didn't miss the flash of humor in his eyes.

A grin, at once impish and tentative, touched her lips. ''Don't you think I deserve one?''

He turned back to his game, and Raine followed the swift low trajectory of the flat stones as they bounced and skated on top of the water.

Still not looking at her, Bran let out his breath in a sigh of defeat. ''I guess I've been a bastard,'' he conceded roughly.

Raine laughed. ''That's not the most gracious apology I've ever had. But it'll do.''

He threw one last stone with a fierce tense energy. "But I still haven't forgiven O'Donovan for trying to seduce you."

"Bran, please!" she retorted, genuine alarm mingling with her soft laughter.

He turned back to her, the lower half of his face shadowed by the upturned collar of his jacket. Now she saw that his eyes, although faintly teasing, still held a vestige of hurt. They stood so close that a half step would have put them in each other's arms. But some new constraint held them back, as if both feared the unexpected vulnerability he'd shown.

The moment was charged with unexpressed emotion. Raine ached for his touch, and as if he sensed her longing, Bran lifted his fingers to her hair and gently brushed the strands back over her shoulder.

Now when he looked at her, his eyes were as dark as the waves lapping gently at the shore. "Shall we try again?" he asked finally, his voice hesitant yet warm for all that.

Raine nodded. "Yes, I think we should."

As they recrossed the slippery boulders Bran's arms came up automatically to assist her, but he withdrew them as soon as her feet touched the smooth sand on the other side. That same odd sense of reluctance hovered between them as they made their way back to the village with the moon at their back like a watchful duenna.

RAINE BALANCED on pointe, her supporting leg straight and strong. The late-afternoon sunlight pouring into the room had a curious richness to it that warmed her to the very marrow. She had rehearsed all day without letup. In fact, the entire week had gone that way—work and more work. The pain and the stiffness that had once haunted her were nothing but a memory now. She only wished her emotions could have come through the preceding months with the same resiliency.

Because Raine wanted desperately to try again with Bran, she had accepted his invitation to visit the Roman ruins near St. Rémy. Still, she was more afraid than ever of being hurt. So much of herself was at stake now. Perhaps that's why she'd taken refuge again in the discipline of her art, clinging to Madame T's carelessly given praise. The old woman might believe that Raine was one of the company's finest dancers, but Raine still felt bound to prove it to herself.

She hadn't even noticed when the others had drifted out one by one, discussing their own plans for dinner and jokingly inviting one another up to their rooms for games of Monopoly or poker. She was too busy concentrating on a particularly difficult series of *sautés* she was determined to perfect. In the back of her mind was Bran's injunction that she be ready at five sharp when he came over to the pension, but Raine told herself she had plenty of time yet. So she turned the album over, and falling in with the cadence of the music, did a series of exuberant *grands jetés* across the empty studio.

The sound of a door slamming behind her caused Raine to turn with a start. She looked at Bran with surprise, demanding breathlessly, "What are you doing here? I thought you had a backlog of paperwork to finish."

He leaned back against the door and crossed his arms. "And I thought we were going to meet at the pension."

A little taken aback by his tone, she replied uncertainly, "We were...we are."

"I waited for you for half an hour."

"A half hour! What time is it?"

"Quarter to six."

She hurried across the room toward him, her lithe body an exquisite, well-tuned instrument over which she'd gained absolute control. She was so radiant, in fact, that he barely noticed the contrite look in her eyes.

"Bran, I'm sorry!" she said quickly. "I lost track of the time, I guess. The days are already getting longer, so I thought it was still early, and I just got so engrossed in the role...." She broke off her trailing list of excuses, realizing how hollow they must sound. There was no excuse for having stood him up, and she was suddenly anxious to make it up to him. "Let's just go straight from here. I'll grab my jeans and we can be on our way."

Long before they reached the sleepy provincial town, the sun had disappeared behind a hilltop church spire, so that they arrived at the ancient ruins of Glanum just as the first stars were coming out. There was an eerie beauty to the great slabs of hewn stone and broken columns that had once been a Roman theater. A cool wind blew off the hill behind it, rustling through the trees that bordered the site.

Raine stood in the middle of what had once been the stage, her eyes roving over the fan-shaped amphitheater that must have held hundreds of spectators. "I wonder what it was like to perform here," she said aloud, surprised at how far her voice carried in the night air.

"Go ahead," Bran said from behind her. He'd been in a needling mood ever since they'd left Stes-Maries.

Raine whirled around to face him, tired of his festering anger. "Bran, what's the matter?" she demanded softly. "I apologized for being late and ruining your plans. But it's not that big a deal. We can come again tomorrow," she added in a coaxing reasonable voice.

Sitting down in the first row, he rested his elbows on the quarried stone of the tier behind him. "God, you sound so much like her," Bran observed at last, his eyes roving restlessly to the stars that gleamed more brightly as the night deepened around them.

Raine took a couple of steps toward him, her head cocked at a questioning angle. "Who?"

"Lucille." He muttered his mother's name in an impatient dismissing tone. "It was always the same—apologies for what we couldn't do today and promises of what we'd do tomorrow—until she was finally gone completely."

Raine sat down on the cold stone next to him, her chest tightening as she stared at the broken stage ruins and attempted to envision the man beside her as a vulnerable boy of four or five. "Don't you think it's time you forgave her?" she ventured at last. "She was a gifted dancer. Her only crime was wanting it all—a career and her child. She loved you, Bran. She left because she had your own best interests at heart."

He shot her an angry look. "Since when have you become Lucille's advocate?"

"Since I visited her at her villa."

Bran exploded. "You had no right!"

"She invited both of us, if you'll remember," Raine defended herself, eyes flashing. "I decided to accept, and I'm glad I did. She needs you, Bran."

He turned his head sharply. "When I needed her thirty years ago, where was she?" He breathed a sigh of pent-up frustration. "Lucille is more a stranger to me than anything else. The anger isn't really there anymore, but then neither is the love."

"You can't blame her for what she is," Raine countered.

"I don't, not anymore. To a point, I even understand her."

"Yes, you should," she answered softly. "After all, you've chosen the same life for yourself."

Bran laughed bitterly. "Haven't we all! Take you, for example." He shot her an accusing look. "I watched you rehearsing this afternoon—so caught up in your work that you were oblivious to everything else."

The tightness in her chest intensified as the implication of what he was saying finally dawned on her. "You're afraid that I'll be the second Lucille in your life?" she said, her hushed voice rising on a note of disbelief.

"Aren't you?" His mouth was drawn into a thin line.

"No!"

He ignored her denial. "You have so much love for dance, Raine. I can see it brimming in your eyes.

You give so much to it that there's not enough left for anything or anyone else.''

Hot tears burned at the back of her eyes, so that they gleamed with an anguished brightness against the night. "Damn it, you won't even let me try!" She reached out to touch his arm, but he withdrew it.

"I don't want to take the chance," he muttered, and Raine listened to him with a growing sense of desolation, her eyes following the rigidity of his upper body as he leaned forward and rested his elbows on his knees. His head was bent, his eyes fixed on his hands as he kneaded one palm with the other thumb in a gesture of frustration. "I don't want to risk that kind of pain."

She shook her head, still trying to fight back the tears. "Can't you forget I'm a dancer and see me simply as a woman?"

Bran stood up, radiating a tenseness that was alien to the lithe easy power of a dancer's body. "No, I cannot," he ground out slowly, his eyes as they raked her reflecting a jagged edge of pain. "I can't, because in part it's been my doing. I can't separate your transformation into dancer and woman, because they're one and the same. And with every step closer that you take toward your goal, I know I'm losing you."

"Bran, stop it!" she cried in a strangled voice. "What are you saying? Are you asking me to give up dance, just like your father asked Lucille to do? Are you going to force me to make an impossibly difficult decision?"

He leaned down to grab her arms, pulling her roughly to her feet. "Damn it, no," he bit out between clenched teeth, "because I'm making that decision for you." His harsh words released the tears she'd tried to hold back; they filled her eyes and overflowed down her cheeks. But no broad thumb came up to gentle them away, as it had once before on a night that now seemed so tragically distant. He had hardened himself to her tears. "I'm telling it to you simply, Raine. I was wrong to say we should try again. There's no chance for us. None at all."

CHAPTER SIXTEEN

PARIS WAS STILL GRIPPED by winter, a succession of overcast and bitingly cold days that sent Raine's spirits plummeting even lower. Bran's rejection had so devastated her that her heart felt as frozen as the fountain in the middle of the square. Here she stood, a woman on the brink of realizing her full artistic potential, and the success tasted like ashes in her mouth. Over and over she asked herself if Bran had to be right—that she couldn't have it both ways.

Her weariness was lightened a little by a visit from Margrit Blake the day after the company's return to the city. Vivacious and blooming, the Englishwoman told her gleefully how well their sly ploy at Chez Martinique had worked. It had been the coup de grace, helping Pierre to finally get over his hopeless infatuation for Riva. Now he and Margrit were most definitely a couple. And so she chatted on in blithe contentment, oblivious to her friend's distant expression.

Raine felt a little guilty after Margrit had left, because she'd listened with only half an ear as the woman boasted jubilantly about Pierre's upcoming exhibit. Now she took out the invitation, a beautifully designed card announcing the special one-man show at the Tabor Gallery on the rue du Dragon.

She went over to the telephone, but before she could pick it up Riva breezed into the apartment and tweaked the end of her sister's hair. "What are you so deep in thought about?" Riva demanded.

Raine glanced around in surprise at her sister's buoyant manner. "Nothing you'd really be interested in," she answered in the same offhand manner, her eyes focusing on the blouson mink jacket Riva wore so casually. "Margrit came by this afternoon."

"What's new with her? I hope she's convinced Pierre to sue that old curmudgeon of a grandfather," Riva answered as she riffled through the stack of mail on the table, obviously indifferent.

"I'd ask what's brought about the change in your mood, but I don't think I need to," Raine observed, her eyes still on the mink.

Smiling, Riva looked up. "You have your little secrets, *chère soeur*, and I have mine. Besides, you'll find out soon enough."

Raine had the distinct feeling that she'd just as soon never find out what more Riva had up her sleeve. The ballerina had been somewhat chastened after the brouhaha she'd caused in Stes-Maries. Yet for all that, Raine suspected something was still simmering beneath Riva's calm exterior. She hadn't forgotten the challenge that had amounted to a threat: I haven't changed. I still play to win.

Humming the prelude to *Swan Lake*, Riva disappeared into the bathroom. Raine stared after her, then with a shrug reached for the art-show invitation and propped it up by the lamp. Her eyes on it, she picked up the telephone receiver and dialed Monsieur Santandre's number.

Monsieur himself answered with a testy, *"Bonjour."* His voice was congested and gravelly with a cold.

"Good morning, *monsieur*. It's Raine," she greeted him cheerily. "The company is back from Provence, and I'm calling you as I promised."

"Et bien, but I'm delighted to hear from you, child. Paris has been cold and gloomy, to match my mood."

"I'm sorry to hear that," she replied sympathetically. "I was thinking you might enjoy having lunch with me today—my treat. Nothing fancy, mind you, but I feel I'd like to repay you a little for all you did for me."

His voice warmed a little. "Thank you, child. I would be honored. I half feared you wouldn't call me again after our little spat. Shall I pick you up?"

Raine laughed again. "I'm still trying to stand on my own two feet, thank you. Let's meet instead."

BUNDLED UP AGAINST THE COLD, Raine stood beneath the stone arcade opposite the Louvre and watched for the familiar silver Rolls. When it drew up to the curb, she stepped forward to greet Santandre as he climbed out of the rear seat.

She bit her lip in anxiety as her eyes swept over him—his sparse gray hair, his eyes rheumy, his shoulders a little stooped. Some spark of vitality seemed to have left him, and the urgency of what she wanted to do pressed upon her. Taking his arm, she reached up to kiss his cold dry cheek.

The restaurant Raine had chosen for their meeting wasn't elegant, but it was cozy. The small English tearoom was on the second floor of the arcade, over-looking the bustling rue de Rivoli.

After they'd ordered a simple meal, Raine reached across the table and briefly touched his hand. "You look a little under the weather, *monsieur*. I'm half regretting my impulsive invitation."

He shook his head. "I'm an old man, *chérie*. I need the warmth of friendship now more than I need doctors or medicines."

Raine smiled. "That's true for everyone, young or old."

"Perhaps so," he muttered ruminatively. "We're too busy to realize it when we're young. There is always too much going on, too many goals to attain. And all of a sudden there's nothing left."

Raine caught her breath at that, the truth of it striking painfully close to home. Bran had accused her of that more than once.

She sighed as she looked across the table at her friend. "Some things endure, though—love, family ties."

"I have neither," he replied sharply.

"That's because inside you're still that ambitious young man, worrying about business and careers and...and forgetting that they're all unimportant if they have no basis in human feelings," she chided.

His bushy brows quirked downward in feigned anger. "I get the feeling I'm being lectured to, *mademoiselle*."

"You are." She smiled in return, though her eyes were a little sad. "Still I think my little lecture is meant for me, too."

The waitress brought their wine then, and they

were silent for a while. Throughout their meal, one name remained unspoken—the reason for their being together.

Surprisingly it was Santandre who finally made the opening. His eyes fixed on the wineglass before him, he began to reminisce. "Pierre was a delightful child, charming and quick. I remember one particular birthday many years ago. He must have been all of ten. I was sitting in the breakfast room with my coffee when he appeared in the doorway, some bit of frippery hidden behind his back. He marched right up to me, his expression solemn but mischievous. '*Grand-père,*' he said. '*Grand-mère* has told me what the doctor told you—more exercise and more fun to make your heart stronger. So I have made you a present to help you get both.' He pulled out a kite then from behind his back. It was as brilliant as a butterfly's wings, and he'd made it himself. He was quite proud of it, too."

Santandre looked across at Raine, his gaze sharp and bright and stubborn. "Do you see what a gift he had for dealing with people? He'd made something that he wanted, yet he made it seem as though it was done for my own good. I was charmed and impressed, believe me." The old man shook his head with regret.

"And the butterfly's wings?" Raine pressed softly. "Wasn't the kite also the expression of another part of him even then?"

His eyes narrowed at that, but he seemed too tired to argue the point. As they ate, Raine encouraged him to reminisce some more. And he did so, touching on a lovely patchwork of memories: hilarious, sad, endearing.

"But *monsieur*, how could you give all that up for

the sake of a silly feud?'' she exclaimed at last, her eyes warm as they rested on him. "That kind of shared past is beautiful. You've talked so much about family traditions, but the real tradition is the common history between you and your grandson. You're so lucky to have each other. It would be a tragedy to destroy that.''

"He destroyed it, not I,'' the old man growled, though his manner was a little less certain. Perhaps the wine and the long afternoon of remembering had mellowed him just a little.

Raine let the argument drop. She had one more trick up her sleeve. "Monsieur Santandre, there's something else I'd like to treat you to this afternoon.'' She looked over at him with guileless eyes.

"And what is that?'' he demanded a shade suspiciously.

"It's a surprise.''

"Not a good omen,'' he grumped. "In the past few years, the only surprises I've had were unpleasant ones.''

Though she fretted inwardly, Raine fought to keep her expression serene. "Then I hope this one is different,'' she said with feeling.

The chauffeured Rolls was waiting at the curb on the busy boulevard when they came downstairs. As they climbed into the back seat, it was Raine who leaned forward and murmured an address into the driver's ear.

The car motored through the great Place de la Concorde and slipped into the stream of traffic threading beside the Seine. Within minutes they'd crossed the Pont Neuf, and the driver was weaving expertly along the narrow back streets of St-Germain. Raine kept up a light patter of conversation as they swept past the ancient church, the colorful flower market and small shops and galleries of the picturesque quarter.

Her pulse was racing when the car drew at last to a smooth stop. Belatedly she found herself cursing her own temerity as Monsieur Santandre stood on the sidewalk gazing up for a long, heart-stopping moment at the Tabor Gallery sign. When he glanced at Raine his brows were drawn together in a thunderous scowl. But he didn't turn back to the waiting car.

Dozens of people milled around inside, their conversation animated. The newcomers were greeted at the front desk by a smiling woman, who handed them cups of hot wine punch and an attractive printed brochure from which Pierre's bearded face smiled up at them. The artist himself was not in sight. With another mutinous look at his companion, Monsieur Santandre stalked off to examine the paintings. Raine, still nervous, perched on the edge of the desk, her eyes following him.

The skylighted gallery seemed to absorb warmth from the color-splashed canvases covering its walls. Taking them in for the first time, Raine realized that Pierre was really coming into his own as an artist. But her attention soon reverted to the elderly, slightly stooped man as he moved from canvas to canvas, studying each with the keen, hawk-eyed stare of a critic.

She was so intent on observing him that she jumped when someone took her arm. She looked up to find Pierre beside her, his expression disconcerted.

"What the devil brought him here?" he demanded as his eyes followed Santandre.

"I did."

"He came willingly?"

Raine flushed. "I'm afraid I had to use a ruse. He had no idea where I was bringing him."

"But why did you bother?" he asked angrily.

"Pierre," she chided, "you know that you love one another and are too stubborn to admit it. It's a crime to forsake all that because of pride. Your grandfather doesn't have all that many years left. This should be a rich contented time in his life. The two of you still have so much to share."

His expression was no longer quite so hard. "I admired him when I was a boy," Pierre muttered. "So many times now I've wanted to ask his advice. He gave me so much of himself when I was a kid. A lot of my art is drawn from that part of my life." He shook his head in regret, much as the old man had done at lunch.

A smile tugged at Raine's lips. "He told me about the kite you made him for his birthday once."

"He remembered that?" Pierre asked, amazed.

Raine nodded, but the artist was no longer looking at her. He had turned back to watch his grandfather, and she, too, turned just as Santandre walked up to a small blue-splashed canvas and took it down from the wall as if it were in his own home. With mingled alarm and curiosity, they waited to see what he would do.

He marched back toward the door, his step quickening when he saw his grandson. "Pierre," he said a little stiffly, "I wish to purchase this. It reminds me of our summer holidays at the shore when you were just a boy. There's a spot just right for it on my library wall.''

The younger man's expression was rather uncertain. "No. Please, sir, accept it as a gift.''

There was a long silence. "Thank you, son,'' Monsieur Santandre replied at last. "It means a great deal to me.'' His eyes were bright and moist, perhaps from the effects of his cold, perhaps from emotion.

Pierre put his hand gently on the older man's shoulder. "Come on, *grand-père*. Let's see if there's any other you'd like to have. I don't make kites anymore,'' he admitted with a laugh. "I haven't made one in years. But perhaps something else will catch your fancy.''

Santandre's answering smile was wry but warm and loving, too. "Perhaps.'' Knowing she wouldn't be missed, Raine took the opportunity to slip away.

Once she was outside the cozy brightness and warmth of the gallery, the winter day seemed even grayer than before. But Raine no longer feared the cold. Her leg had healed completely; it was her heart that now bore the brunt of pain. She left the narrow street, heading away from the noise and bustle of the boulevard St-Germain. She wandered into the quiet of the Place St-Sulpice, where the naked branches of a dozen plane trees were etched sharply against the church walls. Even the fountain in the middle of the square was silent, its four statues mantled with a light covering of frost. Raine turned back and walked toward the nearest *métro* station. For all the cold dreariness of the day, she wasn't eager to get back to the studio. Suddenly she felt she had no joy left inside her, not even for her work.

Leaving the subway in the rue des Abbesses, she slowly made her way back to the ballet company. But even as she climbed the stairs to the second floor, her thoughts were five hundred miles away in the heart of Provence. She was so distracted that she didn't notice Bran coming around the corner to Madame Tarsamova's office, and they nearly collided in the doorway.

Her eyes took in the attractive but unfamiliar gray suit and the tie knotted carelessly at his throat. He looked like a stranger. They exchanged hesitant hellos, their eyes averted and unhappy. It was a tense awkward moment for Raine as she struggled within herself, wanting desperately to say something, yet afraid even trying would be futile.

She might have moved past him without a word if Madame T hadn't chosen to step out of her office at that moment. The Russian woman shot Bran a quick inscrutable look. "Ah, you're here." She noticed Raine was with him, and her lips tightened almost imperceptibly. "This involves you as well, Raine, so you had better come in."

As the ballet mistress turned to go back inside, Raine looked up at Bran with a questioning glance. But his shoulders lifted in a puzzled shrug; he apparently had no idea, either, what this was all about.

Raine perched on the edge of the floral chaise, half turned toward Madame Tarsamova, who sat regally erect behind her desk. Bran had shoved his hands into the pockets of his trousers and taken a stance before the window, his eyes fixed on the withered carnations that had fallen into decline during *madame*'s month-long absence.

"What's this all about, Nina?" he began impatiently without turning around. "I'm late and I've got rehearsal in ten minutes."

"Then I won't waste any more of your time," she began acidulously. "I will go directly to the point. I have decided to overrule you, Brandon. I have decided against Raine for the role of Odette. That role should never have been split in the first place. Odette-Odile will be danced by Riva."

Raine stared at her, numb with shock. Though the back of her throat was dry and burning, she'd lost so much in the past week that the deeper pain buffered this one a little.

Bran expressed enough fury for both of them. Whirling around, he planted both hands squarely on the edge of the desk. "What the hell do you mean, Nina? Raine's worked on it for weeks. She dances like a dream, damn it!" he growled, muttering another imprecation under his breath. "There's no one more deserving of a solo role."

Raine listened to him with bated breath, deeply touched by his passionate advocacy. Then she remembered what he'd said their last evening together. "And with every step closer that you take toward your goal, I know I'm losing you." And now, as then, she wanted to cry in earnest.

The volatile discussion raged around her as if she weren't there, but she was only half listening to it, anyway. Finally Madame Tarsamova stood up and looked from one to the other with her piercing eyes. "I must be honest with you both," she said at last.

"This has not been entirely my decision. I have to confess that I've had a visit from Riva's Signor Chiari. He has promised to make a sizable contribution to the Ballet du Monde—given the one stipulation."

Bran ran impatient fingers through his hair. "Massimo's a friend of mine. I'll talk to him myself. I can't let this happen."

"Chiari is far more than a patron," Nina replied, her thin brows lifting a fraction of an inch as she glanced over at Raine. "I think the man is in love with Riva. Given that, the words of an old friend would hold remarkably little sway."

Bran's expression hardened. "You know I respect you, Nina, and I understand the financial problems of running a company. But I can't let you get away with this," he added harshly. "If you take that role away from Raine, I'm severing my relationship with the company."

Raine's head shot up. "Bran, you can't do that!" she cried, her hand automatically reaching out to cover his where it still gripped the desk edge. "I don't want that kind of sacrifice made for me!" she whispered in a strangled voice, her eyes seeking his.

It was as if they were alone in the room then. Bran's eyes traveled over her slowly, his expression at once loving and troubled. "You worked for it. I gave it to you," he said with a grave touching simplicity that bruised her insides.

It was with great difficulty that they tore their gazes from each other as *madame*'s strident voice interrupted their private exchange. "I was prepared for this, too, Brandon," she began in her acerbic way. "And I am also prepared to make a compromise."

He straightened and regarded his wily old colleague with a faintly sardonic look. "What?"

She ignored the irony in his tone. "I've been watching the genesis of your new dance, *Sweet Seduction*, and I like it very much. To be frank, I believe it's the best work you've ever done. I'd like to incorporate it into the company repertoire—beginning with our first performance Saturday night." She paused, waiting to see the effect this announcement had. Satisfied, she went on. "The role was modeled on Raine—in fact, I think it was made precisely *for* her. She'll dance that. It will be a far lovelier and more individual signature piece for a new ballerina than *Swan Lake*."

Bran shook his head slowly, exhausted from arguing. "But that's impossible, Nina. We've got no time to prepare a male partner for the lead."

Madame paused another long moment before showing her trump card. "I was assuming you would take the part," she countered with a remarkably innocent expression on her lined and world-weary face.

Raine's own expression was tense, agonized as she waited for his reply. But he said nothing, stalking out of *madame*'s office with his mouth set in a grim line. After he'd gone, Raine's shoulders slumped. So often she had half teasingly demanded the same thing of him. Now it hurt her to think that even if he relented and agreed to dance with her, it would not be out of choice, but out of duty.

MUCH LATER, after all the other dancers had gone and the pallid, late-afternoon sunlight was slanting into the theater, Raine made her way down the cor-

ridor toward the familiar studio. The battered old
piano had been moved there during the company's
absence, and now someone's fingers were moving
with a hesitant slowness over the out-of-tune keys. For
all the funny discordance of the notes and the player's
indifferent plunking, Raine picked out the familiar
sweep of music, and her heart rose to meet it.

She stood quietly in the doorway. Bran sat at the
piano, deep in thought, the sunlight gleaming off his
dark hair as he bent his head over the keys. She was
reluctant to intrude. But he must have sensed her
presence, because he looked up. Slowly she crossed
the wide expanse of polished oak and sat down beside
him on the piano bench, watching the idle play of his
long sensitive fingers over the keyboard.

"I get the feeling this isn't something either of us
expected," she began softly, her lips curved in a
semblance of a teasing smile. "Getting the coup de
grace like this from Madame T and Riva. I . . . ." She
faltered. "I just wanted to let you know that I don't
expect you to dance *Sweet Seduction* with me. It
doesn't matter now anyway because—" Raine swallowed painfully before going on "—I've decided to
go back to the States."

His fist came down on the keys. "Where will you
go?" he asked roughly, though his eyes searched hers
with disturbing intensity.

Raine shrugged. "Boston, New York. . . . Does it
matter?" She looked past him to the window where
the sunset sky burnished the Parisian rooftops.
"There'd be too many painful memories here. Besides, I've . . . I've paid my dues, so I suppose it's time
to move on."

Once again she felt the intensity of his gaze that compelled her to meet it. "*Sweet Seduction* is your role, Raine," Bran said, his voice infused with passion. "You have to dance it."

"With whom?"

Bran looked at her now with an expression that was curiously veiled. "With me."

Her heart skidded, but she tried to keep her tone light. "Are you sure you want to?"

"I couldn't let you go without seeing you get the praise you deserve. I'd never forgive myself," Bran said slowly in a voice that had been carefully stripped of any emotion.

"I see," Raine conceded with a stiff nod. "It will be a...a kind of farewell gift, then." She found it incredibly difficult to utter those last words, because tears were scalding the back of her throat.

Without waiting for his reply, she stood up and ran from the room.

CHAPTER SEVENTEEN

THERE WAS AN AURA OF MAGIC to a theater that no other place could capture. But for once Raine was impervious to it. Every bit of her concentration and thought was turned inward as she stood alone in the wings, waiting for Tchaikovsky's rousing finale to *Swan Lake*.

Now the curtain had descended, and Riva, glittering and beautiful in her black Odile costume, ran up breathlessly and brushed her sister's cheek with her lips. The hard topaz eyes shone from the mingled effects of her public and personal triumph. Her performance had been a dizzying tour de force that would go unmatched for a long time, for this was Riva's last surprise—she, too, was leaving the Ballet du Monde. Riva had accepted Massimo's proposal of marriage and his promise that she could form her own dance company in Florence. The ballerina was leaving Paris in a blaze of glory.

Raine no longer begrudged Riva the Odette-Odile role. Her methods had been undeniably devious, yet the work she'd put into its success had been disciplined and real enough. "A fighter," Bran had once called Riva, a woman who was willing to go after what she wanted.

The thought lighted a flame in Raine. Why, after

all, shouldn't she do the same? Just then the stage manager pushed past her officiously with his velvet-tipped cane in hand and struck it three times on the stage floor—*les trois coups*, the traditional signal in French theater that the curtain was about to rise again.

Slowly Raine smoothed down the gossamer white skirt of the costume that left her arms and regally held throat bare. She was half seductress and half virginal bride, ready to work her own brand of magic upon the stage. As she reached up to touch her hair for one final check, Raine gave brief thought to the hundreds of nameless unseen faces in the audience.

Her mind touched, too, on Madame Tarsamova, and a smile glimmered in the depths of her eyes. She still didn't know if the clever ballet mistress had engineered this final performance because she wanted Raine to dance or because she wished to see Bran on stage again. No matter. Raine was deeply grateful for the chance to enfold herself in Bran's arms, this one last time, at least.

The orchestral prelude to her entrance began, but a part of her remained detached. For the first time she felt completely that she was a woman coming into her own, a woman who knew herself. And with that same sense of detachment, she had to acknowledge the enormous debt she owed Bran, for what he'd done. She remembered, too, the first time she'd seen him in the studio and—from that first moment—the pride and clear sense of self-awareness he'd aroused in her. Raine had been angry when he'd stressed technique over and over again, but she truly felt now what her mind had known all along—that it was from confidence in technique that the power of emotion could flow unimpeded. Long before she'd believed in herself, Bran had recognized that her body would be a powerful instrument of expression, and he had guided her to see it, too.

How much he'd given her! And now there was this farewell gift—the dance. The terrible thought again struck her that it might be the last time she ever saw his face, but she could not dwell on that.

Now the dreamy music swelled up from the dark orchestra pit. Rising effortlessly on pointe, Raine moved forward from the upstage wing. And curiously, as she began to dance, something like fire smoldered within her.

Bran stepped out of the downstage shadows. Black tights molded the lower half of his body, but his muscular torso was bare. Now his arms reached for her. Like a lonely bird in flight suddenly brought down, she lost herself in that embrace for one brief tentative moment. Glancing up into his face, Raine saw that his eyes were dark as a moonless night, and for an instant she despaired. Then their depths flickered into hot awareness as if kindled by the fire in her own, and no thought existed but for each other. There was no theater, no auditorium, no outer world.

They danced joyfully together, their movements spare and pure against the emptiness of the stage. They had no sets or props to impede them. Bran moved with that animallike grace, each step a powerful impulse that touched an atavistic chord deep within her. All the feelings he'd held in reserve throughout their weeks of rehearsal now surged with breathtaking force. His every emotional response was fresh and vital, totally alive.

The first sequence of the dance was playful, a coquettish give-and-take of strangers meeting and sensing an instantaneous attraction. With arms outstretched, she leaned away from him, her tenuous diagonal balance maintained by the sure grip of his fingers around her wrist.

Then, as if tiring of her elusiveness, Bran bent his arms and drew her inexorably toward him. Raine's feet slid out in a controlled, lightning-quick *échappé*. With legs extended far out to either side of her, she balanced on pointe against him, her elbows resting in the crook of his arms as her hands gently framed his face and his hands just as gently cupped her tilted head. Through the thin fabric she felt the heat of him against her hips and uptilted breasts. For several long beats their gazes collided in sultry confrontation, the now mingled heat of their bodies a catalyst that touched off a spiraling inward tension.

Then, with reluctance, they moved apart, the quick whisperings of her toe shoes against the stage floor blotting out the fluttering beat of her own heart. Like the gossamer net of their emotions, each step they took meshed in a dizzying erotic pattern. They stood back to back now, her leg curved in arabesque around his hips as her arm slid beneath his to clamp his shoulder.

Step by step, she shed her mantle of maidenly reserve in response to a male vitality that was at once magnetic, sensual, mysterious. Bran moved with a lightning brilliance and controlled power that inspired in her a new willingness to dare.

In a twinkling the intimate pas de deux became a desirous interplay, wild and abandoned. Their moves were so intense yet so free that the well-rehearsed roles seemed as spontaneous as life itself. A quick twist of his shoulder brought his hands up to grasp her waist, and Raine's arms and head were flung back in ecstasy. He spun her around, so that her head brushed his chest for an instant. His sheer masculine strength took over as he swung her up off the stage until her back arched above his head and her arms drifted backward to either side of her face in a timeless gesture of feminine surrender.

Gone was the last vestige of her cool restraint. All the fire that had simmered tantalizingly just below the surface now erupted with tempestuous grace. Her female form was imbued with a feral beauty that expressed her innermost longings in a moment of unforgettable richness and poignancy.

The music rose to a crescendoing clash, leaped to a quivering finale on the high note and then drifted earthward again in a muted tremolo. Ever slower and slower, the dancers spiraled until, as if under a magician's spell, they sank to the stage floor. They lay curled in touching intimacy, inverted, her head resting on his bent knee while his cheek rested against the swell of her hip. The last trembling note of a flute died away, but all that tinged Raine's awareness was the exquisite pressure of his bent arm against her breast and the gently possessive pressure of his splayed fingers against her thigh.

A hush so still and deep gripped the entranced audience that the man and woman on stage might indeed have been alone in a magical world of their own creation. Instinctively the silent watchers understood that they had shared a unique moment in the lives of two lovers. Then the curtain fell, and belatedly, like a far echo, the applause began to build and swell.

But neither of them was aware of it. With agonizing reluctance Bran pulled himself up from the gentle curve of her hip, his hand sliding in one long and delectably fluid velvet motion along the contour of her inner thigh. Inflamed by the sensuality of his lingering touch, Raine made her fingers a delicate echo of his own as she withdrew them from around his crooked knee and reluctantly lifted her head. From beneath her lashes she shot him a swift look that mingled shyness and a bold unabashed hunger. Bran's senses leaped to the unspoken eloquence of her gaze, and in one lithe spring he was on his feet, drawing her up beside him. Before the curtain could rise again in response to the audience's wildly enthusiastic cries of "Bravo!" they were gone. Now amid the excited milling of the other dancers, Bran and Raine slipped away along the shadowy half light of the wings and moved hand in hand toward the theater's back stairs.

The audience's approval had grown to a thundering roar, for the theatergoers had recognized the poignancy of what they had been a part of. Far more than a dance, it had been an intensely personal and moving experience. But neither Bran nor Raine wanted applause; they wanted only to be alone together.

As they climbed the second set of curving stairs, the clamor below receded like a distant wave. But still they climbed upward until they reached a narrow landing that opened onto a studio. Impatiently he pulled her inside, and even before the door had shut behind her, he was crushing her to it, his lips seeking hers with an ardor that engulfed them both.

At last their mouths drew apart, but Raine clung to Bran's arms as though she'd never let him go. She rested her cheek against his bare chest, breathing in the mingled sweat and musk of his male body. The scent of him excited her, and with softly parted lips she began to tease the dark hairs that grew in lush profusion over his muscled torso as she drank in the heady salt sweetness of his skin.

Uttering a muffled groan against the smooth cap of her hair, Bran brought his hands up to drag the pins free and run his fingers through the lustrous uncurling wave of mahogany. Then in one swift movement, he reached down to scoop her into his arms. With two steps he scaled the raised platform at the far side of the room and set her across the faded damask chaise that was tucked beneath the slanting studio windows. He bent over her, his lips and fingertips caressing and teasing every inch of her until she whispered for him to lie beside her.

In an instant their costumes were a tangled heap of black and white on the dusty floor and Bran was lowering himself to her, a forceful man in his prime, yet infinitely tender for all that. Like stars colliding in a black velvet void, their bodies fused in a hot explosion that rippled through their heightened senses. All thought was obliterated as they joyously became one, moving to an exquisite rhythm that was the ultimate fulfillment of the implied promise in their dance....

Much later they lay side by side, their passion spent, as reality crept back inexorably around them. The black spangled sky over their heads had the brittle clarity of a frost-laden night, and they could just see the square medieval towers of Notre-Dame below in the city. The frigid winter air had crept into the studio, so Bran had pulled an old velvet robe from some long-forgotten production up around them.

Though he held her closely in his arms, Raine sensed his preoccupation, and she swiveled her head around to look into his face. Bran's expression was tender, and when he spoke his voice was curiously rough yet gentle. "During the performance tonight you looked so beautiful and self-contained. It scared the hell out of me."

Raine's lips curved in a teasing smile. "You're supposed to take pride in your creation—like Pygmalion."

But he refused to be teased. "You're far, far more to me than that," he said huskily as his hand came up to grip her jaw and he caressed its beloved contour with his thumb. "You're so much a part of me that I can't tell where your flesh and blood ends and mine begins."

She stared up at him with a sense of wonder.

He bent his head to brush his lips against her forehead, then spoke again. "When you came toward me on stage, I looked into your eyes and knew I couldn't let you walk out of my life, Raine. Loving you was so painful for me because it reminded me of everything I'd never had. I wasn't ready for it; I didn't *want* to be ready for it. I don't know what frightened me more—loving you, or the prospect of having to let you go.''

"And now?" Raine lifted her head from his chest, her fingers curling tightly in the matted hairs.

He grinned down at her, his expression tender and teasing. "I'm a risk taker; I always have been. But I honestly believed that sending you away would have been best for us both—until tonight.''

Her eyes shimmered. "Oh, Bran, you put me through hell last week!''

"I know that and I'm so sorry, my heart," Bran whispered as he drew her more closely to him. "I've put you through hell from the beginning, accusing you of all the things I was guilty of myself. I was the one who was afraid to feel for fear of being hurt. I was the one who used people—women. I guess in a way it was my subconscious revenge on Lucille. Every dancer represented her in my mind.''

"But not me?''

His answering laughter was husky with emotion. "You most of all, Raine! You forced me to believe that love was real and not just some childhood myth I'd long forgotten.''

Raine was touched deeply by his revelation, yet one issue still loomed. "I'll love you, Bran, all my life and with all my heart, but...." She paused, her luminescent eyes intent on his. "You have to understand that I won't give up my career. I'll always be a dancer.''

Bran caught her fingertips to his lips and kissed each one in turn. "You danced into my life, Raine, and I'm not going to let you dance out of it. I'm not haunted anymore by fears out of the past. You were born to be a ballerina, and you will be," he whispered, his eyes caressing and cherishing.

Radiant with happiness, she reached up to touch the outline of his mouth with gentle fingers. "Lucille will be surprised by our love," Raine said softly. "She told me it would never work between us."

"You talked to her about it?" he replied in disbelief.

Raine nodded. "She's afraid for us both. She's suffered so much." Raine paused, as if searching for the right words. "Don't you think you should stop punishing her?"

Bran was silent for a while. "I suppose it's been hard for her these past few years," he conceded reluctantly. But when he looked up again, Raine was surprised to see a subtle sparkle of amusement in his gaze. "I'll tell you what," he said at last. "I'll agree to your request—on one condition."

Her eyes widened with curiosity. "What's that?"

He grinned. "Marry me, Raine, and give me a child."

She reached up to twine her arms around his neck. "I'll gladly give you that, and a lifetime of devotion, too." Then she drew his mouth down to hers, kissing him with sweet hungry fervor.

Breathless with desire and mischievous laughter, Raine drew back to look up at him again with gleaming eyes. "There's just one thing, Bran," she began with an air of solemnity. "I've promised you a child, but . . . you have to make a promise in return."

Wary amusement glimmered in his own eyes. "What?"

"That you won't be angry if 'it' turns out to be twins." She chuckled impishly. "They run in the family, you know."

Bran threw back his head with a shout that was somewhere between a groan and wicked laughter. "Now that's one thing—or two—I think I can learn to handle."

Harlequin reaches
into the hearts and minds
of women across America
to bring you

Harlequin American Romance ™.

Enter a uniquely exciting new world with

Harlequin American Romance™·M·

Harlequin American Romances are the first romances to explore today's love relationships. These compelling novels reach into the hearts and minds of women across America... probing the most intimate moments of romance, love and desire.

You'll follow romantic heroines and irresistible men as they boldly face confusing choices. Career first, love later? Love without marriage? Long-distance relationships? All the experiences that make love real are captured in the tender, loving pages of **Harlequin American Romances.**

What makes American women so different when it comes to love? Find out with **Harlequin American Romance!**

Send for your introductory FREE book now!

Get this book FREE!

Mail to:
Harlequin Reader Service

In the U.S.
2504 West Southern Avenue
Tempe, AZ 85282

In Canada
649 Ontario Street
Stratford, Ontario N5A 6W2

YES! I want to be one of the first to discover
Harlequin American Romance. Send me FREE and without
obligation *Twice in a Lifetime.* If you do not hear from me after I
have examined my FREE book, please send me the 4 new
Harlequin American Romances each month as soon as they
come off the presses. I understand that I will be billed only $2.25
for each book (total $9.00). There are no shipping or handling
charges. There is no minimum number of books that I have to
purchase. In fact, I may cancel this arrangement at any time.
Twice in a Lifetime is mine to keep as a FREE gift, even if I do not
buy any additional books.

Name	(please print)	
Address		Apt. no.
City	State/Prov.	Zip/Postal Code

Signature (If under 18, parent or guardian must sign.)

Now's your chance to discover the earlier
books in this exciting series.

Choose from this list of great

SUPERROMANCES!

SUPERROMANCE

Complete and mail this coupon today!

Worldwide Reader Service

In the U.S.A.
440 South Priest Drive
Tempe, AZ 85281

In Canada
649 Ontario Street
Stratford, Ontario N5A 6W2

Please send me the following SUPERROMANCES. I am enclosing my check or money order for $2.50 for each copy ordered, plus 75¢ to cover postage and handling.

☐ # 26	☐ # 32	☐ # 38
☐ # 27	☐ # 33	☐ # 39
☐ # 28	☐ # 34	☐ # 40
☐ # 29	☐ # 35	☐ # 41
☐ # 30	☐ # 36	
☐ # 31	☐ # 37	

Number of copies checked @ $2.50 each =	$	
N.Y. and Ariz. residents add appropriate sales tax	$	
Postage and handling	$	.75
TOTAL	$	

I enclose _____

(Please send check or money order. We cannot be responsible for cash sent through the mail.)

Prices subject to change without notice.   Offer expires 29 February 1984.

NAME_____
(Please Print)

ADDRESS_____APT. NO. _____

CITY_____·_____

STATE/PROV._____

ZIP/POSTAL CODE_____

30856000000

Just what the woman on the go needs!

BOOK MATE

The perfect "mate" for all Harlequin paperbacks
Traveling • Vacationing • At Work • In Bed • Studying
• Cooking • Eating

Pages turn WITHOUT opening the strap.

Perfect size for all standard paperbacks, this wonderful invention makes reading a pure pleasure! Ingenious design holds paperback books OPEN and FLAT so even wind can't ruffle pages – leaves your hands free to do other things. Reinforced, wipe-clean vinyl-covered holder flexes to let you turn pages without undoing the strap...supports paperbacks so well, they have the strength of hardcovers!

SEE-THROUGH STRAP

Reinforced back stays flat.

Built in bookmark

BOOK MARK

BACK COVER HOLDING STRIP

10˝ x 7¼˝, opened.
Snaps closed for easy carrying, too.

Take these 4 best-selling novels FREE

Yes! Four sophisticated, contemporary love stories by four world-famous authors of romance FREE, as your introduction to the Harlequin Presents subscription plan. Thrill to **Anne Mather**'s passionate story BORN OUT OF LOVE, set in the Caribbean.... Travel to darkest Africa in **Violet Winspear**'s TIME OF THE TEMPTRESS.... Let **Charlotte Lamb** take you to the fascinating world of London's Fleet Street in MAN'S WORLD.... Discover beautiful Greece in **Sally Wentworth**'s moving romance SAY HELLO TO YESTERDAY.

Harlequin Presents...

The very finest in romance fiction

Join the millions of avid Harlequin readers all over the world who delight in the magic of a really exciting novel. EIGHT great NEW titles published EACH MONTH! Each month you will get to know exciting, interesting, true-to-life people .... You'll be swept to distant lands you've dreamed of visiting .... Intrigue, adventure, romance, and the destiny of many lives will thrill you through each Harlequin Presents novel.

Get all the latest books before they're sold out!

As a Harlequin subscriber you actually receive your personal copies of the latest Presents novels immediately after they come off the press, so you're sure of getting all 8 each month.

Cancel your subscription whenever you wish!

You don't have to buy any minimum number of books. Whenever you decide to stop your subscription just let us know and we'll cancel all further shipments.